HOT
MESS

Look for Emily Belden's next novel
Husband Material
available soon from Graydon House Books.

HOT MESS

Emily Belden

GRAYDON
HOUSE

**GRAYDON
HOUSE**

Recycling programs
for this product may
not exist in your area.

ISBN-13: 978-1-525-81141-8

Hot Mess

BookClubbish.com
GraydonHouseBooks.com

Printed in U.S.A.

For my grandmother, Jane.

HOT MESS

1

"Are you going to be okay?"

His question gives me pause. Will I be okay? Was "okay" a hypothetical three exits ago?

All things considered, I'm hurtling through time and space with a guy whose recovery from a serious cocaine addiction matters as much as the rise of his chocolate soufflé tonight. So I answer honestly.

"I don't know." My voice sounds far away.

"Well, if you're not sure, change. You'll be walking at least five miles between ushering people to tables and the bathroom and running back and forth from the kitchen."

"Oh, shoes. You're asking if I'm going to be okay in these shoes." I glance down at my black platform wedges.

"Yeah, babe. What the hell else would I be talking about?"

He grabs the bottom of my chin and plants a quick kiss on my lips before he rinses a whisk in the sink.

The shells of seventy-five hard-boiled eggs are in the trunk of a car I rented to shuttle all the shit required for tonight's guests, I took an unpaid day off from work to be here to help and my parents are about an hour away from arriving to this special "comeback dinner," which will be the first time they've seen Benji somewhere other than the headlines in the last thirty days.

And he's worried about my shoes?

"I'll be fine," I say sweetly, knowing now is not the time for a true audit of my emotional well-being. Tonight is about

Benji's big return and my confidence that all—including my shoe choice—will go as smoothly as the house-made butter at room temp that he's just whipped up.

I find my reflection in a nearby Cryovac machine and take out a tube of my go-to matte pale pink lipstick from my makeup bag. I sweep it across my bottom lip, then fill in just above my lip line on the top for the illusion of a slightly fuller mouth. After all, I know at least half the guest list is here to see what the woman behind the man looks like.

Speaking of lists, I can see Benji in the reflection as well, leaning over a stainless-steel counter consulting the prep list for tonight's dinner service. He takes a black Sharpie from the pocket of his apron and puts a quick slash through each item as he recites them out loud to himself.

I come up behind him and cast my arms around him slowly; my touch puts him at ease. He curls his left arm up to hold my arms in place and continues to mouth ingredients one by one to make sure he hasn't forgotten anything. It sounds like sweet nothings being whispered to me in a romance language I barely understand.

Benji crumples the list, a sign he's successfully on track with everything from the dehydrated goat's milk to emulsified caramel, and I snap out of my schoolgirl daydream. He turns to face me, shuffles a few steps back in his worn kitchen clogs and bends down to shake out his longish dark hair.

I know what he's about to do. And for as ordinary as it is, especially to girls like me who *routinely* wear their hair like this, watching Benji shimmy a hair tie—my hair tie—off his right wrist to tie his mane into a disheveled topknot is like the start of an exotic dance. For anyone who says the manbun trend isn't their thing, they're lying.

The hair tie snaps when Benji tries to take it for a third lap around his voluminous bun.

"Goddamn it!"

"Relax, babe," I tell him as I zip open my makeup bag and pull out a spare. Crisis averted, I think to myself as I put another mental tally in the "Saves the Day" column.

He reties his white apron for the umpteenth time over a tight black T-shirt that shows off his tattooed-solid arms. I know for a fact he doesn't work out (unless you consider lifting fifty-pound boxes of pork and beef off the back of a pickup truck getting your reps in) but somehow he's been blessed with the body of a lumberjack. The only thing missing is the ax, which has been appropriately swapped out for an expensive Santoku knife custom-engraved with some filigree and his initials: BZ.

No doubt he's got the "hot and up-and-coming chef" thing down: tattooed, confident, exhausted and exhilarated. Hard to believe this isn't a casting event for *Top Chef*.

Harder to believe this is the man I get to take home every night.

"FUCK! Are you kidding me, Sebastian? Where the fuck is the lid to that thing?" Benji's words effectively snap me out of the trance I was in danger of being lulled into. It takes me a minute to realize what happened: his sous chef, Sebastian, has pressed Start on a Vitamix full of would-be avocado aioli, except the lid to the blender is nowhere to be found. Green schmutz has gone flying, marking up Benji's pristine apron like the start of a Jackson Pollock piece.

"Sorry, chef. I got it on now." Tail between his legs, Sebastian gets back to work as Benji furiously wipes at the streak with his bare hand. He's making it worse.

"Benji. Breathe." I grab his half-drunk can of LaCroix and pour a little onto a clean kitchen rag. While tending to the stain in the hot kitchen, I look directly into those deep brown eyes and give him a reassuring smile. He smells of cigarettes and sweat, garlic and onions. It's intoxicating.

"I know, Allie. This is just…huge for me. Huge for us. The press is going to be here tonight." He wipes some sweat off his brow.

"And my parents," I whisper.

"Oh god, them, too." He releases the tension by cracking the bones in his neck. A poor substitute, I imagine, for his true preference: a shot of whiskey.

But even a slug of 120 proof wouldn't take the edge off the fact that Benji's pop-up dinners are the new It Thing. People salivate at their screens just waiting for him to tweet out the next time and place he'll be cooking. Why? Because he's the hottest chef in Chicago and you can't taste his food at any restaurant. So when he announces a dinner, it's a mad, server-crashing race to claim one of only twelve spots at the table. And when everyone wants to see how the reformed addict is faring, they'll cancel all their plans for the day on the off chance they'll be one of the first to submit a reservation request, followed by prompt prepayment—which all goes to me, the fan-favorite girlfriend of Benji Zane.

I can't blame his followers for the obsession. Our flash-in-the-pan love story was covered by the most-read food blog earlier this spring, and since then, there have been myriad articles chronicling his love-hate relationship with hard drugs and high-end cooking. Between his unlikely relationship with me, his checkered past and his unmatched kitchen skills, Benji's managed to divide people like we're talking about health-care reform or immigration.

Half see him as a prodigy in the kitchen who was given a second chance when some no-name poster child of millennial living suddenly inspired him to get clean. The other half of Chicago views him as an all-hype hack who uses the media attention to rob his patrons of their hard-earned money so he can get his next score.

Fuck those people. Because the Benji that I know, that I live with…well, he's a stand-up guy whose brunch—and bedroom—game happens to be on point.

"Listen, babe," I say. "What did I tell you? I'm not going to let you down tonight, okay? I'll pace the seating however you need me to. I'll greet the press and spot the critics, too. We got this, okay? I believe in you." And I do.

I don't always agree to help Benji at his pop-ups—usually I just accept the reservation requests and keep the books straight. But tonight is different. Benji told me yesterday that he's got an outstanding dealer debt to pay off and so he's oversold the dining room by about twenty-five chairs to try to make a little extra cash. Without me here to help host a guest list of this size, this highly publicized dinner would look and feel more like a dysfunctional family reunion. Something I'm sure the piranha-like press would love to write about.

I wanted to be pissed about this little "oops" moment. How careless could he be? Now, by over-inviting a horde of geeked-out foodies, and in the past, by racking up a $2,000 coke bill. But he assured me it's just one of those things that *needs* to be handled in order for him to move on with his sobriety. And that's what I signed up for by being his girlfriend: unconditional support and a back that would never turn on him.

He's even arranged for Sebastian to be the one to hand over the cash tonight after the last diner goes home. Consider it just another example of how hungry people are to work alongside Mr. Zane. The same set of hands is willing to debone fifty squab *and* pay off gangbanging drug dealers from the South Side, all in the same night.

I don't blame Sebastian, though. There's something about Benji that makes you want to strap in for the ride. It's like rushing a sorority: you'll do what you need to do to get in, because ultimately, you end up part of something bigger than yourself. I just don't think any of us know what that *something* is yet.

At least that's the way I see it from my vantage point, which is currently the groin area of a brand-new apron that was marked with an unsightly stain until I stepped in.

"See, babe?" I say. "All clean."

Benji pulls me in for a kiss, his hand cupped around the back of my neck. With my French twist fragile in his palm, I feel the stress in the kitchen disintegrate. I'm no superhero, but if I were, my power would surely be managing to make it all okay for him, every time. It doesn't even matter that there's garlic burning in a sauté pan, my lipstick is now smeared, or that my work email is probably blowing up with a hundred notifications an hour.

"You're my rock, babe," he tells me, tucking a few strands of loose hair behind my ears. I love hearing that I'm doing a good job, because it's not always easy.

"Okay, so here's the final guest list," he says, getting back to business. Benji hands me a piece of paper from the back pocket of his charcoal gray skinny jeans. At the top, *Aug. 20 Pop-Up* is underlined in black marker. I give the list a quick once-over.

"So seating begins at seven, tables are set as rounds and the largest group is a party of six. Simple enough," I say.

"Well, it's more than just ushering people to their chairs." He tenses back up. "After everyone's seated, I'll need you to run food and bus tables if we get in the weeds."

"Weeds?"

"Busy as shit."

"Ah. Okay."

"And water. Constantly. You should be carrying the pitcher and filling any glass that's lower than two-thirds."

"Got it."

"Pay attention to what people are saying. Any issues, come find me immediately."

"Obviously."

"And as we're wrapping, make sure you call a cab for anyone who's too drunk to drive. The last thing I need is bad press about a deadly DUI from someone I fed."

"Anything else, your highness?" I jest to lighten the mood. I get that he's on edge, and rightfully so. So am I, to be frank. This mini-romper won't be forgiving in the derriere area should anyone drop a fork while I'm rehydrating them. I also barely know the difference between kale and spinach, and am about to play hostess to a room full of people who are jonesing to fire off a photo or two of this year's culinary celeb couple to their judgmental social sphere. It's a lot.

"Very funny. And yes, there is one more thing. Mark and Rita just texted me. They can't make it tonight. Couldn't find a sitter for Maverick or something."

While it would be great to finally meet Benji's sponsor, Mark—and his wife, Rita—I'm okay with the last-minute cancellation. Two less comp seats means more profit and less work for Benji. It also means two less people who I need to impress on the spot. Especially people whose job it is to spot bullshit. They'll be missed by Benji, I'm sure, since they're basically the parents he never had from what I gather. But hopefully he'll just shake it off.

"I'm sorry, that sucks. It's tough with kids," I say, like I know.

"Yeah, it's whatever. I told them we'll see them next weekend. Anyway, can you just promise me something?"

"Of course."

He looks me dead in the eye and says: "Promise that you'll fuck me after this is all done."

Blood rushes to places it hasn't since I lost my virginity on Valentine's night my freshman year of college. I know, I know. That's totally cliché. But what was your first time like? Okay then, let's not judge.

Speaking of clichés, now would be a good time to mention that I fell for the bad boy. And being "that girl" doesn't end there: just imagine a more basic version of Selena Gomez with a day-old blowout, tucking her leggings into Uggs when the temperature falls below seventy degrees. Give or take a Pumpkin Spiced Latte and a *Real Housewives* viewing party, and you've just about got me—Allie Simon—pegged. I'm the last person someone like Benji Zane would want to date and the first person the food blogosphere has been able to confirm he actually is dating. I give him a wink and turn toward the dining room. I've got a little time before our first guests are set to arrive and I need to get my game face on. I need to feel less like someone whose superhot boyfriend wants to ravish her across the very counter the amuse-bouches are being prepped on and more like someone who knows on what side of the plate the fork goes.

Tonight's pop-up is in a small ballroom on the forty-fifth floor of a high-rise luxury apartment building way up on the North Side. For a Friday night, it'll be a bit of a clusterfuck for anyone who lives in the heart of Chicago, the Loop, or out in the suburbs like my parents, to get up here, but the views of the boats on Lake Michigan and the sunset reflecting off the buildings in the skyline will be so worth it. This summer evening is the kind of night Instagram was made for.

How Benji secured the venue this time is a doozy. He put an ad on Craigslist: "Party Room Needed." Said he couldn't pay money for the space, but would leave all his leftovers behind *and* the secret to "a roasted chicken guaranteed to get you laid." Thirty minutes later, some teenager whose parents live in the building dropped off the keys to the penthouse floor. It never ceases to amaze me the things people will do just to feel like they have a personal connection to the Steven Tyler of the food world. Alas, here we are.

I push on the balcony door handles fully expecting they'd be locked. But they pop down with ease and the warm summer wind hits me in the face. I grab the railing, close my eyes and suck in that city air.

I don't breathe enough. Not like this, deep and alone. I have to admit that being Benji's girlfriend sometimes feels like sitting in the passenger seat as he drives 110 miles per hour on the freeway in a jalopy with no seat belts. It's easy to get overwhelmed, but I remind myself that Benji came into my life for a reason. Every douchey, going-nowhere guy I dated before him was worth it because they led me to him: a beautiful genius who knows exactly who he is and what he wants. A guy with talent, charisma and nothing but pure adoration for me. So what if he had a flawed start? All that matters is that I stopped the top from spinning out of control and now we're good. We're really fucking good.

Just then my phone, which I have stashed in my bra (hey, no pockets, okay?), buzzes with a text. I dig around in my cleavage and read the message from Benji.

2-top off elevator. It's time, babe.

My feet are aching and I'm sweating, but as far as everyone can tell by the smile on my face, I'm having a grand old time filling water glasses. By now, we're more than halfway through the service and so far, Benji's only used the bottle of bourbon in the back for a caramel-y glaze on the dessert course, not to ease the kitchen chaos. In fact, in the ten or so times I've popped my head in to check on him, he appeared to be keeping his cool entirely.

"And how are you two enjoying your evening?" I say, hovering over a couple at a round-top table I haven't checked on yet.

"There she is." My dad wipes his mouth as he stands up to give me a hug. My god, he's wearing a wool suit and a silk tie. Overdress much?

"What do you think of the food?" I ask.

"It's outstanding, Allie. Say, can we get another one of those Sriracha Jell-O cubes?"

"Goodness, Bill, don't embarrass me like that. Just ignore him, Allie. Although, yes, the Sriracha cube was..." My mom, Patty, closes her eyes, puckers her lips and explodes an air-kiss off the tips of her fingers. I think that's mom code for amaze-balls.

"I'm really glad you guys could make it," I say. And I mean that. It's not easy to accept the fact that your daughter is dating the most talked-about, tattooed chef in the Midwest, let alone show your support by attending a BYOB makeshift dinner party on the far North Side.

"Wouldn't miss it for the world. And hey, I couldn't figure out how to get the flash on this dang iPhone to work, but I took a bunch of pictures," my dad says. "You'll have to explain later how I'm supposed to send them to you."

I'm positive they will all be blurry, but it's the thought that counts.

"Is Benji going to come out?" my mom asks, playing with the pearls on her necklace. Her question captures the attention of strangers sitting across the table and now everyone's eyes are on me.

"We'll see," I say, knowing that answer isn't good enough.

Not for anyone in the room who paid to be here. "You'll have to excuse me. I've got to keep checking on other tables. Love you guys."

As I make my rounds, everyone seems to be gushing over the fifth and final course of the night: grilled fig panna cotta with a bourbon, honeycomb drizzle over vanilla bean gelato. I hear one person whisper it was better than Alinea's dessert. Another says she just had a foodgasm. At that, I set down the water pitcher and offer to clear a few dirty plates back to the kitchen. When no one is looking, I dip my pinky into some melted gelato and run it through a glob of the bourbon honey before quickly licking it off my manicured finger.

Heaven. Pure heaven.

Even though there's no negative feedback to report to the kitchen and everyone is stuffed, I can tell people are saving room for one more culinary delight.

They want to see Benji Zane.

Put it this way: sure, the tenderness on the squab was on point. And yes, the scoop of gelato was spherical as fuck. But as rock-star as his dishes may be, these people are here for something else entirely. They've ponied up to get up close and personal with Benji Zane and not just because he's easy on the eyes. To them, this is the Reformed Addict Show. It's their chance to witness firsthand if he's turned over a real leaf this time, or if he's just moments away from the downfall more than a few food bloggers think is coming.

My money is on the former.

Does that make me a naive idiot? Maybe. But these people don't know Benji like I do. The one thing I'm sure of is that I am Benji's number one supporter. If I waver from that, I know the chances of a slip are greater, so it's not something I'm willing to do. Especially not since we live together. I mean, *you* try staying ahead of the curve when your roommate has a kinky past with cocaine.

"Benji?" I say, cracking the kitchen door open a few inches. "Can you come here a sec?"

He puts down his knife roll and heads to the doorway, tapping Sebastian on the way over and telling him to take five.

"What is it? Everything good?" I can see the anxiety in his eyes. Whether it's an audience of one or a roomful of skeptical diners, Benji cuts zero corners when it comes to his cooking. He wants tonight to go seamlessly and if he's not pulling a huge profit in the end because of some dealer drama, well, then, his reputation among these unsuspecting people needs to be the thing that comes out on top.

"Everything's great," I whisper. "But are you going to step out? I think people want to applaud you. They loved everything. Honestly, it was the perfect night."

Benji's not shy. Not by a long shot. But I can tell he's delayed making his cameo until I offered up the reinforcement that people really are waiting in the wings like Bono's groupies.

"Really?" he asks.

"Really. Look at table eight. Bunch of food bloggers who wet their panties when they ate the deconstructed squash blossoms. I'm pretty sure they'll have a full-blown orgasm if you just come out and wave to them."

He peers over me to check out the guests. Table eight is all attractive blondes with hot-pink cell phone cases who must have taken a thousand photos so far. I'd worry, but when your reckless love story has been chronicled on every social media platform since its hot and heavy start, that makes it pretty official: Benji Zane is off the market, folks. Has been since the middle of May.

"Alright, fine. Give me a sec."

Benji ditches his apron and grabs my hand. Together, we

walk into the dining room and all chairs turn toward us. I feel a bit like the First Lady, just with a trendier outfit and a more tattooed Mr. President by my side. I bite back the urge to wave to our adoring fans.

"I just want to thank everyone for coming out tonight. I hope you enjoyed the food. It was my pleasure feeding you. Feel free to stick around and enjoy the view or see Allie for a cab if you need one. Good night, everyone." Benji holds our interlocked hands up and bows his head.

The crowd goes wild—well, as wild as forty diners who have all just slipped into a serious food coma can go. It's a happy state, the place Benji's food sends you. Kind of like how you feel after a long, passionate sex session. When done, you've got a slight smile and glow on your face, but just want to lie down for the foreseeable future and possibly smoke a cigarette.

I spot my father standing in the back, filming on his phone as my mother claps so hard, her Tiffany charm bracelet looks like it's about to unhinge and fall into what's left of her dessert. Seeing them both smile proudly across the room at who their daughter has wound up with warms my heart. It's been an uphill battle, but I'm confident we've won them over.

Benji whisks me back to the kitchen and before I can congratulate him on a successful evening, he pushes me up against the walk-in fridge. His tongue teases my mouth open and I am putty in his hands. With his right hand, he pulls down the collar of my romper, exposing my black lace bra. He frees my breast and kisses my nipple. My neck turns to rubber and my eyes roll back.

"Benji," I pathetically protest, very aware that all that separates us from a roomful of people who are currently picking a filter for a photo of the two of us holding hands is a swinging door that doesn't lock.

He continues kissing my neck, my breast still exposed. "I couldn't have done any of this without you, Allie."

"Oh, really?" I say, recognizing that the natural high he's on is most certainly fueling whatever is happening here. He slips a hand up my thigh.

"You made everyone out there have a good time tonight."

"I know," I playfully agree. He pulls my panties to the side. I know where this is going.

"And now it's my turn to get in on it."

Before I know it, he's inside of me and we're officially having sex against a cooler with forty people standing fifteen feet away, two of whom are my doting parents.

Sex between me and Benji has always been explosive. It's like he knows exactly what I need and where to touch me without me having to give a lick of instruction. Sex has never been like this in my entire life. Granted, I've only got about five solid years of experience, but nothing rivals what Benji has introduced me to in the last three months. There's virtually nothing I'll say no to with him. Pornos, toys and now public places. Who am I?

I'll figure it out *after* I get off. A few hushed moans later, and I'm there.

"You did so good tonight," he whispers in my ear as he helps adjust my outfit. "Now I need you to go back out there and get everyone to leave so I can fuck you again over that balcony with the view of the lake in the background. Okay?"

I come back down to earth and reply, "Yes, sir."

Back in the dining room, I brush shoulders with Benji's sous chef, who's on his way back to his station. I give Sebastian a nod and return to my post, trusty water pitcher in hand.

There are a few stragglers left in the dining room, including my parents, finishing the last sips of their BYO selections. From what I can tell as I clear empty dishes and put the tips in a billfold, people liked dinner. They *really* liked it. The average gratuity being left on the prepaid meal is about fifty dollars cash per person.

After subtracting the dealer's cut, it's looking like we'll walk with about $2,000 cash for ourselves and I can't help but feel like a bit of cheat. I know nothing about this world—this high-end foodie club that I got inducted into overnight—yet people are emptying their wallets of their hard-earned cash to show their gratitude for what we've done. Do they realize just hours ago, the black squid ink from course two was being stored on ice in my bathtub? Regardless, we need the money. Benji may have kicked his expensive habit, but I'm the only one with a steady job right now and being a social media manager for Daxa—yes, the organic cotton swab brand made famous by Katy Perry's makeup artist on Snapchat—isn't exactly like being the CEO of Morgan Stanley.

"Excuse me, where is the ladies' room?" a tipsy guest asks. Benji might not have taught me how to sous vide a filet mignon, but he did tell me you always walk a guest to the bathroom when they ask. I promptly put down the dirty glasses and the wad of tips and walk the boozy babe to the loo.

Upon my return, I nearly collide with another guest, this one quite a bit soberer.

"Allie." The prim-looking thirtysomething woman with a bleached-blond pixie cut says my name matter-of-factly. I stand up straight; this chick has *CRITIC* written all over her face.

"Yes, ma'am. Can I help you? Do you need a taxi?"

"No, thank you. I just wanted to give you a tip."

"Oh, that's so kind of you. You can actually just leave a gratuity on the table."

"No, I meant, like, some advice."

I tilt my head to the side and try not to lose my grip on my smiley service. She's five foot nothing, but her demeanor is as bold as her bright red lipstick.

"I'm not sure Benji would be cool with you leaving a bill-fold with what I'd guess is about $2,000 in it just sitting on a table in a room full of drunk people who don't know that it's time to go home. It would behoove you to keep an eye on your shit."

She jams the billfold into my chest and proceeds to walk right past me to the elevator bank.

And just like that, I've officially been felt up twice in one night.

2

It's been two days since the pop-up and I'm meeting my girl-friends, Jazzy and Maya, for a *very* belated birthday celebration they arranged at Tavern on Rush, a glitzy Gold Coast eatery whose only meal I can afford is this one: Sunday brunch.

I've known Jazzy and Maya since high school. We ended up going our separate ways for college, but stayed in touch through thousands of group texts and visits home over the holidays. The four years flew by and it was no surprise that we would all wind up back in the city after graduation. The two of them live together in a cute two-bed-plus-den walk-up in Bucktown. They asked me if I wanted in on the lease but the could-be third bedroom was more like a *Harry Potter* closet and by that point I had determined my days of trying to hook up with a guy on a twin-size mattress ended the moment I was handed my bachelor's degree. So that's how I wound up solo in a studio in Lincoln Park, but it's all good—especially given how things shook out with Benji.

Admittedly, it's taken longer than it should for our little friend group to get together and celebrate my big quarter-of-a-century milestone, but I've been...well, I've been with Benji. Regardless, today we've got reserved patio seats looking out onto an area of town called "The Viagra Triangle" and the change of scenery, no matter how perverse, is welcome.

There's no direct route from Lincoln Park to this part of town, but the people-watching is worth the public transportation shortcomings. Everywhere we look, there are men sixty

years and older valeting drop-top Bentley convertibles and
ushering around girls my age with tight bodycon dresses and
fake tits. What these ladies will do for a Chanel purse the size
of a dog crate is...well, come to think of it, pretty similar to
what people do to get near Benji. I just hope no one petitions
us for a foursome while we're sitting out here.

"Thanks for putting this together, you guys," I say as a mon-
tage of mimosa flutes and Bloody Mary tumblers connect in
the center of our table.

"Cheers to twenty-five!!" they harmonize back.

"Oh, wait. Keep your glasses like that," I say. "This is a
great Instagram."

I pull out my phone to get the bird's-eye shot: Jazzy's champagne flute angled slightly toward Maya's Bloody Mary tumbler. Fresh pastel-colored gel manicures and just a hint of the
robust bread basket overflowing in the lower left corner. It's
perfect for my Sunday morning social streams.

Too bad I'm not actually taking the picture. I'm really just
checking my phone to see if Benji has tried to reach me. I
know if I pull it out at the table and start texting, the girls
will give me major shit about the fact I can't go two hours
without looking at it.

But what they don't understand is how tough it really is to
leave Benji alone knowing he doesn't have a pop-up to prepare
for this week or a bank of trustworthy friends of his own to
hang with at the moment. I worry that the boredom may lead
to something more sinister. Alas, there are no new messages
from him, which could actually mean he's at an NA meeting.
I take a calming breath at the thought and strive to be a little
more present at my special birthday brunch.

"Did you get it? My arm's getting tired," Maya says.

"Oh, damn, my storage is full. Let me delete some photos
and we'll try again when our food comes."

The three-egg veggie omelet on the menu catches my eye. Sometimes, the simpler the dish, the better when Benji isn't around. Because when he is, it's always something like evaporated pancake mix with bacon jam. Delicious? Yes. Swoonworthy? Totally. But filling? Hardly. And even though gourmet is my new normal, I enjoy the simple throwbacks, especially when they come with a side of home-style hash browns. When it's time to order, I make a game-time decision to go sweet instead of savory, locking in the cinnamon brioche French toast and a promise to go for a jog by the lake later.

"I feel like I haven't seen you in forever," Jazzy says as she hands her menu back to the server, who trots off to put in our orders. I can't tell if she's peeved that I've dropped off the radar a bit, or just stating a fact. "I have bangs now."

I love how Jazzy is using her bold hair choices as a milestone for our hangouts. From now on, I wouldn't be surprised if we refer to things as "BB"—Before Bangs—and "AB"—After Bangs—which coincidentally aligns with Before Benji and After Benji. Either way, they suit her well. But when you look like Padma Lakshmi's little sister and work as a buyer for Nordstrom, how could a trendy haircut betray your already perfect sense of style?

I think back on when the last time we all got together actually was and realize it was for our book club meeting a few months ago. It was my turn to host and Benji was only about a week sober at that point. I hadn't yet told the girls he was living with me, nor had I filled them in on any of the gory details about his addiction, but I couldn't cancel on them the day of. I also couldn't tell Benji to get lost for a couple hours while we girls drank half a crate of wine and discussed periods, recent blow-job mishaps and a little bit about the book *Gone Girl*. So I explained that I was having friends over to talk about a book we were all reading and would try to hurry it up.

"You don't have to rush because of me," he immediately said. "If these girls are important to you, they're important to me."

"I know, but there will be wine. A lot of wine."

"There will always be wine, babe. It doesn't tempt me anymore, though. So why don't you just sit down, relax and let me make you ladies some canapés."

Before I had a chance to answer, my doorman was calling up to my unit to let me know my first guests had arrived.

As they filed in, I glossed over the introduction and explanation of Benji. He waved and smiled and looked hot in his apron while whipping up some hors d'oeuvres in the kitchen. The girls took their seats around the coffee table in my living room as I fetched a wine key from the utensil drawer.

"Sorry, babe," I whispered as I grabbed the bottle opener from the drawer next to him.

"Stop apologizing, Al. *Enjoy yourself*. Please."

On my tippy toes, I reached up to plant a kiss on his lips. That's the first moment I realized I had it all.

A half hour later, Benji walked into the room with a tray of snacks. I know the girls were expecting some crackers and brie, but when he placed the canapés that could be on the cover of *Plate* magazine in front of us on the coffee table, everyone took their phones out and started Snapchatting like crazy.

"Holy shit. Does he cook like this all the time?"

"Oh my god, is this for real?"

"Did he just whip this up for us?"

Yes, yes and yes.

As the night went on, so did the culinary surprises from Benji. Deconstructed *elotes* featuring yellow corn, homemade mayo and parmesan cheese. Crispy cucumber slices with fresh-made garlic hummus and dehydrated cranberries. Mini toast points with guacamole made from avocadoes that were sitting on my countertop earlier that day. All of these treats came from ordinary groceries I happened to have in my fridge and pantry.

I soon recognized the infamous Benji Zane food coma coming over my girlfriends. At that, a few excused themselves by way of an Uber, leaving Jazzy, Maya and me to sit and chat while Benji cleaned up the kitchen and fixed himself dinner with the leftovers. That's when I decided to tell them about my new living arrangement. I figured doing so after they'd experienced the Benji Effect firsthand would lessen the judgmental blowback that comes with telling people you've reached a major relationship milestone seemingly overnight.

Jazzy: "He's living here now? God, you're so lucky."

Maya: "Agree. Maybe *book club* should morph into *supper club*, and permanently be at your place."

Me: Mission accomplished.

"Sorry, it's been crazy," I say, returning to our brunch conversation. It's minimal, but true.

"Speaking of crazy, can we talk about this?" Maya flips her wavy red hair over her shoulder and holds her phone my way. Her gap-toothed smile gets bigger by the second. I squint to see what's lit up on her screen but before I can make it out, Jazzy grabs it from across the table for a better look of her own.

"'Hot in the Kitchen,'" she reads. "'Zane Stuns at North Side Pop-up.'"

"No way," I say. "Gimme that."

"Oh yeah, your face is all over *FoodFeed*," Maya confirms, spiraling a curl around her pointer finger.

She's right. *FoodFeed*—the quintessential dining-out blog of Chicago—has posted their review of Friday's pop-up and chosen a photo of Benji holding my hand and bowing as the article's hero image. Damn, we look good together.

Skimming the post, I see that *FoodFeed* approves of everything from the courtship to the courses. I scroll down to the comments and aside from one that says, "The fuck is she wearing?" in what I assume is in regards to my romper, it all seems positive. I text myself the link from Maya's phone before giving it back to her.

I never used to care what *FoodFeed* had to say, mostly because I never knew what *FoodFeed* was. But since Benji's name is as common on there as a photo of a doughnut on Instagram, I figured I had better familiarize myself. Not to mention, they're the ones who broke the news we were dating in the first place.

When I hear the ding from inside my bag, the link to the article isn't the only new message I've received. I've somehow missed five texts from Benji in the last few minutes.

Hi.

How's brunch?

When R U coming home?

How do I go from TV to DVD with this remote?

Hello???

I picture him on the couch struggling to figure out how to put on *Little Miss Sunshine* but the directions are too much to type without being rude to Jazzy and Maya. So I quickly forward him the article in hopes that it distracts him long enough to realize he can probably just find the flick for free OnDemand.

Moments later, our brunch order arrives. The food runner places my French toast in front of me and our server follows behind him with a plate of ricotta pancakes.

"You're Allie Simon, right?" he asks.

"Yes, why?"

"I knew it." He puts the plate down and smiles proudly.

None of us ordered the short stack, but the fluffy pillows of perfection with their golden-blond hue look and smell delicious.

"I had the kitchen make these for you as a thank-you. I was at the pop-up Friday. My girlfriend got us tickets for my birthday."

"Did you enjoy it?"

"Did I? Pardon my French, but holy shit, your boyfriend can cook. I mean, seriously, I have been dreaming about those squash blossoms ever since our Uber ride home. Do you know when his next dinner will be?"

"No, I'm sorry, I don't. It all depends on securing a venue. But if you follow him on Twitter, he usually announces them there."

"Oh, I already do. And on Instagram. And on Facebook. And I follow you, too, actually," he says, completely fangirling out.

"Wow, thank you for...all your support. And for the pancakes."

I can feel my face turn as red as Maya's hair. I'm used to attention when out with him, but the fact I'm now being recognized on my own takes the reality of this high-profile relationship up a notch.

The server scampers away, looking like he just got laid. I've completely made this guy's day and I'm not really sure how.

"Unreal," Jazzy says.

"You literally have the craziest life," Maya echoes.

Yeah, I guess this ain't too shabby, I think to myself as I forklift the top pancake and plop it onto my plate.

So how does a girl like me wind up even crossing paths with a guy like Benji? We don't hang with the same people.

We don't like the same things. Before him, the hardest drug I'd ever been around was pot smoked out of a water bottle at a frat party. On the food side of things, I never knew what a Michelin star was, nor could I fathom a world in which people paid $400 for a single meal. Before Benji, I could be found shopping the Nordstrom anniversary sale with Jazzy's discount, hanging at some lawyer-laden soiree with some of Maya's coworkers or out fulfilling my quest to collect as many punches as possible on my frozen yogurt loyalty card. None of that lent itself to meeting a guy like Benji.

Well, as it happens, while manning the social streams for Daxa-related news one day, I saw a chef tweet a video of plating a really beautiful dish of food using tweezers and our very own cotton swabs. I clicked on the guy's profile and realized he was someone with some social media worth, 16,000+ followers. According to his bio, he was the executive chef of a restaurant I hadn't heard of in the heart of downtown Chicago and seemed to enjoy chronicling his every moment in the kitchen online.

So I did what Daxa pays me to do: I "at-replied" him and retweeted his picture with a cheeky caption. Cleans your ears, cleans your eats.

In the moments that followed, my professional responsibilities combined with my personal curiosity and down the Google rabbit hole I went. I punched his name into a blank search bar and was blown away by what I found next.

One of the first hits back was a YouTube video of him sitting in front of a computer with his feet up on a desk looking remarkably cool. The cameraman sneaks up behind him to catch a glimpse of what Benji's watching on the screen. Surprise! It's a porno. "So what's on the menu tonight, Chef Zane?" says the person filming. "Cream pie?" Benji jumps, lets out a loud "Fuck you…" and the room explodes in cackles. Thank god I had my headphones on.

I then clicked over to the Images tab and saw no shortage of eye candy there. Hell, there were entire Pinterest boards dedicated to his glorious man-bun. Most of the pictures were candid ones of him cooking, but there were definitely quite a few—some in color, some in black-and-white—of him hamming it up for the camera.

I got stuck on one photo in particular. It was connected to a write-up in *GQ* titled "Knife Fight." He was pictured standing with his shirt off holding a butcher's knife that was covered in red pepper puree meant to look like blood dripping off the blade. He was tatted up to his chin with everything from olive tree branches to a pig being roasted over an open flame. Over his left knuckles, the word *RARE*. Over his right, *WELL*. Kudos for having a theme, I thought. His face had a wicked, smug stare on it as if he was thinking, "You can't tell because the photo is cropped, but I'm getting an awesome blow job right now."

He was hot—at least, I guessed that's the word you'd use to describe someone who's both intimidating and alluring all at the same time. Even though he wasn't my usual type, a small part of me wondered right then what it would be like to walk into his restaurant, sit alone at the bar with a view into the open kitchen and wait to see if a girl like me could catch the attention of a guy like him as I sipped on a glass of wine.

I hit on a few more links that day and caught myself reading what others were saying about him in the comments section of some blog.

"Just what the city needs. Another druggie chef."

"He's not on drugs, you idiot."

"Doesn't he only cook while super high?"

"He's been clean for years. Get your facts straight."

"I heard he powders their doughnut holes with cocaine."

"I'd let him powder my doughnut hole with cocaine."

Okay, so he may or may not be the Charlie Sheen of the culinary world, I thought to myself. But despite his sordid past, he clearly was a fan favorite. Whether people were loving or hating on him, the one thing that was inarguable across the board was that Benji Zane came with an obsessive following.

But at the first mention of a drug problem, I tightly closed the lid on my digital crush. There's always a catch with guys in Chicago, right? Just as I finished x-ing out of all the tabs I had opened about him, he tweeted back at me—well, Daxa I mean.

See America? Even @DaxaSwabs knows I'm clean LOL

Yes, he went there. #Awkward.

I wanted to say I was shocked, but something about the frequency at which he was firing off random thoughts of 280 characters or less told me he wasn't the kind of guy who'd ignore attention from a major brand—be it America's favorite cotton swab or Calphalon—when he could spin it in his favor.

It was never my intention to allude to his could-be sobriety in a tweet, a subject that was well over my head for sure, but according to my job description I needed to continue to engage with him. Daxa's social media policy states that when engaging with an influencer, we should never be the ones to drop the conversation—let them tire, get distracted or sign off. So I cracked my knuckles and got down to business trying to steer this conversation into more neutral territory.

Hey @BJZane, we got your back. But mostly your ears.

@DaxaSwabs if I can get your tongue, U R welcome 4 dinner at my resto anytime. #NotAPervyTweet #JustTryingToBeNice

As we bantered back and forth behind the safety of our respective avatars, I began to find him palatable. Where was the big, scary addict dude that everyone was gossiping about on the blogs?

That's when the fantasy I had of meeting him got the best of me and I did something typically frowned upon in the Daxa social media handbook. I reached out to him from my personal account, introducing myself as the voice behind the cotton swab conversation.

He replied right away and said I was really funny. And hot. Funny and hot? I'll take it.

We spent the rest of the day exchanging DMs. I even forwent a company lunch outing to stay back at my desk and keep the flirt fest going, telling everyone I had a mini crisis with a user who had a swab stuck in his ear. A couple hours later, he had to leave for a restaurant meeting. But not before he publicly tweeted, Everyone go follow my new friend @AllieSimon— she's a real cool chick.

Wait. *Really?*

A few days later, Benji sent me a direct message. He said he had only one night off from the restaurant and if I wanted to meet him, now would be the time and a little dive bar in the Logan Square neighborhood would be the place.

I didn't respond right away.

Did I want to meet him?

It's not that I had other plans. It's just that I hadn't actually thought about crossing the IRL threshold with him. It's a lot easier to converse with a tattooed guy who may or may not be addicted to drugs when you have the luxury of thinking about what you'll say next as you hide behind your double monitors from the comfort of a cubicle.

So, for the time being, I resolved I'd table the in-person option and just ignore his ask.

Thirty minutes later, he sent another DM, one that couldn't be ignored: It's now or never. Are you meeting me tonight or not?

On one hand, he seemed aggressive. A little too intense for me. On the other, it was intoxicating that this quasi-celebrity chef dude wanted to hang out with me so badly, he had to wave a limited-time-only offer in front of my face to get me to act.

Another fact about me: I'm not one to pass up a good deal.

Yeah, I'm in, I coyly responded back, even though I was terrified at the thought of stepping out of my comfort zone.

Good choice, he typed back.

A few hours later, I put on some eyeliner and walked over to the meeting place with zero expectations. When I saw this rough and tough hottie sitting at the counter drinking a generous serving of neat whiskey, I knew I was in for more than I bargained for. I probably should have run before he had a chance to see me. I could have easily DM'd him, said my bus broke down or I got stuck at work. But I just couldn't turn away.

"There she is, Miss Allie Simon, everybody," he said along with a slow clap.

I looked around and there was no one else in the bar, which made his intro of me both silly and sweet. I could feel my nerves dialing down a notch.

"Hello, Benji," I said, putting out my hand for a shake. He grabbed it, flipped it and kissed the top of my hand.

"Hi, Allie."

"What can I get for you?" the bartender asked, putting a cocktail napkin down in front of me.

"Uh, how about a sauv blanc?"

"You're at a whiskey and burger bar, babe," the condescending bartender said back. "We don't have *sauv blanc*."

"The fuck you don't." Benji stepped in. "Go ask your chef what he puts in the mustard glaze. And bring an empty glass back there while you're at it."

The bartender gave us side-eye, realized it was Benji Zane shouting that order and grabbed a tumbler as he departed to the kitchen.

"Fucking idiots," Benji whispered to himself as he took a sip of his drink. "So, how are you?"

He put his hand on my thigh as he asked the question—an action I would normally reject from a guy who wasn't physically my type. After all, I was drawn to dudes who looked like they were sent home the first night on *The Bachelorette*. Clean-cut, maybe wearing a little concealer, just trying to be nice until we took things to the Fantasy Suite.

Like I said, walking, talking cliché.

Before I could answer, the bartender came back.

"Sorry, we don't have wineglasses. But here's your sauv blanc."

"Well, cheers," said Benji.

"How did you know…"

"It's a burger place. They have mustard."

"So?"

"I assume if they're charging $15 for a basic hamburger, they probably make the mustard in-house, meaning there's got to be a crisp white wine in the walk-in cooler back there or they wouldn't be able to get the recipe right. He knew they had sauv blanc. He was just being a douchebag who was too lazy to walk ten feet and get it."

I had been out with straitlaced stockbrokers sporting impeccably tousled hair who had held doors for me, brought me flowers for a first date and pushed in my chair for me at dinner. But no one in the last two months had ramped up my mojo as much as Benji had in that first five minutes. He stuck up for me—and my girlie drink order—all while showing off his culinary chops just a little bit.

From that point on, I knew he was going to be trouble. But I never imagined he'd become *my* trouble. Big difference.

Throughout the night, Benji excused himself a handful of times to go to the bathroom. Sure, a part of me wondered if he was doing coke in there, but I had to remember we both were drinking. I, too, would be in and out of the bathroom all night had I broken the seal earlier. Also, I had never done coke, nor did I know anyone in my social circle who had, so what was I looking for anyway? White powder to be coating his nostrils? A nagging itch at his nose? For what it was worth, neither of those things were happening, so I shrugged it off and stopped counting his trips to the bathroom. After all, I wasn't in this for the long run, so what the guy did in the men's room was none of my business. All that mattered was that he kept rejoining me back at the bar and picking up right where our scintillating conversation left off.

A one-night stand was inevitable. But by the time I realized the drug thing was real, and it was serious, we were way past just one night.

3

It's late in the workday Monday when I get an email from my alma matter, Mizzou. It's the quarterly journalism alumni update wherein they compile a list of about a hundred bullet points, all just quick mentions of who got hired where, which people have been promoted at their jobs and which of the former editors are now stay-at-home moms and freelance taste testers for Nabisco. Being three years post-grad and still happily working for an ear-cleaning company, this digest is basically my version of *Page Six* news.

Which is why I'm particularly shocked to see my name about a third of the way down the list.

Allie Simon is dating celebrity chef Benji Zane. They live together in Chicago.

Normally the chairman of the department solicits for these kinds of updates, and this is most certainly a blurb that I did not submit myself. So the fact that one of the best journalism schools in the country has scooped this intel straight from a popular food blog *and* finds my personal life newsworthy makes me feel like a goddamn celebrity, I must admit.

I don't blame them for not including a word about my role at Daxa in the roundup. In fact, it's kind of a shameful career choice considering I was at one point the managing editor of the school paper. But the truth is, I never wanted to be a reporter and by the time I pocketed my degree and moved back to Chicago, the way the world works had changed. People wanted to speak and read in bursts of 280 characters or less and Daxa, headquartered here in the River North neighborhood, was looking for someone to help them get in on a conversation of that caliber. Couple that with my need to pay bills and suddenly tweeting about cotton swabs became my calling. Or something like that.

It's always a bit difficult to play catch-up on Monday mornings since we switch over to an automated community management system for nights and weekends. Unfortunately, the "NightHawk2000" has the personality of a bad first date and sometimes misses an influx of tweets if the system has to reboot itself—which it does, often. I want to say that today is no different, but it's actually worse. Taking off last Friday for Benji's pop-up set me back about 300 replies before 9:00 a.m.

I somehow make it through the day and am now standing outside my office waiting for the Route 22 bus up to Lincoln Park while group texting with Jazzy and Maya about tonight's premiere of the new season of *The Bachelor*.

Maya: Starts @ 7. My Place?

Jazzy: Can BZ whip up some garlic hummus?

Suddenly, I'm interrupted by a tap on my shoulder.

"Babe! What are you doing here?" I pull my headphones out as Benji brings me in for a clammy hug. He clearly walked to my office, which is a good forty-five minutes at a brisk pace. He smells like a cigarette accompanied him and deodorant did not. Still, I'm happy to breathe him in, although I'm regretting the fact I haven't touched up my makeup at all today. It may sound shallow, but in my defense, I'm not like Benji. I can't just throw on a white Hanes V-neck with a sweaty man-bun and automatically look like I should be on the cover of *People*'s Sexiest Man Alive issue.

Plus, this is an ambush. *He* surprised *me* outside my work. Now, what for is the question.

"Remember how I told you there were a few VIPs on the dinner list at the pop-up? I circled their names on the sheet I gave you before service…" His eyes are big and intense. Kind of like how they always are, I guess.

I squint as I rack my brain. I don't remember any one person in particular, but immediately panic wondering if they all got food poisoning or something.

Benji doesn't wait for a reply.

"The guy who runs Republic, Ross Luca, invited us in tonight."

Ross Luca is a Chicago restaurateur—an iconic one at that. I know this because *FoodFeed loves* Ross Luca. They seem to run a blog post about him daily. At first, I wanted to know who he was paying off for all the good press, but then I realized there's a lot to cover about Ross. For one thing, he's both a businessman and executive chef. In something like two short years, he's managed to open everything from a kitschy Jewish deli to an over-the-top steak house and rotates cooking at them all, six days a week. It's rare to find someone like that, who can fire from both sides of the brain. Who can be artistic in the kitchen *and* savvy in the boardroom. Everyone in the industry knows that Ross Luca is that prodigy. Hell, even a typically jealous Benji agrees Ross is the shit. Which is why his name was highlighted and starred on the VIP list— that I recall for sure.

While he may have just about every cuisine in this city cornered, Republic is Ross's fine-dining spot. *FoodFeed* called it "an instant classic" when it opened about a year ago and the reservation list hasn't dwindled one bit since then, despite the $150+ per person price tag. Which leads me to my next point: we can't go.

"Well, that's exciting. But…Republic is for very wealthy people."

"Or for normal people pretending to be rich for the night," he casually volleys back.

"Right. Either way, a $400 meal for two is pretty grotesque. Don't you think?"

"I do."

He's not at all picking up what I am throwing down. The majority of our profit from the pop-up Friday has already been used for bills, groceries and drug debts, and I've set the rest aside for September's rent since he hasn't scheduled the next pop-up yet.

"Relax, Allie. It's on the house. No charge for us."

"Holy shit!" Yes, I'm a grown woman squealing in middle of the sidewalk. If people weren't already staring at us, they are now.

"Wait, so let me get this straight," I say. "Ross Luca invited you and me to eat *free* at Republic tonight? That's so freaking awesome. What time's the reso?"

"Eh, right now, actually. Sorry, I know it's kind of early for multicourse dining but I expect we'll be there awhile."

The expression on my face sags a bit as I remember my plans to watch *The Bachelor* at Maya's.

"Something wrong, babe?" he asks.

"No. Nothing." I smile big to reassure him I'm so in for this.

"Great. Can I get the cash?"

Although having to ask your girlfriend for money to treat her may not feel like the most graceful display of chivalry, he knows the drill. That I'm the keeper of the cash. So I hand over a portion of the tips we made at the pop-up, our "fun money" as we like to call it, as discreetly as I can. In exchange, he grabs my chin and kisses me directly on the lips.

"Wait here, I'll flag us a taxi," he says, bolting to the curb.

I could call us an Uber from my phone. It would make trying to hail a cab during rush hour in River North a nonissue, but it's linked to my credit card. And I can tell Benji wants full credit for this date so I let him hunt and gather while I text Maya that I won't be able to make it to her place tonight.

Maya: It's kind of tradition, A...

Me: Sry! Republic = MAJOR. Can we watch tmrw?

Maya: Jazzy's already on her way. Can't cancel.

Me: OK. Will watch online over my lunch tmrw. Next wk 4 sure!

I toss my phone back into my bag and cringe as I look down at my pencil skirt, flats and button-up shirt. I'm dressed like a district attorney. I dig around in my trusty Marc Jacobs tote for some lip gloss and a hair clip, then spend the rest of the ride over touching up my makeup and trying to pull my day-old hair into a decent-looking chignon. Before we get out of the cab, Benji uploads a selfie of the two of us to his Snapchat story, tagging Republic in the post. It's been live for all of five seconds and I can already feel the notifications vibrating my bag.

"Welcome, Benji. Hello, Allie." The hostess knows who we are without us having to introduce ourselves. I feel like a celebrity. "Follow me."

As we trail the blonde hostess into the main dining area, I soak in the interior of the restaurant. Right away I see they run a silent kitchen—ten chefs, all with their heads down. Benji always says the quieter the kitchen, the more expensive the meal. Thank god this is getting comped.

We are led to a table in the middle of the dining room, close to the window nearest the entrance. It's a strategic move on the restaurant's part—so we can see everything and be seen by everyone. Once seated, we aren't handed menus. When you're a guest of the guy in charge, you eat what he cooks, end of story.

"Congrats on the *FoodFeed* review. Well done, Chef Zane," the blonde says before walking back to her post.

It's apparent she's seen the article. Perhaps that's how she knew exactly who I was.

The table attendant pours our water after ascertaining our preference for still. "Hey, nice going with the pop-up. *Food-Feed* said you killed it," he whispers to Benji.

"So, has *everyone* in the industry seen this post?" I ask with a hint of sarcasm as I unfold my napkin and place it on my lap. Doing this promptly and coyly is something Benji once said separates the restaurant pros from the Friday-night novices. In fact, it's a tactic I used while hosting the pop-up last week to measure the ratio of actual VIPs to slutty chef-chasers (1:5).

Benji takes a sip of his water and cracks his knuckles on the table. "Well, babe, we showed them what's up. They fucking loved everything."

He pulls out his phone, normally a faux pas at a fine-dining restaurant unless you're quickly snapping a photo of some rare black truffles. I think it's to check the number of views on our selfie, but he actually references the *FoodFeed* article for the hundredth time. I suspect he's a little addicted to the good news, but that's a vice I can handle.

"… From the high-end venue, to the bone-china soup bowls, it appeared that no corners were cut this time."

"… Zane seemed remarkably poised despite a crowded dining room. Especially for someone who's rumored to have a serious past with hard drugs…"

"… We'll be dreaming of the bourbon honeycomb panna cotta dessert until the next pop-up is announced."

As he reads the praise, I can't stop staring at this man who I call mine.

"Don't look at me like that…" He catches me.

"I can't help it. You're kind of incredible."

"Only because of you, babe." I smile at the credit given. "And I said don't look at me like that or I'm not going to be able to wait until we're home to fuck you."

He may be blunt. He may be crass. But his matter-of-fact confidence in my feelings for him reinforces that we are working.

"Benji, Allie, good to see you both." Ross graces us with his presence at the table. Did he hear Benji discuss his plans for me later? The thought causes my face to heat and Benji to smirk at me before getting up to shake Ross's hand. I get up to do the same but Ross waves me back down. "Please, sit. Relax."

All eyes in the restaurant turn like magnets in our direction. I remember Ross from the pop-up looking remarkably dapper for a fortysomething-year-old. His slicked-back brown hair contrasted his piercing blue eyes, not to be one-upped by the purple gingham shirt with a navy bow tie he was sporting. Tonight Ross is dialed down in a long, all-black apron and dressed to cook. It's his turn to show off what he's got.

I wonder if he feels like because he ate a good meal, he now owes us a favor—or if it's more of a pissing match. A "you cook good, but I cook better" type of thing. Who knows? I'm just hungry.

"So, no allergies, right?" Ross asks.

"Nope, just…three months sober," Benji says with a nervous laugh. Has it been three months already? Damn, now that's something to celebrate.

"Got it, so we'll hold off on pairings, then." Ross's tone

is matter-of-fact. "Well, I hope you brought your appetites. I'm going to head back to the kitchen and get going on your first course. If you need anything, we've got Steve as the lead server tonight and Felix is his assistant." Felix is the guy who got us our water. He nods in the background.

Ross departs and I spy a few rogue eaters awkwardly trying to make it look like they weren't just taking a picture of us from across the room on their phones.

"To three months and a great *FoodFeed* review," I say, clinking my water glass against Benji's. "Proud of you, babe."

Moments later, a plate arrives with a single tortellini on it. I grab my knife and fork and prepare to dig in.

"Whoa, whoa. Hold up," Benji says. "That's the amuse-bouche."

"So?"

He swallows his portion and replies: "It's a one-bite."

From across the table, Benji uses his fork and shimmies my tortellini onto it.

"Open," he directs.

I close my mouth around the tortellini.

"Now chew slowly. Take it all in. Let the taste hit your palate like a slow leak."

Nothing like the manic addict telling *me* to slow down to show the world how far he's come.

We're six hours into what I can only describe as a food coma meets a red carpet event. The three-hour premier of *The Bachelor* has come and gone, and every half hour Steve and Felix have brought out some mind-blowing dish featuring food I've never heard of, and certainly never dreamed I'd be eating.

Our tenth course of the night arrives and by now, the restaurant rush is over and the dining room is starting to filter out. After all, it's only Monday.

"I'm literally so full," I whisper, trying my best to tap out.

"You have to keep eating, babe."

"I can't, I feel like I'm going to burst." I'm a petite girl being suffocated by a pencil skirt, for crying out loud. Benji knows I'm struggling, especially since we're still on the savory courses. He looks around to make sure Ross is nowhere to be seen and takes a forkful of venison from my plate, devouring it in one bite.

"Jesus. How are you still hungry, Benji?"

"I'm not. It's just rude to leave food behind when they're doing what they're doing."

"Showing off?"

"Basically."

Ross makes his way back out to the dining room. As he approaches our table, he unties the knot on his apron, a sign that the white flag has been raised—no more food, thank god.

"How was it?" Ross asks.

"Fucking delicious, man. Everything was bomb. Seriously, dude."

"Nice, that's what I like to hear. I've got our pastry chef working on your dessert courses now. Figured I'd leave the sweet finish up to the pro in this case."

I put my hand over my stomach like my food baby is kicking.

"Listen, Benji. If I don't see you while I'm breaking down the kitchen, I just wanted to say thanks for coming in. I loved what you did at the pop-up last week and if you ever want to come in and stage, just hit me up. Cool? And hey, congrats on the sobriety, man. That's killer."

Benji gets up and gives Ross a hug. I follow. It's the first time I've stood in several hours and my legs feel like jelly. I'm wondering if that's because of the lack of blood flow or the fact that I've gained twenty pounds since being here.

Dessert is an orgasmic chocolate cake with little gold flakes throughout the ganache, served with a pot of gooey, warm caramel, which shockingly I manage to find room for. Afterward, Felix comes to bus our plates as Steve tells us the cake course completes the evening. He wishes us both a good night and departs to the back-of-house. That's it. There is no check presented, no paperwork that shows we came, we ate, we conquered.

Benji stretches his arms and protrudes his food-filled belly forward. He must feel like a king right now. He digs into his pockets and proceeds to count the rest of the cash I gave him earlier.

"What's that for?" I say.

"Kitchen tip-out."

"Are you going to leave it all?"

Instead of verbally answering me, he puts the twenties down on the table one at a time like he's dealing cards from a deck until there are none left.

Though it's a bit hard to see him spend everything that's left from what we made on Friday, I know it doesn't cover a fraction of what this dinner would cost a regular patron.

But between everything I saw and tasted tonight, I'm now 100 percent convinced we are anything but regular.

"Ready, babe?" he asks, helping me out of my chair. We walk hand in hand toward the front of the restaurant, where we pass the blonde hostess who sat us so many hours ago.

"Have a good night," I say to her.

"Excuse me..." she says back, checking over her shoulder for management. "Could I take a quick picture with you guys?"

The three of us squeeze in together as Benji extends his arm out with her phone to press the button. *Anything but regular*, I think to myself again as I smile big for the camera.

4

"Babe."

One Mississippi. Two Mississippi. I award myself a mental grace period in hopes that Benji realizes the sandwich I'm making requires actual skill. For me, at least. I don't cook much anymore—well, let's be frank, I never really did—now that an esteemed chef shares my address. But when I'm hungry and he's exhausted, it's back to a basic turkey-and-cheese for me.

I didn't think I'd ever feel hungry again after last night's nonstop food fest at Republic, but Benji picked up a crusty-on-the-outside, soft-on-the-inside loaf of bread with actual chunks of roasted garlic baked right in it from the Farmer's Market while I was at work. And it's a beacon of carby goodness that won't stop calling my name.

Just like Benji.

"Hey, sweet babe?" he asks again.

"Yeah? What is it?" I finally respond after a lengthy pause.

"Come here. Come look at this email. I'm pretty sure I'm getting a fucking restaurant."

Benji has left my laptop open on the couch, I'm assuming for me to peruse said email at my leisure while he grabs one of the last Camel Lights from a dingy pack in the pocket of his gray hoodie. I bought that pack for him earlier this morning as he walked me to the bus stop and it already looks like it's been through a shredder. Stressful day of buying fancy bread and checking email on the couch?

I've always thought there were two kinds of smokers: the

James Deans and the truck-stop loiterers. Benji is a James Dean, so I let it slide, especially since a cig hanging from his lips means he's not smoking coke through a foil pipe.

I humor him, taking a seat on *my* couch and grabbing *my* laptop. To be clear, I'm not fighting some sort of custody battle over inanimate objects. It's just that ever since Benji moved in with me a few months ago, boundaries have become a bit... blurred? Most days, I really like sharing my space with Benji. But every once in a while, I start to feel a little claustrophobic. It could be the 500-square-feet cabin fever kicking in, but today is most definitely one of those days.

Last night, I was famous, he was sober, and we were more in love than ever before when we had amazing sex until two in the morning. Then come 9:00 a.m., I was sluggishly pushing out tweets about a cotton swab while wondering why Jazzy and Maya wouldn't text me back about some stupid TV show and if my direct deposit will hit when it's supposed to so my bills aren't late. It's exhausting going from cloud nine to nine-to-five over and over.

Again, not the time for an emotional audit. Not when I need to see what this email is all about.

Dear Benji, the email begins. Before I read more, I peek at the sender's address: a.blackstone.82@gmail.com. The email rings a bell, though I can't quite place it.

My name is Angela Blackstone. I was a patron at last week's pop-up dinner.

Bingo. It all comes back to me. I picture pasting her name and email into an Excel spreadsheet and recall her paying for two tickets to last Friday's penthouse event.

As a fan of the Chicago food scene and industry professional myself (I'm the General Manager of Florette just outside of Chicago), I can confidently say you are doing some of the most interesting, flat-out genius stuff I have ever seen in a kitchen. From the carrot mousse as the amuse-bouche to the bourbon honeycomb panna cotta for the sweet finish, it was all so theatrical. Meaningful. Complicated. Appetizing. Amazing.

Now to be candid, as much as I follow your culinary delights, I am also privy to what they say about your lifestyle. Regardless, I want to talk to you about an opportunity.

I know what goes into a five-hour, five-course dinner like the one you hosted Friday. And so long as blood, sweat and tears don't count for shit as seasonings, I know you are not actually considering doing pop-up dinners for the rest of your career. You are one of the best that ever has been and ever will be. It would be a shame if all of that capped at these fly-by-night dinners.

Like I said, I am in the industry. I helped open some of the best restaurants just outside of Chicago and earned accolades of all types less than 12 months after the doors opened. The gentleman financially behind those places is looking to invest, finally, in a space in downtown Chicago. As a result, he has excused me from my current role to start scouting for this forthcoming restaurant. After the location and talent is secured, it will be a fast, hard open. I will become the new GM and I'd like you to be Chef de Cuisine.

This is not a joke. This is not a drill. Reply for further details and give my best to Allie. She was a wonderful hostess on Friday night. Just tell her to keep an eye on her billfolds if you keep doing those pop-ups…

-Angela

Ah-ha.

So the bitchy blonde firecracker who damn near broke my sternum shoving a folder of cash into my chest wants to give my boyfriend a restaurant. Well, she's going to have to get in line with the fifty other people who, for their own selfish reasons, like to dangle shiny false hopes in front of a guy who is trying to focus on getting his life together.

I take a bite of my sandwich and the crusty bread roughs up the roof of my mouth. The nerve of this woman and her sadistic little email has also managed to suck the saliva from my mouth, and now I'm rage-chewing and wishing I hadn't forgotten my Diet Coke on the counter.

"What do you think?" Benji says as he blows a thick stream of smoke out the window.

"Still reading," I say. *Still processing* is the real answer.

In Benji's defense, yes, Angela's offer sounds legit. But there's a good chance she's like all the rest: just someone who wants fewer degrees of separation between herself and the beautiful lunatic they see portrayed in the media.

I've got one job when it comes to Benji, at least until he gets a little more sobriety under his belt. And that job is to protect him. Protect him from the people who want to either glorify his addiction, or sabotage it.

I've got to look out for myself, too. *"Give my best to Allie."* A cordial sign-off from a woman who just four days ago let me know exactly what she thought of my ability, or should I say *inability*, to command a room? I smell bullshit—even through the aromatic cloves of garlic six inches from my nose.

"I think this could be good for my reputation," Benji says, ashing out the window before taking his next drag.

Here's the thing about his reputation. He may be the one responsible for trashing it, but I care about building it back. I know that's mostly his job, but we need people not to lose interest in his pop-ups. If he switches gears and takes the bait Angela's hooked, we risk losing out on the type of cash flow that can be made with the snap of a finger. Or the sear of a scallop, I should say.

I get the allure of what Angela is offering: steady paychecks from a hot, new open. But Benji has sabotaged anything and everything that could have been good for him. In fact, he admitted that verbatim to me the first time we met. I thought it was the whiskey talking, to be honest, so I just giggled, asked for another glass of sauv blanc, and looked past it. I mean, who just matter-of-factly states that if it's a good thing, he's going to throw acid on it?

Perhaps not taking that warning seriously was an oversight on my part during the whole getting-to-know-him phase. But as his current girlfriend, I am now very familiar with his former MO. So while I should be supportive and excited at the thought that someone wants to give him a chance—a real, substantiated chance—I just can't see the light when so many red flags clog my vision.

Angela has no idea how fragile Benji really is. Her job is to taste his food, catch a glimpse of him in the kitchen, post it on her Instagram and feel like the popular kid in school when the likes roll in. That's it. She has no idea the size of the pot she's stirring by promising sunshine, rainbows and restaurants. But I've managed to show him the way thus far and I'm not letting him take a detour on this dead-end offer. Go ahead, call me his part-time girlfriend, part-time game keeper. It's true. God, Facebook "it's complicated" relationships have nothing on us.

Then why the hell am I sticking around? Because the sex is just that good? I mean, it's the best I've ever had *by far*, but that's not what keeps me here. And neither is the cooking, although that's a hell of a hook. So have I bought into the delusion that I'll be the *one* thing that changes Benji, that sobers him up, shakes his shoulders and turns him into the Top Chef the whole country knows he can be?

Well.

Kind of.

I haven't failed at much in my life so far. At least, not this quickly. For all the irritation and frustration a situation like this can carry, part of me really does believe that I could be the missing piece. Benji seems to think so, too. He tells me every day that no matter what success he has, it's because of me. Everyone can see he's doing so much better now that we're together. And last night—three months of sobriety—is proof.

Benji rejoins me on the couch. My apartment reeks of cigarette smoke and mustard. I hate to admit that it's not a terrible combo.

"That email's crazy, right, Al?"

That's one word for it. I don't know what to say back, so I let Due Diligence Debbie chime in.

"Sure, but do you even know anything about this chick?" I decide not to tell him that I do, that she nearly football-tackled me over the little slipup I made when busing tables.

He takes the laptop back but doesn't answer the question.

"Also, what happens with your pop-ups? You're just going to ditch doing those right after *FoodFeed* announces it's the one can't-miss dining experience of Chicago? You finally have a real, passionate following, Benji. Just the other day I was at brunch and my server was begging me to spill the beans on your next dinner. Do you realize how easily you could sell them out? You'd be booked the next six dinners if you scheduled them."

Full disclosure when it comes to his pop-ups: I front all food and supply costs. It's not something I wanted to do, but when he came to me with a solid plan about how to pull off these pop-ups and contribute financially to our household, the Bank of Allie was really the only one willing to give the loan needed to get his idea off the ground. Plus, it was the only way to do this while avoiding his number one trigger—easy access to cash.

It works like this: Benji announces a pop-up on social media after he secures a "venue." I use that term loosely since he never actually acquires any permits or paperwork. Therefore the destination for these dinners depends on who's willing to say yes to letting him take over their space for a few hours, which usually means it's only a matter of days between the initial announcement and the dinner itself. By that point, I will have withdrawn anywhere from five hundred to a thousand dollars from my personal account to purchase the last-minute ingredients and supplies.

Fronting the money isn't as scary as it sounds. When someone wants a seat at the pop-up, they have to pay immediately online. The money goes directly into my account so I can pay myself back. After I'm reimbursed, the profit is enough to cover stuff like his cell phone bill, our gas and water usage, a fraction of the cable bill. We could probably stand to make even more of a bottom line, but there are only so many seats available to sell and Benji has a habit of insisting he needs just twenty dollars more for bigger sea urchins...or for a new slotted spoon...or to pay Sebastian in cigarettes. Even though the ebb and flow of things has become my obsession in the last few months, I can't begrudge him twenty dollars. Plus, when I see people post gorgeous pictures of his beautifully composed dishes, I know there's no possibility he's abusing our system.

So if the pop-ups alone just cover the basic bills, where do we really rake it in? With gratuities. By the time the dinners end, patrons forget they've prepaid for their meal so it feels weird to them leaving the table empty—especially since they had a good time and ate great food. They dip into their wallets for whatever cash they have stashed away and make sure to leave it all as a token of their appreciation. It's exactly like last night when Benji cascaded twenties like a waterfall onto the table at Republic before we got up to go home. But we were just two people, and stone sober at that. When an entire roomful of overserved celeb-chef chasers are involved, the result is hundreds of dollars just for a glimpse of the man-bun and a taste of his Sriracha Jell-O cubes.

I've thought about looking into legitimizing this business but the thought of figuring out an LLC for a guy whose credit looks like it's been through a meat grinder is daunting as fuck. For now, I'm not worried as long as we continue to keep the gratuities as all-cash and totally under the table.

And as long as Angela is not in the picture.

"The pop-ups are what they are," he says. "But this…this could be legit. Like, some real steady shit."

He cracks his knuckles—the gesture I know means he's getting excited about something. The first time I saw him do it was the second time we ever hung out. He had just gotten a text from a buddy who'd scored an eight ball (aka a helluva lot of cocaine) from a dealer known for having the good shit.

"I don't know, Benji. I don't have the best feeling about this proposition," I say.

"Come on, Allie. You know I want my own restaurant. That's always been the goal. To get four stars from the *Trib*. To have Candice Allegro give me a James Beard Award."

To get what? From whom?

"All I'm saying is: Why would I slave my dick off doing pop-ups anymore if I don't have to?"

This is a wee bit frustrating to hear considering he's spent about two-thirds of his tenancy in my apartment basically just sitting on my couch focusing on his sobriety. The pop-ups are new and exciting. They're just starting to get off the ground. Should he already consider retiring?

"But you're making a profit that you don't have to split every which way," I remind him. "And you get to do what you want to do with the menu. Wasn't *that* the goal?"

"You've got to think bigger than these pop-ups, babe. These dinners were always just supposed to be a distraction. A means to an end. And it looks like the end is coming real fucking quick."

Benji hits Reply and starts pounding letters on the keyboard. I already know he's drafting a note back to discuss this more so I excuse myself to put my dirty dish away before he asks me to proofread it.

Moments later: "Boom. The bitch already wrote back. We're on for coffee tomorrow."

The speed at which he propels himself into these head-on collisions is beyond my understanding. Sometimes, the chasm of difference between us repulses me, though I wish it didn't. I just think about relationships like my mom and dad's and wonder if I'm on the right track. They've been married for thirty-some-odd years and together even longer than that. Whatever the secret to a lasting relationship is, they know it. Would my dad ever do something rash without discussing it thoroughly with my mom? Before I play it out in my head, I stop comparing. This is *my* love story, I reason.

I rinse my dish under the sink as Benji comes up slowly and softly behind me. He puts his arms around me and lays his head on my back.

"Put that down," he says. "I'll clean when you're at work tomorrow."

I'd rather not leave filth in the sink overnight, but Benji starts kissing my neck and suddenly I lose my motor skills. He guides me a few steps to our bed and lifts my shirt over my head.

★ ★ ★

Benji had his own place for a hot minute. He invited me over sometime around our third date and made me dinner while sipping out of a fifth of whiskey he kept by the oven like a handy bottle of olive oil.

He plated the meal and slid it across his large kitchen island. I climbed up on a bar-height stool and he sat down next to me a moment later.

"Dig in, baby girl," he said.

As I looked down at the plate, I was so intimidated. Scared I didn't know how to cut into whatever he made and that I would proceed to eat a part you're not supposed to. I was unsure if I'd even like the way it tasted.

But one bite in and my world was rocked.

"You like?"

I could only nod as I swallowed my food.

"Next time, dinner at my place. I'll make you my famous grilled cheese. I use tinfoil on an ironing board," I said.

At that, he spat out his most recent pull of whiskey and let out a laugh from deep within his chest. I hadn't ever heard a laugh like that, especially not from him. It softened his edgy demeanor even though I'm pretty sure he was mocking me for my lack of kitchen skills.

"You know what? An ironing-board grilled cheese sounds hella good. Sign me the fuck up for that," he said.

The rest of the night went just like that: jokes and drinks. He was way more palatable than I had ever imagined him being.

"Okay," Benji had said as he cleared away our dirty plates. "Now, you're going to fuck me."

It wasn't a demand. He was simply right. I *was* going to sleep with him. I *wanted* to sleep with him.

The next morning, I awoke to the sound of my alarm on

my phone around six in the morning. I had set it extra early so that I could get back to my place, shower the sex off and get to work looking somewhat put together.

As I reached to silence my phone and sneak out of bed, Benji pulled me back like a magnet, burrowing me into the nook of his chest. I was the small spoon, which in itself wasn't so outstanding. But he held me closer, tighter, harder than I had ever been held by anyone before.

And in that moment, when even in his sleepy haze he still objected to my leaving, I knew this wasn't going to be just a onetime thing. Was it a lifetime thing, or even a long-term thing? Who knew? But contrary to my story with Benji being over, I was sure whatever was coming had only just begun.

5

It's too early in the day to do math, but I find myself staring at yet another utility bill on Wednesday morning. I really don't understand how a person whose worldly possessions include just six T-shirts, some skinny jeans and a pair of Dansko kitchen clogs can rack up such a high cost of living.

Every month since Benji moved in, a small part of me has died when I open the bills. My studio apartment is far from enormous. Yet lo and behold, the electric bill feels like it's for a four-bedroom house with a pool. I'm not trying to point fingers, but as I look to my left, there's a rack of lamb that's sitting in a sous vide and will be for seventy-two hours straight. Seriously, if the health inspector could see the shit that Benji pulls from up here on the tenth floor, he would never be allowed to cook again.

Not far behind is the cable bill. While Benji was getting sober, he insisted he shouldn't work. Like, at all. I didn't doubt the process, but then he claimed he was so bored while I was at the office that he feared a relapse. Could you imagine the *FoodFeed* headline? Zane Relapses Due to Girlfriend's Lack of Robust Cable Package. So I gave him the green light to set it up.

I'm sure there's a way to scale back on the bill now that Benji attends regular NA meetings and has his pop-up work to distract him, but I just don't have the energy to sit on hold with the cable company and negotiate what premium channels should stay and what DVR features need to go. So I pay the bill and accept it as part of the price you pay to keep your boyfriend on the right track.

It's still odd to think how we achieved "couple" status in the first place, since the path there was about as rinky-dink as the food prep that goes on in this apartment.

Before we were living together, he accidentally left a hoodie at my place. So I put it on, kept it unzipped with no bra and sent him a little sext. Not my best moment, but tempering myself around him was (still is) damn near impossible and I thought I'd tease him a bit with a smoky eye and a little side boob. Clearly, he liked what he saw, because he saved the photo to his phone and blasted it out a week later directly from his Twitter account while on a bender. He captioned it: My girlfriend is hotter than yours. cc: @AllieSimon.

To set the record straight, I was his side chick at best. Not a title one is usually proud of, but a role that accurately described the state of our relationship at the time. You know, one of probably a few people you call for a sloppy bar make-out session, or a 5:00 a.m. cuddle-fest. I was just someone who answered his calls with a wave of butterflies instead of a pit in my stomach. The pit was reserved for a woman daring enough to be his actual girlfriend; someone willing to take Benji on full-time.

The following morning, his dedicated fans saw the shocking 2:00 a.m. tweet and as such, my phone buzzed with notification after notification. The combination of dings and glows woke me up before my alarm did. A lot of people were sending their congratulations, concurring that I was in fact "hot." Others said he could do better. A few girls tweeted back, I thought I was your girlfriend, you dick. Or just a plain and simple Fuck you @AllieSimon.

Whether or not Benji was actually in the market for a girlfriend, this tweet heard 'round the Chicago food world was the moment it all went down for me, a no-namer suddenly thrust into a controversial limelight without any warning.

@FoodFeed: Hey @BJZane, congrats! Would love to do a blurb on you and @AllieSimon. Favorite this tweet if OK.

Moments later, Benji of course gave it a like, which gave *FoodFeed* permission to go even more public with what was just a private guilty pleasure to me at the time.

That pic was only 4 U, Benji, I texted him with the slightest bit of rage/embarrassment.

ppl should know, he promptly wrote back.

Know what? My bra size?

U R my gf

<3 How is this going 2 work?

IDK.

I had learned from previous exchanges with him that short, intense, rapid-fire texts were a telltale sign he was high.

Cocaine talking? I had to ask.

I'll get clean 4 U. I told U.

I turned my screen to dark and clutched the phone to my pounding chest as I sat up in my bed. *Is this really happening? Do I want it to be happening?*

Before this public display, what we did was in the dark. It was a secret he and I kept, and we capped it at booze-fueled conversation and fiery hookups. Sure, Jazzy and Maya knew that I was dancing with the devil, but my parents—and certainly the entire city of Chicago—didn't need to know I was spending a few nights a week rounding the bases with a ticking time bomb who would sniff white powder off the nightstand before going down on me.

When Benji came into my life, keeping my distance was both the first and last thing on my mind. Every time we'd finish having sex, my internal battle was always, do I gear up for round two? Or do I leave now while he's toweling off in the bathroom and block his number for good? Before I could make up my mind, he'd come back into the room, lock his arms around me and ask me what I wanted for breakfast the next morning.

How do you put a lid on that? Any of that? Had I known how it all was going to shake out a few months later, maybe I would have pumped the brakes a bit. But with a guy like Benji, I learned there are none.

And now here I am four months later—figuring out our expenses on a hot and sticky late-August morning. In times like this, I wonder about the girls who assumed this role before. Did they have to pay a monthly entertainment tariff just to keep our mutual acquaintance from getting bored and looking for drugs?

Do you know who else I think about? The girls who'll *never* be in my shoes—and how they are free of obligations like this, and so many others. A pang of envy hits me right in the gut. I remind myself Benji's the prize, and it goes away.

Standing at the kitchen counter, I write out three checks, stamp the envelopes and tuck them into my purse. Even though he's clean now, the entire internet and everyone I know tells me I should be paranoid about a possible relapse, the provocation of which can come from anywhere. Spare cash lying around, compounded by a bad day or, I don't know, a teaspoon of baking soda spilled on the counter, can lead to disaster. So I've learned to worry that if I pay these bills online, Benji will figure out a way to reroute the money somewhere it doesn't belong, which is why I'll personally be delivering these checks to a mailbox before setting foot into my office this morning. No one tells you what it's like to live with a drug addict, but the trick, apparently, is that you can never be too careful.

"You going to work?" he groggily asks from his side of the bed.

Perhaps it's just early, but the question rubs me the wrong way. He makes it sound like I have a choice, like it's feasible that I'm on my way to grab picture frames at World Market or something. It's 7:45 in the morning. Where the hell else would I be going?

"Yup."

"Love you," he says, getting up to kiss me and pull me in for a tight hug. The smell of stale cigarettes lingers in the patchy start of a dark brown beard. He's either out of razors and waiting for me to notice so I pick some up on my way home, or he's sporting a new, burlier look. Whatever the case may be, I don't mind it. I let the smell take me back to another place and time; namely, the bar where we first met and first made out.

The fluttering feeling in my gut comes back in force, the strangeness and danger and possibility of him swirling together in my heart and mind. In these moments, I experience a high of my own that makes so much of what I'm struggling with fall away. Debt might be high and resources low, but when he crushes me to his chest this way, it's all good. A man who loves me is enveloping me in his arms. And I am all in. In retrospect, I have been from the moment we first met.

"Love you, too," I say back, calm and sweet, though what I really want to say is, "Maybe I should stay home and fuck?"

Then I think, why don't we? Sex has always been the perfect equalizer for us. No matter how frustrated I can get by day-to-day life with Benji, in the bedroom it all melts away.

I glance over at the clock to see just what I'm working with. It's enough time to unzip his pants and blow him. Oddly enough, giving him head does it for me as much as it turns him on. Seeing him utterly tantalized by something only I am capable of doing is probably how he feels when he's putting the perfect sear on a piece of halibut as I wait for my plate at the table.

A few moans and groans later and the deed is done. I freshen up in the bathroom and hear him say, "Babe? Can I borrow twenty bucks to cab it to Randolph Street?"

Whatever tender moment I thought we'd just shared ends abruptly with the financial ask.

"How about I leave you my bus pass?" *Bargain with me, pal. Please.*

"I can't exactly roll up to this meeting with Angela on a city bus. And I can't risk being late because I had to take six different routes all over this fucking city. It's impossible to get to the West Loop from here on public trans. You know that."

He's pitching it as if he's interviewing for a job at the Board of Trade. I thought it was just coffee with some fan?

"Then text me when you want to go and I'll order you an Uber. I have a credit."

"You're so obsessed about money stuff sometimes," he says. He's correctly identified my hesitation to give him what he wants, so he's going for the hard sell. "But when I have a very important business meeting that could take care of you and me for a really, really long time, I can't get twenty bucks to make sure I'm there on time. I seriously don't understand you, Allie. I really don't."

Here it goes. The temper tantrum. Sometimes dating Benji

is like raising an unpredictable teenager. One minute, we're best friends. The next, he's pissed I won't let him ride his bike by himself to the movies. It's hard to play mom with a guy you really enjoy fucking—and trust me, there's no fetish there. I've explored it.

Still, I wonder, how is he so good at making it seem like I'm the one who's so goddamn—

"You're just being selfish," he says offhandedly. I want to castrate him with his own paring knife. I'm not an ATM machine, for crying out loud. I'm his girlfriend.

"Benji. I literally do not have any cash on me. You—we spent it all at Republic." It's the truth.

"Well, then, I'll walk downstairs with you and we'll stop at the bank on the corner. It's not that hard. And we can even get Starbucks before you head in to work."

A Starbucks date with your bae before work sounds so romantic and cheeky. The ironic thing here is that when he kisses me goodbye and sends me off to show up fifteen minutes late to work with a vanilla latte in hand, he really doesn't have a clue what I do. He knows I tweet about cotton swabs but whether or not this is my dream job, how long I've been working there, who my coworkers are, what the watercooler drama is…those are all things that never come up. It's almost painful how indifferent he is about the details of my career, but then I remember there probably isn't room for two at the top. And right now, and most likely always, what Benji's got cooking matters much more, and to many more, than my day-to-day.

"Fine, but let's go. We need to hurry," I concede.

On the elevator ride down, I think about what *We can get Starbucks* really means—that I'll be buying for the both of us. But as a recovering addict, Benji's two green-lit vices are cigarettes and caffeine—neither of which he seems to get enough

of. At least three times a week, Benji wakes up in the middle
of the night and brews a pot in my little kitchen. It's like he's
a prisoner to the hankering. I almost feel bad for him. At least
it's better—and cheaper—than blow.

Hey @AllieSimon...you need to come pick your boy up lol,
read the tweet from someone I eventually figured out was a
coworker at his old restaurant. I wasn't sure on what planet
something like this warranted a "lol," but the kid uploaded a
picture of Benji curled up in the fetal position, passed out by
a Dumpster. *Good god*, I thought.

This took place before Benji had announced to the world
that we were an item, and it was my first clue that maybe our
rendezvous wasn't so secret after all. How this kitchen worker
knew to tag me in a tweet like that was equal parts unsettling
and flattering.

I ignored my phone the rest of the day, denying that this
could actually be my responsibility (no, really...we're just fucking. Call someone else!). But at around midnight, a text that
woke me up became a text I couldn't pass over.

Can I come over? Please? Need 2 C U.

He *needed* to see me. And regardless of the circumstances,
I liked the way that sounded and said yes.

When he stumbled into my unit, shaking and pale, I immediately settled him onto my couch and wrapped him in a
blanket. I asked him what the hell happened, but the details
were fuzzy. I'm not sure if he was being vague to spare me,
or because he couldn't recall all the gory specifics.

"Are you high? Can you at least tell me that?" I begged for
more information.

"No. I swear. But I did get high Monday. And Tuesday. And yesterday. And now I think I'm having withdrawals."

FML.

"Okay, so, what do I do? Do you need water? Crackers? Tylenol?" I didn't realize then that treating withdrawal and nursing a hangover are two very different things.

"No, none of those things. It's just gonna suck for a few days. Can you rub my back?" he asked me amid his distress. I placed my hand on him and felt a bulge the size of my fist under his skin.

"What is that?" I asked, grimacing slightly. I didn't want to freak him out, but I was assuming the worst. A blood clot maybe?

"When I do too many drugs, I get these knots in my back. I don't really know, just, can you keep rubbing?"

Scared as I was sitting that close to an overdose, it brought me comfort to know this wasn't the first time he'd experienced these bulbous mutations.

"I think I'm going to go," he said a few seconds later.

"Right now? You just got here. I feel like you should lie down."

"No, I mean to rehab." Boom, there it was. The first time Benji admitted that his drug use had evolved into something far more out of control than just a casual sniff off a credit card in a bathroom stall. But why to me, I wondered? Who was I in his life that he could so suddenly come to me in the middle of the night with his desperation as visible as the toxic lump protruding from his back? He must have known I wouldn't judge him, call him a loser and tell him to get the hell out. Even I hadn't known I was capable of such compassion until the need for it was physically and inescapably in front of me.

"What about your restaurant? Don't you have to go to work?"

"It's over," he said.

I didn't know if he quit or got fired, but I figured I'd let the food blogs figure that one out.

"Okay. So when would you leave?"

"Tomorrow."

"What? Why so soon?" A part of me selfishly couldn't fathom our road coming to an abrupt dead end.

"This is going to get really bad, Allie. Soon. You aren't going to be able to take care of this. I've already made the appointment. They're expecting me to check in at 6:00 a.m."

I took a big breath and looked at the time.

"Well, then, let's get you back to your place to pack."

"You can't come over," he said. "I can't have you see what's going to happen next. You're too good for that. Trust me, okay? Please."

At that point, I called him an Uber and walked him back down to my lobby. His eyes were the dopiest I had ever seen. From the withdrawal? Maybe. From the fact that both of us weren't ready to accept this would be the last time we'd see each other for at least a month? Definitely.

I had planned to pull the plug many times before on things with Benji, but now it was all coming to a forced stop. I should have been grateful—this was my out. But instead, I was sad. I didn't realize that at some point, I had fallen for this guy. And it wasn't just about the mind-blowing sex or handmade pastas. I cared about him.

I also didn't realize that once I shut the door of the car and watched it take off toward an all-quiet Lake Shore Drive, Benji was going to partake in one last hurrah before rehab.

A bottle of pills, a fifth of Jack and whatever else he could get his hands on fueled this particular bender. And this is when he tweeted out my photo. This is when he outed me as his girlfriend. This is when I decided that accepting my new identity was easier than dismantling a bomb.

The next day, I slogged through work, worried and sad and happy and confused. I tried to Google what rehab was really like, but feared IT would hack my history and I'd get canned for being a liability with a double life.

From what I had seen on *Celebrity Rehab*, going away for help was going to be the right thing for Benji. I grappled with the idea that once sober, Benji might not see me the same anymore. That whatever drug-induced infatuation he'd had with me would subside. It'd be like sleeping off a hangover and realizing that the 3:00 a.m. order of extra-large cheese fries from the Weiners Circle was a bad idea. And I was okay with that. I had to be okay with that. I told myself a complicated story about how difficult people don't deserve love any less than the simpler ones. If we only allowed ourselves to care deeply about those who can reciprocate our affection the way we've grown accustomed to, did we have any business calling that "love" at all? Whatever hurt or emptiness I felt in Benji's absence was in the service of something much greater, and I made peace with it.

And then I came home from work and found Benji—the very same!—sitting on the foot of my bed.

"No. No, no, no, no. You can't be here," I remember saying adamantly as I threw my keys down on the counter. "What are you even doing here? How did you get in? You have to go!" I felt like I was hiding a fugitive. This kid needed serious help, even *he* admitted that. Who let the monkey out of his cage?

"Babe, calm down," he had said, placing both of his hands up like I was about to shoot. "I know what you're thinking, but trust me: I got this. I'm going to start going to NA meetings every day, twice a day. I already have a sponsor. His name is Mark. I even picked up the books. See? See?" He held up the Narcotics Anonymous literature like church propaganda. "My first meeting is tomorrow at 8:00 a.m. I'll be gone before you even leave for work. I'm serious this time."

This time? How many other failed attempts were there? And how serious could he be if he hadn't even given rehab a single day to kick in? Which made me wonder…

"Did you even go?" I asked.

He didn't say yes or no. Instead just offered a flippant, "Rehab isn't for me."

I had heard that line before. On *Intervention*. Right before they rolled the updates that said the subject hadn't been heard from in months and was last seen smoking crack under a bridge.

"But you said it was. Right here on this couch, like fifteen hours ago. What the hell happened?"

"I don't know, a lot of shit. My phone got stolen last night, I ran out of cigarettes and I don't have the money for it unless I go to that freebie clinic in the ghetto. I'm not doing that. Get stuck with some fuckin' weirdo roomie. No way. I'd much rather do it on my own terms. I'm going to do this my way with Mark and the meetings."

"What about the withdrawal? I thought you said it's going to be bad?"

"It will be. But I'll stay tough and fight through it and call Mark if I need anything. He helped me get a new phone today. It's a fresh start, only your number and his are programmed in it."

I'm pretty sure this was when I started crying. I was already in a state of complete emotional exhaustion and this, food pun unintended, just took the cake. Worse, I couldn't tell if I was happy he was back or scared he'd never leave. All I knew for sure was that I didn't want to be in this situation anymore. It was all too much.

"Oh, babe. Come on. You're breaking my heart. What's wrong? What can I do?" Benji had stopped me from pacing uncontrollably by holding me in the way only he could—the way that managed to hit the reset button no matter how haywire my system was going. My body warmed up like I had just downed a shot of vodka. I slowed my breathing and let myself fall into him. I felt swaddled like a baby—safe and warm. The swirl of insanity instantly simmered down and the relief set in; this was real.

And we were going to be okay.

Underneath his messy front, there was *something*—a lot of things, actually. There was a lost soul that needed direction. A man with a good heart and an insane amount of talent. Benji had the wisdom to know he needed help, but not where to find it or how to get it. And then there I was, this beacon of normalcy shining in the night, and he had clung to it. I was like the *Carpathia* coming to pull him out of icy waters. How could I have blamed him for that? For thinking his source of rescue came in a little five-foot-three package, was a good lay and had a kind heart?

Plus, when a person asks you to help save his life, you can't exactly turn him away. Or at least I couldn't.

"I just want this to work," I muttered through an ugly cry. There were another six words that would have been just as easy to fire off—*I just want you to leave*—but they would have been a lie. No matter the circumstances, I needed to be within arm's reach of this man.

"I do, too, babe. And it will. The coke stuff…it's over. *For good*. And with you by my side, I know staying clean is possible. Regardless of everything that's going on right now, I still feel like I'm the luckiest guy in the world. I'd take slipping up, losing my job, the Twitter shit storm I started last night—I'd take it all again because I know it brought me you. The greatest gift of my life. I really mean that."

He wiped a tear from the corner of my eye and went on with the monologue.

"But you gotta promise me one thing. You gotta stick by me, let me *show you* I can do this. I'm not going to let this fall through my fingers. I've never had anything like this, like you. I've wanted this my whole life."

I stared out beyond him through the windows of my apartment and shook my head—what was he going to tell the press about losing his job? What part would everyone think I played in sidelining their favorite chef?

"So remind me, what's the plan, then?"

"I'm going to NA twice a day. You should try to go to some programs, too. Nar-Anon and Al-Anon are good. Stay away from CoDA, it's bullshit."

I'd had no clue what any of those things were, or how I would fit them into my schedule. But I soon found out these were just nicknames for meetings designed to make me feel less crazy. Like I wasn't the only one in a relationship with someone who doubled as a nuclear button. My biggest problem would not be finding a meeting—they happen all day every day in big cities like Chicago—but rather how I would go about hiding my attendance from my friends and family.

"And I'll do my coursework each night. Look—I've already started. I'll work the program with Mark."

"Who is Mark again?"

"My sponsor. He and his wife, Rita, actually want to meet you. They host a picnic every Saturday in the summer at North Avenue Beach. We can go this weekend."

"Benji, I don't know if I'm ready for this."

"Sorry, I know. I'm getting ahead of myself. When the time is right, we'll do the picnic thing. And I'll make some rad side dish, or you could bring your ironing-board grilled cheeses, and we'll blow everyone's mind. In the meantime, I'll keep things between Mark and me. Okay? Sound good?"

I didn't know these Mark-and-Rita people from Adam or Eve, but something about their names, or the fact they hosted a weekly picnic, made me feel like Benji was in good hands. And just like that, I felt myself starting to turn. Slowly.

"And what about work? What about your apartment? Your rent?"

"Babe, look at me." I wasn't sure how much closer he could have gotten, but he nuzzled in a little more and held my shoulders tightly. I granted him blotchy, tearstained eye contact.

"That place I was living in...the landlords...they terminated my lease."

"They *what?*"

Just when I thought I was calming down.

"It's my fault. I was late on rent, they had trouble verifying my work and after last night...things got a little trashed."

"So, where's all your stuff? Where are you living now?"

"Well, all I really had was cooking stuff and Sebastian is holding on to it all for me."

I pictured his apartment on the night he cooked for me; there really was no furniture over there. Just a mattress on the floor and some bar stools. That's when I realized that in the corner of my studio was a black duffel bag. His life, whatever scraps of it he was able to pull together before being evicted, was most certainly zipped in there.

"You want to stay here." It was a statement, not a question—let me make that clear. "And get sober." Again, not a question.

"I'll make you lunch every day, I'll cook dinner for you every night. Your friends, too. I'll keep the place clean for us. Run your errands. Do whatever you need for me to prove how bad I want this and how committed I am to our future.

This is a good thing, Allie. For our relationship. I can get better at my own pace, figure out what to do for work and take care of you."

I don't know how Benji got into my apartment that day. My doorman must have recognized him from the night before and figured he was on the let-up list. As far as my unit being unlocked, I was tired that morning. Really fucking tired. It's entirely possible I forgot to lock up. Point being, as I looked around, I noticed my place was immaculate. Bed made, TV stand dusted, towels in the bathroom folded. He'd picked up while waiting for me to come home.

It had seemed ironic to me that the trade-off for accommodating a drug addict was a series of proposed housekeeping services and a promise that I'd eat like a queen. But sometimes when you're just that tired, worn down and desperate, the vision of a decent lunch and coming home to a clean bathroom is enough to make it all seem worth it.

"I'm not going to starting cooking tonight, though," he said.

My heart fell through the floor. I couldn't put up with another night of mayhem or another false promise.

"Because tonight, I'm going to order you a pizza. I'm going to get your favorite—butter crust with crispy pepperoni and extra sauce on the side. And we're going to share it, eat the whole goddamn thing. And we're going to watch a movie, *The Lake House* or *P.S. I Love You*...one of those girlie DVDs I keep seeing in your collection that I'm too embarrassed to admit I want to watch. You can pick. And then, we're just going to hold each other and talk if we need to talk, be quiet if we need to be quiet, and at the end of the night, we'll go to bed knowing it's just you and me against the world, and that tomorrow is a fresh start and a new day."

He never let me object. Not once did I poke a hole in his

plan or tell him no or force him to at least pick up a part-time shift at CVS. Yet still, the relationship that every girl wants was right in front of my face. The one where you can throw on some sweats, get comfy on the couch and curl up with your boyfriend, a greasy pizza and a chick flick, and still feel like the prettiest princess in all the land. And best of all, I wasn't begging him to be on the same page as me. That was all Benji. He was laying it all out there for me.

Twenty minutes and two slices in and I had felt the stress and tension ebb out of me. How I was going to tell my mom and dad, or Jazzy and Maya, that an ex-addict was now sharing my address was going to require politician-like spin. But I'd deal with that later. Because right then, we were on the right track. Benji was there for me to rest my head on. The *FoodFeed* comments section and the Twitter speculation were out of sight and out of mind at that moment.

Later on, his warm hands rubbed the small of my back under my favorite Mizzou hoodie.

"I love you," he whispered to me.

"I love you, too," I said, knowing with certainty that *I* was his fighting chance, not some dark, dingy rehab center on the far West Side of Chicago.

6

I like going to work for two main reasons. First, it's a place I can go to escape my strange home life. The near-constant sound of a blender, prep bowls always piled high in the sink and the occasional sous chef asleep on the floor is enough to drive anyone crazy. Here in my River North office, I can table what's going on in my world and tune in for eight hours to what other people, sometimes worlds away, are going through. Granted, these online conversations are almost always about cotton swabs, but I still find ways to engage with hordes of people who seem really nice, really normal. Sometimes I wonder...do any of them have a Benji?

I'm good at what I do, too. So that helps. Our boss, Connor, doesn't spend a ton of time with our social media department—he's got bigger, more corporate fish to fry. But he checks in with us formally every six months to see how we're feeling about things and where we want to go with our jobs. He and I last met together five months ago, when I hinted at creating a new role for myself: Creative Director. Essentially, I'd step back and oversee Stacey and Dionte, our graphic designer and copywriter, respectively, then lead a team of monitors who would divvy up responding to all the social streams. Though I've been a little distracted with my home life, I plan to pick up the conversation with him during our next one-on-one review, and remind him he'd been tentatively on board.

The other main reason I like coming here is that people ask me about Benji. And because there are only a few office-appropriate sides of him that I can discuss with my coworkers, my office is a place where I get to bask in the more delicious reasons I love him. When I can only talk about the good, it helps me reaffirm that my feelings for Benji are stronger than ever.

"What's for lunch today, Allie?" Stacey asks, waiting her turn for the microwave.

"Um, not too sure. Looks like Benji reimagined some of our dinner leftovers," I say as I stir them around and nuke them for another fifteen seconds.

I'm not giving the man enough credit, I just don't know the technical terms for what he concocted and threw in a Tupperware for me. I do know, though, that whatever it is is a long way from barbecue sauce and mac 'n' cheese—the first things he ever learned to cook on his own from scratch.

I've never asked him to explain the history of his culinary career to me because I feel like that's a job for a fawning food blogger—not his other-side-of-the-industry girlfriend. But I know his first kitchen job was when he was in high school. His dad left his mom for a much-younger woman and Benji wrote him off completely. He chose to live with his mom, who moved them to a small apartment in Austin, Texas. That's when he got a job as a dishwasher at a BBQ joint to help her with the rent.

A few months into the gig, the owners gave him a bit more responsibility—let him toy around with rotating chickens in the smoker, stirring the vat of coleslaw every thirty minutes so it wouldn't crust over, things like that. One area they did not let him play around in so freely was the bar, but his teenage angst led him to a habit of topping off his free shift fountain drink with a shot of Jim Beam when no one was looking. One day, he got a little more buzzed than usual and decided the mac 'n' cheese tasted like shit and the barbecue sauce was bland. So he afforded himself the liberty of redoing them both and sent the next twenty dishes out to the dining room with his altered menu choices. Regulars started complaining that something was different, which was when the bosses figured out the root of the problem was the teenager in the kitchen who smelled like whiskey.

From there, Benji bounced around at a few more restaurants. Meanwhile, his mom became depressed and started acting crazy and belligerent from all the medication she would take mixed with the vodka she kept on her nightstand. She was impossible to be around, according to Benji, so he started hanging out with the cooks after work instead of going home. From them, he adopted new kitchen skills along with some bad habits.

Eventually, he tried coke. The drug allowed him to be fearless behind the stove, unintimidated by any ingredient and never in the weeds despite his age or lack of any traditional training. No one could deny that Benji had talent. Talent that went beyond just scrubbing dishes or spicing up a few condiments. But no one in the Greater Austin area was willing to let a teenager who required two smoke breaks an hour be in charge of the kitchen.

At eighteen, he packed up the same black duffel bag that's currently in my apartment, left his mom $500 cash and bought a Greyhound ticket to New York City. Through the power of social media, he built a following and made connections, setting up a staging gig at a new restaurant every year in all the major foodie destinations. Next came DC, then San Francisco, Miami and Vegas to name a few.

One hot spot at a time, he added skill after skill to his culinary repertoire. One hot spot at a time, he added drug after drug to the shit he was willing to try, ultimately always coming back to coke. Lots of it.

Ultimately, he wound up in the Windy City. He says that's because it's the capital of modernist cuisine. I say it's because Chicago is the capital of girls who put out for chefs. (Guilty.) Regardless, he came here to "settle down"—meaning, to take his first ever full-time cooking job. While the same people who offered him the gig ultimately let him go, it was the first and only time he could really say he made it as a chef.

"Oh my god, that smells amazing," Dionte says when he happens to catch a whiff in the break room. I have to admit, I feel special. Food may be the way to a man's heart, but as my colleagues assemble around me, I'm convinced it's the way to a woman's ego. It's like I'm dating da Vinci and I've just hung the *Mona Lisa* in my cubicle. Everyone is oohing and aahing, reminding me just what an awesome perk it is to be dating Benji Zane. I'm the cool kid at the lunch table, just like I was at Republic.

"What did he make?" Dionte asks.

"She's not sure, but it looks like ditalini pasta with cream and pancetta," Stacey answers for me. It's like they're gathering enough info to send TMZ a tip.

"You're *so* lucky," a girl from a different department gushes from the kitchen table. I don't even know what her name is, but she begrudgingly stabs at her lackluster salad and shoots jealous death rays my way.

I escape the public scrutiny of the lunchroom and return to my desk to eat quietly alone in my cubicle. Words cannot describe the peace I feel in this little cubby. I used to think my apartment was my own safe haven. Now? Not so much. My cubicle, though, that's indisputably mine. All twelve and a half square feet of it. I close my eyes and inhale a big whiff of the ditalini-whatever before taking a bite. It is pure heaven indeed. My mouth waters and I am reminded just how talented this beautifully flawed man is. And just like this lunch, I'm not sharing.

I go to throw away my brown paper bag and a few scribbles of black Sharpie marker catch my eye. I flatten the bag out on my desk. A love note.

Allie Simon. Every day, I thank my lucky stars that you are making me a better man. Deciding I wanted to do what it takes to be with you was the best thing I've ever done. I LOVE YOU. -B

My favorite three words from this man (other than *dinner is ready*). The first time he said it was when I was sitting there on the floor with puffy, red eyes in an oversize college hoodie, stuffing my face with thousands of calories of pizza and wondering how the hell this thing was going to work, but not really worrying about it either. Because next to me, tucked away in our own little enclave in the city, was somebody I was never supposed to meet but was always meant to have.

A few things have changed since then; some for the good, while others...well, like I said, the momentum is rolling and it's hard to know whether I'm keeping up or falling behind. But a surprise note like this tells me that, for the most part, he's keeping his promises. He makes my lunch most days of the week, keeps the place (somewhat) tidy and has (sort of) figured out what he wants to do. Or at least, he *had* that last part figured out, until Miss Angela Blackstone decided to come out of nowhere and dangle a restaurant in front of his face.

I finish my lunch and I still haven't heard from Benji. Under ordinary circumstances, I would take the silence to mean the worst: an overdose or an arrest during a drug deal gone bad. I know I saw him just hours ago and he was totally fine, but I usually hear from Benji at least five times by lunch; his addict's personality makes him incessant. Everything he likes, he loves. Everything he hates, he abandons. Everything he wants, he needs now or better, yesterday. And most days, what he wants is to talk to me. All the time.

But today is different. Today he has his meeting with Angela, and I'm sure she's still blowing smoke up his ass or I'd have heard from him by now.

I look her up on LinkedIn to verify she is, in fact, the chick who scolded me for leaving the money unattended. I'm in the social media business, after all, and frankly curiosity got the best of me.

From what I can tell from her profile, Angela checks out— which is both a good and a bad thing in this case. I mean, according to her résumé she worked where she said she worked during the times she said she was there. And she was definitely a manager, too. Not just some entitled server who appointed herself with a new title after claiming to "practically run the place." No, she's a bona fide back- and front-of-house professional with ten people who have written recommendations for her. Glowing ones, too.

In the time it takes me to rinse out my Tupperware and return to my cubicle, I somehow miss six calls, four texts and an email from Benji. Apparently, Benji's meeting is finished.

Of all the communication, the email is the most frantic. It says: Why the hell aren't you answering? Bout to call your desk phone.

I've made it very clear that Benji is never to call my desk line. For one thing, I don't have a direct number, which means to reach me, you have to call our receptionist, Linda, and ask specifically for me. Then she forwards the call to my landline. He did this once a while back that day he wanted permission to splurge on cable. I was busy in a meeting, away from my desk, email and cell—but that didn't stop him from asking

Linda to personally go find me for a wellness check. I'll never forget Linda's face as she stood outside the all-glass conference room and tried her best to nonchalantly get my attention. I thought there was an emergency. I thought my dad's blood pressure problems had finally gotten the best of him.

Benji seemed baffled that in the corporate world, you can actually be fired for having your boyfriend pull you out of a meeting to find out what channel *Shahs of Sunset* is on. But once I explained that no job would mean no way to make rent for our cute little Lincoln Park abode, he cut the shit. Since then, he's been pretty good at steering clear of Linda and my landline, but that doesn't stop him from blowing up all other mediums of communication.

His texts grew more frantic by the second—literally:

Yo. U around?

Hello??????

ALLIE. WHERE THE HELL R U

Ugh, just checked Locator. I know UR @ work. CALL ME.

I know it sounds insanely controlling for him to track my locale with an app. But adding Locator to our phones was an even trade; I'd put it on mine if Benji put it on his. I rarely check his anymore, but I used to, just to confirm he was always near Lakeview and Diversey, the intersection of my apartment. And before you tell me the plan is flawed because an addict could just leave his phone there while out hunting for drugs, let me remind you that Benji wouldn't part with the device that links him to his social media feeds. Plus, how do you complete a drug deal without unlimited texting?

Relax, was eating, I write. Call u in a min.

K. Love u.

Like most things concerning Benji, communicating with
him while at work takes a bit of science. I used to chat with
him on Google Hangouts. I thought that was safe because I
could just minimize it when someone walked by, but one day
I saw IT run a company-wide troubleshoot, which proved
they have the ability to see what's on our monitors at any
given moment. Since then, I blocked Benji from contacting
me that way during work hours. He was pissed at first, but
the last thing I need is for someone to let HR know that at
10:13 a.m., Benji Zane wrote Allie Simon, My dick still smells
like your pussy and I kind of love it.

Most people would keep a thought like that to themselves,
but not Benji. Benji will talk about life's more personal details
the way other people talk about the weather. I have to give
him points; a good lover is a good communicator, and Benji
never hesitates to tell me what he wants, when he wants it.
But highly graphic instant messages about my lady parts while
I'm at work? I have to draw the line somewhere.

I grab my phone and make my way to the server room.
There are about 150 people who work on computers on our
floor, so essentially this room has rows and rows of hard drives
stacked about five feet high that hum, flicker and vent a slight
amount of heat. Buried in there, four rows down and one row
in, is the perfect place to take five and call Benji back. In this
nook, no one can hear us argue about money. No one can hear
us discuss what days I need to take off for his pop-ups. No one
can hear us chat about the amazing sex we had that morning.

Not surprisingly, he picks up on the first ring. "Hey." Real casual, like he hasn't been in a complete frenzy for the past fifteen minutes.

"Hey. What's going on?" I ask.

The good thing about chatting with Benji is that he's direct. Whatever he wants, whether it's sex with me, twenty dollars from the ATM or for me to put his cell phone bill on my credit card so it doesn't get shut off (he always gives me cash from a pop-up after), he doesn't beat around the bush.

"It's happening," he says. "I'm getting a restaurant."

I was afraid he was going to say that.

"Really?"

My stomach fills with anxiety. I should probably see my doctor, get something prescribed for these moments when his antics send my nerves into overdrive. But a bottle of mood levelers would be too big a trigger for Benji. Even if I hid them somewhere, he's like a bloodhound with narcotics. It's a risk I'm not willing to take.

"I met with Angela. She's a cool chick. Knows her shit. Totally legit."

"Yeah, I looked her up online earlier."

"She has this investor guy," he goes on, as if I hadn't spoken. "The one from the 'burbs. He's ready to make his city debut and they want me to design the culinary concept. Get this: they have a space in mind already and he's basically ready to buy the space and make it happen for me."

"They already have a location?"

"Not just a location. An actual restaurant that's ready to be flipped. It's a pocket listing."

"What's that mean?" I ask.

"It's basically like a secret listing at this point. The previous owners need to sell it quick. Their Realtor was friends with Angela's investor, so they called him to see if he had any interest. Now he gets first dibs and it stays off the MLS or some shit like that."

"Got it." *Eight ball, in the weeds, pocket listing*...the vernacular I learn from Benji is the gift that keeps on giving.

"Right now, they're the only people who know about it," he continues. "If they don't strike by the end of the week, the building goes to auction and they'll be outbid by someone who wants to turn it into a trendy office space just so they can say they're on Randolph Street."

"Wait. It's on Randolph Street?"

"Sure is," he says.

I've learned to basically take everything Benji says with a grain of salt, but if what he just told me has any merit, then he, Angela and this investor dude are onto something.

Admittedly, I don't know much about the food industry. But even I know Randolph Street is Chicago's famed restaurant row. Every nice dinner we've had since being together has been on Randolph. In fact, it's where Ross Luca's place, Republic, is. Though the area had basically been decrepit for years, it's since turned into a mecca for the Michelin-minded because rent downtown is way too high. Granted, the West Loop is getting pricey due to the celebrity chefs, hour-long waits, prix fixe menus and artisanal cocktails—but hey, that's Randolph Street for you. A foodie's paradise.

"You have to be kidding. How does no one know about this?" asks Due Diligence Debbie.

"I don't know. I told you, it's some secret listing. We've got to move fast here."

We. An interesting if undefined pronoun that I'll sweep under the rug for now. No time for semantics. The server room is making me hot; I need to get back to my desk.

"Can it wait until I get home? Can we talk about it more then?"

"Sure, yeah, that's fine. But can you come home a little later today? I didn't get a chance to do the laundry and cleaning and I have no clue what I'm going to make for dinner yet."

Benji's brain is in a constant state of overdrive, especially when he's excited about something. So the fact that housekeeping is at all on his mind in the midst of believing his dream is coming true right before his eyes helps me regain my bearings. No matter what's going on with the restaurant on Randolph Street, Apartment 1004 will at least be clean and tidy.

"No problem. See you around six thirty."

Back at my desk, I find an email sitting in my inbox from Angela Blackstone. For a second I assume it's something Benji's forwarded, but, sure enough, it's a note directly from her, addressed to both Benji and myself.

Benji,

Great meeting with you today! Thank you so much for taking the time to speak with me about 900 W. Randolph. I think we can both agree it's something spectacular, and an opportunity we cannot afford to pass up.

As per your request, I am copying Allie, and will on all future communications. As I understand it, she will play a large role in moving forward with our plans and I am delighted to welcome her to the team. I have no doubt that you two are a true power couple and am so excited to get to know her more in the coming days, weeks, months.

I spoke with the Realtor this afternoon. He gave me the entry code and we are a "go" for a self-guided, private tour of the space on Friday, August 27th at 11am. Craig will meet us there and Allie will be there too, correct? She really should see this for herself.

Finally, attached you will find the blueprints of the space, as well as the proposed budget I put together based off of the initial investment numbers we talked about today. This all can be tweaked, but it shows you where we need to hover around in order to move forward—plus or minus $10k.

See you Friday.
-Angela

What. The. *Breathe.*

I won't read too much into it. I won't overreact. These phrases become my mantra and I run them through my mind on repeat. Still, it's hard to ignore all those pesky plural pronouns. And this budget...what has Benji promised? And how am I involved?

It's just an email, I remind myself. It's just an email that can be deleted as quickly as it came through. But instead of pressing delete, I press the pause button on my freak-out. Maybe this is one of those things that's best not to bubble up.

I try to look on the positive side. Benji and I are a couple. We freaking live together. He obviously wasn't receptive to committing to the pop-ups much longer, so I'm in no position to give the cold shoulder to anything that could potentially mean more income. I cling to the small, bright hope that maybe this isn't as bad as it seems. What's definitely a pleasant surprise is the fact that he's requested that Angela copy me on everything from here on out. Hey, Ang, remember the girl who couldn't manage to handle the tip-out to your standards? Well, we're a package deal, so get over yourself.

My email dings again. Please, no more from these two, I think to myself.

Google Alert is the sender. I click to open and read a paragraph from a blog that this handy little tool has scraped from the internet.

Dating in Chicago is a complete and total nightmare. Aside from Benji Zane & Allie Simon (omg, can we please start calling them Zimon?!), who after last week's pop-up dinner are basically Relationship Goals, the rest of us are screwed...

It takes seeing my relationship from another angle, this time from some chick on the web who calls herself a dating expert, to loosen the knot in my stomach. I may have no idea what we're getting into, but the world seems to think Benji and I have something special and I happen to agree.

And that's when it hits me: maybe this whole restaurant thing is actually that "something bigger" I always knew was in store for us.

Since Benji requested I come home late, I find myself with an extra hour to kill after I get off work. So I hit up Jazzy and Maya for a quick Happy Hour at a place that's central to all our offices.

At Roka Akor, a swanky steak house, Maya shoves her blazer into her work bag and Jazzy clips her bangs back with two bobby pins as our first round of cocktails is served.

"Okay, guys, before you say anything," I begin, afraid of how hard they may come down on me, "I have to admit I haven't watched *The Bachelor* yet so no spoilers, please."

"Oh my god, don't freak me out like that," Maya says. "I thought you were going to say something crazy...like you and Benji got engaged."

I can't tell if that would be a good crazy or a bad crazy in her opinion.

"Speaking of Sir Benji, what's the latest?" Jazzy asks. "Any more pop-ups we can finally get on the list for?" She nudges me as she takes a sip of her mojito.

The two of them wanted to come to Benji's dinner last

week and I told them it wasn't a good idea. We were already oversold and I'd comped my parents' meal, obviously. If I ate the cost on two more free seats, it would have created more work for Benji in the kitchen and less profit for us. If they knew how hard it was worrying about my paychecks for the first time in my life, maybe they'd cut me some slack. But of course, I'm not letting them become privy to the gloomier side of things. Instead, I decide to hit them with the good news.

"Well, actually, no. Because he's in talks right now with some investors about opening a restaurant. On Randolph Street."

"WHAT?" They react in unison with the same big eyes and high-pitched exclamation. It feels so good to get that off my chest to people who actually care. Who get what it means to have a spot in the West Loop.

"Yeah, it's really early on and I don't have many details, but it sounds like it could be happening. Soon."

There's a longer pause than I'm comfortable with given the big news I've just shared. I want them to ask me what kind of food he'll serve, if it's located next to any of our favorites, if they can get on the list for opening night. But, nothing.

Eventually Jazzy says, "Wow. That's cool," and Maya just sips on her drink.

"Okay. What am I missing here, guys? I thought my boyfriend having his own restaurant would be a good thing?"

"It is," Maya confirms. "It's just that…I mean, my dad knows this guy who's a chef and he, like, never sees his wife and drinks a lot. He said he's surprised they're not divorced yet."

Oh, well, if your dad knows a guy…

"Yeah, opening a restaurant is great," Jazzy says. "But it's going to be super stressful. And on Randolph Street? Every eye is going to be on him."

"Every eye is *already* on him," I correct.

"My point exactly. What happens if he slips?" Jazzy asks.

"If he *slips*?"

"He's only been sober for what, like, a few months?"

"Three." I lick the salt off the side of my margarita glass.

"Maya and I just want to make sure you're prepared if he relapses."

There, she said it. The R-word. The word I've barely let myself think. I'm surprised how much it hurts to hear it aloud.

"So that's how it is. You have no problem eating his food, screenshotting the articles we're in and talking about how hot he is on our group texts. But deep down, you just think he's going to relapse? Maya, do you think that, too?"

Maya goes pale. But if an intervention is what they're turning this into, then I have no choice but to flip it on its ass.

"Maya?" I prompt.

"I mean, statistics show—"

"Oh, don't even go there with me. I live with the guy, I see him work his program every day and every night. I kiss him goodbye before he goes to his meetings and have his sponsor's number written on a piece of paper taped to the fridge. He's going to be just fine, ladies. In fact, he *is* just fine. So you know what I say? FUCK statistics. That's what I say."

I set my glass down as my hands start to shake. I fix my gaze to the left and stare out into the bar at nothing in particular. I just know that if I make eye contact with my so-called friends, I'll start to cry. Or drop another round of f-bombs.

"Try to understand where we're coming from." Jazzy jumps in to play referee.

"I can't. Because I was under the impression that you two supported me. Supported *us*."

"We do!" They sound feeble and unbelievable. I just shake

my head and take my phone out. For once I'm not concerned about the shit they might give me for doing so.

When I look down, of course I have a text from the man of the hour. Benji wrote to let me know it's now safe to come home. Dinner is just about ready and he can't wait to see me. I smile and reply with a single heart-shaped emoji.

That's when Maya puts her hand over my screen.

"Yo, can you stop texting and listen to us?"

I tighten my grip on my phone and spring my arm back. Something about her attempting to put a physical barrier between me and Benji just to drive home a moot point sends me into a blind rage. As if I wasn't in one already.

"Yo, can you stop poking holes in my relationship? Both of you need to either find your own or get a hobby that isn't dissecting my life."

I throw down a wrinkled twenty that I keep in my purse specifically for this cash-only frozen yogurt place I go to and tell them that should take care of my margarita plus tip. Then I grab my bag and head home to the meal Benji's prepared just for me.

7

"Smells so good. Burgers?" I ask, inhaling greedily as I walk through the door. The drama with Jazzy and Maya dissipates upon first whiff.

"Not quite, babe." Benji pops out from the galley kitchen and kisses me, a warm oven mitt gently cradling my face. "Chicken with roasted carrots and broccoli, and mashed sweet potato gnocchi."

He's nailed it and he knows it. Benji's soft, pillowy gnocchi recently dethroned his infamous macaroni and cheese as my favorite meal. Plus, I'm a sucker for sweet potato anything. Coming home to this will never get old, I tell myself as he dips back into the kitchen to put the finishing touches on our meal for two.

"Do I have time to change?" I ask as I kick off my shoes.

"You do, but..."

"But what? What's the problem?"

He takes two steps toward me, kisses my lips, then works his way down to my neck. I roll my head back and feel the goose bumps start to surface. He and I both know that when he gets to my neck, we go to the bed. But before he spends too much time on my sweet spot, he stops himself and heads back to his post at the stove.

"The problem is I want to fuck if you're already going to be undressing, but I can't right now because I'm at a critical spot with these potatoes."

I feel my face flush. It's unimaginable that I'm with someone who is as creative and passionate in the bedroom as he is in the kitchen.

Benji makes me feel like a woman. A desired woman. A wanted woman. And even though it's *his* libido that's amped up, it's mine that's just getting discovered.

Before Benji, I was doing the whole single-in-the-city thing. Not necessarily by choice, but Chicago is an epicenter for Peter Pan Syndrome—that thing where grown men still think drinking until 6:00 a.m. in Wrigleyville with their buddies on the weekend is a good look. I swear, no guy here is in a rush for any sort of committed relationship.

So I did what all other twentysomething females with a Chicago zip code do: embraced it and rotated through guys on Tinder. Clearly I'm not one to scoff at meeting someone from the internet (hello, @BJZane), but you could say there was something a little too casual about my love life in the time between moving back after college and finding my way with Benji.

"You just have to get to the third date," Maya would say. "*Cosmo* says that's a morally acceptable amount of time before sleeping with a guy." But three dates with a person I knew I didn't have a future with felt like a slow race. And when we managed to finally get there, sex felt like something I needed to squeeze in like a side of vegetables because it was good for me.

I was never truly needed by a guy before Benji came along, and so I never realized just how powerful that feeling is. Dirty talk? Yeah, sure, whatever. But tell me you *need* me, and I'm halfway to an orgasm. I may have learned this about myself from Benji, but he's learned from me that saying it gets him what he wants—both in and out of the bedroom.

It may not be outlined in the official NA handbook, but I've read enough lifestyle blogs to know that regular sex is part of a normal, healthy relationship. And that's what I'm after here—normal and healthy—no matter how I have to go about getting us there.

"How about in a little bit?" I bargain. "We'll put on an episode of *Lost*."

"Putting on an episode of *Lost*" is essentially code for "we're going to screw." I don't know what it is about that show, but every time we watch it, we wind up naked on the couch within the first twenty minutes. I have no idea what's actually happening in the season two story line, but it does a good job washing out the occasional moan that could be heard by those waiting for the elevator in the hallway.

"Okay, deal. Go change and let's eat."

We eat dinner together every night unless he's got something pop-up related going on or an evening NA meeting with Mark. Most of the time, we stay at the apartment. Partly because preparing me a home-cooked meal is a term and condition in the stay-sober deal he made with me, and partly because going out to eat in this city is almost always a spectacle. Don't get me wrong, it feels incredible—to be the woman behind the man like I was at Republic. But tonight I'm craving simple and delicious in all facets of my life, so I'm pleased it's just us.

Sprawling granite countertops are not part of the amenities in my tiny unit. So Benji hinged a piece of butcher's block to the wall for added prep space a few weeks ago. I have no clue how sturdy it is, or what kind of damage he's caused to the drywall, but tonight he's set it up as a makeshift table for two. There's a single yellow flower, plucked from the landscaping near the front door, poking out of a highball glass. It's a romantic touch and I quickly forget how cramped we are when he puts a steaming plate in front of me. I'm in awe this was made right here in my underequipped kitchen.

"How is it?"

"You know I'm obsessed with this gnocchi."

"Good, babe," he says, pushing the flower into frame and snapping a photo of his plate before uploading it to social media. Not everything can be sacred, I guess. "I made extra for your lunch tomorrow."

There are times I doubt that I'm doing this right—this whole keeping-an-addict-sober thing. It's like losing your virginity or graduating from college: there aren't manuals for this kind of stuff. But when I hear him say that he's made a double batch of my favorite food so I can eat well at work tomorrow, I know something's working, something's clicking. He's thinking about someone other than himself and it's a relief seeing that he's on the right track. Not to mention empowering to know that I helped steer him there.

But he can't distract me with food forever. There's something I need to bring up, even if it means derailing our *Lost* plans.

"So what's with the email I got from Angela?" I keep my voice calm and pop another gnocchi in my mouth.

"What do you mean?" he asks, peeling the crispy skin off his chicken with his bare hands and stuffing it in his mouth. I guess two can play at this keep-it-casual game.

"She emailed us this afternoon. Said that you said to keep me looped in on everything."

"Well, yeah," he says, chewing thoughtfully. "She needs to know that I'm only in if you are. If she thinks I can be successful without you in the picture, she's dead wrong. Made that crystal fucking clear today."

My face flushes again; this man trusts me with his life, his career, his everything. It's an incredible responsibility and an honor. I only wish I could put it on my résumé.

"So I don't have to do anything, right? I don't need to reply?" I want confirmation that this is his pet project, not mine.

"Did you look at the attachments?"

"No, why?"

"They detail the investment." His voice takes on a salesy quality.

"Isn't that for some old, rich, white guy to peruse?"

"Craig is his name. Yeah, but he's not the only investor here," Benji clarifies. "*We* have to own a part of it, too, or this isn't going to work."

Bomb. Dropped. And something tells me this isn't "an extra twenty dollars for cab fare" kind of investment. I can feel my blood start to come to a slow boil. I set down my fork, which still has a gnocchi dangling from the spears.

I accept that Benji cannot do much on his own at this stage in the game. And I don't mind helping. Having him in my life has shown me how much of a natural-born problem solver I am. Couple that with my need to feel needed, and I understand why he feels comfortable running everything by me. But sometimes I wish I had the option to RSVP "no" before getting roped into the real clusterfucks.

"What are you talking about? Either this Angela chick has an investor who's footing the bill or she doesn't and this is just a bullshit scheme to bleed you dry and use your name." My appetite suddenly disappears.

"What are *you* talking about?" Benji snaps back.

I know where this is going—to the land where civil conversation goes to die. My only hope is that we don't emotionally drain each other before dessert is served.

"Do you have any clue how these things work, Allie? Obviously not. Yeah, sure, Craig could front the whole thing easily. But if he does, we have no say in what the hell goes on there."

Please stop saying we.

"I'll just be a slave to whatever some sixty-year-old fuck-face from the suburbs wants to do. I'm not taking that kind of a risk. Not on Randolph Street. Not at this stage in my career."

Career is hardly a word I'd use to describe what goes on in here between his jimmy-rigged food prep and the micro profit we pull, but I throw no flags. Yet.

"What do you want for me, Allie?" He continues with the diatribe. "Do you want me working at a place with some laminated spiral-bound menu that can be wiped off when someone's kid throws up on it? That's going to be my big return to the food scene? Loaded baked potato skins and early-bird specials? Please, I'll get laughed straight out of Chicago and have to spend another six years staging around the country before I find my way again."

Subtle as it may be, I recognize that as both a threat and a jab. The likelihood that Benji would actually throw away this cushy Lincoln Park setup to go back to coast-to-coast couch surfing is slim to none. But he's certainly attempting to get me to believe that this life I've helped him create isn't good enough.

Needless to say, this is not the first time a normal conversation with Benji has gone sour. What hasn't killed him has indeed made him stronger. But it also has caused him to develop unhealthy coping mechanisms and an uncanny ability to turn a neutral chat into a straight-up confrontation. Most of the time, I can defuse the situation before one of us throws something. A reminder that one call to the front desk from an angry neighbor is all it will take to get us kicked out of our building usually gets him to lower his voice. Tonight, I don't see that tactic bringing him down. I'm just glad the days of him running to a pile of cocaine to feel better are over.

That said, I need to find solid ground again. So I take a breath and try a different approach.

"Why don't you fill me in, then. What was in that attachment, Benji?" I keep my voice calm and, I hope, curious.

"The number."

"What number?" I say, willing my hands not to shake with suppressed frustration as I resume eating.

"Thirty."

"Thirty *what*, Benji? Just tell me, okay? Please."

"Grand."

I put my head in my hands and rub my eyes. "You need *that* kind of money to do this deal with them?"

"No. For them to do the deal with *me*."

It might be my head spinning, but this is not adding it up. The confused look on my face signals Benji to explain his rationale.

"If we can't buy in, I tell them I'm out and this whole thing capsizes. Angela said so herself, they're not doing this open with any other chef. If I bow out because I can't have part ownership, the space goes straight to the MLS where it'll be scooped up by someone else, probably Ross Luca to be honest, and the opportunity for Craig to have a restaurant on Randolph Street is over. So it's ten percent, or I tell them to get fucked."

"And ten percent is $30,000?"

"Yes."

"Well, then, tell them to get fucked."

With a steak knife in his grip, Benji slams his fist to the table.

"God fucking damn it, Allie. You're missing the point. Opportunities like this don't wind up in your lap every day—or at least, not in mine, okay? You know my past. Angela knows my past. And this whole city knows my past. And guess what? She and Craig are *still* willing to do a deal with me. They're willing to give me a chance that no one else is ballsy enough to offer. They know I'm the right person for this regardless of what they've read about me on that hack-job *FoodFeed* blog."

FoodFeed's given him his platform in this city and he knows it. He may claim now, in this moment, that he doesn't care about what they write, but he and I both know it's the first and last thing he looks at every day.

"Well, if they know so much about your past, they should know you're still in recovery and ought to give you another six months to get your shit together." It comes off snide, but I'm just being defensive of him.

"Look, I've known I wanted to do something like this since I learned how to make barbecue sauce from scratch. Since I learned to make a roux for *real* mac 'n' cheese. Since I said fuck you to my dad and turned my back on my deadbeat mom. Since traveling thousands of miles, sleeping on hundreds of floors and making shit money while staging at places that didn't care about me. I stuck all of that out because I knew it would lead me to something like this. And now that something is finally here. I'm not saying no. I can't."

Benji gets up from his seat, crouches down like he's doing a squat and grabs my hand.

"I've been sober for ninety-two days, Allie. That's ninety-two days of doing nothing but sitting in this apartment, fucking around in this tiny ass kitchen and busting my dick doing one-off pop-up dinners for people who have the audacity to call themselves 'foodies.' Aren't you tired of that? I'm tired of that."

I've been cheerleading so hard for these pop-ups; rooting for him not to give up on them. I don't know what my obsession is with them, to be honest. They're a lot of work, a little bit of money and would be completely frowned upon by a handful of governmental agencies if they knew about them. But they give me a sense of control that I find comforting.

The moment I hop into the Excel document that shows his food costs or his current guest list, I see exactly what he's up to—who, what, when and where. And I can breathe easier and sleep better at night.

But if I remove that from the equation and make this not about me, then the truth is that, yes, I am already tired of the pop-up scene. Tired of having to wait for someone to submit their reservation payment so that I can buy a new shirt. Tired of black-market squirrel meat purveyors doing drop-offs in my lobby at 2:00 a.m. Tired of there being corn silks in my sheets at night because there's never enough counter space. Tired of snapping at my friends because a conversation about these stupid dinners can turn into a full-blown fight about my relationship.

But still, a couple hundred dollars every week makes more sense than $30,000 all at once. I mean, that's just basic math, right?

"So what are you asking me, Benji? What's the endgame here?"

I watch brown butter cool and solidify around what's left of my gnocchi. If I tried to swallow another bite right now, I'm pretty sure I would choke.

"I'm not asking for anything, Allie. I'm telling you that we're so close—so, so close—to not ever having to worry about money again."

Is this reverse psychology? Okay, sure—I guess I can see the logic here. But—

"Benji, where is this magical $30,000 going to come from?"

He gets up and sits back in his own chair.

There's a small chance he's going to say the investment could come from me. Why? Because occasionally I send him to get the cash he needs for his pop-ups with my ATM card. It's a risky move given the fact he's a recovering addict, but

I feel like every instance when I can show my faith in him makes him stronger—makes *us* stronger. He hasn't proved me wrong so far. That said, he's obviously seen my account balance, which is roughly $31,783.44 (but hey, who's counting?). He knows that I technically have enough to cover the ask.

My savings are, well, mine. They are the result of nearly a decade of work. A *decade*. I cobbled that impressive sum by babysitting at age twelve, sweeping up hair at a salon at fifteen, working at the mall at sixteen and slinging beers at a bar by my college damn near every day for four years. By the time I got hired at Daxa, I was doing pretty well for myself. A five-grand signing bonus and a decent salary was the icing on the hard-work-pays-off cake.

But what I have in my account now, I'm fairly certain, isn't meant to be spent in one fell swoop, and not by the ripe old age of twenty-five. I'm smart enough to know a woman's life savings isn't meant to be blown owning 10 percent of some dude's dream, no matter how good in the sack—or the kitchen—he is.

Benji knows this, too. On some level, he must. So I've got to be missing something here. I just can't see it yet.

"Babe." His tone is suddenly, dramatically different, like honey on warm toast. He reaches out from across the table and grabs my hands again. This time, his are noticeably clammy.

"Hear me out. We invest ten percent now, just enough to make sure we get a little say with things from the start. After the restaurant pays out salaries and costs, whatever's left in profits is yours and Craig's. Then, we work it into the contract that at a certain level of revenue earned, our ten percent grows to twenty-five, then fifty-one, then seventy-five, and finally—in a few years—we're at ninety and Craig's at ten."

I literally.

Cannot.

Even.

He's asking me for $30,000. *Thirty thousand dollars.*

"And when we're at ninety percent ownership," he continues, blissfully unaware of the sirens blaring in my head, "we'll be living in a brownstone a block from the lake. Four floors, all to ourselves, a little yard. We'll have popped out a kid or two by then with one more on the way. You won't have to work at all. And we'll be having dinner, just like this, at a massive table—kids will be in bed, cute dog asleep at our feet—and you know what? We'll look back at this conversation and laugh. I'll say, 'Remember when we talked about doing this five years ago? Weren't we having dinner in your little studio or something?' And you'll say, 'Yeah, I remember fighting about Randolph Street while eating that shitty chicken you roasted. I can't believe we ever hesitated.' How does that sound?"

Funny enough, it still sounds like he's asking me for $30,000.

He releases my hands, lets out a sigh and scoots back a few inches in his chair. The spell he cast on himself has been broken.

"Babe, look. I know you have the money. I'm not asking for it right now. But I *am* asking you to come with Angela and me to meet the investor at the space. I want you to be part of that conversation. Will you at least do that for me? Be part of a conversation? That's fair, right?"

The sensation of being drowned in a sea of Benji's pretty words starts to subside, his intensity ebbing back out to the wide-open ocean where it belongs.

"Yes. I can do that." The pressure valves have been opened.

"Thank you," he says, like we've just settled on terms to end the Cold War. He rises and takes our plates to the sink.

Now would be the ideal time to take a sip of wine, but a

deep breath will have to suffice. As Benji rinses the dishes, I take mental inventory of what just happened.

Benji tried to speed through a yellow light in asking outright for the investment. When he saw he was going to crash and burn, he diverted, suggesting that he merely wants a second opinion on the space. There's no need to call him out. In fact, I feel bad for him. After all, someone is dangling his dream scenario in front of his face and I'm the only one who can help him reach it.

"Dessert, babe." Benji returns to the table with deconstructed cannoli, my favorite. This is the same dish he plated using tweezers and Daxa before uploading it to the Twittersphere for me to find all those months ago. This sweet finish is the reason, roundaboutly, that we are here, doing life together. I'm warmed by the throwback as I take a bite.

"Who are you texting?" I ask as I get a sinking feeling that he's sitting across from me firing off a message to Angela about the restaurant right now.

"Mark. I'm asking him if he can take me to a meeting."

"Right now? What about *Lost*?"

"I'd love to, trust me. And we will. But right now, I need to prioritize my sobriety. This was a tense dinner, babe. And I'm sorry for the role I played in that. If I head to a meeting, it'll help me hit the reset button and that's a good thing. Mark's on his way now to get me. That okay?"

A welcome smile hits my lips. I'm impressed that self-awareness has joined us at the table. Benji taking this kind of initiative with his well-being is as attractive as his tatted arms and command over the kitchen.

"Of course," I say. "Tell Mark I said hi. And thanks."

8

Hi Connor,

I have a doctor's appointment at 11am today so I'll be taking my lunch a little early. I should be back around noon but will call Linda if anything comes up. Stacey and Dionte will watch the social streams for me while I'm OOO.

Thanks,
Allie

Send.

It's Friday. Our appointment to see the space with Craig (or should I say "Doctor" Craig?) is coming up in just a couple of hours. I haven't slept soundly since—well, to be frank, since I met Benji. But I've been especially restless since our conversation two days ago over roasted chicken. While Benji was able to escape promptly after things got heated and attend a support meeting with his sponsor, I still haven't been able to find a similar source of instant chi. Even if I did drag myself to a support group like Nar-Anon, I'm not sure how it would change the enormous ask I know is coming from the man I'm supposed to be loving and supporting in his recovery in any way I can.

I also can't just call a friend to reaffirm that I'm not crazy. If I respond to Jazzy's and Maya's apology texts and fill them in with what's going on, it'll just give them more material for a relationship they already think is a joke. I know the three of us will work our drama out in time, but right now I need them to sit and stew a bit so they understand it's not okay to haphazardly mention over drinks that they think my boyfriend is going to spiral out any minute.

Aside from them, the remaining members of my circle of trust are some girls from book club who I never really hang out with unless Jazzy and Maya are there and my coworkers, Stacey and Dionte. I'm friendly with these two, as friendly as you can be with people you spend forty-plus hours a week with. But the daily woes I face with Benji are hardly fodder for watercooler gossip.

So I guess that leaves my parents—or more specifically, my mother.

Ever since I was a kid, my mom would say, "As long as you tell me the truth, I won't be mad." I tested this theory once in a toy store that sold rolls of scrapbook stickers. I peeled off six inches worth of sparkly smile faces and put them in my pocket.

When I got home, I immediately stuck them on my school notebooks. Soon after, she asked me where I got the stickers. I told her I found them in a bush outside of the toy store. She then promptly grabbed my arm, tossed me in the car and drove me back to the toy store where she made me tell the owner what I did, apologize profusely and give them all back. I got grounded for a month.

Flash forward to the night I graduated high school and confessed I got caught underage drinking at a house party. She was disappointed, but helped pay my legal fees and get it expunged from my record like it was NBD.

That said, I'm sure I'll have her support, but it just doesn't feel like the right time to tell her about Benji's restaurant proposition. But I guess it's always the right time to just hear her voice. So I call her.

"Hi, honey," she says. "Is everything alright?"

I try to call my mom most days on my way home from work. It makes the smell of BO on the bus less noticeable. I forget that a call from me this early in the morning could be cause for concern.

"Yeah, it's fine. I'm just, um…" *bad at lying*, I think to myself. "I had a few minutes before my next meeting and wanted to get the phone number of your hair lady. I'm in dire need of a root touch-up and everything in the city is booked."

I'm not in need of a touch-up, nor do I need the phone number of a lady who does hair for middle-aged women in the suburbs. But what I do need is my mom's care and concern, even about something as trivial as caramel-colored highlights.

"Sure. I do have it written down somewhere, but I'll have to call you back. I'm on my way to tennis. I read in the paper that the girl I play doubles with got caught shoplifting at Kohl's and I want to see if she says anything about it."

"Cool. Have fun playing detective, Mom."

"I will. Love you, Al. 'Bye."

Oh, normalcy. How I've missed you.

Benji has been exceptionally polite to me for the past twenty-four hours. He even went down on me, which he hasn't done since being fueled by cocaine. Not because he's against it when he's sober, but because he says his taste buds are too sensitive to do it. I'm not sure how much truth there is to that, but it seems like a good excuse for a high-profile chef to get out of doing some dirty work.

This morning I woke up to the simplest, sweetest email. Benji sent it to me sometime after I fell asleep last night (note: a chef and a nine-to-fiver have completely different circadian rhythms) and I've reread it probably twelve times already today.

You are my princess. Everything I ever wanted but never knew I needed.

Lunch is in the fridge for when you leave to catch the bus. Love you SO SO SO much.

-B

The email, the lunch, the cunnilingus—I know it's all leading up to our meeting with Angela and Craig. And Benji knows, too. Anything he can do to lessen the blow of asking me to sign over just about everything I have to my name, he'll do. And while I must admit that the steak sandwich with caramelized onions and leftover gnocchi for lunch is a nice touch, it doesn't make my decision any easier.

My phone buzzes with a text.

On the way w/ Angela. Pick U up @ 10:45. White Jetta.

I can feel the anxiety start to flow through my veins the way you can feel the buzz of alcohol, except this is nowhere near as fun as being tipsy. *It's just a conversation with this Craig guy,* I remind myself.

This Craig guy. I wish I had his last name, or the name of his investment firm, so I could have done some online due diligence. I picture someone tall and tan (probably because he just got back from playing golf in Palm Springs) with sandy blondish-gray hair. I'm expecting porcelain veneers and a personality to match: fake, flashy and distracting.

Could a guy like him—or at least, a guy like the one I imagine Craig to be—even be serious about financing a restaurant with someone like Benji? I know Angela was candid in her email, saying she knew about Benji's past, but the first three Google hits for "Benji Zane" revolve around drugs, firings and going off the deep end. Wouldn't that scare any practical person away?

Then I remember the first time I Googled Benji and answer my own question. Nope. In fact, it does the opposite. It pulls you in like the suction from a drain.

Downstairs, reads the text from Benji. I take a deep breath, throw my phone into my purse and slither out for my appointment without so much as saying "I'll be back soon" to Stacey or Dionte.

As I trot down the back access stairwell, my heels clicking on the metal steps, I wonder how Angela is going to treat me when we meet again in just a few moments. After all, the last time our paths crossed, the encounter was essentially a less intense version of a strong-armed assault. She can't possibly be that rude to me in front of Benji, right? I have to imagine pissing off the chef's girlfriend/bankroll is a huge faux pas if she wants to get this restaurant off the ground.

Angela's white Jetta is parked in front of the entrance to my building in a fire lane with her hazards on. Benji is in the passenger's seat but quickly gets out when he sees me coming.

"Hi, baby, you look cute today," he says, giving me a kiss and letting me sit shotgun for the ride over. He's in a gray blazer and black skinny jeans looking like a more burly, more built Adam Levine. I buckle my seat belt, remind everyone I have an hour, hour and a half tops, and get ready for the awkward ride over.

"Angela, meet Allie. Allie, meet Angela." Little does he know, we've already met; hell, we've already been physical together.

We both say, "Hi, nice to meet you," at exactly the same time. It's a truce.

"Thanks so much for coming to get me—excited to see the space," I say out of respect for Benji.

"My pleasure," says Angela, pulling back out into traffic. "Full disclosure, there's a few things you've got to look past. It hasn't been maintained as well as it should have over the years, but the possibilities are endless. It's a real diamond in the rough, as they'd say. You're going to fall in love with it."

Is she describing the restaurant? Or the man sitting behind me?

Take the money aspect out of the equation, and I *am* excited to see the space—truly. I know how big a deal Randolph Street is, and the fact that there's a soon-to-be-abandoned space up for grabs is major. No matter who winds up there—whether it's us or some other chef (god, I hope it's the latter)—the square footage will inevitably convert into something press-worthy, and we'll have seen it first. Even with all the anxiety about what will happen next, I can still appreciate the exhilaration of it all.

As we weave under the El tracks and over the Chicago River, I note that Angela is in business attire and looks just like her profile picture—part lesbian, part Swedish model. The unforgiving sun reveals she's wearing a full face of concealer two shades too light and her signature bold lipstick is cracking. You would think a front-of-house professional would get a grip on her makeup game, but whatever. I shake my lingering bitterness toward her by engaging in obligatory conversation about traffic as we make our way to the West Loop.

"And...we're here. Nine hundred West Randolph," Angela says, throwing the car in a loading zone spot directly in front of the door and shifting into Park.

Benji grabs my hand as I step to the curb, taking in the digs. It's as if a Realtor is showing us the entryway to our first home. I feel grown up.

She fidgets with the code on the lock and finally we are

in. The space is small, but it has character—starting with the fact that the entire storefront is a glass garage door. I like it.

"That'll be the first thing to go," Angela announces as if she was reading my mind.

"It's so 2012," says Benji with a hint of elitism.

Well, at least their hatred of receding glass doors is in rhythm.

Angela continues to walk the space and spew off facts and figures about the foundation, piping and electrical—stressing that all will need to be inspected and likely replaced before opening.

"Hey, babe, real quick," Benji starts softly. "Just want you to know, there's no pressure here. Okay? You really do look beautiful today. And I love you."

No pressure? Is it possible that he had a bit of a heart-to-heart with himself over these last forty-eight hours and re-alized asking for $30,000 from his girlfriend of four months is a bit much? Or maybe he realized that a little humble pie might not be a bad thing to put on this particular menu. As in, maybe he doesn't need 10 percent ownership off the bat. Maybe just being employed will be a big enough step up from where he is now.

Whatever the reason for his sweet reassurance, I'm grateful.

"Thanks, babe," I say as we continue the self-guided tour.

The restaurant that Benji was the exec chef at before things went south held approximately 300 people and served break-fast, lunch *and* dinner, seven days a week. As alluring as it is to have your name on a menu for a beast of a place like that, it's understandable how someone could crack from that amount of pressure. But this spot is quite the opposite. It's not built out yet, but it feels like the same size as the venue for the pop-up dinner. If I were to guess, I'd say the maximum capacity would be about fifty people at a time.

I follow the thought. If this restaurant only does dinner service, and plans on being closed one day a week, then Benji could approach it the same as one of his curated dinners. He could probably handle it.

The restaurant is long and narrow and smells like mothballs and sweet-and-sour sauce. Even though we entered together, Benji has since dropped my hand as he beelines to the back, where the kitchen is. I imagine he wants to see firsthand what his headquarters look like and if there's sufficient space for a sporadic walk-in cooler romp session.

I stare at him standing in front of the current oven. He's dragging his pointer finger across the range. While he's probably imagining a brand-new appliance as he cuts through the filth and dust, I imagine him stirring that balsamic reduction whatever-whatever from the first night he made me dinner.

The flashback reminds me that I've never seen Benji cook in a proper, professional kitchen. Since we've met, it's been a hodgepodge of his kitchen, my kitchen and portable burners at whatever pop-up space he could secure on a whim. So even though this space would drastically change *if* it became his, there's a certain magic that envelops him in a setting like this. I see him calling orders. "Two scallop, no butter. Fire asparagus. Fire broc." I see him tasting a sauce with the tip of his pinky finger and ordering some sous to add more salt. I see myself stopping by, entering through the back door because he forgot his favorite apron at home, and in front of everyone, in the middle of the weeds, he stops everything to kiss me.

In the moment, I want this for him. I want the dream to come true.

"What do you guys think?" Angela asks, coming back into the main dining area, snapping me out of whatever nostalgic, flowery moment I was experiencing.

"It's so fucking beautiful." Benji sounds like he's touring the Smithsonian.

I can feel his extremes flaring up the way you can feel lightning in the air just before it cracks across the sky. Not surprisingly, he's falling hard and fast for this place.

"Shit. Is that Craig?" he asks Angela as he spots a man—scratch that—as he spots precisely the man I imagined getting out of a Porsche convertible parked across the street.

"It sure is," she proudly confirms.

The guy looks spry from here, jogging across the street with an outstretched wave to slow an oncoming sedan.

"Angela, sweetheart, how are you?" he says as he enters the building, air-kissing both of her cheeks. "This place is just as incredible as you described! What a find!"

I wonder briefly if they've slept together, which would debunk my theory she might be exclusively into girls, but don't have time to investigate their body language before Craig fixes his sights on Benji.

"Craig Peterson…" Angela trills, "…meet Benji Zane."

Peterson, Peterson, Peterson. I need to remember that for online-stalking purposes later.

The two shake hands.

"So Angela told me she had an orgasm when she ate your food. Do you think you could share the recipe so I can give it to my wife?" Craig cackles and brings Benji in for a hug. "I'm just kidding. It's good to meet you, Chef!"

Oh god. It begins.

Addressing a chef as "Chef" is one thing when you're standing next to him in the kitchen chopping onions. But Benji's in a blazer and Craig is essentially a stranger, so this move is a total ego stroke on Mr. Peterson's part. I find it irritating, but the twinkle in Benji's honey-brown eyes tells me he's flattered.

"And who's this?" Craig asks no one in particular as he looks my way.

"This is my girlfriend," Benji asserts. "And my business partner. Allison Simon." His chest puffs a bit as he rolls the full, three-syllable version of my name off his tongue.

"It's great to meet you as well, Allison."

"You can call me Allie," I say as we shake hands.

"Allie, then. Let's have a look around, shall we?"

When Angela and Craig turn toward the kitchen, I raise my eyebrows in Benji's direction to let him know I'm not particularly fond of my new dual role in his life. Simply fronting him some money is a drastically different level of involvement than being a "business partner." He gives a conciliatory smile and mouths, *Sorry.*

"So what are they asking?" Craig asks when the tour is over and we've arranged ourselves near the clunky old host stand.

Angela digs through a folder stuffed with printouts to find what I assume is the listing sheet. "It looks like we can get in here at 300 initially. Granted, there are some issues the city is going to flag before we're approved to do the deal. I spoke with the Realtor and the seller can't afford to fix them, so it's on us to prove funds and clean it up."

"So three-hundo to get in, and how much more to greenlight it with the city?" Craig asks.

"It's too soon to tell without the formal inspection," Angela says. "But I'm guessing it could be three times that."

"Well, even at under a mil, that's a fucking steal for Randolph Street. Ben, what do you need to outfit the kitchen?"

Who's *Ben*? Ugh.

"I can do a kitchen for forty."

The conversation is moving fast. It dawns on me all at once that not only are we speaking in thousands, but these are numbers Benji has already calculated and considered. *No pressure, Allie. No one can force you to write a check...*

"And how long 'til open?"

"Depends," Benji says. "Do you want to open this year? Or next?"

"Hmm, let's see...do I want to make money or do I want to sit with my hand on my dick? I want to open this restaurant as soon as humanly possible."

Have I mentioned that Craig is *exactly* the guy I imagined in my head?

"Fair enough," Benji says, appreciating the crass sense of humor. "Well, assuming you guys handle the structural and architectural changes, I need maybe a month? Forty-five days?"

"Staffing and equipment done in forty-five days? So it's a month and change 'til we're making money?" Craig wants to confirm. I want to object. How is a full-blown restaurant going to manifest itself before the time my next period comes?

"Yes. Tops," Benji says. His confidence is terrifying. And sexy. And terrifying.

"Wow. That's faster than I thought. This ain't the suburbs anymore, is it, Ang?"

He nudges her with his elbow and she smiles. It's about to be game over if he calls me "Al" next.

"Alright, Benji. What do you guys want here?" Craig's question is directed at the two of us. I know things are getting serious because, all of a sudden, I exist.

"I want to be able to execute my vision, my menu, my way. Everything from the people to the pots and pans."

"Interesting. Go on," Craig says.

I don't get it. Does he actually want to hear what this tattooed kid has to say? Or is he just taunting him because he knows he can steamroll Benji at any time with the wad of hundreds protruding out of the back pocket of his khakis as we speak?

"Well, for starters, there will not be a pot pie of any sort on my menu, or any of the safe shit you and your golf buddies are used to eating back at the clubhouse. Food is going to get gnarly here, okay? We're going to push a lot of boundaries. Some people are going to hate it, others will love it, but the bottom line is anyone on the inside has got to be okay with it or I walk right now and you can get some no-name banquet chef from the W Hotel to be your yes-man."

His parting words indicate the whole thing could implode right here, right now. I'm probably the only one praying for that, though.

"We've talked about this." Angela steps in, her face finally as white as her ivory concealer. "And there's no one else we're positioning to be chef for this space."

I'm not sure if she's reminding Craig or calming Benji, but either way the absence of a Plan B raises my heart rate.

"So you want some say," Craig says haphazardly. "Well, that comes with a price. But I'm sure you and your…business partner…already know that."

He chokes on the description as much as I would have. I don't take offense.

"Yeah, we know."

Benji's gesturing with his hands more than usual and I can tell it's to bring his tattoos into frame. Ink like that is tattoo-speak for "I'm not fucking around here," and Benji is turning up the volume for Craig while I secretly hope it's turning him off.

"So you're prepared then to put down the standard ten percent upon contract execution, I take it?"

"So long as that's ten percent on the initial price, and not the all-in markup for that structural shit you guys mentioned, then yes. We're prepared for that and a contingency plan for more ownership over the next five years."

Benji has gone completely rogue at this point. Short of withdrawing the money himself, he's verbally committing to tying up my wealth with that of a man whose fake teeth and splotchy tan are nothing compared to the loudness of his tie.

We all stand silent, unsure of whose turn it is to talk next.

"Hell, cash or check, Angela? Let's call the Realtor and get something in writing by close of business today. I want to start throwing lipstick on this motherfucking pig come Monday." Craig throws up his hands like he's at a surprise party.

My heart palpitates in my chest like kernels of popcorn erupting in a hot, oiled pan. I wonder if anyone can hear my breathing, which has gone from shallow to heaving. I can feel the panic literally flowing through my veins into the tips of my tingling limbs. "Wait," I finally hear myself say. "Wait just a minute."

Actually, I want to scream, *let me rephrase: I'm five seconds from a nervous fucking breakdown.* Only falling apart isn't an option. Isn't there some unwritten rule that only one member of a couple can go totally off the deep end at any given time? How peculiar that my only options for a calming force are a perfect stranger in a wrap dress, a wealthy son-of-a-bitch or my just-this-side-of-drug-addiction boyfriend. Of the three, Angela is looking more and more like the only one who can talk me down.

"Angela, can I talk to you outside? Alone?"

9

All that separates this nice sunny day from the makings of a nightmare is a single storefront. If the sliding garage door behind me that's about to meet its fate with a sledgehammer could talk, I know it would say the same thing.

"Well, Allie? What can I help you with?" Angela huffs hot air onto the lenses of her big black sunglasses and wipes the smudges off with the fabric from her chevron-print dress. This is the first time I'm seeing her in broad daylight with nothing between her eyes and mine.

"Angela, I'm freaking out."

"And here I thought you just needed a tampon. In that case, let's move a *little* to the left so we aren't in plain sight of the guy who thinks you're stable enough to go into business with."

Angela puts her sunglasses back on and ushers me toward the alley. I lose sight of Benji through the front door and pray to god he and Craig don't take the liberty of making any permanent decisions during my momentary absence.

"Okay, talk to me." She pops a piece of gum into her mouth and runs her fingers through her platinum hair.

"I have no clue. I'm lost with all this." I can hear my voice quavering but can't seem to make it stop.

"Oh, sweetie, don't worry about it. I'll take care of all the phone calls and logistics this afternoon. You'll just have to sign a few papers later this evening."

"No, no. That's not what I mean." That's when I realize it: none of us are on the same page. She thinks Benji and I have talked and come to a unified decision—that we're skipping toward the finish line together, when really, the extent of my involvement caps at an argument over roasted chicken and a fake doctor's note this morning. Today was only supposed to be a *conversation*. Remember?

"I'm sorry, I don't understand," she says. "Is there something wrong with the space? I know the building is old, but our construction crew is brilliant. Even if the foundation is sinking, they can handle it. So don't worry."

"No, it's not that. It's just, we don't have the *money*." There. I said it. Well, whispered it.

All the features of Angela's face protrude. Her jaw drops and her brows rise above the tops of her shades. "Wait, what? Are you serious? I made Benji swear on his mother's life that he had the funds to go through with this."

"Well, that's problem number one," I mutter under my breath. She doesn't hear, which is probably for the best. Now doesn't seem like an appropriate time to delve into his unfortunate family dynamics.

"Fucking A. I figured this was too good to be true. I'm going to rip him a new one right now." She starts to storm off but I grab her wrist.

"Angela, stop. Relax for a minute." Did I just tell someone *else* to chill out? "Let me back up. We have the money, technically. Well, I do. I have around $30,000 to my name, but that's it. There's nothing left in my savings after that. No trust fund. No added allowance from mommy and daddy."

I watch her shoulders ease down an inch. The little voice in the back of my head that's saying, "This is crazy, Allie. RUN."—I can tell Angela hears it, too. But right now she's choosing to be poised and factual instead of compassionate and worried.

"Well, thirty grand is enough to cover a share of owner-ship," she states.

"I'm aware, Angela. But up until now, the most expensive thing I bought was a computer. I don't do stuff like this. I don't make *investments*. Alright? Especially not in something that I won't even be involved in."

"Ha!" she blurts out. What could possibly be funny?

"You *are* involved, Allie. You're Benji's girlfriend...or should I say, business partner. He's made it quite clear he's not going to wipe his own ass without you. So, you're going to be a part of this whether you like it—or even know it—or not."

"I know that," I say, waving away this happy family thing she's invented with a flick of my wrist.

I want to be his right-hand woman, so long as that caps at helping fill waters at a pop-up and being his date to fancy foodie dinners. This? This is something else entirely and I can't do it. Hell, I hate when I have to be the one to pay for our dinners. How am I going to foot the bill for his biggest move yet?

I break away from Angela for the moment and pace around the alley. Approaching the noon hour, I can see, hear, feel Randolph Street is already abuzz. Produce trucks are making their final deliveries of the day for the restaurants that are only open for dinner, while hungry foodies are dribbling across the bridge over the river for lunch. I see a table of four women across the street check in with a hostess at a restaurant called Rosalind's. She proceeds to offer them a table outside. They hang their bags on purse hooks being handed out from their server like a blackjack dealer. There's nothing like soaking up the sun on a nice patio day. Summer goes by so fast in Chicago.

As they settle in, I start to grow more uncomfortable with what's happening on our side of the street. If I go forward and say yes, I'll never again get to be like any of those ladies who lunch. Randolph Street won't be a place I meet my friends for special occasions. It won't be a destination for Benji and me to be wined and dined. It'll be the story of Benji's life, and so the story of mine, too. It'll be a beast.

Maybe I just say no and tell him if he really wants this, he's going to have to figure it out himself. I mean, that's certainly the cheaper option, although it may mean I wind up single and gossiped about in *FoodFeed* for the foreseeable future.

"Yoo-hoo." Craig ducks his head out from the front door. "Is there a problem out here, ladies?"

There are several. But Angela cuts me off before I have a chance to let the first one bubble up.

"It's all good, Craig! We're just discussing possible loading zones for deliveries. Tell Benji we'll be in in just a minute."

He winks and points at us before disappearing back into 900.

"Al-Dog, we need to get back inside. What are you thinking here?"

As I ponder the question, I'm back to being transfixed by the patio table across the street at Rosalind's. The ladies are now imbibing a bottle of rosé, the remaining few sips of which are comfortably resting tableside in a stainless-steel white wine cooler waiting for whomever is brazen enough to claim them. It's common knowledge that there are four glasses to every bottle, so I always wondered how there could be any left after a waiter pours for a party of this size. That's when Benji told me a server will always leave a little in the bottle and set up a complete wine display on the table to inspire other diners to order similarly. Meanwhile, a food runner has brought out a tower of bread—Rosalind's is famous for their cheddar biscuits—and the gals are clinking crystal wineglasses and laughing. Can we please trade places?

"Listen, Angela. I can't cook for shit. I hate oysters. And

I don't know why wineglasses have different shapes. Beyond appreciating some good Indian food, I really don't have any ties to this industry."

"You *do* know who you're dating, right?"

"Yes, of course. And I love Benji—don't get me wrong. But why would I invest all of my hard-earned money into something that has virtually nothing to do with me? This isn't my dream. It's Benji's. And yours. And Craig's. Something... I don't know. Something just doesn't feel right about this. It feels like a pyramid scam or something."

The stress of the moment washes over me. It's the first time I've voiced my feelings out loud, which makes it real. The fact my confession is to a woman I hardly even know causes me to start crying, apparently my favorite thing to do when I can't handle life anymore.

"Allie, let me explain something to you." She removes her sunglasses and looks me square in the face. Her eyes look like greenish-brown kaleidoscopes as her pupils adjust to the light.

"People make investments because their money comes back tenfold, and usually without them having to do much. Now that man in there, Craig, he's a super successful businessman who wouldn't waste his lunch hour doing something that wouldn't put money in his pocket, so you should take that as a really good sign. And then that other man in there, your boyfriend, well, he's a genius in the kitchen. I don't care how tired you are of hearing that, it's true. And then there's me. Now, I know you don't know me from Eve, but I'm pretty damn good at what I do, too. Okay? You're basically looking at the dream team, Allie. If anyone else knew what we were up to right now, they'd jump at the opportunity that's in front of you—to be a partial owner in what we've got brewing. Take a look around you. This is fucking Randolph Street! Pardon my French, but every patio table in a three-block radius is sat. You've got the expressway right here, the river right over there, Google headquarters here, McDonald's there and four El stops within a half mile…we're going to get eaters from every angle. You see dollar signs going down. I see dollar signs going up. Way the hell up."

She jams a finger to the sky to drive her point home.

"How do I…make my money back?" I choke out through some pathetic tears.

"When the restaurant makes money, you make money—simple as that. And the restaurant is going to make *a lot* of money. Trust me, okay? Do you trust me?"

That is the million-dollar—or rather, thirty-thousand-dollar—question.

Angela's vague explanation falls somewhere between pep talk and matter-of-fact. I try desperately to allow a nugget of confidence to work its way into my brain but nothing transpires to words. I shrug my shoulders and wipe my nose with the top of my hand.

"Are you still crying? Jesus, you're still crying." Angela digs a tissue out of her bag and hands it to me. "You need to put your big-girl panties on here and pull yourself together, okay?"

"I'm sorry I'm a mess right now." I blow my nose into the tissue, which I'm fairly certain has already been used.

"Okay. New tactic," she says. "Story time. I'm going to tell you a little something about this industry that you know nothing about, that you say feels like a scam. This industry? I love it. It saved my life."

"What do you mean?" I manage.

"I mean, eight years ago, when I was your age-*ish*, do you know where I lived? I'll give you one hint. It wasn't in some studio apartment in Lincoln Park, that's for sure. I lived on the street."

Truth bomb detonated.

"Yeah, I lived in whatever little nook in between two buildings I could squeeze my fat ass into to keep warm. To keep from being raped in my sleep. Because *that's* what it's like to be homeless in this city."

I can't picture Angela homeless. But I also can't picture her fucking with me right now so I try to ignore the big Chanel sunglasses and expensive-looking mod haircut as she goes on with her story about more desperate times.

"You want to know what's funny about being homeless?"

"There's something funny about being homeless?"

She smiles, a wry kind of smirk. "All the good spots get taken by the people who have been homeless longer than you. You know, like in the alleys, behind the Dumpsters? Kind of like where the two of us are standing right now. Yeah, good luck claiming a spot like this. You'll get knifed by someone a little more *senior*, if you will, if you even look like you're trying to settle in."

Angela moves closer to a nearby Dumpster and starts to circle around it like she's eyeing a luxury car on a showroom floor. I worry the stink will latch onto her clothes, but she doesn't seem to mind.

"A spot like this blocks the wind. It's a place where chefs throw away day-old bread or the unserveable ends of a rump roast. It's where yuppies toss last year's Marc Jacobs sweaters. I never could get a spot like this. So one day, I grabbed an empty Starbucks cup, one of those clear ones they put the teas in, out of the trash. It still had hot-pink lipstick stains on it, probably from an ad executive or a Macy's makeup artist. Do you know that cup is the reason I only wear red now? Anyway, I held it out and begged for change. I only needed enough to buy myself a ticket to ride the Red Line. Took me three days."

I do the mental math. A ride on the El is three dollars. How can you afford anything making a dollar a day?

"Once I got that ticket, I felt like a new woman. I boarded it, tucked myself in between a girl who looked kind of like you and some Asian guy in scrubs. I didn't know where I was going, I just wanted to take the train as far as I could go. Pretend for just a minute I was on my way to work, or to lunch with a friend, or to a new boutique on North and Clybourn. I ended up getting off somewhere up by Evanston. It was one of the last stops. I figured the further up I went, the less I'd have to compete with the meth heads and hookers jonesing for space by a Dumpster downtown. Are you following me, Allie?"

I nod once, barely noticing that my tears have dried.

"I wound up in Ravenswood. Have you been? People don't walk around there like they do in the Loop. What took me three days to collect in my cup downtown would take me a week in Ravenswood. So while I felt safer and more comfortable, I knew I couldn't stay there unless I got a steady job. So I went to a UPS Store and I asked the lady working if I could borrow a marker to write on a box they had thrown in their recycling bin. I wrote 'Second Chance Wanted. Please leave job applications instead of money. God bless.' I'm not religious, just so you know, but people respond well to the whole God thing.

"Anyway, I held that sign up at the El stop every day around 6:00 p.m. when I knew businessmen who worked down at the Board of Trade would be getting off the train and heading home to their perfect little families. Most were too exhausted to even acknowledge me standing there. Not one person talked to me for six straight weeks. But I kept going back to the tracks every day at 6:00 p.m. And then came Craig."

"Craig, like, the Craig inside?"

"Yes, sweetheart. That one. Craig stopped in front of me and pulled out a folded application from his Jack Spade briefcase. It was for a restaurant called the Rainy Day Pancake House. 'A few of our servers quit this week and I'm short-handed. Fill this out, and bring it back tomorrow for an interview.' He said something like that. It was so matter-of-fact, so business as usual. He needed a server. I needed a job. So then guess what?"

"What?"

"I cashed out my change cup, got a train ticket and aced my interview. Granted, all I had to do was show I could balance four plates on my arms and could accurately describe what was in the Rainy Day Scrambler. But regardless, they hired me on the spot. And guess what else?"

I just lift my eyebrows this time. She knows I want to know—*need* to know—every detail of her story.

"I worked breakfast, lunch and dinner. Every day. This whole time, no one but the head honcho, the owner, Craig, knew that after I clocked out, it was back to my secret little hiding spot in an alley in Ravenswood. Three months later, I could finally afford cheap rent and moved in with another server. Six months later, I got promoted to shift supervisor. A year later, assistant manager. Two years later, I left the Rainy Day Pancake House for Florette."

"The fine-dining place in Hinsdale?"

"That's the one."

"To serve?"

"Hell no," she says, putting her sunglasses back on. "To run the show! Come on, I *know* you've read my LinkedIn profile. I was the general manager...in charge of twenty people front-of-house, twenty people back-of-house, ordering, payroll, marketing, floor managing, you name it. I did it. Guess how many Michelin stars they had when I started?"

"One?"

"Zero. Now guess how many they had after one year of me on the floor?"

"Three?"

"Okay. Are you serious? No. No one's that good. We got one. One Michelin star, which is still a really huge deal. You'll learn more about that later."

"Congrats," I say, wiping any residual mascara from my tearstained face. I tilt my head slightly to peer through the clear garage door. Benji and Craig are both zeroed in on their cell phones, no longer fazed by our absence.

"The point here is this industry literally saved my life. And don't get confused. This isn't the food industry or the restaurant industry. It's the *service* industry. Do you get what that means? Because I don't think you do. It's not the whole 'we'll pamper you and pretend to care about you while seething and hating you behind the scenes' thing. It's the business of making other people feel warm and welcome. The hospitality business is what Craig showed me that day on the platform, and I've been committed to living it ever since. There's not a day that goes by that I don't honor what that man did for me by loving what I do."

I can hardly believe that under that spray tan and behind the veneers, there lies a big heart. While I have no doubt Mr. Moneybags is still in it to win it, I now understand why he's not afraid to give Benji this chance. On one hand, Angela recommends him. And after proving herself for the last eight years, I'm sure that what she says, goes. On the other hand, if Craig's done it before, he'll do it again. Meaning, if he gave a chance to someone who on the outside looks like a person you wouldn't want coming within ten feet of your front door, Benji's sordid past or hard exterior doesn't really weigh much on whether or not Craig pushes forward. So, at this point, it's just me. I'm the only one afraid. I'm the only one clogging this thing up. I'm the only one with hesitations. And maybe…I shouldn't be.

I don't know what I'm supposed to say to fill the silence between us now that her story is over. Of course there's a part of me that wants to ask how she wound up homeless in the first place or if she ever asked Craig why her, but I realize those are questions I don't need answers to. They are sprinkles of the past that should be left exactly there because everyone and everything is alright now. Hell, Angela's driving around in a brand-new Volkswagen Jetta and has a multimillionaire on her speed dial. The woman is a baller in disguise. I can't help drawing a parallel between her rock bottom and Benji's. If the industry saved her…

"Allie, let me ask you this. Do you remember the best meal you've ever had? Now, I'm not talking about anything Benji's whipped up for you, but rather your best meal out on the town?"

"Republic," I say, without hesitation.

"Ross Luca's place. Excellent choice. On track for two Michelin stars this year. Why was it so good? And don't say a word about the chocolate cake, even though I know it's better than sex."

"Benji took me. We were invited by the chef. He cooked us probably fifteen different courses. We were the only two people left in the restaurant after, like, six hours of eating crazy-good food. It felt like some weird *Bachelor*-style date or something. Who gets Republic all to themselves?"

"So correct me if I'm wrong here," she says. "But nowhere in there did I hear it was the best night ever because of the unlimited breadsticks. Or because they let you sub fries for a salad. Or because you had a coupon. This is the big leagues, Allie." She gestures to the door of 900 Randolph with an expansive wave. "There are going to be people who come through this door—*this very door*—and experience the best night of their lives. They are going to transcend reality and live to tell about it the next day. We're going to do that for people. No, let me rephrase that. We *get* to do that for people. Remember, it's a privilege. It's *our pleasure*."

Benji looks up from his phone and sees us outside. He smiles and waves. We wave back.

"You're the lucky one, Allie. You're the lucky one, because all you have to do is sit back and watch the fruit of your investment change people's lives. I, on the other hand, have to do the dirty work. I've got to deal with the people who complain that they don't like the brand of toilet paper we stock, or that there were lipstick prints on their wineglass when really that's just part of the crazy pattern that Benji picked out. I have to try to schedule a horde of twentysomething servers who are just in it for the cash and who all request Fridays off so they can go clubbing. I have to worry about whether our dishwashers can prove they are legal citizens. I have to make sure our sous chefs reek of BO and not whiskey.

"Okay? That's the fun shit I get to do on a daily basis, but let me tell you this—I love it. It's what makes me get out of bed in the morning. The hard stuff. The stuff that no one else wants to do, like…" She looks down at her watch; it's a Rolex. "Like get a contract for this place drummed up in the next five hours before everyone takes off for the weekend and wrangle all you fuckers to sign on all the lines where you're supposed to."

I laugh a little bit at the absurdity of all of this. Of Angela once being homeless. Of me currently dating some rock-star chef. Of there being a bazillionaire ten feet away who wants to own a sick piece of real estate in Chicago with me so we can start a restaurant. Of signing away $30,000 to be to Benji what Craig was to Angela. To give someone a much-needed, well-deserved second chance and let them run with it.

"Grab my hands and look me in the eye," Angela commands. "I need your commitment. Are you in?"

Angela's touch sends a surge of energy through me. It's like I've plugged myself into an outlet in the wall. All of a sudden, it dawns on me that I can relax. She's the Coast Guard circling this sinking ship that I am on with Benji, ready to make a rescue. The onus isn't on me and me alone to save him anymore—not if I sign on the dotted line. It's a huge financial investment, but is it a huge risk? Everything in me believes in Angela. And if Angela believes in Benji, well, then I should, too.

And so I inhale deeply, breathe out and say, "Yes. Yes, I'm in."

10

I arrive back at the apartment late that evening, around seven thirty. I guess you could say my little "doctor's appointment" totally threw off the rest of my day and I got tangled up in tweets. While I was checking out the restaurant space, a pic of Jennifer Lawrence's morning routine featuring our product went viral. We're up to 15,482 retweets, 61,059 favorites and 50 incoming tweets per minute. Work piling up combined with my head being somewhere else entirely made for one hell of an exhausting afternoon.

But the good news is this: I'm home, and I smell garlic and butter.

Benji peeps from behind the kitchen wall as he hears me unlock the door. He kisses me and quickly returns to his post at the stove, where he's rapidly moving around a delightful pan of spaghetti sautéing in olive oil, light cream and speckles of cracked black pepper.

"How was the rest of your day, babe?"

"It was good," I say, throwing my hair up into a messy top-knot (still not as perfect as his) and taking a seat at the already-set table. "Busy."

Benji plates the spaghetti and grates some fragrant black truffle on the top of the perfectly swirled mountain of noodles. The shavings smell heavenly. What a contrast to my former habit of dousing mushy pasta with a glob of butter and Kraft parmesan.

He joins me at the table as I tuck a piece of paper towel into the collar of my black shift dress and prepare to gorge.

"Bon appetit, babycakes." He holds up a bottle of San Pellegrino to *cheers* me.

"Whoa. What the hell happened to your wrist? Did you burn yourself?"

"Oh, this?" Benji remarks, looking toward a piece of white gauze the size of a pack of gum taped to the inside of his left wrist. "Nah, not a burn. Hurt just as bad, though."

Benji slowly removes the tape and peels off the bandage. His wrist is only facing him at this point as he uses the pointer finger on his right hand to gently brush over the spot.

"You like?" he says, finally turning it toward me.

My jaw plummets to the floor.

"You're crazy!" I say through a grin I cannot control. I immediately get up from my chair and jump into his lap. "Let me see that!"

I hold his wrist in my hand and examine the fresh tattoo that says *Allie* in cursive. It beautifully blends with the rest of his gnarly ink; but still this delicate, swirly addition stands out from a mile away.

"What…why…how…?" I'm at a loss for words. He's branded himself with my name and I've never experienced something so romantic in my life.

"I just wanted to show you that I appreciate what you're doing for me with the restaurant and that I'm in this for the long haul. As long as this little doodad is on my wrist, I'm not going anywhere. I love you."

Forget the pasta. Forget wondering where he got the money for a tattoo. Forget the fact I'm about to buy a restaurant. I rip his shirt off over his head and slink out of my dress. He picks me up and I wrap my legs around his torso. The good thing about a small studio apartment is that it's never a far walk to the bed, which is where he throws me down and proceeds to make me feel more delectable than any dish he's ever created.

"Allie, it's Angela. I got the paperwork in by five today as per Craig's request. Our closing lawyers are going over it all day tomorrow. They said they won't have the final green light on things until Monday, but it doesn't seem like there'll be any problems. Long story short—we won't need your funds until then, so just hold tight on pulling that money order. Alright, that's all for now. You kids sleep well and start thinking about what you want this place to be called."

I don't often deliberately send people's calls to voice mail, but I've just had the best sex of my life and I am waiting my turn to shower it off as I casually chow on some lukewarm (but still delicious) *spaghetti cacao e pepe*.

Hours have passed since the conversation Angela and I had on Randolph Street and I'm still replaying it in my head. I don't know if she's secretly a motivational speaker, has a background in theater, or was just using some really good distraction methods—but she was so inspirational in that moment. Talking to Angela felt good for my soul. What can I say? I'm a bit of a sucker for damaged goods.

But now, as I lie nestled in the corner of my deflated Ikea love seat while Benji is in the bathroom, things feel a tad different. Without the immediacy of Angela in front of my face and the endorphins from the celebratory sex charging through my body at a thousand miles per hour, my commitment doesn't feel quite as firm as, say, when Benji was naked on top of me twenty minutes ago.

It's not that I'm going back on my word to her. It's just that alone in the quiet, away from these powerful influencers, I'm seeing this situation from another angle: a really expensive due for dating Benji Zane.

I keep remembering what Angela said about investors only existing because they get a return on their deals. The difference between someone like me and Marc Cuban, though, is that he has the ability to make multiple investments; I only have this one chance, and taking it will leave me close to destitute.

But I still want to do it. And I have to accept that this is it: this is the big-ticket item I've been waiting for. Maybe I thought I was saving for a down payment on a house, or the first year of my future kid's college tuition. But no, it's actually this—part ownership of a restaurant that doesn't even have a name yet. The only thing wilder would be using the money for bail to get my mother out of jail for stabbing my father. That's how outlandish teaming up with two strangers and a drug-addict chef—sorry, *recovering* drug-addict chef—feels.

Bzz, Bzz.

Thankfully a text interrupts what I can only assume was the beginning of a downward spiral.

Hi sweetie. It's Rita, Mark's wife. U guys coming to the picnic this wknd?

Seeing a text from the wife of Benji's sponsor pop up on my phone calms me immediately. She's someone I know I can instantly trust without any strings attached. And even though we haven't met before and this is her first time reaching out directly, the fact that she's not asking me for money or to sign a contract is welcomed. I save her number to my contacts before I reply.

Briefly I wonder how she got my number in the first place. I'm sure that Benji gave it to Mark, who then passed it along to Rita, just to open up the lines of communication a bit more. But a part of me wonders if Benji had to put me down

as some sort of emergency contact in case he…well, let's not
even go there.

4 sure! C U then, I fire back.

OK, hon. Thx.

Being called "sweetie" and "hon" in subsequent texts makes
it feel as if her warmth is exuding through the line. Her dia-
lect reminds me of a school nurse you fake like you need an
ice pack just to go visit, or like a really kind flight attendant
who gives you extra pretzels. I wonder if her voice is soft and
feminine, or smoky and gravelly. I can picture it both ways.

I haven't met Mark either at this point, although I've been
home when he's been parked with his flashers on downstairs in
the driveway to pick Benji up for an NA meeting. I'm itching
to check the two of them out on social media, but since last
names are a no-no in the program (Benji and I get a bit of a
pass due to all the press), I can't just search online for a sneak
peek of what they look like. Trust me, I've tried.

From what Benji has told me, they have a few decades of
sobriety under their belts and know the ins and outs of the
program and how to work it at various stages of recovery. I
don't know how much they know about the space on Randolph Street yet, but I'm sure that when we see them at the
picnic, we'll fill them in.

As Benji's sponsor, Mark apparently has one job: to be a
Life Alert button in the flesh. His and Rita's experience allows them to say the right thing at the right time for people like Benji who are just trying to get back on track. I take
comfort in knowing that if Mark and Rita see Benji veering
off course, they're the perfect people to reel him in. Together,
they are a much-appreciated safety net.

Benji started going to NA meetings the day after he moved in with me. Surprisingly, the meetings are working. Mark is working. And when I see him reading from his books, or texting me when he's off to see his group, I feel hopeful. Even more hopeful now that we're adding Angela and Craig to the total number of people Benji ultimately cares enough about not to let down.

I am so thankful for this newfound motivation. It's exactly what he needed. Maybe a little will rub off on me and I can build up the courage to smooth things over with Jazzy and Maya and tell my parents about the newest crazy thing I'm up to with Benji so they don't have to read about it in the paper.

I remember the first time I told my mom about Benji. He was nameless then. "I'm hanging out with this chef I met," I told her. She was intrigued, but not as interested in discussing him as she was her neighbor's new dog, a three-legged Chihuahua named Chino who wouldn't stop barking. As I got to know Benji, and just how rough he was around the edges, I decided to build a dam when it came to the details I'd share with her. She'd ask, "Whatever happened to the chef?" and I'd just say, "We still talk." Did she know he was cooking for me? That we were sexting? That I was massaging out drug nubs from his back? Nope.

But the dam broke when the news that I was his "girlfriend" did. It's not that Patty and Bill Simon followed *FoodFeed*, but people who knew me and my family posted the articles on their social media feeds and soon my parents got the picture. The whole picture. What started off as happy news—*Benji Zane tweets relationship with Allie Simon*—quickly turned into articles about him no longer working and taking time off to get sober…super heavy stuff. It was as if they had been bound, gagged and held at gunpoint all at once. The only thing I could do was call them immediately and swear up and down that everything was fine. That I was happy and safe. That this was really no big deal and the media was exaggerating. Talk about a tough sell.

Finally I volunteered to prove just how fine everything was by bringing Benji to their house for dinner. They volleyed by requesting his parents join us and we could make it a family affair. I thought about lying and saying his parents worked for the CIA and lived in China, but instead folded and said they were separated, it was a sensitive subject, and don't bring it up again.

When our dinner date in the suburbs rolled around, we happened upon another logistical problem. He had nothing suitable to wear for such an occasion. With no time or money to hit up Macy's before our train departed from the city, he borrowed some khakis two sizes too big and a collared shirt from his sous, Sebastian. For the first time in his life, he looked more like a guy who enters data into a PC all day than a guy who thought a neck tattoo was a good idea.

With a bouquet of cheap flowers from the drugstore to complete the "Meet the Parents" starter kit, we soon found ourselves in my parents' living room, making awkward conversation while waiting for the oven to preheat. The presidential town hall setup made Benji so nervous, he kept having to excuse himself to use the bathroom.

"He's not doing coke in there, is he?" my mother leaned in and asked.

"Mom! No! That's so rude," I whispered adamantly.

"Maybe I should go check on him," my dad offered in the most dad-ish way possible.

"Oh god. Please don't," I begged.

When Benji came back downstairs, my mom was putting the finishing touches on a chicken she was set to roast. She started pumping this olive oil spritzer thing she bought in the As Seen on TV aisle when the cap broke off and all of the olive oil spilled onto the floor. I blamed the tension in the room for her unusually shaky grip.

"Well, there goes my glaze," my mom said as she bent down with a rag. "Everyone watch your step over here, it's slippery on the tile."

"I guess I'll just order some pizza," my dad suggested. "What toppings does everyone like?"

"Wait a sec," Benji said. "I can still roast this without olive oil. Got any butter?"

My mom retrieved a stick from the fridge while Benji rolled up his sleeves and washed his hands. It was like he was scrubbing the nerves right down the sink. He then intuitively opened a drawer with a knife in it and started cutting the butter into pats. He lifted the skin of the chicken up slightly, sliding the slivers of butter between that and the outer layer of the chicken. After stuffing them in there, he cut the twine from the legs and retied the chicken tighter with an impressive yet humble "Let me show you how it's done" flourish. As he pulled on the knot, his muscles surged a bit through his sleeves and the spell was cast. I looked over at my mother, who was salivating. It had nothing to do with the chicken, mind you.

Finally, he heavily seasoned the whole thing in salt and pepper, loosely chopped some onions, carrots and broccoli, dumped them into the roasting pan with some chicken stock and slid it all in the oven. The whole thing took him about six minutes.

"Okay, now give that about forty-five minutes."

"Wow, Benji. Thanks. Can I offer you a—"

I prayed harder than I had ever prayed in that moment that my dad wouldn't slip.

"—Coca-Cola?"

Having Benji in their house that day was like having a doctor on an airplane with a woman in cardiac arrest. He managed to save the dinner and land our first meeting with my parents smoothly, even after so much initial turbulence. A few bites into the moistest, most delicious chicken of their lives, telling them that we were also now living together in my apartment was surprisingly palatable.

That said, I have enough respect for my parents not to let them find out about Randolph Street in the press before they hear it from me. But dealing with their imminent freak-out will have to wait.

What *can't* wait? Chugging a 1.5-ounce bottle of merlot that I remember is hidden in the back of my underwear drawer before Benji gets out of the shower.

I miss the days of being able to drink liberally. Whatever I wanted, whenever I wanted. I don't have a problem with alcohol—not by a long shot. But a tequila flight every now and then with my tacos would be nice.

Benji emerges from the bathroom in black basketball shorts and a white Hanes V-neck. He's toweling off his knotty hair. I can tell he used my shampoo.

"Here," he says.

"Here, what?" He didn't hand me anything.

"That's what I want to call it—the restaurant. Here."

"Shouldn't you call it *There* because you'll be living *there* trying to get the place opened in forty-five days?" I ask, only half joking.

"No, not at all. And don't doubt me on how to open a restaurant. I know my shit."

"Okay, okay," I say, a conciliatory smile on my lips. That mini serving of wine might be hitting me harder than I thought. I need to dial down the sass or I'll blow my cover.

"So why 'Here'? How'd you decide on that?"

"I was thinking about it and I've been to almost all fifty states in the last five years of my life. I tossed fish in Seattle, I fried just about anything you can fry in Louisiana, I staged in New York City. I wanted to learn everything I could about every kind of food, and I did. But the constant running from place to place was just a front for what I was really trying to do…keep away from my family and get high enough to forget about them as much as I could. But for the first time in a while, I don't feel that urge—to run. To get high. Cocaine's a beautiful drug, don't get me wrong. But I've got an even more beautiful life now with you."

He pauses his soliloquy to press a kiss on my forehead.

"My whole life, I've wanted my own restaurant. I've wanted to cook my own food, hire my own people, do my own thing. And now look. It's finally happening. Is it going to be crazy? Yes. Chaotic? Yes. But will having this place and knowing that it's ours give me more peace than I've ever felt? Fuck, yeah. And I want everyone who walks through the door to feel that way, too. Even if it's just for the two or three hours they're sitting down eating, I want everyone to feel like they've finally spotted that little red dot on the map that shows you where you are. Because I've seen it. And now I know: my place is here. My girlfriend is here. My work is here. Everything that makes me feel happy and complete, everything that I truly want forever and ever, well, it's all here. So, yeah. Here."

It might be the wine kicking in, but Benji's little speech moves me to the point of tears. There's something to be said about this sexy nomad of a guy finally hunkering down after years of bouncing around from city to city, thinking drugs would be the only stable thing in his life. He has struggled for so long to find out who he is in relation to the rest of the world and now it's coming into focus. Perspective is some powerful shit and I'm grateful he's sober enough now to see the big picture. It doesn't make handing over my life savings any easier, but I'm reminded of my own place on the map. I am the muse to this sensitive artist.

Before today, I would have told Benji to pick another name. I would have told him "Here" was stupid. That for $30,000, he could and should do better. I would have insisted he push for something sexier—some French woman's name written in a cursive font that no one can read. But I can't discount what Here means to him, nor can I shake how it plays into Angela's past. Something tells me that her involvement in all this merits something more meaningful than an illegible, arbitrary name. Angela deserves a full-circle story. And while Here is clearly just the start to Benji's, it's the perfect ending for hers.

"I like it," I tell him, and I mean it.

11

"There they are, setting up food by the grill." Benji spots Rita and Mark. Catching my first glimpse of those two is like seeing Santa Claus and Rudolph on Christmas morning. I'm giddy.

As we approach, I take Rita in. She looks like a model from an L.L.Bean catalog. Petite with transition sunglasses and blond hair pulled back halfway and clipped in place with a tortoiseshell barrette, she's perfectly PG standing there in a floral day dress holding a package of hot dog buns. I can hardly believe that between her and her husband, there's fifty years of sobriety.

Their high times were in the '80s—Quaaludes for him and heroin for her, Benji said. Now, they're totally clean and normal, and have a trendily named son who goes to a really expensive private preschool. I wonder if any of the other moms know the lady running carpool on Wednesdays has done blow off a motel nightstand about a thousand times.

"Allie, dear. Finally." Rita pulls me in for a hug. Reality reveals she's more soft-spoken than smoky, so there's that mystery solved.

Mark embraces Benji. Then we rotate to the right like we're changing positions in a volleyball match.

"Sorry, I should have mentioned hugging is an NA thing," Mark says to me as he encases me in his Tommy Bahama polo shirt.

"It's a good thing I wore deodorant," I say with a smile.

I don't actually mind the hugging, but I do feel a bit guilty for not having made it to a meeting myself where I could have already learned this firsthand. Going with Benji to an open meeting or finding a support group of my own is something I've been meaning to do ever since he pledged to get sober, but I haven't pulled the trigger. I've Googled them, sure. Even wrote down some addresses and times, but when push comes to shove, I still can't quite picture sitting in a room full of people whose lives took such different paths than my own.

I'm realistic. I know not everyone who attends those meetings has a supportive girlfriend like me. Not everyone lives in a cute little apartment furnished mostly by CB2. Not everyone eats $400 meals for free at restaurants that are impossible to get into. I'm afraid that the stories I'd hear from the faces I'd see would be impossible to shake. And until I get more used to this life, I need to stay away from the darkness as much as I can. I need to stay focused on Benji and Benji alone.

"Hey, Rita, where should I put these?"

I already saw the food table behind her, but I play dumb in order to buy myself a minute alone on the short walk over there. It's a heavy moment, seeing for the first time the only other people in this whole city, this whole world, who have prioritized keeping my boyfriend safe and healthy. I know we haven't had a chance to talk much yet, but I already like them. Probably because I share something with them that no one else does: an inexplicable belief in Benji.

Benji didn't have time to cook something special for the picnic, so I grabbed a package of premade vanilla cupcakes from the bakery section of the grocery store earlier this morning. They have pink and green frosting and a little plastic palm tree decal on top. I catch myself scoffing a bit at such a quotidian confection. If it's not emulsified, deconstructed, double-boiled or sous vide, I don't really eat it these days. Part of me misses the days of microwaved chicken nuggets, but TV dinners do not make an Instagram-worthy picture. I look around at the other selections people have brought—Doritos, Funions, Oreos—and realize what we brought fits in just fine. However, seeing that there's nothing anonymous about Benji Zane being here, I just hope people aren't disappointed with our contribution.

I crack open the plastic container to make the sugary six-pack feel more inviting. For the sake of nostalgia, I swipe a finger along the inside rim of the cupcake packaging, collecting the partially dried frosting stuck to the plastic. The simple sweetness is like holding every one of my childhood birthday parties on my tongue at once: unhurried and uncomplicated, just sugar and butter and simplicity.

I leave the cupcakes and go sit down next to Benji on a picnic blanket. Mark and Rita are in those zero-gravity camping chairs you see in SkyMall.

"We're so glad you could make it today," Mark says. "Rita's always so worried no one will show up to these things and I tell her, 'So what, honey? We've got a babysitter. We're by the lake. We've got Chex Mix. What else do we need?'"

I'm not sure what turnout they're used to, but there's about eight of us here for the picnic. After an initial round of hugs, everyone is now off doing beachy things: Frisbee, swimming, putting ketchup on a burger. From the outside, I can't tell who the sponsors are, how long anyone has been sober or what drugs everyone has been addicted to.

"So tell us what's new, Miss Allie," Rita says.

"Let's see…my college roommate is getting married, a Starbucks is opening in our lobby at work and I'm apparently the only person who didn't go to the Lady Gaga concert last night."

"Was it sold out? Did you check StubHub?" Rita asks.

"I did. But they were, like, $400 a seat or something ridiculous like that."

"Whoa! That's like some Benji Zane pop-up prices," Mark chimes in.

I dig his sense of humor. He's very Bob Saget from *Full House*, feathered haircut, dad jeans and all.

"And, Benji, what about you? Have you perfected the recipe for, I don't know, gourmet mountain lion meatballs?" Rita waves her hand and looks to the sky with a smirk. She's just like everyone else who thinks he's a genius with a knife, but for some reason, when she voices it, I'm not annoyed. I'm proud.

"Well, we're actually opening a restaurant before the end of the year. We secured the space on Friday."

I have to hand it to Benji—or, rather, his extremes. Unless he's being especially subtle because he wants something, he just throws it the fuck out there. Whatever "it" is. I've called him on this behavior before, but he either doesn't realize he's doing it or doesn't care. To Benji, the idea of chatting through this kind of stuff first is totally foreign. It's his life, he thinks, so he can disseminate information about it however he wants. It's part of his impulsiveness but it's also part of his joie de vivre, I guess.

"Oh. Wow. You're kidding," Mark says. He and Rita look exceptionally inquisitive. Their kind eyes are alert but wary, cautious. I don't blame them for not immediately offering their congratulations, but I'm expecting it soon.

"Yeah, it's a 2,000-square-foot space over on Randolph Street. We submit the funds Monday."

"No shit," says Mark. I didn't peg him for a curse-word kind of a guy. "So you found an investor, I take it?"

Benji's rolling through the news like he's talking about his morning routine. But Mark pausing to confirm an investor is involved at least indicates to me that they've somewhat discussed this before. I'm sure Mark is just as shocked as I am that a) it happened and b) this quickly.

"Yeah, Craig Peters."

"Peter*son*," I correct.

"Whatever. He's some hedge fund dude. Ultra wealthy, has a couple spots in the 'burbs, wanted to make a move in the city and now I'm his guy in the kitchen."

Mark squints and nods. "Are you two…similar? You and this Craig guy? I mean, does he get the things you want to do? Your style? Does he know anything about you or your past?"

What Mark is really asking is, *How the hell did you pull this off?* I've had a front-row seat to the whole show and I still have no idea.

"Yeah, he knows about it, and he's cool with it. I'm also part owner so he's going to have to remain cool with it, too, if you know what I mean."

There he goes again, cracking his knuckles and bringing those tats into frame. *Stand down*, I want to say. *Mark is on our side.*

"I see. And did you have a lawyer look over the agreement? Make sure everything's kosher?"

"It's just a gentleman's agreement for now," he says. "The final inspection is Monday and if the space checks out, we'll make it all official next week."

Rita and Mark both pause to take a sip of their strawberry lemonade. I can't read anything in their mannerisms and they don't exchange so much as a raised eyebrow. My heart sinks a little bit, but I give them the benefit of the doubt. This is a lot to take in, and studied encouragement is kind of their thing.

"I'm going to grab my sun hat from the car, if you'll excuse me."

And just like that, Rita exits stage right and Mark hops

up to go flip some burgers, leaving just Benji and me on the plaid blanket.

"Do you think they're excited?" I ask. "They didn't really say much."

"Don't worry. Mark and I will talk about it more during our session this week. He just doesn't want to be rude. These picnics aren't supposed to be about coursework or betterment. It's a day where we can just be normal, you know?"

That makes sense so I drop it. Admittedly, I'm a little bummed I won't get to hear Mark and Rita do their thing, but I respect the process.

After noshing on hot dogs and salty snacks and tossing a stick to a dog who's loving the cool waters of Lake Michigan, we cab it back to Lincoln Park. Just your average Saturday.

Except every other Saturday hasn't ended with an urgent text from Rita telling me to call her *immediately*.

It's almost impossible to have a private conversation in my studio unless one of us is in the shower or taking a shit in the bathroom with the fan on. When Rita's text comes through, Benji is eating crispy chicken thighs he just made and watching an episode of *Pawn Stars*.

"I'm going to check the mail," I tell him.

"I'm about to go down for a cigarette, I can do it," he says, licking the grease off his fingers and springing up from the sofa.

"Nah, it's okay—just smoke out the window." Normally I'm against enabling, but I need Benji to stay put while I talk to Rita. The urgency in her message is making my palms sweat.

My secret hiding space for calls like these isn't actually the mailroom; it's the storage units on the top floor. I take the elevator all the way up and get off on a cold, dark floor. I find a dial to a fluorescent light timer to my left and crank it a half turn. I've just bought myself twenty-two minutes of harsh lighting. I walk through a row of steel cages dotted with Master Locks. None of these are mine, but when I get to the end of the lockers, just below the stairwell to the locked roof access, there's a floor-to-ceiling window facing downtown—the Hancock Building, Lake Shore Drive, the Lincoln Park Zoo, they're all visible from up here. Why they've made the best vantage point in the whole building a space to store off-season ski equipment is beyond me. But when I find my seat on the cement floor, I pretend this is my living room as I look out at that million-dollar view. This is where I take my most private calls.

"Allie?"

"Yeah, hey, Rita. What's up?" I say, noticing how overgrown my cuticles are.

"Are you alone?" Her usually sweet voice is now hushed. Perhaps I'm not the only one hiding out to have a private conversation.

"For the moment. Why? What's going on?"

"Look, I'm not supposed to be doing this—calling you and all. Mark hated that I texted you yesterday. But I just... I really like you. You're a good person. You really are. I confirmed that today. And that's why I feel like I need to look after you a bit."

"Well, thanks, Rita. I appreciate that." I feel like she's petitioning to become my sponsor and I'm not sure I need one. Or that I'm ready for this.

"That's why I have to be honest with you about Benji."

"What do you mean?" I know everything about him. What else do I need to hear?

"Swear that you will not confront him with this information? Just that you will just use it to make your own wise decisions?"

"Sure."

"And you *cannot* tell Mark I told you, okay?"

"I don't even have his number," I reassure her. This is beginning to sound like the start of some juicy high school gossip and I'm not sure I want to be part of it.

"Okay. Here it goes. Benji hasn't shown at the last four NA meetings." Her tone is matter-of-fact.

"What? That's impossible. Mark picked him up the other night. And I saw him leave yesterday morning with the books in his hand. He's been going to the 10:30 a.m. one in the library basement, did you know that? Maybe Mark still thinks he's going to the ones up off Belmont?"

"No, Allie, he hasn't gone at all, trust me."

"How do you know that?"

"He hasn't answered Mark's calls in a week. We were both shocked to see you at the picnic today. That's why I texted you. To ask if you were coming."

And here I thought she'd just wanted to know how many hot dogs to get. Could there really have been another reason?

"Okay, so what are you saying?" I catch sight of a deep wrinkle creasing my forehead in the faint reflection of my face in the glass. I get up and start to pace.

"I'm saying, he's relapsing. I can't say for sure if he's actually done anything hard yet, but I'm telling you he's about there."

My feet freeze. There's no way. *NO WAY*, my mind screams. I *live* with this person. I'm pretty sure I would be able to tell if something was off. And as far as I know, Benji is still the same old sober guy, eating food on my couch, watching TV.

Plus, there's zero possibility that Benji would jeopardize the deal on Randolph Street. I've only met Craig once, but I don't see him tolerating a lot of drug-addict behavior from the chef supposedly at the head of his next enterprise. And Angela? Forget about it. That woman takes no shit, period.

She'd chop his nose off with a butcher knife if she suspected he was snorting coke.

And again, and most importantly, *I* haven't noticed anything.

"I really don't think he's up to anything, Rita." My tone is direct without being defensive. I don't want to disrespect the wife of a guy who's helped Benji come so far.

"I didn't either. But now I do," she says, still treading lightly.

"I've been watching him like a hawk. He doesn't do much besides these pop-up dinners, the occasional business meeting and his NA stuff."

But as I say this, a small voice in the back of my mind starts to pipe up about the Locator app. I haven't checked it in forever, because there has been no activity to speak of. Now the voice says I should rummage through Benji's history when I get off the phone, just to be safe. It wouldn't hurt my peace of mind—or Rita's—to know for sure that Benji has been where he's said he's been for the past few weeks.

"Look, I appreciate that you love and care for him, but I'm not so sure he's being forthright with you, Allie." Again, Rita shows her mastery of the polite understatement. What she means is, "I think you're being fucked over and you're completely blind to reality."

"And if he isn't," she continues, "then let me just tell you this: you do not want to get in the ring with an addiction like his. You are *never* going to win."

I take that statement as the threat it's intended to be. I don't like that she's challenging me, undermining not only the work that Benji has done the last 100 days, but also all the shit I've put up with since Day One to make it work with this guy.

"Isn't there supposed to be some level of anonymity with this whole program? What is your intention here?"

Up until now, I considered Rita to be the fairy godmother

of recovery. Now she's spreading rumors to me about Benji's attendance—or lack thereof—and it feels like some sort of a shitty retaliation tactic. Was it something I said?

"My intention is to prevent him from taking you down. Financially," she clarifies.

"Excuse me?"

"I had a boyfriend just like him twenty-five years ago. It started off innocently enough. He got me high at a party. Then the next day, then the day after. You'd be surprised how quick an addiction kicks in when you've got the hots for someone and your serotonin is out of whack. From there, he convinced me his habit was our habit and somehow I should be the one to fund it. Before I knew it, I had lost $28,000. Do you know how much that was back then?"

I'm about to lose—I mean, *invest*—thirty grand myself, so I have some idea.

"I had a trust fund from my parents, and I blew it all on heroin," Rita adds. There's a tinge of something that might be shame in her voice. "Not a day goes by that I don't regret dwindling that account down to nothing. Because when he realized I didn't have anything left, he picked up and moved on to another girl who did. He left me broke and alone, disowned by my family, heartsick and dopesick."

Rita—sweet, middle-aged mom Rita—is coming completely undone. Nothing I can say will plug the hole, so I let it bleed out even more as I pick at my nails.

"I was in this dark, depressed space." I hold the phone away to protect my eardrums as her voice catches. "And the next thing I knew I was blowing guys for ten bucks' worth of dope so I wouldn't wind up in an alley by myself to die in withdrawal."

I bring the phone back up to my ear, not entirely sure what to say after picturing the woman in a rose-print dress and wide-brimmed hat from earlier today laid out in an alley two decades ago. "Rita, with all due respect, I have never touched a drug. I'm not going to start now. So if you'll excuse—"

"Cut the shit, Allie." Rita's voice sharpens like a Wüsthof. I can tell this is the tone she uses when someone bullies her kid on the playground. "You know what kills me? That most of the girls he gets to give him an allowance, buy him clothes, put a roof over his head...they're really dumb. And insecure. And they're just as broken as he is. Like I was back then. But you are sweet! You are smart! You are sane! How did he manage to do it? To trick you into this *investment*?"

"You don't know what you're talking about, Rita. You don't know what arrangements were made."

"Oh, please. Mark and I know damn well you're paying for his portion of the restaurant. And if you weren't doing it, he'd be on to the next girl who would. Mark and I have known Benji for a long time. Before you were ever in the picture. We know his shtick."

For the second time in as many days, I catch myself thinking, *What the fuck is going on?*

Benji, Mark and Rita go way back? I guess that's a detail Benji purposefully left out when he told me about the nice, all-American couple he conveniently got to sponsor him the same day he was suddenly sharing my address.

Or maybe...none of this is true. Maybe Rita's a whack-job with permanent brain damage from all the drugs she's done and is now trying to get back at me and Mark for being able to successfully manage having a guy like her ex in our lives. And as far as I'm concerned, Benji at this point seems like the only one upholding his end of this anonymity bargain. Which leads me to believe that maybe this program he's working isn't actually all that rock solid if its members can't even follow the rules. Maybe he should start putting some distance between himself and them after all.

Fuck, I can't decide whose side I'm on.

We both pause for a quick pulse check. Rita, the only person on the planet who—I thought—has my back with this whole Benji thing, has just insinuated that Benji's broken and I'm disposable. The lump in my throat is the size of a walnut and the sting of betrayal makes it impossible to swallow, let alone respond.

"Don't get me wrong, Benji's a sweet guy. He's got a lot in there, in that heart of his. And he may still be sober…but he sure as hell ain't clean. And that's a difference I'm afraid you don't know how to spot." She sighs. "It's not too late. Don't cut that check. You will regret it, and it will haunt you."

I take a deep breath. This is not the phone call I was prepared to take, and it's filled to the brim with information I'm not able to process.

"Rita, I don't know how to respond to this," I say, noting the tick of the lighting timer in my beat of silence. "But it's getting late and I need to go now. Good night."

I hang up the phone and set it down on the cement floor of the storage unit. I fix my gaze on the traffic zooming up and down Lake Shore Drive on this surreal Saturday night. I wonder if any one of the people in those cars and cabs is dealing with anything remotely like this. Or are they all just going fun places—to fancy dinners, out to clubs, over to a friend's for a house party?

How is this my life right now?

My biggest fear about dating Benji has always been denial: becoming a codependent enabler. There's a support group for this, CoDA—the one Benji told me to avoid at all costs. Apparently, those are the meetings for the ones who can't quite cut it in Nar-Anon. Who can't stay strong and see through the bullshit. And I agree, that isn't me.

Not yet, at least.

Rita's two cents are what they are, but I remind myself that Benji is innocent until proven guilty—otherwise, what's the point? Why am I housing, loving, supporting and funding this person? I've been so careful, so vigilant this whole time. *And maybe*, says a small voice in my head, *so naive.*

But before I go racing downstairs for a conversation that will most certainly turn into a fight, I settle into my seat on the cold floor and try to take an objective look at the situation. I mean, if he was really trying to avoid Mark, why the hell did Benji insist we show up at the picnic today? Why did we spend so much time chatting together like nothing was up? Why look them in the eye and share the news about the restaurant? And what about them—why didn't they call his ass out for missing the meetings and dodging their calls? Nothing seemed odd today—nothing seemed off. Except Mark and Rita's reaction.

Plain and simple, I can't picture Benji relapsing. And more than that, I can't picture *me* not picking up on the signs.

But then there's the money thing. Rita's warning about him bleeding me dry is slightly jarring, but I've finally come to terms with making the investment. Yes, I'm doing it for Benji—but also for myself. Opportunity doesn't come without risk, and this is one I'm not alone in taking. Angela told me investors make their money back—and between her, Craig and Benji, the bases are plenty covered. We cannot fail. It actually does not seem possible.

I remind myself that Rita was a junkie who chose to trash her trust fund—she said so herself. That is not me. It never will be. But getting high and draining the account your parents set up for you on your doped-out lover has to come with some pretty weighty issues that I doubt go away with time, I don't care how many NA meetings she's been to. Maybe hearing Benji and I talk about our upcoming endeavor today stirred up some bad memories. Benji and I are what she and her heroin honey could have been and it's killing her inside.

Ugh. Why can't people just leave us alone? Just let us be happy together? It's not my fault she hasn't dealt with her shit properly, and my load is heavy enough without carrying her baggage, too.

My phone pings with a Google Alert. I open it and see our names in a Tweet. Throwback to when I met @BJZane and @AllieSimon at @RepublicChi. They are so nice & chill!

It's the hostess from Republic posting the selfie of the three of us from right before we left that night. I didn't realize my eyeliner was smudged and my hair went flat. Nor did I realize that Benji was kissing my cheek while he snapped the pic as if I was still the prettiest princess in all the land.

Benji isn't using. Until I see it with my own eyes, I won't believe it. I won't even check Locator.

And as far as the restaurant, Here is happening; I'm just waiting for the green light from Angela. Until then, I plan to enjoy the rest of my weekend, even if a member of my small support network has just gone AWOL.

I stand and head back downstairs just as the lights go dark.

"Any good mail?" Benji asks. He's tucked himself into bed by the time I return. I have a white lie cued up about the elevators being slow, but as far as I can tell, Benji doesn't realize any time has passed at all since I left.

"Nope, nothing," I say, climbing into bed with him. "What are you reading?"

Benji closes the book, keeping his thumb pressed into the page he's on, and reads the title off: *"The Physiology of Taste."*

In bed. With a cookbook.

Nothing to see here, Rita.

"Hey, can I actually talk to you about something?" Benji says. My heart flutters. Please don't let this be a confession of sorts.

"Of course—what's going on?" I take a seat on the foot of the bed. He leans toward me.

"I'm thinking of doing some pop-ups next week. You know, to get some extra cash before I'm totally committed to working on stuff for Here."

"Is that a good idea? I mean, isn't Angela going to need you come Monday?"

"Did she text you? Is it a go?" His eyes get big as he asks.

"Not yet. I'm just speaking hypothetically."

"Well, then, no. Not really. There's always red tape to get through the first week, week and a half. Money stuff, demo, filing for permits, shit I'm not going to need to be involved in."

It's ironic the thing I've tried to push him into doing more of, pop-ups, is the thing I'm currently trying to get him to pedal away from now.

"Where are you going to do them?" Due Diligence Debbie asks.

"Sebastian met the owner of some small breakfast–coffee shop place in Pilsen that closes at 2 p.m. She said we could pick a day that works for us and take over her space after that."

"And she's not charging you?"

"Nope. Not a dime. We obviously need to clean up after ourselves and not break anything, but she's willing to trade for the press my dinners will bring to her little no-name spot."

"I don't know. I still think you need to support Angela."

"No, I need to support *you*. Allie, once we get really moving on things with Here, I'm not going to be able to cook your meals or pack your lunches for a while and I can't stop thinking about it."

"You're worried about my eating habits?"

"A deal is a deal, babe. And soon I'm going to have to press the pause button on the promise I made you—that I'd keep the apartment clean and have a hot meal on the table for you every night. So please, trust that Angela will be fine and let me work a pop-up or two and put some cash in your pocket so you can at least order Grubhub or something. I'll sleep easier knowing you're not living on that secret stash of Hostess cupcakes in the bottom drawer in the kitchen."

I bite my bottom lip and drop eye contact. Sure, a part of me is embarrassed that I've been caught, but another part is completely flattered that Benji wants to be the breadwinner this badly.

"Okay, babe. It sounds like it could work, but let me figure out the spreadsheets and stuff tomorrow. It's too late now to work on it."

"I love you." He kisses my forehead. "So fucking much it's unbelievable."

My phone buzzes in my hand with a text.

Benji springs up and asks again if it's Angela.

It's not. It's not her, or Craig, or Rita, or Mark, or any of the other cast of characters I can barely stand right now. Instead, it's Maya telling me she is down the block at a bar with Jazzy and asking if I want to meet them for a drink.

I'm shocked she's reaching out, as I'm fairly certain my little temper tantrum last week at Roka Akor caused some serious PTSD in all of us. However, the neutral text asking me to do something so normal and routine right now is comforting. It's been a long day, and I know I need to muster a difficult apology when I get there, but I really want to go. I just hope Benji won't mind.

"It looks like Maya and Jazzy are at Doc's. Do you mind if I meet up with them for a quick—" I catch myself mid-ask and revise to something a little safer. "Do you mind if I meet up with them quickly?"

"Of course not, babe. You need your girl time. I know that's important."

"You sure?" I double-check.

"Positive. I'll be right here, learning how to take my beef bouillon to the next level."

I smile at him. He's come a long way in how he chooses to spend his Saturday nights.

"Hi, Allie!" says Maya as she moves her purse and taps the seat next to her. She and Jazzy have claimed a table in the dimly lit lounge section of the bar. It's busy, but not entirely loud. Some new Justin Bieber song is playing in the background and the girls are sharing a hummus platter.

I give Maya a hug and Jazzy reaches over the table and throws her arms around the both of us. The mash-up of their perfumes reminds me of the fact I'm wearing none. And haven't since before Benji got sober. The smell of Calvin Klein Euphoria is something else I fear may send him over the edge.

"I've missed you guys so much. Thanks for texting me... I really needed this."

"Girl time? Or the wine?" Jazzy says, gesturing to the bottle of pinot noir on the table.

"All of the above," I say as I pour myself a heavy glass of red.

"Well, before you say anything," Maya starts, "I just want to apologize for overstepping our bounds last time we were together. It wasn't my place to rattle off statistics, not that you let me get two words out."

"I know, I'm sorry. I was acting like a total bitch."

"No, you were acting like the proud girlfriend you are,"

she says. "I needed the reminder, however harsh it was, that the only people who know what's best for you and Benji is *you and Benji*."

"Yeah, exactly," Jazzy joins in. They've probably rehearsed this, but I don't mind. "I mean, we've been friends for a long time. I have never seen you with a guy like Benji. But then I realized I've also never seen you this happy. And I love you. And I love him. And I love you guys together. And that's not the wine talking."

"I really appreciate that. Seriously. Can we cheers now? And order more hummus?"

On my walk over to Doc's, I must have recited ten different ways I could swallow my pride and tell Jazzy and Maya that I needed to talk. I was going to unload this whole restaurant thing on them—every gritty detail. I was going to tell them about Mark and Rita and get their vibe on the possibility of a relapse. I was going to tell them they might have been right about Benji.

But they stopped the bleeding before it even started. Their realizations and apologies and affirmations create the trifecta I need to feel at peace again. The universe has worked itself out, and my faith in all of my most important relationships is restored.

12

After a restless night spent tossing and turning thinking about the gigantic withdrawal I'm about to make for my boyfriend's restaurant, I wake to the smell of eggs and sounds of sizzling bacon around 6:00 a.m.

"Benji? What are you doing?" I ask solo from the bed as I wipe the sleep from my eyes.

"Morning, babe," he says softly from around the corner of the kitchen. "I thought we could enjoy a nice breakfast together before you head out."

I creep around the corner and see him flipping and frying strips of bacon in one pan and scrambling eggs in the other. Two bagels pop up from the toaster.

"Uh…can I borrow your hands, babe?"

The sweet way he asks for my help grabbing down two plates from the cabinet before the bagels turn black and the eggs get overcooked is in stark contrast to what I know he'd say to a sous: *Sebastian, put down whatever the fuck you are doing and get over here. Are you deaf? I need hands on the line, NOW.* I consider my ability to disrupt the natural way he'd respond to a situation—with frustration, red-zone anger and f-words—a gift that helps keep him on the right track.

I set the plates down on the counter and Benji promptly assembles two breakfast sandwiches. I'm in shock at their simplicity. Toasted onion bagel, loosely scrambled egg, thick-cut bacon and a single slice of sharp cheddar cheese are all that make up the stack. A no-frills meal? To what do I owe this pleasure? Granted, he's mixed a half cup of sparkling water into the scrambled egg batter—his secret for beyond fluffy eggs—and cured the bacon himself, but what's a meal prepared by his capable hands if he doesn't put a few chef-y twists on it? At least it's not a self-indulgent science project like usual.

He carries them over to the butcher-block tabletop and we sit across from each other. I'm still half-asleep but fully aware of the stop at the bank I need to make before I head into work. It zaps my appetite but is apparently a nonissue to Benji, who doesn't even bother posting a picture of the meal to social media before diving in. He's already three bites in and halfway done with a string of melted cheese dangling from his bottom lip before I even unfold my napkin.

"What's wrong?" he asks, lapping up the cheese loogie with his tongue. "Oh, shit. Sorry." He gets up to walk toward me. Even though he's responsible for my anxiety, a tight hug would help hit the reset button for me. But instead, Benji beelines it back to the fridge, where he pulls out a carafe of orange juice.

"Here you go, babe."

I plaster a smile on my face and force myself to take a bite of the big breakfast sandwich he deliciously dumbed down to keep the attention on me instead of his food this morning.

"Okay, love. I know what's going on with you and I'm not ignoring your feelings. I was just trying to calm your nerves a bit. We never spend mornings together like this and I didn't just want to send you off with a sleepy 'have a great day.' I just don't know how to show you how much I appreciate what you're doing for us. Is there something I can say? Is there something I should do?"

His eyes are wide and puppy-dog-like. All he's trying to do is please me and I'm making it hard. There are a million reasons why I shouldn't make this investment, and only one—blind trust—that I should. It's like I'm *pretty sure* that I have a winning lotto ticket, but I'm afraid to scratch off the foil and actually find out. If I do, it might stop me from fantasizing here and there about this actually working out—about this investment paying off. I mean, what if in five years we really are making it? I'm preggers with baby number two, my feet are up on an expensive leather Chesterton couch from Room & Board, and Benji is helping our kid work on homework at the dining room table of our decked out brownstone before he heads over to Here for the night. All that's missing is a chocolate Lab.

As I bring myself back down to reality, aka the crowded surface of the butcher-block table in my tiny little apartment, I realize how far off that dream really is. No doubt, the inside of my head right now is a battlefield.

"Babe, please. Say something." Tears start to well up in his eyes. Though he's come close, I've actually never seen him cry. If he cracks, so will I. And it's too early for tears. I just can't get anything to come out of my mouth right now.

"Look, I want this restaurant. I'm not going to lie. But I want you to be happy, too, and this silence is scaring me."

It hits me that he's afraid to lose me. That I am still more important than opening Here. That I am still needed, independently and after this investment.

That calms me more than any dose of Xanax could, though I probably wouldn't mind a pill or two for emergencies.

"Sorry I've been quiet. I'm still just waking up and I had a lot going through my mind last night. But, here we are. And I'm excited. And I'm happy for you."

"For us," he corrects me. A beaming smile returns to his face.

"And I appreciate the breakfast, I really do. I'm just not hungry yet."

"That's okay. Tell you what. I'll add some tomato and mayo to this and wrap it up for your lunch today." He gets up and starts clearing the table.

I stand with my plate and Benji takes it from me. He puts it on the counter behind him, then turns back around and grabs my face. He kisses my lips, first sweetly, then more sultrily. His right hand floats to the back of my head, my messy hair in his fingers. His left hand works its way down my back until both of his hands pick me up by the ass as he sets me on the butcher block. This thing is a whole lot sturdier than I thought.

"I love you so fucking much," he says between kisses as he pulls my T-shirt over my head.

The money order is sitting in my purse right now.

When I got to the bank and filled out the paperwork, the banker congratulated me on my new house. She assumed the money was for a down payment. I didn't bother correcting her and now I am carrying around THIRTY THOUSAND DOLLARS in my purse like it's a pack of gum.

Angela calls at 9:00 a.m., just when I'm settling into my desk at work, to let me know we have the green light. A part of me was holding out hope that the inspection would go horribly wrong and this would all just go away, or at least buy me a little time. But no, apparently Craig is willing to fund all the repairs and rush charges that are needed to open and everything with the city went swimmingly. Here is happening. Starting today.

Angela goes on to say that she has already opened a bank account for our business, which is where my money order will be deposited. I can't believe how uber on-top-of-it she is and how quickly things are moving. So quickly, in fact, that she texts me to say she'll swing by over her lunch to pick it up before I've even had a chance to put my lunch in the fridge at work.

This is going to sound ludicrous, but I want more time with it—with my piece of paper that has more zeroes in sequence than I'm accustomed to seeing. This is (was?) my cushion. I love my job, I plan on staying with Daxa for at least another five years, but if I ever got laid off or fired, I felt safe knowing I'd be okay for at least a year (which is really like six months in Benji time.) Am I scared? Yes, of course. But no matter the circumstances, this check represents an accomplishment. Very few other people my age can pull that kind of money out of a bank account and put it toward something this major, and I'll be sad to see my little "nest egg" go. I consider tacking it up on the bulletin board in my cubicle or magnetizing it to my filing cabinet like it's a college diploma. Instead, I snap a photo of it with my phone and store it in my camera roll.

What feels like mere moments later, Angela texts me to say she's a few blocks away. I march downstairs just as her white Jetta pulls up right in front of my office building in the fire lane. She puts the car in Park but leaves it running with the flashers on as she comes out to greet me dressed in gray capri leggings and a neon yellow Lululemon tank top. There's a sweat stain under her cleavage.

"Hi, sunshine," she says, as happy as someone picking up a check for $30,000 should be.

"Hi" is all I can muster.

"You doin' okay, *mamacita*?" she asks, reaching a warm hand to my shoulder. We've come a long way from her jamming a billfold into my boobs.

"Yeah, it's just…crazy."

"Ain't it, though? Told you these cats move fast when they see something they like. Just take it as a sign—there's money to be made, girlfriend."

"Let's hope." I can't sound any more like my dog just died.

"How's B feeling about all this?"

It's interesting that she's already given him a nickname, but I figure they'll probably be spending eighty hours a week to-

gether in the near future, so why not start now with the informalities?

"He's really excited." A flashback to the insanely passionate
sex we had this morning pops into my head and some spunk
noticeably returns to my voice. "I think he'll dive in more
once he gets these last couple pop-ups out of the way."

"Oh yeah. I think I saw something about them on Twitter
earlier. He's still doing those little supper clubs? Does he realize he just bought a restaurant?"

He bought a restaurant? I let it slide. Informalities.

"Oh, trust me, he's psyched about it. I think he's just trying to get some savings going for us while you're busy dealing with the red tape."

"The red tape? I'm not sure if you guys think I'm futzing
around or what, but let me be clear: I get shit done—like the
forty-five-minute, level twelve incline elliptical workout I
just crushed at East Bank Club. You might not think these
thunder thighs could move that fast, but they can. They most
definitely can."

I don't know her very well, but these sneak peeks at her
personality make me like her. I'll give her that.

"Whatever, Allie. Just know that we're forty-five days out—
or less—from needing to be a fully functioning, high-profile,
major-league restaurant on Randolph Street. Speaking of,
what are we calling this thing?"

Is Total Fuck-Show Bar & Grill already taken?

"Here. We're calling the restaurant Here."

I fully expect Angela to poke a thousand holes in the name,
but to my surprise she likes it. Or she nothings it. I really can't
tell because she's already on to her next point.

"Well, does he understand I'm going to own his ass until
Here opens?" The wrath of God is in her voice.

I'm not sure he does, but I certainly do. So I reassure her we're all on the same page.

"I'll give him a call before I head back up. I'll tell him you came to pick up the money and you guys need to connect later to go over the details. Sound good?"

"Love it. Love you. You're amazing. Now get back to work so I can change out of these clothes before I get a yeast infection and deposit this bad boy in the bank."

"Please don't misplace it on the way," I say, the only parting words I can think of as she buckles herself in.

"Me? Leave cash on the table? Never." She winks and drives off.

And just like that, I have $1,000 to my name.

"Benji? Babe? Can you hear me?"

The sound of pots and pans clanking together drowns out all other noises when I call Benji on my way back into my office.

"Yes, love. Sorry, in the middle of something. What's up?"

"I'm just checking in. I gave the money order to Angela. I think she's on her way to deposit it now."

"That's sick, babe."

That's sick? That's it?

"So what are you up to?" I ask.

"Prepping. Sebastian, no! That's too much olive oil. You've ruined the entire batch. Throw the whole thing out and start again. Damn, is this your first time making an aioli? Jesus, what the fuck, man?"

Prepping indeed.

"Listen, Al. I spoke with the coffee shop lady and she said I could use the space every night this week. So I figure, why just do one or two when I can crank out five pop-ups? I already tweeted the times out for each—said they were the last of my undergrounds and sold out every single spot through Friday."

Normally I'm the one who handles stuff like this. Proof-reading the announcement, taking reservation requests and collecting the cash for the prepaid seats at the table up front. It's a lot of work for one pop-up. Now he's attempting to pull off five? My thoughts are with my spreadsheet system. Is he at least logging this? Did he take the payments correctly? Before I can ask, he delves in further.

"I know you're busy, so I set it up as prepay, cash-only. I made everyone who wanted a spot drop off money by 10:00 a.m. to hold their seat, so there's no need for you to front the food cost at all."

"Drop off money where? The coffee shop?"

"No. Why would I trust a lady I've never met with all that cash? I had people drop off their money here. I told everyone they had to bring cash immediately or I'd move on to the next name on the wait list. Let me tell you, people move real fast when you tell them it's their only chance to see me," he says. I think back to the first time I met him and realize just how much I know that to be true.

Part of me cringes at the fact that my doorman probably thinks Benji cooks and sells meth considering all the cash flow that went on in the lobby before noon today. I just pray that none of the drop-offs were from a critic, someone from the health department or an undercover cop. The other part of me is thanking god that he's managed to figure out a way to excuse me from my normal pop-up duties in the wake of withdrawing $30,000 to fund another one of his culinary es-capades. I'm so relieved, I almost forget to bring up Angela.

"Oh, hey. When are you going to start planning for Here? Angela said there's not a whole lot of red tape to—"

"Well, not-so-little Miss Angela hasn't opened a restaurant in the last five years and has never worked in the city, okay?"

"She said everything's approved," I mention.

"She doesn't know what she's talking about. Has the zoning committee come down to sign off on everything?"

"I don't know."

"Exactly my point. The city is going to take issue with a handful of things in the eleventh hour and she better get ready to clear the path." He's getting angry over a simple question and acting like he knows everything. Typical Benji.

"That's fine, she just—"

"Seriously. We don't even need forty-five days to outfit a kitchen and design a menu. This isn't Cheesecake Factory. We won't have 600 different options for dinner. Sebastian! You're boiling these eggs to death. Get over here and pull them...NOW!"

"Well, could you just maybe call her?"

Success! I said something without him cutting me off.

"I swear, if she's going to be this annoying off the bat...yes, I'll call her. Later. And if she brings it up to you again, just remind her that I can do whatever it is in less than twenty-four hours if I have to."

I make a pistol out of my thumb and pointer finger and put it to my temple. "Okay, so back to these pop-ups. How are you going to manage going back and forth from our place to Pilsen five days in a row? Isn't Pilsen, like, on the other side of town? That's going to be hundreds in cab fare alone."

Money in, money out. My recent obsession flares up.

"My friend owns an art gallery next door. He's going to help bus plates and fill waters this week, too. Anyway, he's got a couch in his back room. I'll just do all the prep in the coffee shop, run the dishwasher a few times, then crash on the couch next door at my buddy's place and we'll do it all again the next day. So it actually shouldn't be too bad. I mean, I won't see you a ton, but it'll be cheaper. No cab rides."

I don't know of any friends of his that live in Pilsen, but I know if I ask for specifics, Benji will either get belligerent about me prying when he's trying to do a million other things or he'll say some arbitrary name—Ronnie, Peter, Stefan—and tell me he was someone he knew from his drug days. It's the trump card when he wants to put an end to a conversation and it always works.

I ease up on fishing for details and squeeze in one more important question: "What about your NA meetings?"

I want to make sure the wheels won't fall off while Benji is out from underneath my watchful stare. Rita's call still has me a little rattled even though I'm positive she's bat-shit crazy. If she wasn't she would have called me by now to apologize for the temporary insanity.

"Babe, chill. This is Chicago. There are meetings 24/7 all over the city. I'll go first thing in the morning with all the guys in their business suits. I'll text Mark right now and ask him to recommend some around that area. He knows all the best meetings."

"Well, let me know if you find an open one. Maybe I could meet you at it this week?" It's a stretch, considering I haven't gone to any yet myself, but I'm going to miss him and a little face time on our calendar, despite the setting, might be nice.

"Okay, babe, I have to get going—I'm dehydrating strawberries in the oven and I really need to keep an eye on things. Need anything else or can I call you later before service?"

"No, I guess that's it." I get that he's busy and I'm at work so this conversation will have to pick up later, but I'm a little bummed we aren't going to have the chance to celebrate the fact I've just depleted my bank account to buy a restaurant. Oh, well.

"Oh, wait, Benji? One more thing. What about the cash that's left after food costs? And the gratuities? Maybe I could rent a Divvy bike and come pick it up later?"

"Allie, are you crazy? First of all, that's a really far way to ride a bike at night in the dark—you'll get hit by a drunk driver or something. Plus, you know whatever I make this week is going straight into an envelope with your name on it. When I see you Friday, you can have the whole damn thing. Okay? Don't worry, I'm trying to pocket as much as I can for you. I want you to be set these next forty-five days, babe."

I'm shocked to hear there's no bitterness in Benji's voice. He knows his demons could have a field day with that kind of a trigger and instead he's still dead set on making sure I'm good.

"Well, it's not a big deal if you change your mind and want me to come pick up the cash," I say, silencing the voice inside screaming, *IT'S ACTUALLY A HUGE DEAL.*

There's a beat of silence on the phone. I can't tell if he's rolling his eyes at me for being overprotective, zoning out to check on the strawberries or scrolling through tweets from people who want to know if there's any room left at the table. He returns to the line and says, "I'll be fine. It'll all be fine. I've gotta go. Love you."

I keep my ear pressed to the phone once the call disconnects, letting it all sink in.

The thought of him hanging on to what could amount to a couple grand in cold, hard cash doesn't sit well with me. Especially since apparently I won't be seeing him this week. Then it hits me that Locator is alive and well on our phones. If worse comes to worst, I can always pull up the app. However, I'm going to try really, really hard not to do that. I'm going into business with a person who has tattooed my name on his body. I suppose now is probably a good time to start trusting him.

When I get back upstairs to my desk, there's a bouquet of flowers sitting in my cubicle in a vase.

"Special delivery while you were at lunch," Dionte tells me.

"He cooks *and* he sends flowers. Benji is literally the perfect guy," Stacey says.

I fish around for a note and find one tucked behind a tulip:

There's no place we'd rather be than Here.
-Angela & Craig

13

Four Benji-free nights have gone by, which is so far unprecedented in the history of being his girlfriend. In fact, the only other time we've not slept in the same bed at night was when I went to a three-day cotton conference in Nashville. And even then, I lied and said Benji cut himself with a butcher knife and was getting stitches in the hospital so I could come home the next day.

I thought the hardest part about being away from each other would be worrying about him falling off the wagon. But the selfie he sent me in front of the church where they have NA meetings in Pilsen coupled with a pic of a bright orange key chain that says CLEAN & SERENE FOR NINETY DAYS puts me at ease. He even invited me to an open meeting, but it was right at the start of my workday and prices to Pilsen were surging on Uber, so I just told him to do his thing and we'd catch one in Lincoln Park together another time.

So what actually is the hardest part? Well, this is the longest we've gone without sex and I honestly feel the void. However, several risqué text messages and an occasional dick-pic throughout the day have managed to keep things interesting in his absence.

But even though I miss him, especially since his cookbooks, socks and foodie detritus are still very much all over the place, it's been kind of fun. I've hung out with Jazzy and Maya almost every day this week, I got a three-day guest pass to an expensive gym I'll never actually get a membership at and I walked to get frozen yogurt last night at 11:00 p.m. just because I felt like it. Tonight, my Tour de Allie ends with pretending I'm the only one who lives in this apartment as I sit on the couch in long underwear and a baggy sweatshirt with a mud mask on my face until Benji comes back later tonight.

"Delivery for Simon." There's a male voice at my door followed by two knocks. I forgot I ordered Thai food over an hour ago and spring from my seat, grabbing a kitchen towel from the handle of the oven and quickly wiping the goop off my face as I open the door.

"Ah, yes. Thank you!" I say as he hands off the warm, white plastic bag containing my panang curry. I go to shut the door, but he props it open with his toe.

"Oh, sorry. Was tip not included?" I ask.

"No, it was. I just can't believe I'm delivering food to Benji Zane's girlfriend tonight," he says.

I flip the bag around and notice my receipt taped to it. There it is, clear as day, ALLIE SIMON in big black letters. I give the guy credit for putting two and two together. I laugh nervously and notice his foot is still wedged in the door.

"I went to his pop-up on Wednesday. Shit was so good. I can't believe tonight's the last night. Hey, does he have, like, a spare bandana or something? I'm a huge fan."

And that's my cue to fake an emergency and get this superfan out of my doorway.

"I'll definitely let him know you enjoyed yourself. I've got to get going, though. I'm in the middle of sourcing opossum for him, and I've got the vendor on the phone right now."

Door = slammed. Dead bolt = slid.

Even though I've stayed out of the way of this string of popups, I've been following him and all of the dialogue about the dinners this week on Twitter, Instagram and Snapchat—so essentially it's like I was there. And from what I can tell he's pulling them off and people are loving his farewell run. A few have even asked about me by name. Example/personal favorite: Bummed @AllieSimon isn't hosting. Heard she's smokin' hot in person. I have to admit, I was quite worried this would be a disaster from just about every vantage point, but Benji was onto something when deciding to double down on these dinners. As of last night, he'd racked up $2,200. And guess what else? He wasn't passed out in an alley with a needle in his arm when he called to tell me that.

My iPhone dings with a new email. It's a Google Alert for Allie Simon and Benji Zane—probably the hundredth I've received this week. But unlike the others, this one catches my eye because it's attached to a four-letter word: *Here*.

Zane Part Owner in 'Here' Restaurant on Randolph. *Food-Feed* is officially the first publication to break the news and my heartbeat goes into overdrive.

I click the link and skim the article. A minute into my reading, my phone buzzes with a text from Angela. It's a link to an article in the *Chicago Tribune*.

Zane: Back and Better than Ever with Here.

Thirty seconds later, another text.
Zane's Road to Owning & Opening Here—a piece in *USA TODAY*.
Bzz, bzz.
Randolph Street Welcomes Zane's Very Own 'Here' in *Time-Out* magazine.
And the hits keep coming. So many that I can't keep up with all the breaking news. Clearly she must have blasted out a press release, because every major outlet is picking up the story of Here.

THIS is how u open a resto, reads the newest text from Angela. Get ready.

For what? Surely as a silent partner, I'm not supposed to be doing anything besides retweeting some of these articles for support. So I imagine she's telling me to buckle up for the Benji Show, because it's back and bigger than ever.

The attention has always been on him, so I'm used to it. But she's right, this is a whole new level. A level I thought I was ready for, but the numbness in my fingers begs to differ. Seeing my boyfriend's name in lights like this just three-and-some-change months after he skipped out on going to rehab is shooting a panic through my veins that would make Jazzy and Maya say, "Told you so."

It's just…it's been a while since people associated Benji with something serious—good serious—like this. Announcing a forthcoming restaurant on Randolph Street is like giving the entire city his word. That he's got his shit together once and for all.

But does he?

Why is being his cheerleader the hardest it's ever been right at the very moment when there's something to actually root for? By the time I cycle back around to the original *Food-Feed* post, it's garnered over 1,000 likes and the comments are pouring in.

"Yay! So glad to see he's turned his life around."

"Who gave this fucking douchebag a restaurant?"

"Y'all hear that? I think it's the Michelin Man coming with a star…"

"You mean, 'y'all HERE that?' lol."

"Oh Jesus. Can't wait to see how fast he runs this one into the ground."

"Have my babies, Benji Zane!"

I quickly realize that reading the comments is a slippery

slope and decide that now—during a commercial break in the middle of *Botched*—would be a good time to call my mom and let her know what's going on.

I haven't been avoiding her or anything; we still talk every day like we always have. I've just failed to mention this specific new and exciting thing when she asks what's new and exciting in my life. I thought I could distract her with news of discovering that T.J.Maxx sells Bumble and Bumble at heavily discounted prices, but that only bought me so much time. Now I've got to find a delicate way to let her know Benji's part owner of a new restaurant all because of me. She won't freak out hearing that my entire life savings are tied up in a restaurant venture helmed by my ex-addict boyfriend, right?

Five more articles filter through my Google Alert system and my conscience simply can't take it anymore. The press leaking faster than a ruptured C-cup implant puts a finer point on the matter.

"Hi, Allie! TGIF, honey," she says upon answering right after the first ring.

Here goes nothing.

"Yes, happy Friday to you, too," I say. "Mom, I have some news. Well, Benji and I have some news, I should say."

"Dear god, please tell me you aren't pregnant," my mother says, probably while clutching a rosary.

"What? Mom, no. I'm not freaking pregnant."

"Oh, thank heavens. You know we love Benji and accept him exactly the way he is, but addiction is hereditary. I just want to make sure you two are practicing safe sex accordingly."

"Ew, Mom! Stop!"

Sex-speak from my mom notwithstanding, the idea that maybe a kid would change Benji, turn him into a stand-up guy overnight—you know, be the father he never had, that kind of thing—has occurred to me on more than one occasion. But reality has me popping birth control pills like Tic Tacs and that has nothing to do with the genetic attributes of addiction, but rather the more immediate symptoms. Benji's track record suggests an unexpected pregnancy would lead him to suffer a classic case of freak-the-fuck-out-and-disappear and I'd rather not give him a chance to prove me right.

"And you're not engaged, I hope. I mean, he didn't ask your father for permission as far as I know," she rattles on.

"Relax. We're not engaged," I assure her, only half thinking, *but what if we were?* It's like Benji is everyone's favorite celeb chef to have in their inner circle…until he's not. What's up with that?

"Well, then, what is it? Oh! I know…you two are finally moving out of that shoebox apartment of yours. Tell me you bought a condo—with a guest bedroom! And a chef's kitchen!"

It takes everything in me not to say *"You're getting warmer…"* but I need to get to the point before one of her tennis friends with a Twitter account calls her with the news.

"No. No baby, no engagement, no condo. Long story short, we met an investor about a week and a half ago—Craig Peterson. He opened some fine-dining joint out in the suburbs—in Hinsdale, I think. The ritzy one, not far from your house."

"Florette?"

"Yes! That's the spot. Anyhow, he found this crazy-awesome secret vacant space of sorts on Randolph Street."

"Where's that?"

"West Loop. By Oprah's studio," I say, providing context suitable for Mom's demographic.

"Oh, yes. Go on."

"So, yeah, Craig decided it would be the perfect spot to open his first, real Chicago endeavor and he had his people nail down the deal. They're going to open in forty-five days or something really crazy like that."

"Oh, good for them. I'll have to suggest it to your father for our anniversary dinner. But only if Benji thinks it's good. You know I only take Chicago dining recommendations from him now. That's the bonus when you have a chef in the family!"

And she's back to being his biggest fan. Let's just stay here for a while, shall we?

"Well, they're actually really interested in working with Benji, so they hired him as the chef de cuisine right out of the gate."

"Wow. That IS big news! Is he home? Can I congratulate him?"

"No, he's not, actually. He's working a pop-up tonight. It's the last one before he starts focusing on the restaurant opening."

The restaurant opening. I'm now realizing how much of a done deal this is.

"What's the place called?"

"He's calling it Here."

"Here?"

Yeah, I had that reaction, too.

I redo my ponytail, a nervous habit of mine, and try my best to land the plane. "He got to name it because he's the owner. Well, part owner I should say."

"Oh, really?" she huffs with a spike of sarcasm. "How much does he own? One share for ten bucks that he found crinkled in the pocket of his hoodie?"

She's not being mean, she just knows Benji's financial situation is as big a mess as his central nervous system. This is every bit as painful and shameful as I imagined it would be, and we haven't even gotten to the good stuff. That's when the mantra she instilled in me when I was younger and stole the stickers from the toy store pops into my head: "I won't be mad, as long as you tell me the truth." It's time to put that to the test.

Deep breaths.

"He owns ten percent."

"Of what?"

"Three hundred thousand dollars."

She lets out a laugh, followed by a stark *"How?"*

"I made the investment on our behalf."

"YOU DID WHAT?"

Disapproving doesn't begin to describe her tone, but it's as close as I can get to capturing the throbbing electricity I feel coming through the line. The jolt goes right through my chest: she raised me better than this. Even I know that.

"Please tell me you did *not* write a check for $30,000, Allison Marie Simon."

"I didn't. It was a money order."

"Is it reversible?!"

"No, it's not. It's been deposited and I signed a contract. Benji is acting as the on-site representation for the investment, and I'm the silent owner who pockets the ROI."

I throw in some financial buzzwords thinking they'll quell her concern.

They don't.

"Silent owner my ass. You're broke. That's what you are. When your father gets home from beers with his golf buddies, we're going to start calling every lawyer we know to get you out of this. This is absolutely insane!"

"Mom, stop."

"Send me a copy of the contract, I want to see the agreement. We need to start looking for a loophole or an out-clause or something. I can't believe it. Benji robbed you of everything you had!"

"It's not Benji, okay? We're working with a team of people…

there's Craig the investor and his really smart adviser, this chick Angela."

"I don't care if Peter, Paul and Mary are part of the deal… these people should go to jail! How they could manipulate a young girl in good faith is beyond me. Give me their last names, I have a pen and paper right now. Speak slowly and spell it out."

"Mom, STOP."

"Allie, they lied to you and dangled some fancy restaurant deal in front of your face and now your savings are gone. Flushed down the toilet! Your hard-earned cash…tied up in some loser's bad habit. I knew we should have written to *Intervention* months ago. I can't believe he scammed his way right into this family with some moist chicken and that I—*we* were all dumb enough to fall for it! Oh my god, I need some water. I'm going to pass out."

"Mom, stop! That's enough, goddamn it."

I have never yelled at my mother. Not like this, at least. But she's spiraling out of control, and I can't let her drag me to the other side of sanity. At least I got her to shut up for ten seconds by raising my voice. Now, let the backpedaling begin.

"Sorry, Mom. I obviously didn't mean to yell at you. I just need you to calm down, okay? I still have my job. That's not going to change. I make good money at Daxa and I'm in line for a promotion soon, too."

I can hear her sniffling. I can't believe I've made her cry. I need to keep piling on the good news—and fast.

"And Craig is a very, very *smart*, very, very *rich* businessman. He wouldn't make a bad deal. I'm going to make my money back tenfold, okay? I promise. I know you can't comprehend this right now, but you need to trust me that I am in very good hands. All I have to do is sit back, relax and enjoy my life as my rock-star-chef boyfriend and a baller investor make me a very wealthy business owner. Please, trust me on this. I'm not an idiot. I did my homework. I always do."

That is a lie. I did very little research on any of this, but in my defense, that's strictly a result of everything moving at the speed of light. If I'd had the opportunity to run a background check on Craig and Angela, I would have. But all I could do was plug their names into LinkedIn and verify that they are who they say they are—at least on social media. That's like the gospel these days, right?

"Mom? Hello? Are you still there?"

"Maybe I won't tell your father about this at all. I'm not sure he can handle this right now. His blood pressure issues have been coming back lately."

"Whatever you want to do is fine, Mother. But let me tell you something, okay? This restaurant—it's going to get *a lot* of press. In fact, it already has. So Dad's going to find out about it one way or another, and soon. Between you and me, you've had more than your fair share of finding out news about your daughter's life from opening the paper during your morning coffee. And I apologize for that. It's just the way the world works these days, I guess. That being said, I think it would behoove you to talk to your husband about Here."

In my head, I hear a male voice-over saying, "Be sure to consult your doctor to make sure your heart is healthy enough for Benji-related news."

"Allie, dear. Please don't take this the wrong way, but I cannot be on the phone with you anymore tonight. I just, I can't process this right now. Let's pick this conversation up at another time."

This is reminding me of the way I felt when I needed to hang up on Rita. But I get it.

"Fine. Do you want me to FaceTime you with Benji tomorrow? You can congratulate him or grill him, whatever you want?"

"No thanks."

Well, then.

"Alright. I love you, Mom."

"Good night, Allie."

The moment I hang the phone up, a few texts from Benji funnel through one after the next.

Last course just dropped

Ready 2 sleep next 2 u

Holy shit did u see all the press?!

I reply that I did and that I am proud of him and that it's all going to be so great. At this point, maybe if I just will things to work out, they'll turn out just fine? In the meantime, I curl up on the couch, queue up another few episodes of trashy reality television and enjoy the last few hours to myself before Benji comes home.

14

It's around 3:00 a.m. when I wake up to my phone ringing. I'm in a bit of a fog, but the one thing that is very clear is that I fell asleep on the couch and I'm the only one in my apartment.

I squint at the light and see the caller ID is my building's front desk. Usually they only buzz when the Jimmy John's delivery driver is in the lobby with my sandwich. So either my doorman is drunk-dialing me, or I've got a sleep-eating problem.

"Hello?"

"Allie, it's Quincy from downstairs. Sorry to wake you."

"That's okay. What's going on?" I ask, clearing the hoarseness from my throat.

"Uh, your boyfriend, Benji? He's outside in the front drive. Been outside for the last, I don't know, thirty minutes or so?"

"What? What's he doing?"

"Chain-smoking cigarettes and pacing back and forth."

Oh god. My first thought is that his mom must have called. They hardly talk, maybe twice since we've been together. But for as few and far between as they are, phone calls from Bonnie Zane are never pleasant. Benji always has to excuse himself because she's usually drunk or hopped up on pills as she blubbers about how both Benji and his father left her behind like a piece of roadkill. That really sets Benji off, obviously. I mean, she's the one who turned herself into a lifeless piece of shit while he was doing everything a teenager could to financially support his mom. It sucks that ten years later, she still has the audacity to pick up the phone and call him a bastard. And I thought the phone call with my mom was brutal.

Regardless, Mark suggested it was best for Benji to send her calls to voice mail until he had at least six months of sobriety under his belt and I agreed with the treatment plan. I wonder what made him pick up tonight, but realize he probably wanted to tell her about Here. She's still his mom after all.

"Shit, sorry, Quincy. I think he's probably on the phone with his mom. She calls late like this every now and again. Sometimes the conversations can get a little loud."

"Nah, Allie. I went out there to check on him. He ain't on the phone."

"He's not?"

"Nope, haven't seen him with his phone at all, actually. He's just kinda talkin' to himself, twirling his keys around his finger."

Damn, I'm lost. But I'm waking up fast. Benji always has his phone, usually in his hand. Even if it got lost between the couch cushions, he would immediately make a mad dash for mine to call his like he'd misplaced a seven-carat diamond.

"I poked my head out there," Quincy continues. "Stinks a little bit like booze, Allie."

There's no need for me to be alarmed. Benji's dinners are BYOB. People come to eat, drink (a lot) and be merry. The smell of a good time just sort of absorbs into his hair and clothes, with the unfortunate result of making him reek like a homeless drunk. Ironically, I find it comforting. It's the stench of a man at work in the industry.

"Give me a minute, I'll come down."

Before I get out of bed, I toggle over to the Locator app. I haven't checked it all week, just like I promised myself I wouldn't. Being with Benji means believing in Benji, right?

But if Benji lost his phone and is agitated because of it, it'll help calm him down if I can tell him exactly where it is.

My prying right now is based purely on logic, not paranoia, I tell myself.

The app takes a second to load, but sure enough his phone pops up. At the corner of Hoyne and Cortez in the Ukrainian Village. Nowhere near Pilsen.

I immediately think his phone must have been stolen by someone at the dinner and the thieves have now made it to another part of the city, six miles away from where the pop-up dinners were. But the fact that Benji isn't up here "Babe! Babe! Babe!"–ing me about it until he is blue in the face tells me that theory is off.

I hit the refresh button on the app. Then one more time for good measure. The icon of his phone is like a beacon in the night, still showing strong from somewhere it's definitely not supposed to be right now. I shoot out of bed and get into the elevator, heading to the lobby in my sweats, without so much as a bra on under my washed-a-bazillion-times, practically see-through T-shirt.

As I whiz right past Quincy, sure as shit there's Benji in the driveway, walking in circles, smoking a cigarette and looking like someone who doesn't belong anywhere near this higher-end building. I need to retrieve him before anyone else happens upon a front-row seat to this shit show.

"Benji, what the hell are you doing?" I say, my voice louder than I expect in the predawn quiet. It feels like the whole world is asleep.

"Allie, shhhhh."

I've never seen Benji in this light, at this hour. Frankly, I'm amazed that Quincy even recognized him because the man who was just on the cover of *Men's Book Chicago* now looks like a lunatic with sunken eyes, wild hair and a ripped hoodie.

"Benji, come inside. How long have you been out here? Where is your phone? Have you been drinking?"

"Damn it, no, Allie. Keep your fucking voice down."

He's talking to me like I'm his sous chef and I'm not into it.

"Where is your phone, Benji? Or should I ask, why is it in the Ukrainian Village?" I shove my phone in his face with the screen still on Locator. Exhibit A is irrefutable.

"Get outta here with that," Benji says, walking away. He may be slurring his words but at least he's heading back toward our building, where we can discuss what happened tonight like civilized adults in the privacy of the apartment.

"Everything okay, guys?" Quincy gets up from his chair when Benji starts to stalk through the lobby. This is clearly the most action he's seen on the overnight shift in a long time.

"Just fine, Q. Thanks." I cross my arms across my unsupported chest and walk purposefully past the front desk toward the elevator bank.

The next thing I know we're in the elevator heading up ten floors. Never has the ride up felt so long and painful. I stare at him from just a foot away, waiting for him to say something. Benji refuses to make eye contact with me but his pupils—the size of dimes—have nowhere to hide.

Speaking of nowhere to hide, the elevator doesn't leave Benji's aroma anywhere to go either. I know the smell of kitchen and sweat and other people's drinks usually hangs on his clothes like a patina, but tonight is different. He smells like a bottle of Jack and cigarettes and that's it. I don't get *eau de chef*—I get the sharp tang of hard liquor.

Quincy was right. Benji's been drinking. And my heart sinks to the bottom of Lake Michigan in a matter of seconds as I realize it. I feel hurt, angry and betrayed but most of all I feel sad. This is a huge loss and I don't know what's supposed to happen next because this wasn't supposed to happen at all.

Back in our unit, Benji unzips his hoodie, hangs it on a chair and walks toward the bathroom like he's Ward Cleaver getting home from a day at the office.

"Nothing to say, Benji?" I'm not sure how exactly to bridge the silence. What I do know is that I'm losing my cool. I want answers to a lot of questions. The first of which is, was Rita right?

"I'm taking a shower," he says, slamming the bathroom door. I hear the lock turn into place.

He starts the water and offers no further discussion. I quickly run to his sweatshirt to raid the pockets. I can't believe he's left it, a direct line to clues of where he's been the last several hours.

I fish around his pockets like I'm the experienced mother of a rowdy teenager. I can't believe I'm doing this—that it's come to rummaging through his sweatshirt the moment he turns his back so I can prove some devastating point. It takes me twenty seconds to search every nook and cranny but I find nothing. No cell phone. No cash. No evidence.

Except—my fingers close on something. A tiny, empty button bag.

My heart sinks. I know exactly what comes in a clear plastic bag this size. I clutch it in my palm and take a seat on my sofa. I am numb.

Benji emerges looking refreshed and acting like nothing is unusual. I think he may even be looking for the remote control and when I don't offer to help find it, he haphazardly asks, "What's your deal?"

My apartment may be carpeted, but there isn't a rug in sight to sweep this whole thing under. I explode.

"What's *my* deal? What's *MY* deal? Cut the shit, Benji. Where's your phone, huh? Where's the money from your dinners?" By now, I have to imagine that I've woken up the neighbors. I pray to god they won't call the cops, but I can't keep my voice down.

"You have literally lost your mind, Allie," Benji says, giving up on the remote and climbing into bed. "Do you wanna have sex?"

"What? Are you kidding me right now?"

"God, never mind. I don't know why you're being such a bitch tonight," he says as he pulls the covers over himself and turns to face the wall like a moody teenager.

I walk over to the bed and crouch down next to it. I'm eye-level with him as I shove the baggie right up to his face and demand answers.

"You're using," I say, knowing full well I can't take an accusation like that back.

"What even is that?" he says as I present Exhibit B.

"You're using," I say again.

"No, I'm not," he says nonchalantly.

"You are!" I shout, begging for him to sense my urgency and somehow offer me comfort, even if that means confessing my greatest fear.

"Get that garbage out of my face!" He raises his hand and swings to smack the bag out of my grip. But his palm connects with my eye instead.

The clock isn't the only thing that feels like it stops right then, at 3:46 a.m.—my world as I know it does, too. There's a slight ring in my ears. Or maybe that's just the sound of silence, but not the peaceful kind, returning to the apartment.

I feel my cheekbone start to bruise right away like a time-lapse of a tomato sprouting from a vine underneath my skin. The pain is immediate, but I don't think about it. Instead, I think about the fact that we are now a very long way away from where we began. From a string of innocent, flirty tweets fired off from behind the safety of a computer screen. I want to go back there. In fact, I wish I never left there.

No further thoughts enter my mind in the seconds that follow; none at all. It feels like I'm floating in a pool, completely alone. I come to when I hear Benji's voice.

"Say something. Babe! Say something!"

"You hit me" is what I say, calmly. Quietly. Factually.

Benji springs to his feet. Whatever he's on, I'm completely fucking with his high. I wonder if he'll flee the scene or stick around to clear the air. Suddenly, my studio apartment feels like it's shrinking down to the size of a dollhouse.

"I would never hit you. You know that." Benji's panting like he just sprinted a mile.

"You. Hit me."

"Babe. Come on. Stop. I didn't hit you. Now let me see your face." He moves toward me slowly and gingerly, but I jump back like his fingertips are made of razor blades.

For the first time since I sat next to him at the bar the day we met in person, I see Benji differently. And that's not because he's drunk or high or both right now and so the bags under his eyes protrude, his pupils are large and his demeanor is chill as fuck for just whacking me.

Nothing he did or said before this moment could make a dent in my feelings for him, or my utter belief in him. I never imagined drugs would come before me, or between us—literally, *between* us—and it makes me doubt everything I thought I knew. Who is this man on my bed? Who is this monster in my apartment? And why won't he just flat-out admit what just happened? I need him to admit what we both know so that I can figure out my next move.

"Benji, what are you on right now?"

"Nothing, I swear. Nothing."

All I can do is shake my head. There's no point in arguing.

I feel so defeated. He needs to sober up and then we can talk, but I'm not doing this right now. I can't do this right now. And so, he needs to go.

Against every part of me that has tried to stay one step ahead of him, protect him and make sure his needs were addressed before he even knew he had them, I've got to ask him to leave. I don't know where he'll go or how he'll get there with no phone and no money, but him not being here is the only thing that makes sense right now.

I know I'm taking a gamble when I draw in a deep breath and announce: "Get out."

"What? Babe, please. I'm sorry, okay? I'd never—"

"Leave your keys and get out right now...or I will call the police." My voice quivers as I deliver the threat and I cover my eye, which is swelling shut.

"Seriously? Let's chill out here, Allie."

"LEAVE OR I CALL THE COPS." I hold my phone up in my right hand, finger on the dial button. If worse comes to worst I'll scream as loud as I can. Someone will hear me. Someone will call down to Quincy.

Benji gets up and starts to dress. I swallow hard with relief and sneak toward the front door, where I unlock the dead bolt. Just in case things turn ugly—well, uglier—I can bolt.

All the while, he maintains a steady monologue in a voice I've never heard before. When someone's high, you can hear it. It's like there's a whole other person temporarily inside the skin of the one you think you know so well. It's rather eerie, actually.

I try not to think too hard about this, because I really don't want to cave on what I've just done, but does Benji even realize that he's seconds away from not having a roof over his head, a stove to cook on or a girlfriend to fuck when he wakes up later? Does he even know that once he walks out these doors, he's got to figure out a Plan B? Does a man who lives in the moment even have one of those?

"Babe, I know you think I relapsed. I didn't, okay? I swear," he says, pulling on his left shoe. "I wanted to get drugs, yes. I did. I'll admit that. But only because I saw all the press come in and I got excited. I wanted to celebrate a little." Right shoe. "But when I went to do the deal, they jumped me and stole my phone. Stole all the cash." Hoodie. "I didn't want to tell you because I figured you'd leave me."

So it's my fault.

"Out. Now."

He crosses the other side of the threshold and turns to look back at me. I shut the door on him before his hollow eyes get one more chance to haunt me.

I slide the dead bolt back into place and turn my back to the door. My legs give out and I sink to the floor in a heavy heap. His admission is a weak attempt at a partial version of the truth. I believe him when he says he went out to score drugs. I don't believe him when he says he wasn't successful with the score.

Because through it all, I haven't let go of the tiny button bag. It's still crumpled in my fist, balled up with a little bit of sweat and tears, but I won't drop it just yet; it's my true north in a situation where hope feels entirely lost.

15

My tender cheek and lack of sleep make me feel like I'm hung-over. It probably looked that way, too, when I woke up in a pool of lukewarm water on my carpet. For a second I thought I passed out and pissed myself, but realized I just fell asleep holding a Ziploc bag full of ice cubes, which melted and leaked onto the floor. At least that'll evaporate in a few hours. Unlike the black eye that's just getting started on my face.

This. This is not a good look for me.

Standing in front of the mirror, I turn my cheek from left to right thinking that maybe if the light hits it just right, the area around my eye won't look like the mess it is. Did he really hit me this hard? It's like that zit you popped a little too much, turning what could have been gone in forty-eight hours into a bruised, purple mess that's not going anywhere without a scab first. Couple that with the yelling that went on and I'm convinced that if my neighbors see me this morning, they'll label me the trailer trash of the tenth floor.

I flip the light off in the bathroom and sit myself down on the couch. I look around my quiet, sun-filled apartment and take in the calm after the storm.

I don't know exactly why, but I proceed to check Locator. The thing I've played keep-away with for months is now my compulsion. Benji's phone no longer shows up at all, which means either the battery has died, or everything on it has been erased by the hoodlum who accepted the device as payment for an eight ball because Benji had already spent the cash from the pop-ups. It feels disgusting to realize the latter option is the more probable of the two.

It's crazy because I protect my belongings like they're sacred. My laptop? I worked hard for that. My iPod? The gateway to my soul. My cell phone? My link to everything that is holy—my family, my friends, my Facebook feed.

But these things to Benji are nothing—or rather, they *become* nothing. They are fleeting pieces of hard goods that at any given moment can and will be used against his sobriety. I wonder if he regrets at all deciding in a flash that his iPhone, the thing he uses to tweet his face off, was disposable. Especially since it probably made calling an Uber—or calling anyone, actually—a little difficult at 4:00 a.m.

Speaking of a little difficult, there's someone I need to talk to. ASAP.

Starbucks on Fullerton. 10:30, I text Angela.

Ten seconds later, she replies: U know it's already 11, right?

Fuck, I'm dragging major ass today.

Just be there in 20, K?

Sure thing, sunshine.

I use a whole bottle of liquid foundation in an attempt to even out my face. The cakiness will probably make me break out, but what else is there to cover up the red, blue and purple mark below my eye? And then there's the swelling, which no amount of Maybelline can contour away. For that, I'll turn to big sunglasses.

I poke my head out of my apartment like I'm checking for traffic, then slither a few doors down to exit through the stairwell. That's right, I'm choosing to crawl down ten flights of stairs so that I can avoid my neighbors and bypass the front desk completely. I can't take a chance that Quincy is working a double. No one can see me like this. Not even Angela. The last thing I need is someone calling social services and having them show up outside my door pressuring me to file a report about a situation I still can't comprehend really happened.

Out on the street, the sun feels like a spotlight beaming just on me. I can see the Starbucks and it's just half a block away. Half a block—that's, like, what, a hundred steps? *You can do this*, I tell myself. *Just keep your head down.*

As I tilt my head to the ground, the thoughts come rushing forward, too.

This was an accident, wasn't it? Oh god, if it's not...does this mean I'm a victim of domestic abuse?

And where the hell did he go? I hope he didn't OD.

Wait, did he even do the pop-ups, then? I remember the delivery driver who said he went Wednesday, but what if that guy delivers drugs in addition to Thai food and he's in on this somehow?

"Hey! Watch where you're going, would you?" says a male voice, his tattooed arm knocking into me. I gasp as I look up.

It's not him. It's not him.

My mind is playing tricks on me, which I suppose is the result of three hours of restless sleep and possibly a head injury from the moderate blow I took to the moneymaker. I need to pull myself together, especially since I see Angela already waiting for me just steps ahead on the patio of Starbucks. She's sitting in the sun, so no need to remove my shades. Thank god, because these knock-off Ray-Bans are the only thing keeping my secret, and as long as the heavy gray clouds in the distance stay glued to the horizon, I think I can get away with looking normal. I just hope I can *act* normal.

"Allie-cakes!" she chirps. "What can I get you to drink, baby doll? A little latte to get the blood flowing?"

It surprises me how chummy we are—or rather, she is with me. I'm not sure when we became sorority sisters, but I guess I don't mind the fact she's skipped out on hazing me.

"Nothing, I don't drink coffee," I say matter-of-factly.

"You *did* say Starbucks, right?"

"Yes."

"Well, okay then." I can tell Angela is being facetious, but I don't have the energy to rise to semantics. "So to what do I owe the caffeine-free privilege?"

"I just, I guess, I…" *I guess I haven't really thought about this.* I haven't come here to tell her what happened back at the ranch, that's for sure. But I do need some sort of a sign from her that all hope isn't lost. That from her vantage point, everything is still going strong.

"Spit it out, Al. I've got a budget meeting with Craig to get to after this."

"Well, I wrote the check Monday, almost a week ago. And I know we open in like, what, forty-five days?"

"It's forty now."

I swallow hard against the sandpaper in my throat. "Shit. Okay. So how has it been going? Like, with planning for Here. I'm just kind of…"

"Freaking out a little bit?"

"Yeah. Something like that. I want to make sure you're on track."

"I'm sorry, was closing a deal on a restaurant on Randolph Street in forty-eight hours not fast enough for you?"

She can't see through my sunnies, but I'm rolling my eyes. Sometimes her sarcasm is like a tollgate that just won't let me through.

"Angela, come on."

"Alright, tough crowd. First of all, calm down. What did I tell you? I got this. *We* got this. You have a dream team."

There it is again, that cute little rhyme. I let out a breath and wonder, is it still a dream if one of the players punched me in the face? It might be too late to make a trade at this point, but how much do I reveal about Benji's performance at home when I still don't know how his relapse will affect him on the field? I don't have time to figure it out before Angela plows ahead.

"Allie, it sounds to me like you're dancing around asking me whether or not Benji's reached out to me to get things going on his end. So allow me: the answer is no, I haven't heard from him. Didn't you say he was doing one last round of pop-ups or something? I've been too busy to keep up with social media this week."

"Yeah, they just ended last night."

"Well, then, there you go. Now just because he's been busy doing his own thing, that doesn't mean I haven't been moving forward with everything at Here. We've got three shifts of workers over there to open on time. There's already new flooring, paint, molding, you wouldn't even recognize the place. Signage was ordered yesterday—it's all custom, so it's going to take a few weeks—same with monogrammed cocktail napkins and the fancy cloth paper towels for the bathrooms. The electrician is coming tomorrow to install lighting throughout and we've got chairs, tables and glassware on hold for us at the warehouse."

"Wow, so it's like a real restaurant."

"As real as it gets. And you saw all that press come through last night, right? PR firms are eating this shit up. I've actually never seen anything like it. Normally, it's kosher to announce something like this during the week—I think Tuesdays at 10:00 a.m. are the sweet spot. But I figured with Benji's pop-ups ending last night, we'd hit people with the 'what's next' right away. And it worked! It totally defied everything

I thought I knew about the media. But then again, I've never opened a restaurant on Randolph Street with a reformed addict driving the boat. I really think Benji is our lucky charm here, I must say."

I can't handle another suggestion that Benji Zane shits roses, so I throw a flag. "Well, that all sounds fine and great, Angela," I say, sharpening my whisper. "Really nice job with the press release. But what about Benji? Shouldn't you and he be, like, menu planning? Or talking about seating? I don't know, chef-y stuff?"

"Chef-y stuff? Goddamn, I wish I had a latte right about now," she says to no one in particular. "You're right. It's a little odd that he hasn't been breathing down my neck asking me to help source squirrel meat for opening night, but the kid chose to do a string of pop-ups while we've been clearing the path on some of the nitty-gritty stuff. He's just been busy. Right?"

Busy doing *something*.

I shrug. I'm not going to offer up any details on what happened last night. Whatever it was, was a temporary setback. It has to be for the sake of the bigger issue at hand: getting Here up and running on time. I'm not sure in what order these things need to happen, I just know that I only have forty days to get him to apologize for last night, admit the truth about whatever happened, and somehow still cheer him on until the doors of Here open to the public and a photo of us holding hands and bowing for a clamoring audience shows up for the second time this year on the front page of *FoodFeed*. Difficult? Yes. Impossible? No.

"Look, in my heart of hearts, I think he's just really nervous, okay? This is the biggest deal of his life, Allie. His reputation is quite literally on the line. If he fucks this up, he's out. He's a goner. There's not one single restaurant in this city that would hire him, not even McDonald's. And at his level of notoriety, hell, I doubt he could get a job in any major food city. Forget New York. Forget Miami. Possibly LA, because California *is* the land of fruits and nuts, but honestly, this is it for him. He *has* to succeed with Here."

I don't respond because the only words I can gather in my brain articulate a question about how someone can have the proverbial world in his hands, and risk throwing it all away to get high off some dirty cocaine from the Ukrainian Village.

"And then, Allie, let's not forget you. He's deathly afraid of letting you down. I mean, you're really the only one who has ever given him a chance. Sure, yeah, Craig and I did, too, but that's only because we saw you do it first. We thought, 'Hey, if that shit-together Allie chick is with him, there's got to be something good there.'"

I give her a cockeyed look. "Really?"

"I swear to god, that's how we saw it! And I'm pretty sure that's how this entire city sees it. They trust you. They like you. And so they're willing to give Benji a second chance. Which is exactly why we are already one hundred percent booked with reservations on our opening night."

"Wait. Are you kidding me?"

"It's a perfect sell," she says.

"Perfect sell?"

"Yes. We're fully committed."

"Fully committed?"

"Oh my god, Allie, you're killing me. Let me put it this way: every seat will have an ass in it ALL NIGHT LONG with no room for walk-ins. Been that way since five minutes after the first press release hit Twitter."

"Oh my god, yay!" I give Angela a high five. Is that what you do in this situation? I have no idea, but what I do know is I just showed my age. I also know that fancy restaurant lingo aside, a packed restaurant is a good thing for my investment.

Angela pulls out a travel size of Purell and rubs it on her hands post high five. This bitch, I swear.

"Look, as much as I'd like to stay and chat, I need to go meet Craig. After budgets, it's back to the restaurant, where I'll be supervising the ladies' room build-out. If the mirrors aren't floor-to-ceiling like I ordered, I'm going to flip my shit. The boxes were delivered yesterday. They look a little on the short side. So, are we done here?"

I'm breathing easier, so that must mean yes.

She scoots out her chair, getting ready to dismiss herself from the patio.

"Here's a piece of advice, Allie. Take it or leave it. Talk to Benji. Tell him how much you love him, support him, and how confident you are that he's going to absolutely knock it out of the park come opening night."

"I have been doing that," I say, not trying to sound defensive.

"I'm sure you have. But people like him need more reassurance than people like you. He's got to *always* feel like you know he can do it. And then he *can* do it. And *will* do it."

I let out an audible sigh.

"Hey, it's okay. I know what happened here." Angela says softly, putting a tender hand on my shoulder and looking me square in the eye.

Oh god. Is Angela who he called when I kicked him out?

"I know you're freaking out because you feel like him rising or falling is on your plate. But such is life for the person who's his rock. I'm lucky, he's lucky and the whole city of Chicago is lucky that person is you and that you can handle it. You love him, right?"

The tweet that made me his. The tattoo that's on his wrist. His tender gnocchi and his surprisingly soft heart. Despite the turmoil of the past twenty-four hours, my favorite things about him scroll like pages in a flip-book and the answer to Angela's question is an absolute yes. I do love him.

"Then go home and tell him so. Then fuck his brains out because you won't be seeing much of him after we start planning this beast of a menu tomorrow."

"Got it."

Her thoughtful suggestion, mortifyingly heard by everyone al fresco, seems so distant. Being intimate with the man who is responsible for the throbbing pain billowing beneath my gas-station Wayfarers is the last item on my agenda. I need time to think about what happened and come to grips with the fact that we've got no choice but to work this out. Quickly, quietly and together.

She walks off, adding one more marching order: "Oh, and tell his ass to call me. I'm serious. Ciao, ciao for now."

Her request is simple enough but the problem is, I don't know where to find him and I'm not ready to go back to the scene of the crime and start making calls just yet. If the melted ice hasn't dried from my carpet, then the wound is too fresh.

I check my phone on the off chance he's reached out sometime during my chat with Angela. Nothing but a text from Maya.

Getting a pedi at noon if U wanna come?

Yes. Yes, Maya, I desperately want to have someone scrub the dry skin off my feet while I pretend to be normal for an hour. But what's going on on my face isn't normal and she's definitely a person I can't tell the truth to right now. I think quickly and fire back a reply that gets me the best of both worlds.

Sure. FYI burned my cheek w/ curling iron. Don't ask.

LOL u would, she sends back.

★ ★ ★

Part of me feels incredibly irresponsible. My dog is lost and I'm sitting in a massage chair as a nice Korean woman paints my toes an ironic shade called "Orange You Lucky." The other part of me is dying to tell Maya everything, but instead I divert the attention to someone else.

"Why didn't Jazzy come?" I ask.

"Tinder."

"Oh god, not again. What about you? What's going on in the dating department?"

"Nothing. But I did sleep with an Irishman last night," Maya says proudly.

"Considering this is the first I've heard of him, something tells me you didn't get to three dates first."

"His visa expired today. I had to make an exception."

I plaster a smile on my face. Maya and Jazzy are the definition of twentysomething, big-city living. One of them is out on a date simply because she made a swiping motion with her finger on her smudgy phone screen. The other may or may not have slept with Conor McGregor's cousin. But who cares? Life's good when none of these people smack you in the eye the morning after.

In a time when I should be clinging on to my friendships the most, I'm thinking a little distance might make me feel better. Or at least, stop me from comparing my complicated life to their carefree ones.

Though my phone is on silent, I see the screen light up from my bag and peek into it. My doorman's called me twice, which tells me that a keyless, phoneless Benji must be back. I've got to get going.

On my fifteen-minute brisk walk back home, I recite out loud, "I forgive you. I love you. I believe in you," over and over. By the time the polish on my toes dries, it better sound like I mean it.

The other thing I do on my walk back is imagine where he's been this whole time. I deduce probably on a bench by the lake, waiting for what seemed like an appropriate amount of time to pass in order to come back and try to make peace with me. I'm not over it, that's for sure. But I'm in it. In the thick of it. And right now, it's best that we move this apology along for the sake of the restaurant and my woefully sparse bank account. I hope there's at least a bouquet of roses waiting for me as I escort him back upstairs. Thinking about it, I'm actually somewhat excited to experience his remorse. The makeup sex, whenever we get to it, will be undoubtedly out of this world. As will be the meal he cooks me tonight to show how much he cares.

Upon entering the lobby, I look left and I look right. He's not there. The weekend doorman, some rent-a-cop type guy who looks to be about eighty-five years old, is reading a James Patterson book behind the desk and doesn't even look up to acknowledge me.

"Excuse me," I interrupt. "Did you call me?"

"Who are you?" asks the doorman.

"Allie Simon. 1004."

He leans over to check the call log. "Oh, yes. I did. You haven't confirmed a time for your annual furnace check yet. Are you available Tuesday around 10:00 a.m.?"

"My apartment has a furnace? Listen, did anyone come here looking for me? Asking for me? A tattooed guy with a man-bun by chance?"

"With a *what*?"

"A man-bun." I make a swirly motion on the top of my head. "Ugh, never mind."

Dejected, I make my way up to my apartment trying to wrap my brain around what I'm supposed to do now.

As I step off the elevator, I can see that the door to my apartment is cracked slightly open, so the light from my windows floods into the dark hallway like a laser beam. That's when it hits me: I never locked the door when I snuck out to shimmy down the stairs earlier.

Oh my god. He's inside.

For some reason, reuniting with Benji after our blowout felt much more exciting when I knew it was going to start in a public place with an audience, the lobby of our building. Now I'm proceeding with extreme caution, gripping my cell phone in my hand just in case a loose cannon goes off. Just in case he's thought about it and he's not actually sorry. Just in case he's thought about it and he's pissed. Just in case...he hits me again.

Have I mentioned how far away we are from those first moments with him that seemed so nonchalant? So serendipitous and special? I can't believe I'm now afraid of the man I've had tabs on for the last three and a half months.

"Benji?" I say, pushing the door open. I repeat to the silence, "Benji?"

It's a small studio apartment; there are only so many places he could be. No one in the kitchen. No one in the closet. No one in the living room/bedroom. I circle my way around to the bathroom. The vent fan is on.

At the bottom of the bathtub are about four of the little plastic button bags, all of them empty. There's a makeshift pipe made of tin foil and a lighter near the drain. It smells like burnt hair or something. Something I'm not sure I should be inhaling too deeply.

The coast is clear. No Benji. Just a sure sign he had been watching and waiting for me to leave. Park bench all night?

Ha. Try just down hallway. Clearly, the moment he saw me depart down the stairs, he snuck back in and had one last hurrah at the expense of my recently refinished bathtub. I checked his hoodie for paraphernalia while he was "showering" last night and found nothing, which tells me he was really in the bathroom to hide his stash under the toilet tank before showering the detritus off with my bottle of Pantene. When I kicked him out without a chance to sneakily pack it back up, well, he had to come back for it. Not for me. Just for the score.

My thoughts are eerily calm as I piece together how the crime was committed. First he did this, then he did that, and so on, and so forth—trying to make some sense out of this very confusing situation. Before I came upstairs I was thinking about makeup sex, but now it's obvious he's on a bender somewhere off in the distance.

"Rita called it," I say out loud. "Rita *fucking* called it."

I'm a big believer in trusting my gut, but my gut never felt this coming. The one thing I rely on to make good decisions and keep myself safe and sane has failed me. I have no idea if my intuition is broken or if it's just been outsmarted. Outsmarted by a man who thought it was a good idea to abandon his dream job just days after it had been fully funded by his dream girl.

None of this makes sense and neither does what I see as I look up at the mirror near the tub. There's a note from Benji written in green marker. Scribbled frantically, it says: *I AM SORRY*

The message is hardly cryptic. The handwriting gets progressively more illegible as it trails off to the lower right corner. My instinct is to smudge it off with my fingers but when I try, it turns out it's written in permanent marker. I'm not sure this kind of thing is covered by my security deposit. I'm already not looking forward to the sorry-I-have-a-psychotic-boyfriend conversation with my landlord.

I don't even know where to begin with cleaning up the bathroom, which is only a bloodstain away from being a murder scene in my mind. My confusion has catapulted into anger and I don't think channeling it through scrubbing the mirror is a good idea right now unless I want to wind up with glass on the floor and seven years of bad luck. So I continue on through the apartment in pursuit of any other thoughtful clues Benji may have left behind to help me figure out just how far off the deep end he's launched or where he may have gone.

On my way out of the bathroom, I see that his shelf in my closet is cleared off and the duffel bag he originally moved in with is gone. All that's left is a toothbrush and his knife set.

Leaving his knife set behind might speak even louder than the mess in my bathtub. He would never leave Dodge without the one thing that makes him who he is. Or who everyone *thinks* he is: a master chef; a genius with a blade. Yes, the events that have transpired are complete insanity, but I find some solace in knowing he's not gone for good; he can't be. He'll come back for these knives when the high wears off, the withdrawals subside and he realizes just how shitty it was to risk throwing it all away in the eleventh hour because things got a little stressful. At the sight of the knives, I think: we still have time to figure this out. And we will.

How he's gone from "man on a mission" to total monster in just five days is…well, it's not exactly a mystery, because it's everything Rita warned me about. I want to call her, tell her she's won the grand prize. Guessing he was about to relapse is kind of like winning a baby pool or something, right? Or maybe not. No matter how you look at it, there can't be satisfaction in knowing you were right in a situation like this. There's only embarrassment in knowing that you were—that

I was, completely and utterly—wrong, and I'd rather feel my shame in private.

I take the elevator up to the penthouse storage unit, being triple sure to lock the door behind me. It's the only place I can go right now to feel safe.

I let myself collapse to the ground like I've done so many times before. My phone rings from the cement floor next to me. I look at the caller ID—it's my mom. I send her straight to voice mail.

I resent Benji now more than ever for the simple fact I could not pick this call up. Yes, I'm hurt. I'm scared. And I need my mom. But I can't do this right now. I can't have a casual conversation about her neighbor's dog or her hairdresser when all that's on my mind is the travesty that's just gone on in my apartment. But what's on my mind and what's going to come out of my mouth are two different things. Because *no one* can hear the truth about the last twelve hours. No one.

That's when my mom's mantra trickles into my mind. "I won't be mad, as long as you tell me the truth."

It's the thing she's drilled into me since I was a kid, but this feels like the one exception. This isn't the kind of truth you tell your mom. This isn't your run-of-the-mill breakup story.

Is that what this is, a breakup story? Or is it just a new level of theatrics for Benji? Which one am I wishing for?

She leaves a voice mail. I check the transcript. "Hi, honey. Nordstrom Rack is having a grand opening sale. Need anything? Call me back. 'Bye, sweetie."

I throw my phone across the floor. How dare Benji get between my mom and me to the point I can't even take a call about a damn Nordstrom Rack without risking unraveling, and thus, jeopardizing my relationship with my mother?

That's when the sobs come in waves; I am drowning yet again. I drop my bruised head into my hands and give myself a pass to just lose it for thirteen minutes…the amount of time left on the fluorescent light timer.

When the lights go dark, that's my cue to leave.

Okay, Allie. That's enough.

I pick myself up, dry my eyes and fetch my phone, which now has a crack through the screen.

It's time to go back inside and clean up what I know for sure is one of many messes Benji has left behind.

16

As I plop a scrub bucket, rubber gloves, bleach, black trash bags and a four-pack of Sutter Home merlot on the counter at the drugstore, I realize I'm just a spool of rope and a shovel away from looking like a suspect in a cold case—especially with the dark circle under my eye.

My usual checkout lady asks no questions as she bags up my goodies, other than: "Pack of Camels?" She's already reaching for them from behind her. I had no idea buying my boyfriend cigarettes was such a noticeable habit. I tell her no thanks, not today.

I get home and crack a merlot. I chug it in what feels like record time. Wiping my wine-stained lips with the sleeve of a Mizzou hoodie, I think to myself: Why the hell did I just buy such shitty wine? And in travel sizes, too? After all, there's no one here I have to tiptoe around and I don't know when there will be again. The thought is both liberating and sad as I open bottle number two.

One week ago, I was sitting on a picnic blanket in the warm Chicago sun enjoying the lake to my left and the skyline to my right. I was surrounded by people I hardly knew but who cared about me anyway. Why? Because I was with Benji, which was like having a fast-pass to the front of the line. And now, in just seven days, all of the wheels have managed to fall off. I'm not soaking up the sun, I'm soaking up bleach. I'm not surrounded by anyone, I'm shamefully alone. And the

people who cared about me then probably won't anymore because Benji is currently out of the picture. The picnic is over.

My phone rings as I'm scrubbing black tar from around the
drain of my white porcelain tub with my sleeves rolled up.
It's my mom again. She probably actually needs something
this time, but I still can't talk. I attempt to decline it by tapping the ignore button with my exposed elbow, and instead,
accidentally pick up. FML.

"Hey, sweetheart. I tried to call you earlier."

"I know. I saw. Sorry, I've been cleaning my apartment."

"Oh, that's okay. Where's Benji? Out doing big chef things?"

"Uh, something like that," I say.

"Well, we're going to make this quick. I've got your dad
on the line."

"Hey there, Allie-bear," he says.

My dad. My sweet, simple dad. His calming voice is enough
to get me to pause the madness and peel off the rubber gloves
for a few minutes.

I don't let myself get too comfortable, though. With the
both of them on line, this could be it. The dreaded I-word.
And if it is, they're ironically too late. An intervention would
be pointless now.

"So listen, Al. We don't agree—" he begins.

"*Definitely* don't agree," chimes my mom, his apparent hype
woman.

"Patty, please. As I was saying, we may not agree with what
you did with your money, but it's *your* money. And you're an
adult now. So we're going to let it go."

"We're going *to have to* let it go. That's what the therapist
said, Bill."

I had no idea they were in counseling, but I'm tempted to
ask who they're seeing so I can find out if he or she is taking
new patients.

"Anyway, as a rule of thumb, let's just keep all conversation about money—yours, ours, Benji's, whoever's—off the table, at least until emotions settle down a bit."

"Deal," I say. A free pass not to go into detail about my twisted living situation? Hell, I'll take it.

"But…"

Why is there always a but?

"If you find yourself in any trouble, you know what to do," my dad says.

I do know what to do.

Tell them the truth.

"Hey, Mom?" I start to say.

"Yes, sweetie? What is it?"

"Any idea how to get permanent marker off a mirror?"

"Nail polish remover," she says mother-of-factly.

I finally got to sleep last night by counting all the ripples that make up the popcorn ceiling directly above the bed in my studio (1,783) and polishing off the four-pack of Sutter Home. I'm not exactly sure what time I finally slipped into another dreamless night, but I have to imagine it was somewhere around the time people are waking up to go for a jog before the lake path gets too crowded. I don't even remember what it's like to go to bed and wake up at normal hours anymore, but somehow it's now ten o'clock on a Sunday morning.

I haven't told anyone about the relapse yet. But then again, who am I really going to tell? Who really needs to know?

Angela, yes. I get that. But I'm holding off on sending that text because, even though I didn't see this coming, I *know* that I still know Benji. Always-frantic-to-communicate Benji. He may have had a field day in my tub with some controlled substances, but let's not forget he was coherent enough to leave a well-intended love note behind before exiting the building on his own two feet. My money is on a deep apology and a "come to Jesus" moment being in my near future. I'm certain of it.

So certain, in fact, that I kept my phone on airplane mode all night. That means no texts in, no phone calls out and no email dings before I have a chance to at least try for a solid night's sleep. Now that I'm awake, my plan is to toggle out of airplane mode, pee, check on my eye situation and then be greeted with an onslaught of warm, reassuring messages from Benji saying how this was all just a giant mistake. It would excuse nothing, of course. But at least it would be the proof of life I need to feel better about things. And I know he's phoneless at the moment, but I also know that when his need to reach me kicks in, there's virtually nothing that will stand in the way of getting me on the other line. That's Benji for you.

As I wait for my phone to kick back in, I realize it's taking longer than usual for the pings to come in. So far, silence. I power off completely, then reboot just to make sure my phone isn't still in some weird sleep mode. But even with a hard restart there, it's dead air.

Zero new messages.

Nothing from my mom, nothing from Angela, nothing from Jazzy, Maya or Rita. And definitely nothing from Benji.

"What the actual fuck," I say to myself.

I'm officially up and at it, no longer tempted by the warmth of my bed. I pry open my laptop and immediately check his social media streams. If he didn't have a phone, maybe he had access to a computer. And if he didn't have the balls to contact me directly through email, then perhaps he ran his mouth on Twitter instead. We all know that's his MO anyway, especially when he's been using.

But those are showing no signs of activity either. And according to the time stamp on his last post, mum's been the word now for over twenty-four hours.

With the laptop still open, I do the next sleuthy thing I can think of and pull up the history in my web browser. We share this laptop and like I mentioned, we're on different circadian rhythms. So when I'm trying to go to sleep for the night, he's almost always still up playing video games, reading *FoodFeed* or menu planning. At least, that's what I assume he is doing. Now's the time to find out.

Porn. Lots of porn. The first three hits back on the history report show me Benji has a fetish for wet panties and saggy tits. This is not the kind of porn the two of us have indulged in during foreplay in the past, so I'm curious what's changed. Oh, right. This is your brain on drugs.

Right below the smut-fest is a hit for a YouTube video of a guitar solo during an old AC/DC concert. Benji used to play guitar, so I'm not too floored by this one.

The third hit down looks like it could be the most helpful insofar as piecing together where Benji may be—or where he's gone recently that he shouldn't have. It's a Google Map result for an intersection in the far West Side of Chicago in a neighborhood called Garfield Park. I've never been to this part of the city, for good reason. Namely, I don't want to get shot by a stray bullet. I pull up the URL and poke around in Street View.

The exact pin on the map takes me to what looks like a gravel-filled alleyway with a rusty blue Dumpster. That's when my brain goes to a place I don't want it to. Because there's probably no better spot to score cheap, hard drugs than an alley like that.

The radio silence makes me more nervous than I care to admit. For as high as he's already gotten, the fact that he's not barreling down my door frantic for help getting clean in time to open Here tells me he may be in "Fuck the World" mode and on the prowl for more drugs. He's a man of extremes and

I have a hunch that the excess is what he's after, no matter what it takes to get it.

However I may be feeling right now about my decision to ever get involved with a guy like Benji, I table it. I have to. This is not the time to beat myself up over following my heart. Because at the end of the day, I care about this man. And I refuse to believe this is it. For his sake, my sake, our sake and the sake of Here, I have to try and find him. ASAP.

With my phone still glued to my hip waiting for an SOS from Benji, I think of a quick and dirty plan that starts with a group text to Jazzy and Maya.

Brunch in the West Loop? Meet @ my place first?

Into it, replies Maya.

Same. Be there in 15, texts Jazzy.

Using the lure of some fancy eggs Benedict, I quickly begin picking up the other areas of my apartment. I recycle the empty wine bottles, put away the bleach and toss Benji's knife roll under the bed. It collides with what sounds like a bottle of pills, so I reach my hand through a field of dust bunnies and pull out a clear, orange container. The label is mostly ripped off but from what I can still see clearly, it's a prescription for Xanax made out to some guy named Anthony. No last name is legible before the adhesive behind the label starts to show.

I jolt at the knock at the door. Jazzy and Maya have announced themselves, so I tuck the bottle back under the bed and spring up to let them in, looking through the peephole to make double sure my visitors are who they say they are.

"I really love how we're on a first-name basis with your doorman now," Jazzy says as she makes her way into my unit wearing black yoga pants and an oversize flannel shirt.

"Yeah it's pretty cool how we graduated to VIP status and

don't have to get called up anymore." Maya follows her in, wearing almost exactly the same thing.

I noticed that, too, no call from the front desk. I need to make sure whoever's working down there doesn't grant the same access to Benji.

"Your burn is healing," Maya says.

"What?" I ask.

"The burn, on your cheek, from your curling iron."

"Oh, right."

"It looks like it's getting a little better."

"Thanks, I've been icing it."

"So where are we going for brunch? Did Benji get us a table at Rosalind's? Ooh! Maybe we can tour Here after and say hi to him?" Jazzy asks.

"Jazz, we're a little undressed for Rosalind's, don't ya think? And are you even ready to go, Allie? You look like you still need to jump in the shower," Maya says.

I put a hand to my hair; my deflated topknot is lobbed over to the right side of my head and I'm still in the sweatshirt from yesterday. Hey, you try showering in a bathtub that most recently resembled a crack house and act like everything's normal.

I quickly redo my bun so at least it's centered on my head and reassure them I just need to change my shirt and put lipstick on.

"You drove, right, Jazzy?"

"Yup, and we found rock-star parking in front of your building. Must be all those good Catholic neighbors of yours who got up early for church this morning."

"Perfect. Okay, so I know I said West Loop, but I was thinking we could try another neighborhood. Still west, just not the Loop."

"Where you thinking?" asks Maya.

"Garfield Park."

"You're kidding, right?" snaps Jazzy, her eyes big.

"I was thinking...we can find some cute mom-and-pop place, eat the best greasy hash browns of our lives and then walk it all off as we do some shopping on Mag Mile later this afternoon. It'll be fun!"

"Allie," says Jazzy. "I'm all for trying a hole-in-the-wall restaurant, but not if that means there will be a hole in my car door when we come back out after paying the bill."

"Yeah, maybe just text Benji and see if he can get us a table at Rosalind's. That sounds more our speed this morning," Maya concurs.

This was not how it was supposed to go, and so I do nothing and I say nothing. I just stand there and think about how stupid it was to try to trick my friends into taking a leisurely ride to Garfield Park on a Sunday morning so while they look for parking, I could look for my missing, drugged-out boyfriend.

"Allie? Hellooo? Text Benji. Let's get rolling," Jazzy says, keys in hand.

"Guys. I have to tell you something but you have to promise not to tell anyone. And you can't go calling my mom or some shit like that either."

"What's going on?" Maya asks with genuine concern.

"It's Benji. He...had an accident."

"What do you mean *accident*?" She digs further.

"He, um, he relapsed yesterday." I practically vomit the word out but I can't think of another way to say it while under so much pressure.

"I fucking knew he would."

"Jazzy, don't. Allie, are you sure?" Maya puts her hand on my shoulder. But what she doesn't realize is I don't need sympathy right now. I just need their help finding him.

"Yeah, I'm sure. But, the good news is, it was just a onetime thing. Even though it was pretty bad and his phone got stolen, he left his knife set here."

"Okay, so he's coming back." Maya picks up what I'm throwing down.

"Exactly. But I was thinking, why wait when I have a pretty good idea of where he is?"

"And that's Garfield Park?" Jazzy asks.

"Yeah. I checked the computer history and that's the last place he looked up directions to."

I kneel to grab the pills out from under the bed.

"And then there's these. Xanax prescribed to someone named Anthony. So I was thinking, even if we don't find Benji in Garfield Park, we could ask around for who sells pills, or if anyone knows who this Anthony guy is, and—"

"I'm going to stop you right there," Jazzy says. "Sorry for being the blunt one here, but am I the only one who doesn't even want their DNA in this apartment right now? This is insane and you need to call the cops. Or his sponsor. Or someone."

"No! No cops. And I don't have his sponsor's number—just his wife's. And if I tell her what happened, she'll just rub it in that she was right."

"His sponsor's wife warned you about this?" Jazzy asks.

"Sort of. But it doesn't matter. I'm telling you, if we just go to Garfield Park—"

"Allie. Jazzy's right. This is *not* your problem. It's too big to be your problem. You need to turn this over to someone who's equipped to handle it."

Who could be more equipped than me?

"Here's an idea," Maya continues. "Why don't we just stay here? We can grab bagels and Bloody Mary mix from downstairs and just hang out and chat and go up to your pool later.

You know, a little Sunday Funday action. That way, you're not alone when he comes home."

"If," Jazzy huffs. *"If* he comes home."

"That sounds great," I say. "And we can definitely do all that...*after* we take a quick, twenty-minute drive to Garfield Park. There and back, I promise. Please, Jazzy, can you just drive us?"

"Allie, someone's stolen prescription for Xanax is in your apartment. Your boyfriend is missing. You want to take a leisurely drive to the most dangerous neighborhood in all of Chicago. What is going on with you? The answer is no."

I need them to see this my way.

"Do you realize we could have him back in this apartment helping him sober up with some Gatorade and back massage in a matter of an hour? It's really not that big of a deal. The first time this happened—"

"Whoa. Whoa. Wait. There was a first time?" Jazzy asks.

I forget I never told them—or anyone—about the night before he went to rehab.

"Yeah, but it was a long time ago...we weren't even official yet. And it was different that time. Someone reached out to me because he was at his worst. But the good news is, no one's reached out yet. So he can't be too far off the deep end. We just need to leave. Now."

"Absolutely not," says Jazzy.

It's time to throw out a Hail Mary.

"I thought you guys said you were done making judgments about my relationship. Can't you just be a good friend? My boyfriend obviously needs our help and if you say no, and something happens to him..."

"Nice try making this our problem, Allie. But flash bulletin: we don't owe anything to Benji. I'm sorry if that's harsh, but I'm not going to sit here and let you *try* to convince me otherwise. Like there's blood on my hands if I don't drop you off in the ghetto right now. Take an Uber if you want to go so badly."

I would, but I'm positive any sane driver will refuse the ride.

Maya stands in the hallway and looks at me with compassion.

"Maya, let's go," Jazzy says, heading for the door.

She doesn't move. I can feel her turning. And so what if Jazzy leaves? Two sets of eyes are still better than one. My fingers are crossed in the pocket of my hoodie.

"I'm sorry, Allie. I can't be a part of this." Jazzy's tone softens. "But if you change your mind and decide to stay back, let me know. I'll meet you here with frozen yogurt, margaritas, Ryan Gosling movies, whatever you want. And we don't have to talk about any of this. We can forget it even happened."

"I'm *not* staying back," I insist.

"Maya, please. Let's go."

I dead-bolt the door behind my closest friends. I cannot believe how badly this backfired. For the first time, I chose to be honest about the less-than-perfect side of my relationship and this is what I get? Total abandonment in a time of need? Fuck it. Fuck them.

I move on to Plan B and text Angela.

R U at the resto?

Always, she rapid-fires back. I'm grateful it seems she is never far from her phone.

Can I borrow ur car?

Silence. Ten seconds turns to twenty turns to thirty and beyond. I wait for a full, painstaking minute before she finally writes back.

Was chatting w/ a vendor. Yes. Come get key. C U soon.

For a moment, I'm shocked she said yes. We barely know each other and I offered no explanation of why I need it or where I'm going or when I'll be back. Sure, Angela may consider lending me her whip the least she can do since I've forked over $30,000 so she could be "chatting w/ a vendor" this fine Sunday morning, but maybe she's just loyal and kind. Unlike Jazzy and Maya right now.

I promptly take an Uber over to Here and, again without question, Angela lobs me her keys from a meeting she's having in the dining room with someone from the construction crew. The place looks remarkably different, in a good way— no, a great way—though now is not the time to soak it all in. I mouth *thanks* and walk back out to her Jetta. As I adjust the mirrors and move the seat forward I think about how I cannot let her down. Because if I come back without Benji, it's truth time. And that scares me.

Next thing I know, I'm cruising on I-90 West. I turn the radio off because what's the soundtrack for something like this? Instead, I roll the window down just slightly and let the city air be the white noise as it stings my still-sensitive eye. A text from Angela buzzes in and I glance down at the screen on my phone, which is resting in the center console cup holder.

Having brunch w/ Benji? TELL HIM 2 CALL ME. Important!

I have no choice but to ignore her, which I know is the last thing she'd do to a text from me. *Just give me a half hour,* I think to myself. That's all I need to find him, bring him to safety and get this Here stuff back on track. My relationship, too. But I'll worry about that part later.

And, for the record, brunch with Benji sounds really good right about now.

A few minutes later, I exit the highway and I'm in a neighborhood that looks like it could be the set of *The Wire*. It's probably a good thing Jazzy and Maya ditched out because when I look around, I don't see much in the way of places to get a home-cooked meal. In fact, the only services I see are a dive bar with boarded-up windows and a Chinese restaurant that's closed on Sundays. Everything else is just unmarked, brick, graffiti-laden warehouses and dilapidated flats that may or may not be infested with rats. I continue driving toward the pin I dropped on Google Maps, keeping my eyes peeled for the exact narrow, gravelly alley that Benji last looked up.

That's when I spy two men sitting on the ground. It's the beginning of September but they're dressed for winter in dirty puffy jackets with a patchwork blanket over their laps. There's a bucket of picked-apart fried chicken beside them. Their faces look like leather. The thought dawns on me to pull over and ask them if they've seen a guy with a bunch of tattoos sporting a man-bun, or maybe if one of them is "Anthony," but as soon as I slow the Jetta, they both flash their crooked smiles, which chill me to the bone.

I speed away quickly, barely realizing I just blew a stop sign. A red Honda Civic slams on its brakes, lays on the horn and flips me the bird. I deserve it.

I'm freaked out, to say the least. I can't believe that Benji would voluntarily come to a place like this. That he'd actually spend time researching where exactly to go for drugs in this hellhole, down to the verified Google Map result. This isn't the Benji I know, the one who enjoys the safety of our cushy Lincoln Park digs. The one who never has to worry about opening the electric bill, or how our fridge stays stocked all the time, or how to get his dream restaurant funded. Benji lives the good life with me and I have to imagine he'd prefer to stay on the safe side. Has he really given it all up for *this*?

No matter the answer to that, I can't give up so easily. Obviously Benji's been in the area, which means there's a good chance he might still be here now.

I drive around the block and suddenly see a guy walking alone about 200 yards ahead. Similar hooded sweatshirt, twentysomething...but definitely not Benji. Strangely enough, though, I'm calmed by the sight of someone who could be him.

I pick up speed to catch up with the man. Fifty yards ahead, he stops at the corner to wait for the light to change and takes out his phone. I slow down so as not to freak him out by coming in hot. I've got eight (...seven...six) seconds before the light changes, so I roll my window down in preparation to yell, "Excuse me!" in the most friendly, non-drive-by-shooting voice I can muster. But before I ever get a chance, another man appears from around the corner. The two touch palms and then carry on in opposite directions without so much as saying hello.

Was that what I think it was? A drug deal—in broad daylight—completed in half a second, right before my eyes?

It was stupid of me to come looking for Benji. When drugs are this easy to get, you don't have to hang around here. You can come and go as you please. You can send an eager sous to do it for you. You can roll up in a taxi and not even stop the meter. You can be in and out and on your way in less than a minute.

Reality slaps me in the face. But there's one thing left to check before I can be fully convinced the theme of the morning has officially gone from hopeful to futile.

I survey my immediate surroundings to make sure I'm safe and put Angela's car in Park with the flashers on. I pull up my text string with Benji and access the photos we've sent each other. I scroll to the NA key chain picture he sent me the other day and save it to my camera roll, then drop it into a reverse Google image search and press "go."

My newest worst nightmare comes true. The photo traces back to a Narcotics Anonymous website for a chapter in Philadelphia. It's a photo they have featured on their About Us page. The site hasn't been updated since 2009, meaning that key chain never belonged to Benji and he certainly didn't take the picture of it.

The master manipulator has struck again and I'm the dumb bitch who fell for it. In my gut, I know the truth. Benji is gone.

17

The next morning, I email my boss, Connor, to tell him I need to take a sick day. He writes back and reminds me I don't have any PTO left to use. Between requesting time off for pop-ups and other rehab-related to-dos, I've spent all my remaining paid time off on Benji. So I ask him instead to take it out of my vacation. He says Daxa got rid of vacation two years ago and now it's all just under PTO, which, again, I have none of. He asks me to call him. I don't. He then writes back again and says that if I absolutely cannot make it in today, he can count it as a mental health day.

"I absolutely cannot make it in today," I type back before slamming my laptop shut.

I haven't moved from the couch since I got back from my little journey yesterday. Wait, I take that back. I went down to the drugstore for two pints of Ben & Jerry's and the latest copy of *OK!* magazine. It's probably all made up, but I find reading about other people's drama soothing when I'm in crisis mode. Either way, fifteen dollars and a couple thousand calories later, I'm officially playing keep-away from my life as I know it.

That includes Jazzy and Maya. Short of telling them that yes, I went to Garfield Park and yes, I survived, I haven't communicated any further with them. It was a mistake to delve as far as I did with them into my relationship with Benji in the first place.

Speaking of, I'm not sure if it has sunk in yet about Benji.

I won't go as far as saying he's missing. That's a term reserved for people who go hiking alone in Appalachia or little kids who are left unattended at a gas station in Waco, Texas. My trip to the West Side was a wake-up call, but I've seen enough episodes of *Intervention* to know that addicts don't go down so easy. He's alive. He's not well, but he's alive. And although I have no solid proof of that, the feeling in my gut is all the conviction I need. He'll turn up, I keep thinking to myself. Like a pair of sunglasses or the remote for the DVD player.

It's weird thinking I'm sleeping on top of his knives. I thought about moving them from underneath my bed, but I don't know if I want a reminder of a person I can't find to be so out in the open.

At first, I saw those knives as a glimmer of hope, a sign that he was just giving me space to cool off and let the swelling around my eye subside. Now I see them differently. Clearly, he was too fucked up in the moment he left to realize what was important to bring with him. Knives? To cook? Because I'm a chef? No. None of that registered. At least he didn't sell them for drugs, I guess.

I'm somewhere in season three of *Lost* (which makes a hell of a lot more sense when you aren't stopping every thirty minutes to screw) when the episode is interrupted by a text from Angela. I realize then that I never wrote her back yesterday. Nor did I bring her car back to Here. I suck.

Keeping my car & not responding 2 my txts is a GREAT way 2 open a resto. Just saying.

Just the right amount of sarcasm mixed with the threat of losing my life savings is all that's needed to pry me off the couch. The time has come. I need to meet with Angela and give her the bad news—we're out.

Meet me @ Here in 20 min, I say.
I never left, she texts back.

"Are you sure he's gone? Like, not-coming-back gone?"

"Well, it's not as if I can call him to confirm, but yeah, he's MIA."

As I say the words to Angela, I realize it's the truth. I don't know where he is or how long he'll be there. But when he finally surfaces, I know we won't be a couple. We can't be. Broken promises, lies, danger and complete disregard aren't exactly the pillars of a successful, lasting relationship. You'd think it'd be easy to write someone like that off, but it's not. A huge part of my life is over and I had no say in it and that makes me sad. Too bad I'm all cried out.

"Well, shit," she says bluntly.

"Yeah. Tell me about it."

Before I left my apartment, I did nothing to hide the bruise on my face. Despite what Maya said to me yesterday, it's not better. It's just a shade of green now instead of purple. Angela doesn't ask me about it. I guess it needs no explanation.

"Hey, hey, hey! What the fuck are you doing? Cage lighting goes over the bar, not the tables, guys. Come on. Did you even *look* at the blueprints I gave you? Is this your first time doing a build-out or something? We've got a little over a month 'til open. Get your shit together!" Angela barks.

A little over a month 'til open. It rings in my head like a bad song on repeat because the worst-case scenario is happening: we are sitting in dining room chairs at a dining room table in our soon-to-open restaurant while discussing the head chef's disappearance. Contractors circle around us like sharks, finishing the wiring and hanging expensive lighting for a restaurant I'm positive will never open because Benji won't be their chef after all.

As she barks at the workers, I give myself a moment to take in the progress—something I didn't get to do yesterday as I was trying to slide out in her Jetta with as little conversation as possible. This place looks pretty fucking incredible. There's white subway tile laid in a herringbone pattern going along the wall of the bar, which is made of an insanely long, single piece of lacquered live-edge wood. The stools are vintage feeling with a back on them, which complement the Edison bulbs I see will be installed in cages above them. Inside the dining room, where I'm sitting now, the walls have been painted a taupey-purple color, which is super-trendy and lush-feeling against some serious molding that's all throughout the ceiling. The place isn't huge by any means, but it's been expertly designed to the max, that's for sure. Oh, and these dining room chairs are really comfortable, too.

"Sorry about that." She returns to our conversation. "It just really ticks me off when these city fuckers think they're too cool to look at blueprints. It's like, do they even realize they're installing ten-dollar Home Depot cage lights over a seat that's gonna cost someone $200 for the night? Use some common sense, people."

Even just sitting across from Angela for the last ten minutes, it's apparent she knows her shit. From the decor to prices per person, she's on top of every aspect of this project. It would be a thing of beauty if I weren't so terrified, so consumed with thoughts of Benji.

"So, this doesn't make any sense," she continues through a sip of a cappuccino and a bite of what looks like a Chips Ahoy! cookie. "He left his knives. Even if he's not going to cook at Here, he needs his knives if he's going to find a job anywhere else. Something tells me he doesn't have an extra grand or two to throw down on replacing the set he has. Those are nice knives, you know."

No, I wasn't aware of their worth. But good to know in case I need to sell them on eBay to recoup my losses.

"Trust me," I say. "I thought that same thing about the knives. That they were some kind of a sign that he'd be back… soon. But I'm telling you, after everything I've pieced together since he left, he's probably so high right now, he doesn't even realize he knows how to cook. That's how fucked up he is, wherever he is at the moment."

"And you have no clue where that might be?" I can see it in her eyes: Angela thinks if we just talk this out, we can get to the bottom of it and bring him back. Sadly, I don't agree with her, so I just shake my head.

"And no clue how to reach him?"

"No. His phone's disconnected, he's not responding to email and he's gone dark on social."

"What about calling his sous chef? Or his sponsor? I swear, a guy like Benji needs to come with a phone tree for situations like this. Ugh, hang on. I gotta go have a word with these contractors. Do you see how low they're hanging those pendants? People will have cage lights literally *in* their tomato bisque if I don't show these people how to do their jobs. Why is this so hard?"

Angela scurries off for the moment, which gives me time to think about her suggestions. I don't have Sebastian's number. In hindsight, I probably should have gotten it at some point, but I never needed it. He's not on Facebook, so I really don't know how to reach him or where he works when he's not following Benji around in the kitchen.

I don't have Mark's info either. And as far as calling Rita, I've put it off. At first, I was worried she'd gloat about predicting the relapse, but now I'm thinking I may have just been afraid of hearing her voice go to the place it did when she told me her version of this story. So I do the safer thing, I send her a text.

Hey I think Benji's in trouble. Have U heard anything?

A few moments later, Rita texts back a very helpful: Nope.

How abt Mark? Has he?

I know it's not kosher for me to pry for information like this, but I'm hopeful she can just give me a simple yes or no.

Sry, staying out of it. Hope U understand.

I'm pretty sure that after I didn't take her feedback very cordially when she called me, Rita has vowed to cut me off. Her coldness indicates that my all-access pass to the NA family has officially been revoked.

"Okay, where were we?" Angela asks as she rejoins me at the table, taking another bite of her cookie.

"You were asking me if I've reached out to anyone else and I have. Still nothing. We're totally on our own with this unless you want to tweet out that we'll be assembling a search party at Here later this afternoon."

"Very funny. Not."

"I'm just kidding. Besides, I've already checked the most logical place he could be right now and he's not there."

"Where's that?" she asks.

"Garfield Park."

"Christ. You went all the way out there? In *my* car? Are the hubcaps still attached?" Angela's shocked. I can't tell if she finds me determined or just plain stupid.

But in a moment, she's going to find me a flake. That, I am sure of.

"So how do we do this?" I ask in an effort to hurry along the conversation. "How do we reverse the deal?"

Angela lets out a disbelieving laugh. "I'm sorry, I'm not familiar with that term. What are you asking?"

"How do I get my money back? We're obviously not opening Here without Benji, so the deal's off," I explain, knowing full well just how happy my mom and dad will be to hear this later on.

"Wait. Are you asking for a refund?"

I nod.

"Jesus. Do you smoke?" Angela asks.

"Me? No. Why, do *you* smoke?"

"No, but I could use a cigarette right now so I can wrap my head around this privileged, millennial fuck-show I'm sitting front row to. Be right back—I'm gonna bum one off Hector. He always kind of smells like an ashtray."

"Who's Hector?" I ask her back as she makes her way to the kitchen.

"Our sous chef, Allie. Hector is our sous chef."

As Angela leaves me at the table, a contractor approaches me.

"Excuse me, miss? Can you verify the cage light we just hung is at a good height for you before we drill it in and install the rest?" I'm positive he needs Angela to approve this, but I humor him and follow him over to the bar.

I take a seat in the stool and scoot myself up to the bar ledge and a strange thing happens.

Instead of hearing band saws and people shouting measurements, I hear quiet chatter. Instead of construction workers passing by, I see servers. I imagine the feeling of sitting here having a glass of prosecco and ordering the octopus appetizer.

I picture looking into the dining room at happy couples and four-tops who are whispering to each other because they've spotted me in the bar, cognizant of the fact it's my other half who's been responsible for their multiple foodgasms throughout the course of the evening.

Yes, I'm visualizing Here in all its glory from the vantage point of the bar during the most inappropriate of times, but I can't help it. It's really too bad this all didn't work out. It could have been great. It *would* have been great.

The sound of a chair screeching across an unpolished floor snaps me out of it.

"So what do you think, miss? Is the height good?"

"The height is fine, but it's the placement you have to be careful about. You see, if you have light shining directly above a plate, then look what happens when I try to take a picture of my food," I say, holding my cell phone under the bulb and above where the hypothetical octopus appetizer would have been placed.

"There's a shadow," he says.

"Exactly. Which would make it impossible for anyone to take a decent picture of whatever they're eating, unless they use the flash, which is the kiss of death for a food photo. That said, everything that gets uploaded to social media, Yelp, you name it is going to look like complete shit unless you—"

"Move the lights."

"Six inches to the left and I think you'll be golden," I confirm.

"Thank you so much," the contractor says. "Gents, you heard the lady. Move everything a half a foot to the left."

A few annoyed groans ensue, but I assure them it'll be worth it and return to the table I was at with Angela.

"Okay, here's what has to happen," she tees up, stinking of cigarettes and cucumber melon body splash.

"Lay it on me, Ang," I say, wondering if my portion of the buy will come back in cash or check.

"I just reread the contract, not because any part of me actually believed there was verbiage in there that warranted you a get-out-of-jail-free card, but because I wanted to see how much *more* it'd cost you to terminate your side of the deal."

"Excuse me?"

"Allie, what do you think this is? Canceling your internet service? You signed a binding contract. The thing gets upheld to the laws of Illinois, for crying out loud."

"This is bullshit. Thirty thousand dollars to Craig is chump change and you know it. Tell him to buy me out. Tell him to ask one of his golf buddies to go in on it instead. What's the big fucking deal?"

"The big fucking deal, Allie, is that he will turn that chump change into a big payday when he sues your ass for a breach of contract."

"He wouldn't do that," I say.

"And you know Craig so well *how*?"

"He helped you out when you were in a rough spot. He'll give me a pass, too," I say with confidence.

"Wow, you are even more naive than I thought. Let's get one thing straight: Craig's kindness isn't weakness. Okay? He's not the Easter Bunny skipping around handing out chocolates and toys. He's a businessman with two kids in college, a very expensive-looking wife and a house with a mortgage that costs as much as my entire car every single month. He's not fucking around here. So if you want me to pitch the buy-out situation to him, I will. Just realize he'll have five high-powered attorneys up your asshole by the time you get back to your studio apartment and they'd be happy to remind you just how unattainable the terms of the out-clause are for you."

Angela grabs her phone and pulls up Craig from her contacts. Her finger is on the call button. "Should I?"

"No, wait, don't!" I push her hand back down to the table. She releases her viselike grip on the phone. "Let's just pause for a second and figure this out."

"Finally. The first intelligent thing you've said since getting here. Now, would you like me to get you a cigarette from Hector?"

This is a bigger nightmare than I ever could have imagined. What's worse than the fact that my addict boyfriend has relapsed and disappeared, leaving me to deal with the aftermath, is that no one apparently cares that my addict boyfriend has relapsed and disappeared and left me to deal with the aftermath. Angela doesn't seem to have an ounce of pity, short of offering to go bum a cigarette that I didn't even ask for. She's just sitting there, casually admiring her manicure as she waits for me to say something.

"So what do I do?" I rally.

"Do you really want to know? Because if you really want to know, I'll tell you. I'll tell you exactly what you need to do, Allie Simon."

"Tell me."

"First, let me ask...you're not going to work today, are you?"

"No, I called in," I say.

"Good. You're going to have to do that every day from here on out."

I blink hard. "Huh?"

"Hell, there's no cute way to say it. You've got to quit your job, Allie. Like, tomorrow. First thing. No two-week notice. You're just going to have to walk the fuck out like you've had enough and then come directly to the restaurant afterward and help me get things going."

I didn't realize I could shoot out of a chair so fast until I find myself on my feet, livid.

"What?! No. No, no, no, no, no, NO. This was NOT part of the deal, okay? Maybe you forgot, but I'm a SILENT partner. *Silent* as in, 'doesn't have to say much, doesn't have to do much, doesn't have to quit my job much.'"

"Allie, listen—"

"No, YOU listen, Angela. This is bullshit! *Bullshit*." I start to pace, feeling like a caged tiger. Suddenly the walls of this restaurant have become barbed wire fences in a prison yard— or maybe I'm only realizing in this moment that it's been this way all along.

"I never wanted to do this. I only put the money in to shut you all up, get you losers off my back. This was the way to get Benji out of my goddamn house for once and give your ass a second chance. Or is this your third? I've lost count. Either way, thirty thousand dollars seemed like a reasonable price for peace of mind, I guess. But damn it, Angela—now you're telling me I have to quit my job to be a slave at a restaurant that I'm only standing in because of a guy who is probably slumped over, high as hell, in an alley somewhere? No. No way. This restaurant is like a bastard child that I have zero personal connection with. I need it out of my life. Like, gone. For good."

"Allie, what are you doing?"

"I'm calling my mom," I declare, phone in hand. "She always said that if I just tell her the truth, she can help me. I'm coming clean."

"Well, that's cute and all, but your mama is not going to be able to get you out of this one. In fact, there's no *out*. There's only *through*. And, frankly, I'm the only one who can help with that. So do your dear mother a favor, spare her the heart attack and put your phone away. Please."

I don't know if she's wrong or right, but she's convincing.

I slip the phone back into my bag and wait for her to give me my next direction like she's an officer negotiating a hostage situation.

"Good, now sit back down."

"I think I need a drink."

"And if our liquor delivery was here, Allie, I'd pour you one. But that won't be for another thirty-four days. So let's try to relax the old-fashioned way, woman. Deep breaths. In through your nose, out through your mouth. Good. Very good. See? Now stop worrying, I will train you on everything. This isn't rocket science. At the end of the day, it's about taking care of people. And I know that's something you're already good at."

"But what about my money?"

"Jesus, it's always about the money with you. News flash: you working here means you get paid *and* you still make your money back. Okay? So your investment will be fine. We just need a new chef."

"Ha. Ha. HA."

"Uh-oh, that's a crazy laugh, isn't it. I'm scared. What am I missing?" asks Angela.

"How convenient that you can just boil Benji down to a mere *thing*. Like he's some kind of worn-out mattress. You just get a new one and life goes on. Let's not forget that just a week ago, he was a real person—a real person you weren't going to do this deal without. What happened to that?"

Angela puts one hand over mine from across the table. It's the first sympathetic move she's made all morning.

"Listen, no matter how attractive a person is or how attractive their potential may be, we do a deal based on reality and we always have a backup plan. Now, I can't say that you did the same insofar as dating him. And for that, I am sorry. Because that shit hurts, I'm sure."

She's going deep. Much deeper than I'm prepared to go while sitting at a table in the restaurant he was supposed to open.

"Benji loves you, Allie. He just loves cocaine *way* more. In your defense, it was probably never a fair matchup. I'd reckon Benji and that other White Girl have way more history than the two of you."

She taps the top of my hand twice and pulls back in her chair just as I finally figure out that White Girl means cocaine.

I wipe away what I hope is just a solo tear, but before I know it, salty streams are flowing faster than my fingers can keep up with. So much for being all cried out. The reserve supply is flowing steadily now and I know I'm making a scene, but I'm an emotional wreck who's sick of having to be the one that holds it together. Benji's gone, I've just been reminded he chose cocaine over me and now I'm being strong-armed into quitting my job so I can serve food or something. It's my turn to be unpredictable and dramatic.

"Allie, come on. Do you see me freaking out at all? No. So just calm down."

"Do NOT tell me to calm down!" I slap the top of the table with both palms to drive my point home. "I'm tired of drawing the short straw. How many times do I have to tell you, I DON'T WANT ANYTHING TO DO WITH THIS RESTAURANT."

Angela finally gets up from her chair. It feels like all the air in the room is suddenly rushing toward us to swirl around Angela like a gathering storm. But Angela isn't Benji; she's not out of control. She's the eye of the tornado, not the destructive cyclone itself.

"Two can play this whole stand up and shout game, Allie. But I suggest you sit your ass down and act like someone who owns a restaurant because guess what? *You do.* And like I explained already, you aren't getting your money back."

I can't see myself, but I know I look like a deer in the headlights.

"You heard me right," she says, putting her finger to my sternum. Classic Angela. "You. Are not. Getting. Your money back. And I'm sorry about that, I'm really sorry. But that's just not how things like this work. I'm not a customer service counter, I'm a fucking general manager. You need to get this idea out of your head that there are exchanges and refunds in this business. Craig can't issue you a store credit to go franchise a Jamba Juice in the Loop. There are contracts and clauses and a bunch of other legal terms that are way over your pretty little head."

She removes her glasses as she puts her face up to my ear and begins to whisper.

"So if I were you, I'd cut this flailing lunatic routine before one of these hourly crew guys calls Craig and tells him you're having a mental breakdown and I can't control it. Because if that happens, and his Monday morning tee time is interrupted, he'll *really* take your ass for broke. So do yourself a favor and calm the fuck down before you make the both of us look bad."

Angela puts her glasses back on and smiles a toothy grin at me. She must recognize that I am frozen, as she proceeds to lead me back to the table and my chair and I allow it. When I sit down, my legs start to tingle like they've just woken up from being dead asleep for hours. I shake my head a little to keep the sensation from traveling to my brain.

"Now I'm going to forgive you for the very hurtful things you just said about me being a loser because I understand you are in a very, *very* stressful situation."

Wait, did I really call Angela a loser? I honestly have no

recollection of the things I said while coming undone, which is super embarrassing.

"Thank you," I say graciously.

"Just know that I'm here for you as your friend and as your new coworker. And as both of those things, I cannot—and I will not—sit here and do nothing. I am the manager, right? That's what you all hired me to do. So I need to *manage* this. But I can't do it alone, Allie."

"Okay, so then let's hire someone," I say. "I can put out a tweet right now saying we're looking for a few industry professionals to help us with the opening of Here. I'm sure we'll get a bunch of hits."

"That's a great idea! Do you have an extra $60,000 to swing it?"

"No, obviously not."

"Well, then, that's off the table. See, in my last budget meeting with Craig, I promised him we had capped the overhead. That means no more salaries out. As of last week, he was under the impression Benji was going to split the opening tasks with me. I was counting on him to take the lead with menu planning, first week ordering, kitchen outfitting, things like that."

Planning? Ordering? Outfitting? I'm already lost.

"But without him, and no one else in his place yet, I can't exactly go back to Craig at the eleventh hour and say hey... actually, the whole thing is imploding so we need to staff up ASAP. It's too late for that. We're going to have to divide that stuff, and a few other things, amongst the people we have now."

"Which is who?"

"You and me, darling. Just you and me. Now before you get your titties in a bundle, I know you don't know how to do the things I mentioned. So chill, I'm not asking you to. I can handle them, but you're going to have to step in and take the burden of some of the other stuff I was originally going to do."

"Like what?"

"Floor manage, captain the staff, front-of-house stuff."

"Oh good god."

"Allie, deep breaths please. Deep breaths. You've helped Benji at a pop-up or two, right?"

"Right, but only when he forgot to ask someone else to step in and I knew he was going to crash and burn if I didn't show up and try to keep the peace by distracting people with funny stories and fake smiles while they waited for the next course to come out," I explain. *Was that all one sentence?* My mouth is moving faster than my brain.

How strange that my memories of helping Benji at pop-ups are now tainted with bitterness and resentment. I swear it didn't feel like that at the time, but maybe this is how I felt all along? I suppose I could only rock the "everything is fine and dandy with my bad-boy chef boyfriend" look for so long until it eventually goes out of fashion, until I want to smash the water pitcher on the floor and just scream.

"Perfect! Funny stories and fake smiles are the gist of it. You'll be fine."

"What? No, I won't!" I didn't realize I walked into a trap with my previous answer.

"Yes, you will. Especially because there's no other choice if you don't want to see your $30,000 go down the drain. Now stay right here, I have to run to the office real quick."

The words "there's no other choice" echo in my ears. Alone at the table, I start to realize my back is against a wall. This may not be my fate, but working at Here is quickly becoming my future. And the sooner I can embrace that, I guess the better off I'll be.

It's just hard to think that a few weeks ago, I was gearing

up to pitch my case for a promotion at Daxa. My review is supposed to be Thursday. But according to Angela, I won't get to see the day where Connor finally names me creative director. I will never know what could have been as far as my career path there because I'll be washing dishes at Here.

And then there's Stacey and Dionte, who I'll just be abandoning like day-old puppies. Do they know that Alt+Shift+F4 is the shortcut to show the last ten tweets we sent? Do they know you have to restart the computer every Monday morning or the streams freeze? Do they know we don't just plug Spanish tweets into some free translator website because Pedro in shipping is bilingual and likes to help?

I guess I can't worry about the wheels falling off over there. They're a corporation with real money to hire real experts, unlike what's going on at Here. I'm sure I'll be replaced before I finish cleaning out my drawers.

"Alright, Allie, good news. I got approval from Craig for you to be my AGM."

"AGM?"

"Assistant General Manager. I spun some nonsense about how since this is a fall/winter opening and not a spring/summer opening, I could use the extra hands and he approved a *small* budget increase."

"So I'm in for $60,000?" That's at least a livable wage.

"Nooooo-ho-ho, that's a pie-in-the-sky number, sweetie. Take a look at the numbers."

Angela slides some papers toward me. The size-6 font is dizzying, but the last time I breezed over a contract before signing it, I sold my soul with no way to get it back.

"Where am I looking?" I ask.

Angela guides her pen to a section that covers payment.

"See here? It shows you'll be taking a salary. That's this tiny little number right here."

Tiny indeed.

"And you'll also be getting paid on your investment as the restaurant makes money, which is detailed in Appendix A, which is here." She flips the page over. There's a bunch of pie charts and graphs. Whatever.

"Oh, and there won't be any health benefits either, so be sure to wash your hands a lot and get a flu shot while you still have that cotton swab insurance. Now just sign on this line to accept the position and then let's get this show on the road."

"Can you give me a minute, please?" I ask Angela.

"Sure, I'll be right back."

I pull out my phone from my purse on the off chance that while I've been sitting here discussing my lack of options, Benji has found a way to reach me. But alas, zero missed calls, zero texts and still no activity from any of his social media handles.

So I instead call the most accountable person I know, my mother.

"Hey, Allie, how's work?"

I could easily say fine, but the theme of this call is honesty. It has to be.

"Well, I took today off, actually."

"You're not helping Benji with another pop-up, are you? I thought he was done with those," she says.

"Mom, Benji relapsed." My mom gasps.

"I don't know exactly on what, or when, or how, but none of his stuff is in my apartment anymore and we're obviously not together."

"Oh, honey. I am so sorry. So, so sorry. Is he okay?"

"I'm not sure. I don't even know where he is right now."

"What can I do? Do you want me to come downtown? Do you want to come here?"

"No, that's okay, Mom. I've got plenty to distract me," I assure her. "I just don't want you to be mad at me."

"Mad at you? For what?"

"For picking Benji. And then having it all turn out like *this*."

"You didn't ask for this, Allie. Remember that. And you did everything right."

"Yeah, I'm not so sure I did."

"Well, I am. I didn't want to say anything because we don't really talk about it anymore, but Uncle John had a major drug problem in the '80s. Everyone wanted me to stop talking to him, to refuse to let him see you, but how could I do that? He was my brother and you were the only grandbaby. I thought *you* would be the thing that could change him. So I went behind everyone's back and made a standing date with Johnny at the park so he could see you. Tuesdays, 11 a.m., right after your midmorning nap. Every week, I felt like he and I were proving the world wrong! Occasionally he'd ask for bus money or money to grab a coffee for the way home and I'd give it to him. A dollar here, a dollar there. So what?

"Then, three months into our little routine, he was a no-show. I instantly got a bad feeling. So I drove by his house on the way home and there he was, needle in his arm, passed out on the floor."

"I was with you?"

"Yes. You were. Paramedics came and revived him, thank god. Do you know how big of a dummy I felt like? I figured all I needed to do was love him, support him, let him see his baby niece and give him some money for coffee. I was wrong. I don't regret what I did—spending all that time and money trying to make him better, but that was the worst thing I've ever gone through."

People always say my mom and I are so alike, but I really didn't think an affinity for drug addicts was something we'd ever bond over.

"Oh goodness. I was not expecting to relive that today, Al," she says. That makes two of us.

Her honesty inspires me. "Look, I can't take another secret. And I don't think you can either. So listen: I need to let you know that I've got to step in with things at the restaurant—full-time—or I risk losing my investment. I know Dad said we shouldn't talk about money stuff as a family anymore and I realize I'll be throwing away my dream job just so that I can pick up the pieces some selfish druggie left behind. But I have no choice. And I don't want to lie about where I am or what I'm doing anymore. My last day at Daxa is tomorrow. I'll be working at Here after that."

I squint my eyes as I brace for impact. This is not what they had in mind when they funded my college education.

"Well, I'm not going to pretend to be happy about this. But you've got to do what you've got to do. I understand that. But I need you to understand something, too. I know you thought Benji was the main character of your life story, but that's actually you. *You're* the star of your own show and that show must go on."

When I get off the phone, nearly weak with gratitude that that went as smoothly as it did, I stare blankly at the table. It's just me and the contract and a semiclear conscience. I take a deep breath, grab the pen and click it open.

"I can't believe I'm doing this," I mumble to no one within earshot as I sign my name on the dotted line.

Angela must have been watching from around the corner, because before the ink even has a chance to dry, she swoops back into frame.

"Congrats on your new position! I'll start working on a press release this afternoon. Now, if you would be so kind, sign this one, too." She pulls out another piece of paper and slides it my way.

"What's this?"

"This is your resignation letter for Daxa. Connor has two *n*'s in it, right?" It's almost shocking how beyond blasé she is about me quitting my beloved job.

"You know I was up for a promotion, right?"

"Sorry. I just can't risk the chance you won't sprout a pair of balls tomorrow when you walk in there at 9:00 a.m. I need you working at Here, Allie. You know I wouldn't ask unless I meant it."

"You're not really asking, you know," I say. This printout has far fewer words but is even tougher to sign. I have to steady my hand from shaking as the pen makes contact with the page.

"Beautiful signature, I really like the open dot on the *i*. Now, like I mentioned, we don't have a lot of time. In fact, we have about two hours. Maybe three."

"Why? What happens then?"

"What happens then is we extend a job offer to our next chef de cuisine. It's got to happen today."

Angela places a stack of papers on the table, whisking the just-signed contract and resignation letter out of sight.

"What are these?" I ask.

"Résumés. I'm not stupid, Allie. Yes, Benji was my first choice to be our head chef. But if for one second I thought opening a restaurant with a guy like him was going to go down without a hitch, well, then, I'd most likely be all hopped up on whatever he was smoking in your bathtub yesterday."

I give her a cockeyed look.

"Too soon? Sorry. Look, we know guys like Benji and what they need to hear to move forward on an opportunity like this. Did Craig and I bait him a bit when we assured him there was no one else we were looking at? Sure. But the truth was, we *weren't* looking at anyone else. In fact, I didn't pull these résumés until *after* he signed on as a way to cover my own ass. Just know, we never doubted his caliber. Only his character. And I'm bummed he proved me right, but I can't stop the train now."

I have to admit I'm envious of Angela. She saw coming what I didn't and she prepared herself. Smart woman.

"So what do you want *me* to do?"

"Replace him. There are five qualified backups right here. All of them are local, so we don't have to relocate anyone. Some of them are between jobs and some are currently working at other restaurants, so you need to call them quickly before they go in for their shifts tonight. Get them on the phone, then get them in here. I want all of them interviewed today and an offer made no later than tonight. Any questions?"

Yeah, like a thousand.

"How do I know if they're good enough?"

"They are," she says. "I've researched them religiously and tasted their food already. They may not have the Benji Zane Effect, but any one of them would be a great fit from a culinary perspective. Next question?"

"How do I pick?"

"Choose whoever you're least likely to sleep with. Anything else?"

"Why are you trusting me with this?"

"Because I like the way you see people when you don't have all the time in the world to get to know them. Plus, you talk to strangers on the internet all day, every day. You'll be fine," Angela says as she starts gathering her things.

"And what are you doing right now, might I ask?"

"Okay, Questions McGee. Easy. Someone has to let Craig know his superstar chef is knifeless, homeless and missing. Did you want *that* job?"

This place is cursed. And I'm the AGM of it.

18

The first three guys I interviewed were both bearded men working for some arbitrary hipster restaurants that have already seen their fifteen minutes of *FoodFeed* fame. Could they cook? Sure. Were they on drugs? Probably not. But when they couldn't get past who I was and what happened to Benji, it felt less like I was interviewing them and more like they were interrogating me.

Before the interviews began, I Googled common interview questions for chefs and printed them out. Having made a decision from the heart about a certain chef before, I'm not willing to go totally off-script this time considering how that turned out. I'm learning, however, that asking "What dish best describes you?" over and over is as exhausting as listening to the answers. One more canned response containing the words *beautifully composed* or *well-balanced* and I'm skipping straight to "Let's play Marry, Fuck, Kill...Celebrity Chef Edition." It may not be on the recommended questions list but I feel like it could tell a lot about a person.

"Tabitha Johnson in the house," I hear a deep woman's voice say. My fourth interview is about to begin—and, I'm sure, end.

I turn and see a six-foot-five middle-aged woman with short, spiky brown hair and Coke-bottle glasses wheeling in a cooler like it's a rolling duffel bag. She's wearing a pantsuit that's about to bust at the seams and Crocs. We shake hands. Her grip is firm as fuck.

"Let me just get this out of the way: I have absolutely no

idea how to dress for these kinds of things," she says, gesturing to her eclectic getup. "Plus, I'm butch. So I have no idea how to dress, period." She laughs like Santa Claus and takes a seat.

Well, at least I already know there's a zero percent chance of falling in love with her, so please, Tabitha, when can you start?

Kidding. Due Diligence Debbie continues by scanning through her résumé. It shows that her most recent position is listed as a private chef to the mayor, which tells me it's highly unlikely that her hobbies include illegal activities or recreational drugs. But the downside here is that I feel like cooking for the mayor is a good gig, so why give it up to work for this shitty-salary, no-benefit hellhole (in comparison) called Here? I ask in more PC terms: "What makes you interested in joining our team?"

"Well, I work third shift at the Mayor's Mansion. That's midnight to 8:00 a.m. and the hours—and the cuisine, quite frankly—are just brutal. Making a pepperoni pizza at 2:00 a.m. and pouring cereal at seven doesn't exactly allow me to hone my craft," she explains.

"So what do you like to cook? You know, if you could make anything you wanted."

"Hands down...my famous bleu cheese burger."

A burger? Really? Does she realize we are trying to replace a guy who topped his spaghetti with parmesan mousse? I thought Angela vetted these people...

"With all due respect, Tabitha, I think your style—well, *cooking* style—may be a little rudimentary for Here," I say, hoping that rudimentary means what I think it means.

"I figured that's how you might react. Which is why I brought the cooler. Please, can I show you?"

She unzips her bag and in it are the ingredients to make her "famous" dish. I didn't plan for there to be a practical part of this exam, but I like that she has taken it upon herself to really prove her worth. Plus, I haven't eaten today so I don't object.

I follow Tabitha back to the kitchen. Yes, that's right. I follow her through a restaurant she's never been to where I happen to be the owner. Her instinctual command over the space is impressive—it's like she instantly understands the familiarity component that we want people to revel in when they walk through these doors.

Once back in the kitchen area, which is hardly set up yet (thanks, Benji), she sets out her knife roll and a few prep bowls, and heats a pan with a dollop of oil. Nothing about her screams Rachael Ray, but I'm drawn to watch her nonetheless.

"Sorry, our kitchen isn't exactly up to snuff yet," I explain as I prop myself up on a steel counter across from her.

"No worries. This doesn't require any fancy equipment. Now here, smell this," she says as she holds a garlic clove under my nostrils. "It's from the best produce vendor in Chicago, Marcel & Sons." She then brings the garlic back to her nose and inhales with a smile on her face and exhales with an "Ahhhhh."

She goes on to mince the clove in what feels like a nanosecond and then adds it to the hot oil.

"Three types of ground meat: brisket, pork and beef." She points to each before dropping them all into a mixing bowl.

"One quail egg." She holds it up like she's showing me a bicentennial quarter, then cracks it into the meat. "It's less runny than a chicken egg, but richer in flavor."

Noted.

"Then you pull the garlic before it burns, and drop it right into the meat and egg mixture. People always add raw garlic to their ground beef. That makes no sense. The garlic flavor comes when it's been sautéed, so that's when I put it in. Now you mix it gently with your fingers, never with a spoon, and let the yolk of the quail egg be the glue. Like so."

I hunch over the bowl to watch.

"It's not every day I get to work meat with my hands, but when I do..." She nudges me with her elbow. "If you know what I mean."

I love her sense of humor. It's such a stark contrast from the way Benji would act behind a stove—yelling at everyone, head down, always so intense. I get that cooking at a busy restaurant is a serious operation, but confirming our chef is also a human being is a check in the positive column. At least it is to me.

"Okay, the pan is still hot from the oil, so I'm going to pour the meat into the pan."

"Wait, don't you have to first make them into patties?"

"Please, Allie. My burgers aren't famous because they look like everyone else's."

She stirs the meat for about a minute until the individual pieces look like they amount to a nice medium rare. She pulls the meat, plates it, crumbles fresh bleu cheese on top and then unzips a few things she handmade before coming here: sourdough toast points, tomato jam and pickled onion. When everything is plated, it looks almost like a beef tartare.

She slides the plate toward me.

"Dig in."

One bite in and I can tell I'll be dreaming about this deconstructed burger later on. One bite is also all I need to realize I would spend $50 on this dish. Or if we served it as an app, $25—easily. There's nothing glamorous about this woman, except for the fact she can create a polished, composed dish like it's no one's business. Which is why I need to beg her to take this job.

"Tabitha, this is incredible," I say, and I mean it.

"I agree. Now can you see why it sucks that I'm stuck in a

job that has me cutting crust off peanut butter and jellies for the mayor's kids?"

"Yes, I can totally see that, and you'd have creative freedom in this kitchen—that I can promise. But I do have a question, and forgive me for being blunt. But...have you ever cooked for more than just four people—the mayor, his wife and their two kids?"

"You mean like the fifty-person catered lunch they call me in for three times a week in his office? Or his sister's 300-person wedding at The Peninsula? Or how about—"

"Okay, okay. Got it." My face is red with embarrassment for even asking. Of course Angela wouldn't bring in someone whose experience capped at family dinnertime.

"Look, if you're wondering if I know how to cook under stress, I don't. Because I don't get stressed. I get focused. And, yes, I'm proficient in how to pace my courses, order my product, things like that."

"Quite honestly, you sound perfect for the job," I say, not caring that I'm showing all my cards. "But I need to be frank with you. This is obviously a brand-new restaurant. Hours are going to be long, we're going to attract obnoxious foodies and our build-out was expensive, meaning the salary may not even be worth it to you. Plus there's the whole 'Benji Zane thing.'"

"Who's Benji Zane?"

"Seriously?" I ask in disbelief.

"Yeah, sorry, I'm kind of behind on pop culture. Any free time I have, I read *Lord of the Rings* fan fiction online. Wait, is he the host of *Chopped*? No, that doesn't sound right..."

"Can you wait here for just a sec?" I ask Tabitha politely and hold up the one-second finger. "I'll be right back. Don't move."

I scurry out of the kitchen over to the office where Angela is holding up two forks.

"Right or left?" she asks.

"Left."

"Thanks, that's the one I was going to pick, too."

"Angela, listen. I think I found our next chef. Clean pee test, not going to fall in love with her and top-notch amazing cook who works for the mayor."

"Oh, yes. Tabitha Johnson. I remember her. What's the catch?" she asks.

"She doesn't know who Benji Zane is," I say.

"And that's a bad thing because..."

"Because 'Tabitha Johnson' packs zero punch. Her name means nothing at all to anyone who we expect will be spending money eating dinner here. She's not mentioned anywhere in *FoodFeed*, doesn't come up on Google until the fourth page and loves *Lord of the Rings*. I'm just worried that if we hire her, we lose the draw."

Angela starts cackling.

"This isn't funny! She's waiting for me to tell her if she got the job. Can you please offer up an opinion?"

"An opinion? No. But I can offer you the cold, hard truth. And that is that *you*, Allie Simon, are the draw. I put the press release out that you were stepping in as AGM three hours ago and the internet has been abuzz ever since."

In an attempt to start moving on from Benji, I canceled all Google Alert notifications I had previously set for my name and his after I got back from Garfield Park last night. Without Angela telling me, I never would have stumbled upon said press release.

"I am?" I ask. "Why?"

"Because. You're pretty, you're smart, you're likable. You went from an industry no-name to everyone's favorite person to snap a selfie with on the street."

"But that's only because of Benji. And he's not even around

anymore. I'm sure everyone will be disappointed when they realize we aren't together. In fact, they'll demand I step down and go answer phones at a dentist's office. I don't belong in this industry without him."

"Allie, do us all a favor. Shut up and go hire Tabitha Johnson. Would you, please? Tell her she's got the job, then send her to my office for paperwork and next steps."

Angela goes back to comparing forks. I'm genuinely impressed with her ability to dilute my concerns, but I still trust her. I walk back out with my marching orders.

"And, hey," she calls. "I'll see you in the late morning tomorrow, right?"

The color in my face drains thinking about what has to happen between my leaving now and coming back tomorrow. For as exhilarating as hiring Tabitha is, there's another thing I need to do that will be just as impactful on my blood pressure: I've got to hand over my letter of resignation.

"Right," I say, as if there's a choice.

I have been dreading this moment since Angela ordered the hit on my job. It's the last time I'm powering up my work computer…ever. And as soon as the screen comes alive, I'll be IM-ing my boss to meet me in Conference Room B before his 9:30 a.m. meeting.

I grab a cup of water from the break room; my throat feels like a shag carpet in the desert. Stacey trots in from behind me to dump out yesterday's coffee cup.

"What's on the lunch menu today?" she asks, per usual.

"Nothing," I say. Her face reacts as if I told her the world was flat.

"Oh, I get it. You two are having lunch together. That's so cute. You guys are adorable. Want anything from Starbucks? I'm so over the coffee here."

"No thanks," I say. *It was nice knowing you, though.*

I'm holding the letter as I walk over to meet with Connor. My hands are sweating so profusely, the page is dampening and curling. I should have put it in an envelope. Or a waterproof Tupperware.

"Good morning, Allie. Come on in," Connor says. He's so nerdy and lovable. His red hair and dad bod are perfect complements to his button-down bowling shirt that hasn't been fashionable since 1994.

"Just so you know, I didn't forget about our review on Thursday so if that's what this is about, just know it's already on my calendar and I'm looking forward to it. And... you should be, too, if you know what I mean," he hints with a smile.

This is gut-wrenching. The comfort of my routine. My coworkers. The work itself. It's all about to become shrapnel as I detonate this bomb.

"Actually, Connor, it turns out I won't need that review. Because I...I quit," I say as I hand him the paper.

He crinkles every part of his face as he looks at the paper I've just handed him. It's like I've subpoenaed him for court or something. I feel awful.

"What is this? I don't understand. Is it about the promotion? You were going to get it, I swear."

"No, it's not about the promotion. And thanks, that would have been great."

"Is it a money thing?"

Kind of.

"You know we're on a salary freeze but I can see if I can get you an extra three percent or maybe a year-end bonus or something if that helps."

"No, it's not that either," I say.

"Are you going somewhere else? I thought you were happy here, Allie."

"No, it's none of that," I say. "I just, I need to quit. Right now."

"Like, today? Is there anything—"

"Connor, let me stop you. There's nothing you can do. There's nothing anyone can do. I typed up a robust transition checklist and saved it on the C: drive. So please just let me go so I can pack up my cubicle and try to get out of here before Stacey gets back from coffee and Dionte comes in for the day."

I can tell he's equal parts dumbfounded and irritated. No two weeks' notice and seemingly no talking me out of it.

"Allie, as you know, Daxa is a hire-and-fire-at-will company. I can't *make* you stay. But my wife's a social worker. And we talk about her patients sometimes. I know, HIPAA, but we do. And all the PTO you've taken, your impromptu mental health day, the bruise around your eye and now a swift letter of resignation two days before you knew you'd be getting the promotion you've been after for years…something's going on. I don't know what, but if you need to talk to my wife, I'd be happy to connect you two."

I cry a little as I fight to keep the sloppy, horrible truth from pouring out of me in Conference Room B at 9:05. He's one sentence away from saying "Blink twice if you need me to call the cops," but thankfully I'm able to cut him off.

"I appreciate your concern, Connor. I really do. And I appreciate everything you've done for me and how you've believed in me and helped me grow in this role. You're a really good boss and whoever you hire next is going to be lucky to be on this team." I nod as I turn around and head for the door.

Inelegant as it may have been, it's done and it feels like a friend of mine has died.

I get back to my apartment with my cubicle belongings

and grab my mail before heading up. Arguably, I've been a little too preoccupied to check box #1004 these last few days so of course it's overstuffed. I'm sure my mailman hates me.

Sifting through the mail upstairs, I see what looks to be a bill addressed to Benji. It's like seeing a double rainbow because normally the money stuff comes to me. But alas, it's from his cell phone provider and that's one bill I never took over. He always paid it with his share of profits from the pop-ups. In fact, I distinctly remember handing him $86 on the thirteenth of every month so he could walk over to the Verizon store and take care of it. I'm convinced this is a letter to confirm what we already know: that the line has been disconnected.

I tear it open, because why not, and discover it's a final letter from collections. He owes a whopping $760 in overages, late fees and dues. According to this document, he's pocketed every cent I gave him that was meant to square up with Verizon. He's also done a good job of checking the mail before I came home from work and intercepting any evidence that might have told me what he was really up to with this designated cash.

I call the number on the bill and politely tell them to stop sending letters to this address. I could have easily gone into exactly why, but the person who answered my call clearly doesn't make enough money per hour for that. When I hang up, the silence and stillness in my apartment is too much to handle. I grab my keys and lock up.

"What's this?"

"*This* is everything we need to do in the next thirty-seven days and how to do it. Do you want to look through it and pick something that interests you, or would you like me to just assign you a task?" Angela says as she slaps a binder down in front of me in the back office of Here.

I thumb through it. There's probably 300 pages or more

all printed, hole-punched and organized behind their respective tabs and sub tabs.

Ordering
- Liquor
- Food
- Supplies

Menus
- Food
- Drinks

Restaurant Setup
- Layout
- Furniture

Staff
- Scheduling
- HR

Systems…

And approximately a hundred other things that make absolutely no sense to me. I slam the book shut before I have an aneurysm, and slide it back her way.

"Dealer's choice, Ang," I say with a smile.

"Well, then…"

She opens the binder with her perfectly manicured nails—this time there's just a touch of color to them like ballet slippers—to the exact page she's thinking of on her first try, unclips the rings and pulls out a sheet of paper.

"Take a look at this. I had Tabitha put it together last night. It's everything we need to order for opening and how much of each. Now this list isn't going to change until the spring when we update our menu for the season, but the quantities we have to order will. For example, we're going to do more covers—"

"Covers?"

"Asses in chairs. We're going to have more of those on the weekends, so we'll be ordering more product on Fridays and Saturdays. We'll dial down our order on Tuesday so we don't have waste. Make sense? It's simple supply and demand, really."

"Yeah, I think I get it. What do you need me to do with it, though?"

"Cool your jets. I'm getting to it, woman. I need you to source vendors for each of the ingredients, put in the order for opening night with them and then set them up in our bookkeeping system so we can pay them when they invoice us."

Upon first glance, I'm familiar with most of the items on the list. Broccoli, strawberries, onions…

"Can't we just get these things at Costco?"

"Really? Really, Allie? This isn't Thanksgiving dinner. We order vegetables from the produce guy, meat from a butcher, fish from the fish guy, tea from the tea seller, and so on and so forth. We need the freshest ingredients possible, delivered to our door the morning before service. Do you see eggs on that list?"

With my pointer finger as my guide, I scan the list and spot them about halfway down. Tabitha is requesting forty-six dozen.

"Yes, right here," I say.

"Okay, so that means I want the chicken to have literally shit that egg out an hour before it winds up at our door. We want to shop local, we want to keep our relationships strong and we want the best of the best available no matter what. We don't need to be losing business to Applebee's because a diner finds a piece of wilted lettuce in their salad."

She's playing with the emerald pendant on her necklace as she shoots the order at me.

"Alright, alright. I get it. So how do I find these vendors?"

Finding Tabitha was easy when Angela did all the research and left me just five to pick from. But something tells me this is going to be more needle-in-the-haystack and less Restaurant 101.

"You're going to need to research. I know who's the best in the 'burbs, but not so much in the city. I assume everyone decent is in the Fulton Market."

The Fulton Market is an industrial neighborhood just a few streets north of the West Loop. It's pretty much just produce warehouse after warehouse along a cobbled street that's laced with forklifts and fish guts.

"I will say, however," she continues, "that the trick is finding one vendor that's solid, then asking them who they recommend for all the rest. It's insider knowledge that way, word of mouth. Oh, and another piece of advice: don't let them bully you with the menu. Tell them it's already set in stone. Vendors will always try to get you to change your offerings based on what they want to push, which is either shit that goes bad quickly, or the real expensive stuff. I'm counting on you to stay strong."

I make a fist with my hand and pound my chest to show my allegiance to Tabitha's menu.

"Speaking of, turn to page 98—there's a copy of the working menu. This isn't what the customers will see, but it details how everything's made and what exactly is in everything. That way if a person with a nut allergy wants to go hard-as-a-motherfucker on our sweet potato mash, our servers will be able to warn them there are pecans in it before someone goes into anaphylactic shock on our restaurant floor."

"I will learn to recite in my sleep," I say.

"Good. Now I've got to go supervise the hanging of our sign outside. I just got a text that it arrived early...so that marks one thing that's actually going to plan!" She claps with excitement and puts her jacket on.

Then she tosses me a ring with three keys on it.

"Back door, front door, walk-in fridge and freezer…you'll figure out which is which."

She leaves me alone in the office and I just stare at the keys in the palm of my hand. It's like somebody asked me to hold their baby and then took off running. I'm overwhelmed to say the least, but I'm afraid of what Angela will do if she mistakes my paralysis for slacking. So I throw the keys in my purse and focus on my assignment.

I begin with the first ingredient on the to-order list: garlic. This is an easy one because I recall being in the kitchen yesterday with Tabitha as she prepared her test meal. The clove of garlic she held in front of my nose was so fragrant, but where did she get it? I know she mentioned it…something "& Sons"?

I punch what I can remember into a search bar and Google does the rest for me. Next thing I know, I'm on the phone with a guy named Jared from Marcel & Sons. He offers to swing by for a meet and greet, complete with a lesson on how to submit my order online and a complimentary apple tasting. Because apparently that's a thing. He'll be here in fifteen minutes.

"Well, I sincerely apologize if I offended you by assuming you would also sell coffee…Yes, I am now *fully* aware of the differences between tea and coffee. Thank you very much."

I'm trying to wrap a less-than-pleasant conversation with a tea vendor when in walks who I assume is the produce guy. He's carrying a box with some apples, paperwork and a clipboard sticking out of it. I wave hello to him and gesture to Angela's empty chair and desk as a place he can unpack for a few.

"Okay, I'm not an idiot so you can stop talking to me like one…You're right, I did hear that you had the best tea selection in Chicago, but I don't appreciate your tone with me, sir. So you know what? You can just cancel the entire order and

I'll find someone else...Yes. Cancel the whole thing...Oh, I
will. Don't you worry."

I slam the receiver down in a fit of rage.

"Are they all like this?" I ask the stranger who just heard
me lose my shit on the phone.

"You mean are all vendors pompous assholes? Yes. For the
most part. Let me guess, that was Gary Schweitz at the Tea
Seller?"

"Yeah, how'd you know?"

"He's a bit of a diva. Hates when people assume he's a one-
stop coffee/tea shop. Why don't you try The Tea Lady...she's
much more flexible and has great coffee, too. She sources
from Dark Matter roasters so it's all local. Maria Montene-
gro is her name."

I scribble it down so I can Google her later and then realize I haven't yet caught the name of the person who threw
out the helpful suggestion.

"Thanks for that. I'll give her a buzz. And hi, I'm Allie
Simon. You are?"

He wipes apple residue on his jeans and walks closer to
shake my hand. "Jared Marcel, Marcel & Sons produce. I come
in peace." He holds the infamous StarTrek/Spock fingers up.

"And also with...an apple tasting."

I still haven't eaten today, which explains the fact that the
seemingly bland, albeit healthy, offering is making my mouth
water right now. I get up and follow him back over to Angela's desk, where he's set up a charcuterie-like selection of
apple slices and dips.

"Gala. Fuji. Honeycrisp. They're in season right now and
you cannot beat the flavor on them. I'd start there."

I pick up a slice of his recommended favorite and bite into
it. It's just an apple. A snack I've had a thousand times in my

life. But this one sends little tingles all through my mouth like pops of lightning.

"Holy shit, that's good," I say. "I mean, those apples have a lovely tasting profile. Can we order some of them?"

"Absolutely," says Jared. "But let me see a copy of your working menu first so I can make sure it fits with something your chef is already planning on serving. While I'd love for you to order 3,000 Honeycrisps, I'm not going to sell you a product you can't use. It's just not my style. Got a copy of that menu for me?"

I pull open the binder Angela made to the page with Tabitha's menu draft and slide it his way for review. He turns his baseball hat backward for a better view, then hunches over the page and begins studying it.

In the quiet moment, I take this man in. He appears to be not much older than thirty and a Ben Affleck (circa *Armegeddon*) look-alike. After the day I've had chatting with snobby vendors, it's refreshing to share just five minutes with a non-judgy industry professional. I was beginning to think people like Jared did not exist in this world.

"Okay, cool. So if you see here, Allie, your chef has a salad under the 'greens' section with spinach and seasonal fruit, but it doesn't specify *what kind* of fruit. I see no reason why you shouldn't suggest that it be sliced Honeycrisp—at least for the duration of the season. Want me to show you how to put in an order? It's really simple, actually."

"That'd be great," I say. "And don't let me forget, I also need to order a bunch of mackerel after we're done with the apples."

"Okay, well, that's actually not a fruit *or* vegetable. But you're in luck, because I have the number for a great fish guy, too."

Embarrassing as it is to not know my food groups, it's obvious Tabitha was right about Marcel & Sons being the best. This guy is good—and he's being good to me. One vendor down, probably ten more to go.

19

"Hi, you must be Allie?" All six foot three leans toward me to shake my hand. "I'm Andrew."

He runs his left hand through his Superman-like brunette locks and my knees buckle.

"Feel free to take a seat," I say, gesturing to an open chair in our bar.

Because I did such a good job selecting Tabitha, Angela gave me a list of all the roles we needed to fill—three dishwashers, three sous chefs, five busers, two captains and ten servers—so I'm on a hiring spree. But most of the people who have come through have been far less refined than Tab—just a bunch of industry fledglings hoping for a glimpse of the King. And when that doesn't pan out for them, they instead leak grainy iPhone pics of the restaurant on social media. While I know it scores people major cool points to say they've already been to Here, it's the sole reason I've had to confiscate cell phones upon arrival.

I don't, though, with Andrew, my latest interviewee. He's a referral from one of my recent hires, a service captain named Jessica, who will take our most difficult tables, largest parties or diners we need to impress most. She's a twentysomething who came from the now-closed L2O, an iconic, Michelin-starred restaurant in Chicago. It's a good get.

His insane good looks cause me to draw a blank on how to begin. I want to ask him why he isn't a full-time male model, but instead lead with: "Tell me why you want to be our second captain."

My words spill out like tumbling bowling pins.

"First off, I've worked with Jessica and she's incredible. But, I've actually been following *you* in the news and really respect what you've done. I think I could learn a lot from someone who has a different angle on things. I've served at Michelin-starred restaurants and worked for a ton of industry vets, but I've never followed direction from someone young, fresh and with a really great energy like yours."

A good part of his response could just be him blowing smoke up my ass to get the job. But he seems genuine, his eyes are the smoldering kind and I like the way he double-knots his Converse.

I ask him a few more targeted questions and offer him the job. After filling out the paperwork and his requested days off, he offers me his digits.

"I know Benji could probably answer them for you, but if you have any industry questions, I'd love to help where and how I can," Andrew says before leaving.

I fan myself with his paperwork after he goes.

Getting my feet wet at Here has been nothing short of a whirlwind. After two straight weeks of sixteen-hour work-days, I'm only about halfway through Angela's bible, aka the book on how to open Here, which is exactly three weeks away from opening. Granted I've been flipping around to different sections depending on my mood, but it still feels like I haven't even made a dent in everything I need to master before we take our first seating.

Right now, I'm up to basic accounting. The numbers make my eyes gloss over and I hate looking at anything that resembles a bill—call it PTSD from when Benji was living with me, or just difficulty accepting that money that's needed to pay a vendor cuts away at the investment I'm trying to make back.

I've accepted that there will be no days off at this point, or the foreseeable future. So I break up the tasks by looking on Pinterest for centerpiece inspiration. I call this research and development. Aka, the closest thing to a break.

"OMG. Would you just look at this POS?"

"Can't. Busy right now," I reply, gaze fixed on the screen where I'm this close to generating my first schedule after what feels like hours of data entry. "But if it's a piece of shit, might I suggest boxing it up and bringing it to the post office before it closes?"

"POS stands for Point of Sale, Allie. Not Piece of Shit. And this here machine that you didn't bother to watch get installed by a man who looked like Chris Hemsworth just now is the top of the line."

She has me at "Chris Hemsworth."

"Seriously, it doesn't get any better than the YeltonXT. It's a thing of beauty, I tell ya."

Angela is probably the only person on the planet who can get excited about a computer system that allows servers to send orders back to the kitchen. But I get that these machines are an integral part of opening Here and I remember filing an invoice for them last week. The software and the four systems we'll have planted throughout the restaurant—front of restaurant, back of restaurant, back office and bar—cost a cool $18,000. That's enough for me to pause where I'm at on When I Work and give Angela and the YeltonXT my complete attention.

"Isn't she gorgeous?"

"*It's* something else," I say, not as stoked to assign the machine a gender.

"Whoa, Nelly. Is that a YeltonXT?" Tabitha asks as she

walks in, putting her backpack down on the floor next to her desk. She's in houndstooth-print kitchen pants, a black button-down chef's shirt and Dansko clogs. When she's not trying to dress like someone who works at the DMV, she actually looks great. Or at least, the part.

"It sure the hell is," Angela boasts. "Hey, now that the three of us are all here, we need to talk about something."

Angela grabs some papers off her desk and hands us each a copy.

"This came to my inbox this morning," she says of the email that's apparently from an editor at *FoodFeed*. "If you look down at the second paragraph, they want to know why Benji's been so silent on social media. They're onto it. Everyone knows it's not like him to keep his mouth shut about anything, let alone the most buzzed-about restaurant in the city, aka the one he's in theory about to open."

Any excitement I felt from Andrew's uplifting remarks earlier quickly deflates.

"I don't get it. Can't you just hit Reply and say he's missing and we don't know?" Tabitha asks.

Over the past few weeks Angela has given her the abridged version of the life and times of Benji Zane. Tabitha said he sounds like a character in one of her fan-fiction stories. It's so odd to think she never tasted her predecessor's food, hasn't seen his man-bun, wouldn't recognize any of his tattoos and will never fall victim to his intoxicating charm.

While I like Tab's suggestion to just call a thing a thing, it's not that easy. Clearly she has no experience having to lie or cover up someone's tracks so the whole world doesn't simultaneously demand a wellness check on all involved parties— which is a good thing, don't get me wrong. But in this case, we've got to be strategic with how we handle this unwelcome reminder that the chef everyone thinks is at the helm of this opening is nowhere to be found.

I realize then that it's moments like this, when I'm busy cleaning up his dirty laundry, that I forget how sad and mad I am.

Every inch of this restaurant still screams Benji. It's not like he's the one who's picked out the tile or the lighting fixtures. And he's certainly not the brain behind the menu draft. But these four walls that are currently entrapping me stand only because of him. Distractions like never-ending to-do lists, hot servers and fancy software systems that need to be learned only go so far in the way of preventing me from scratching the itch that is wanting Benji to come back and be okay.

"Well, the way I see it we have two choices…one, like you say, Tabitha, is to be honest. We release a very concise, black-and-white, official statement in writing and distribute it to the press on behalf of Here."

"Bad idea," I say, sharply cutting Angela off. "If we give the press an inch, they'll take a mile. They'll have a field day running stories about what may or may not have happened. And since we don't know the truth ourselves, how will we ever be able to wrangle the rumors and set them straight? Social media will just end up blaming me for whatever everyone *thinks* went down now that I'm in and he's out. And when that happens, you can kiss me being the draw goodbye. It'll be a witch hunt after that."

"Well, what other choice do we have besides telling the truth?" Tabitha asks me like I know. I just look to Angela for the light.

"Option two is telling a *version* of the truth. We say, 'He's simply focused on opening Here and maintaining the element of surprise for the individuals who were lucky enough to score opening-night reservations.'"

Hmm. I guess that's not entirely false. I'm sure wherever he is right now, he's got to be somewhat thinking about Here. And, yes, our opening-night patrons *are* going to be in for a treat. "Go with option two," I order.

Tabitha's eyes, magnified by her glasses, teeter back and forth between Angela and me like a cat clock on the wall. I can tell she's lost.

"Copy that. And sorry, Tabitha. She's part owner, I have to go with her direction on this one. But hey, I swear we won't be stuck in the shadow of this douchebag much longer, okay?"

Angela grabs the handouts back from us and puts them through a shredder before queuing up a new email.

Just when I'm about to hit the wall each night, Angela shoves me in her Jetta and we drive to make the last seating at a different fine-dining establishment. I wish it felt as glamorous as it sounds, but it's all just for the sake of research—a crash course in multicourse dining, if you will. It is for this reason that I now keep a change of clothes at Here. At just two weeks until we open, I might not know everything there is to know about this industry, but I can tell the leggings I haven't washed in ten days and a pair of one-dollar Old Navy flip-flops that are flat as a pancake by the heel don't pair well with a crystal glass of Côtes du Rhône full of notes of cherry and oak.

When Angela told Craig that Benji was out, he freaked. Even though she assured him that I was very much still in, he didn't care. In fact, to say he was concerned would be an understatement. He couldn't imagine how I could go from a job that required me to think in bursts of 280 characters or less to successfully running a high-end, high-traffic restaurant.

I can't say I blame him for holding off on sending in his RSVP for the "Allie Simon is the draw" party that Angela swears is happening. Even I'm not so confident in my identity or my abilities now that Benji Zane isn't next to me in every picture that hits the internet concerning the opening of Here.

Even though Angela is far more positive about my potential, she had to side with her ride-or-die, Craig, and validated his fears on the status call she had with him wherein she went into details about Benji's disappearance. Our desks in the back office are just three feet away from each other, so there's no privacy. I wasn't meant to hear the conversation they were having when she downloaded him, but Craig was screaming so loud that it was tough to miss. Angela tried to signal for me to leave, but I was busy inputting Tabitha's entire menu into the YeltonXT and didn't want to lose my place in the system. Moments later, I learned how shitty it feels to be dedicating your whole life and all of its savings to opening a restaurant, and then have the guy who's really in charge not think you can do it.

Before he had a chance to tell us all to get fucked, she magically convinced him that she saw something special in me and that trial by fire would be the only way to bring it out. So, thanks again to her quick thinking, she swindled a hefty $5,000 research budget from him that's meant to be spent by live action role-playing at some of Chicago's best restaurants. All hail Craig and his seemingly never-ending bank account.

"So where are we going tonight?" I ask Angela as I trade my workout pants and hoodie for a navy blue pencil skirt and white button-down shirt. I look more like a generic flight attendant than a sexy industry pro, but these are the cheapest things to send to the dry cleaner each day.

"Paragraph," says Angela as she shuts down her computer. "So you might want to go one button higher on that blouse and throw on some nylons considering you haven't shaved those stems in what I'd guess is two weeks."

Caught.

The average Chicago foodie follows every food truck on Twitter. They are the ones first in line each morning at the Doughnut Vault, cash in hand for a classic vanilla glazed. They've checked in to 487 places on Yelp. And they've all snapped the same photo looking down the center of Restoration Hardware's trendy restaurant concept, the 3 Arts Club Café. But Paragraph is not for your average foodie—although they wish it was.

Paragraph is the number-three restaurant in the nation and seventh across the globe, according to the esteemed World's 50 Best Restaurants awards. The rankings may be based out of New York City, but Chicagoans pay very close attention to this annual list. If Paragraph rises or falls even just one slot, the blogosphere erupts.

Ironically enough, Paragraph isn't in the West Loop on Randolph Street at all. They're actually near my place in Lincoln Park. In fact, I've walked by it a thousand times before dating Benji and had no idea the culinary clout it had. Now when I pass it, I want to shake the shoulders of whoever is near me and ask them if they realize this is one of *the* most famous restaurants in the whole world.

On the rainy drive over, the two of us are unusually silent. The only thing I can attribute it to is nerves. Not about opening our own restaurant in less than two weeks, but about dining at a place so fancy that even Angela doesn't have a hookup to get in.

"Remind me again how we got a reso?" I ask to cut through the quiet.

"I put my name on the list fifteen months ago. The first available table for two was next March. I was counting on going then. But they had a cancellation tonight and I was next on the wait list to call."

"Oh, well, isn't this our lucky night," I say. "Who were you originally going to take?"

"What do you mean?" she asks, upping the speed of her windshield wipers as the rain crushes us.

"You booked a two-top for March before we knew each other. So, who were you planning on going with?"

"That's a good question. I never really thought about it. Maybe I assumed I'd be dating someone by then?"

We never really talk about Angela's personal life, so her answer catches me off guard. I'm not sure what type of guy I picture her with, actually. But that doesn't stop me from throwing out my best guess.

"Someone who would be willing to sit through a sixteen-course prix fixe meal for $175 per person?"

"It's actually $275 with pairings," she corrects.

"Get the fuck out. Well, when you find that guy, do me a favor and see if he has an identical brother for me."

Angela pulls her car to the curb and I dig around for some coins for the meter. Paying for our parking is the least I can do. But before I can scrounge up enough change, a gentleman opens the passenger side door.

"Good evening, madam. Welcome to Paragraph." He grabs my hand to help me out of the car and ejects a giant umbrella for me to step under. Before I do, I look over at Angela and she has her own hot-guy-with-an-umbrella helping her out the driver's side. I'm looking for the sign that says how much the valet costs, but I see nothing. I don't even see a sign on the front of their restaurant to reassure us we're in the right place.

"How much is valet?" I whisper to Angela as we walk through the front doors together.

"Expensive," she replies.

The hostess ushers us up to the second-floor dining room, where she passes us off to another maître d'. That gentleman then walks us to a two-top table located in the far cor-ner, which is actually now back to the front of the restaurant. We are right by the window overlooking the street below. The raindrops look like glitter as they catch the glow of a streetlamp that is eye level with our table.

Whoever canceled this reservation is missing out. Majorly.

"I could use a drink. Do you see a cocktail list anywhere?" I ask Angela.

"It's Paragraph. There are no menus," she says, taking a sip of sparkling water. "And we're not drinking tonight either. I need you paying full attention to everything that happens here. If our captain adjusts his junk, I want you to note it. Study it. Learn from it."

I roll my eyes, but it's probably a good idea not to get to-tally sloshed. I haven't had wine since chugging the Sutter Homes after Benji trashed my bathroom, and I don't know how well I'll be able to hold my liquor. Considering that after this, we are heading back to Here for an all-nighter, I prob-ably shouldn't test it.

Speaking of all-nighters, this'll be my third one in six days. For what it's worth, I'm getting used to pushing two chairs op-posite each other—which equates to the length of my body—and covering myself with a tablecloth meant for a six-top and calling it my bed for the night.

"What about food menus?" I ask. "Are they going to bring any of those out? I'd like to at least peep the design."

"Okay, so here's what's going to happen. Our server is going to approach the table in the next fifteen seconds. They'll ask if you have any allergies and that's all the cooks need to know."

"How do you know it'll be fifteen seconds?"

"Because if you don't address the table in the first forty-five seconds, it's considered extremely minor league."

"Good evening, ladies, and welcome—" dramatic pause

"—to Paragraph. My name is Emmett and our chefs have a fantastic night lined up for you. They have requested, however, for me to find out if there are any allergies or dietary restrictions that we should be aware of."

I have a flashback to the night Benji and I ate at Republic. "Three months sober," he reminded the chef when we were asked that very same question. I remember how proud he was to say that. How proud I was of him. That wasn't even that long ago, was it? I put my hand up to my eye and gently touch my cheek. It's been at least a week since the swelling and discoloration completely subsided but I'm taken back to that moment when it all went wrong. Without that mark on my face anymore, without any communication from him on my phone, it's like Benji never existed at all. The fact that so much has changed in so little time sends a lump of sadness to the back of my throat, making it hard to swallow, hard to concentrate.

Angela must sense that I'm in la-la land, because she answers Emmett's question for the both of us.

"No, sir. No allergies."

"Very well, thank you." Emmett disperses.

Angela dips her fingers into her water glass and then flicks them my way. The few splashes that hit my face snap me out of it.

"FYI, Craig's not spending $500 on the two of us tonight so you can sit here and daydream. Are you focusing or not?"

"Yes, sorry," I say as I blot my face with the softest, most luxurious linen napkin I've ever felt.

"Good. Now, you see that man right there?" Angela asks as she hunches low to the table like she's giving me some secret agent intel. "He's the FOH captain. I want you to watch him all night."

The man is in a tuxedo. He's probably midthirties, black

and extremely polished looking. He doesn't look like he's lost a staring contest in his life, the way that he makes contact with each one of the servers on the floor and directs them using just slight movements—a head turn, a change in eye direction, the extension of his fingers, one digit at a time, despite relaxed arms hanging naturally on the sides of his body.

"What about our server, Emmett?" I ask. "Shouldn't I watch him?"

"No. He may have the most adorable dimples, but he's as good as a robotic arm. The captain is in control of everything. He calls the shots. Watch how he commands the room."

"Isn't this Jessica's job? Andrew's, too?"

"It is. But who's in charge of them?"

"I am."

"There you go, then."

The first course arrives. It's a spoonful of butternut squash soup that has the consistency of cake batter. The spoon is horizontal and balancing on a metal stick. We lick them clean with one swirl of the tongue.

"Damn, that was good," I say.

"It was. But don't pay attention to the food."

"What do you mean? We're at the nicest restaurant in Chicago and I'm not supposed to care what I'm eating?"

"No. Not tonight. This is all about service and back-of-house. In a minute, we're going to get up and find their expeditor. I want you to see how that all works."

"Their expi-what?"

"The expeditor. The expo. Arguably the most important role in a restaurant. Come with me."

We leave our napkins and shimmy out of our seats.

"Normally, this is a no-no, FYI," Angela says. "All members of a dining party should never get up at the same time. It sends a signal to the waitstaff that we're dining-and-dashing."

Finally, a term I know.

"But take a look at what our server is doing now for what it's worth," she says.

I glance back and Emmett is diligently refolding our napkins and pushing in our chairs. Even if we're not there, the people at Paragraph care how the table looks to others. I like it.

Angela and I are standing at the landing on the second floor, looking down into the open kitchen below us. Among the chefs is a man in a suit and his back is to us. He grabs a ticket off their printer, holds it momentarily, then places it in front of him like a tarot card.

"That's the expo right there. That's who you're going to shadow."

"You think *that guy* is going to be cool with me standing in his peripheral taking mental notes as he's trying to do whatever he's doing?"

"Good point. Maybe unbutton two buttons before you go down to see him. Now let's get back to the table."

A few more courses go by and even though I'm not supposed to be paying attention to them, they're fucking delicious. Everything is rich, yet delicate. The amount of care in the flavor is the same for the presentation. A cycle of edible art that I can't help but wish Benji was able to enjoy with me. I know for a fact he's never been to Paragraph—not to stage, not to eat. I thought about trying to get reservations for us had he made it to six months sober, but I guess it doesn't matter now. Not only did he not make it to that milestone, but I have now learned that getting a reservation at Paragraph isn't like calling ahead for a table at the Olive Garden.

"That right there! Do you see that? Do you see what that man just did?"

"He pointed at something?"

"He's not *pointing*, Allie. He's *gesturing*. Big difference. Whenever anyone asks you where something is, you—"

"Walk them there. I already know that. Benji taught me."

"Well, good, that means your relationship had some value, then. But to drill down further, you *only* do the walk if it's a guest. If it's a colleague asking where they can find an extra apron, you open-palm gesture. Bend your thumb to your palm and keep the rest of your fingers erect. Try it."

"Like this?" I try the motion for myself.

"Exactly."

Angela goes on to explain that pointing with one finger is considered rude. That's why it's a full hand motion with an open palm. The open palm represents an open heart. And from there, it's sunbeams and rainbows and gratuities around 20 percent or higher.

"I've got to piss. Where's the bathroom, Allie?"

"I think I saw it over by that server station." I point in that general direction.

"Fail."

She trapped me. I bend my thumb and try it again. "I believe that the bathroom is just over by that server station," I say, *gesturing*.

"Nice. Now if you'll excuse me, I actually do need to pee."

Nice.

That is fast becoming my favorite food industry word. I remember Benji saying it a lot, too. Whether he mastered the perfect plating of a poached egg or I gave him a warm hug first thing in the morning, he'd say, "That's nice." And he'd mean it. I guess when things felt right, they were just *nice*. Ironically, no other words were needed, even from the man of many extremes. Though I haven't adopted it myself—or maybe I just haven't identified a situation where it was worth it to say it yet—when I hear someone else use the word, it's a reminder that something good did exist with a man who's probably nose deep in a pile of white powder right now.

And there it is again, the pit in my stomach. It's really not fair that I am forced to feel every emotion that this situation has to offer while he gets a pass. I suppose I could also choose to numb everything with drugs—I know the exact corner of the city to get some—but that just isn't my style. Call me a masochist, but I guess I prefer to feel the pain.

Even though I don't have an eight ball in my pocket right now, I have something else to distract me: the keys to Here in my purse. Considering I'm not alone very often and there's an endless amount of tasks to tackle concerning the opening, my mind doesn't often get a chance to wander to the point where I feel sorry for myself. Sure, I'm toeing the line right now thinking of Benji, but Angela will be back from the ladies' room before my tear ducts can catch up with my brain.

In that respect, it's a good thing that I'm too busy learning how to void a guest check in the YeltonXT to worry about all the what-ifs with Benji. What if he's been trying to reach me but can't? What if he's been hurt? Like, *seriously* hurt? And mainly, what if he comes back? But as I count down each day as one closer to the opening of Here, it's also a tick in the other direction—one day further from the last time we were together and happy and safe. And now that it's approaching the one-month mark of him being gone, I can probably stop worrying about his return. I think it would actually take a zombie apocalypse to see him walk through the door at this point.

I snap out of my Benji reverie and bring my attention back to Angela as she returns to the table.

"That was a hella nice bathroom," she says. "Now, are you ready to go slut it up for that expo?"

I look down at my cleavage and decide I'm as ready as I'll ever be.

20

"I can't believe you two ate at Paragraph without me," Tabitha says as she buttons up her chef coat for the day.

"Not just *ate*, Tab…we got a private tour of the kitchen," I feel compelled to clarify.

"How the hell did you pull that off?"

"I squeezed my boobs together when I was shadowing the expo."

"Hmm. I guess I'll have to try that next time."

Into the back office barges a more intense than usual Angela.

"Guys, we need to talk."

"What now?" Tabitha and I say in tandem.

"We're scratching FFN," she says.

"Well, that's a bright idea. Said no one ever…" Tabitha replies.

"It's not like that's my preference. But we just don't have the time and we definitely don't have the budget."

"Can we back up a sec?" I ask. "WTF is FFN? These acronyms are killing me."

"Friends & Family Night," Angela clarifies. "It's a soft opening—a chance for us to work out the kinks while we comp the meals for our invitees. You know, the people who won't go straight to Yelp or social media to bitch if their food came out too slow or if their venison was dry."

"Hey, hey, hey." Tabitha steps in. "It's not always about problems with the food, okay? The computer system could freeze up, we could discover an area of congestion on the floor, or one of our servers could no-show and throw the whole night off. Basically, it's a dry run that ensures our actual opening night is not a total shit show for the public."

"Well, then yes, let's do it. Let's absolutely do the Friends & Family thing," I vote.

"You guys, you're not hearing me," Angela says. "I've run the numbers every which way and it's not possible. We grossly underbudgeted the final touches on the kitchen build-out because the proposal Benji submitted…well, let's just say he was probably high when he sent it."

No. Not another thing crucial to the smooth, successful opening of this restaurant gone straight to the dogs because Benji dipped out. Seriously, at what point do we just call the governor and ask him to declare a state of emergency?

"What do you mean? What's missing in the kitchen?" Tabitha asks.

"Take the walk-in cooler for example…we only have sixty-four inches of space to fit it before walls will need to be knocked down. Now I'm finding out that's a very custom size. What he slated as $2,500 is actually going to be closer to six grand."

"Jesus. And you're just realizing that now?" I can feel my tone sharpen. My frustration is getting the best of me.

"Sorry I don't walk around with a tape measure everywhere I go. He was a pro, I thought these recommendations were solid," Angela says.

"Don't you know by now you can't trust a single thing he's ever said or done? Now you've got me worried. What else is just floating around out there that you haven't double-checked for accuracy? This is ridiculous. He was only a part of this team for, like, five total days. You had one job, Angela—to babysit him."

"Actually, I had about 560 jobs, but who's counting."

"This isn't the time for snark," I say, fully aware of the nervous breakdown that's developing from deep within. "It's not a movie premier for a film that's been in editing for two years. We're opening a fucking restaurant for the first time. Tabitha hasn't done this before. I haven't done this before. And you came from a sleepy suburban spot that took all week to generate the business we're slated to do in a single day. We *need* a trial run or this whole thing goes to shit."

Angela's eyes zero in on mine as she takes three steps toward me.

"Tabitha, can we have the room for a moment?"

Tabitha grabs a paperback copy of *Lord of the Rings* from her backpack and scurries out the back door.

"What the hell is your problem, Allie? Why are you being such a bitch about this? Don't you think that if I could snap my fingers and spit out another 20K in comped food and beverage I would? The reality is…we cannot do it. Our doors open in less than two weeks. Do you know how much this whole shebang cost?"

"I'm familiar with the financials, thank you very much," I say back.

"No, you're familiar with the sticker price. Once we drove this thing off the lot, Craig dumped $2 million into making sure this was the most gorgeous restaurant in the entire city— hell, as far as he's concerned, the entire nation. And also, you know, rush charges were about half of that. So if you want to hold this whole deal up until spring because you aren't confident enough we'll make it unless we serve free food to 100-plus people, fine. I'll let you make that call to Craig. And if for some reason he's suffered head trauma and says, 'Sure, why not, let's delay *everything*,' then I'll happily go back to Florette and keep managing my 'sleepy' restaurant where at least I'll still be collecting a paycheck for six more months. You, my dear, not so much. So, love you, but you need to shut your mouth, accept reality and get it together for the grand opening, which is all that really matters anyway."

I look at her and shake my head.

"What? What now? Just say it, Allie."

"It's just...I'm the assistant general manager. On paper, our jobs aren't that different—yours and mine. Yet, for some reason, I have no say in anything. Ever. Unless it has to do with how we break the news about Benji to the media, you've never cared about my opinion. You just steamroll me into whatever you want me to do or say. And I'm tired of it."

"Is that what it's about for you? Control? You're going to have plenty of chances to call the shots once these doors are open. But now's not the time to right-fight with me."

Angela gestures her hands toward herself: "Ten years' experience." Then gestures toward me: "Ten days—ish—experience. Not trying to downplay your contributions or anything, but you need to trust me on stuff. Look, I'm sorry that you didn't get to dictate the fate of you and Benji. But this restaurant isn't your relationship. It's a business. You can't take it out on Here, okay?"

It's been a long time since I've gotten to do what I wanted to do, when I wanted to do it. Whether it was the liberty of having a glass of wine with my dinner, or going out with my friends and not really specifying when I'd be home, or not having to purchase cable or spend my Saturday at an NA picnic, the world has revolved around Benji since the day he came into my life. And all I know right now is I'm obsessed with being the one to drive the boat. Maybe the sheer exhaustion is taking its toll and this is just a false feeling after all. Or maybe I'm—dare I admit it?—starting to get into a groove with this whole restaurant thing and I actually *want* to feel like my opinions are valid or that I have good ideas.

"Can we move on, or do you want to continue to waste time and argue?" Angela asks.

"We can move on," I resolve. Not like I have any real say (again) about whether we continue to sit here and hash it out longer.

"Now do you want to know what would actually be helpful?" she asks. "If this restaurant had plates."

"You've got to be kidding me. Benji fucked us on plates, too?"

"Well, salad plates to be exact."

"Wait, I thought those were ordered weeks ago. I know I processed an invoice for them."

"They were, but I just got an email saying the ones we picked out are on back order and not due in stock for at least three months. So they refunded us—you'll see it hit the P&L in a couple of days."

"Alright, well, what do we do now?" I ask.

"*We* aren't going to do anything. *You* are going to take these, though." From her purse, she hands me the keys to her Jetta and an American Express Black Card. It's metal. It's Craig's.

"You're an authorized signer now, so just show your ID when they run the card, but try to stay under a thousand dollars. Okay?"

The weight of the credit card in my hand gives me pause.

"So, just to clarify: you're asking me to go pick plates out... by myself?"

"What's the big deal, Al? It's just one plate that you're going to get a hundred of. Choose a design that you like—they don't have to match the main course plates, they just need to be white—and then come back with a full order. Remem-

ber, they've got to all be the exact same—no rinky-dink garage sales, okay?"

"And what are you doing right now, might I ask?" I'm not
trying to show any hesitation about my newfound freedom,
but I am curious how this seemingly large responsibility has
fallen into my lap and why she's not needling me to death
about specifics (has to be this, can't be that, make sure it's got
this, but not that, etc.).

"Tabitha's got me all worried our floor plan is jacked now.
I need to focus on the layout and figure out if any areas are
going to be a server's nightmare once our dining room is full.
Send her back in when you go out, would you?"

Angela sits back down at her desk and opens up a document with the floor plan. She proceeds to drag and drop the
tables like chess pieces on the screen. It's impressive how she's
always able to revert back to business-as-usual no matter how
high I let my freak flag fly.

As I climb into her Jetta, it hits me. I don't know where to
go to complete this task. Restaurant Depot? Bloomingdale's?
Goodwill? But the thought that I get to choose my own ad-
venture is more exciting than the fear I feel about potentially
getting it wrong.

"Good news, Angela," I say as I trot in through the back
door. "I got plates!"

Six inches in diameter and a perfect circle—this Crate &
Barrel find features no fancy geometric angles or weird cuts.
In fact, just the opposite. Simple, like the plate you'd microwave a meal on. And the best part? I came in a whopping 48
cents below my $1,000 budget.

"Yeah, and you got McDonald's, too, apparently. What the
hell, Allie? No text to see what I wanted?"

"Don't you want to see the plates? They're so cool, they're like—"

"Don't you know that every Saturday at noon I sneak out and shame-eat a Happy Meal in my car?"

"Not really. But I guess I noticed a few wrappers on the floor of the front seat, now that you mention it."

"*Please* tell me you didn't go to the one on Ogden and Lake."

"Yeah, I did. It was on the way back. Why are we still talking about McDonald's?"

"You're killing me, Al. Because they always give me an extra toy at that location."

"You're thirty-eight years old, right?"

"Ugh. Never mind. Just go find Hector and ask him for help carrying the plates to the kitchen, will you?"

It's late in the afternoon when my mom shoots me a text. I haven't talked to her in a few days and seeing her name pop up on my screen is a welcome distraction from my current task: stocking the ladies' room with tampons.

Hey Allie Boo. I'm downtown for an art fair. Can I tell cab driver 2 drop me @ Here and say hi?

Let's be honest. I haven't taken anything close to a break in the last three weeks, short of stopping for a greasy burger and fries a few hours ago, and I doubt Angela will harass me about slacking in the presence of my own mother. If anything, it'll allow me five minutes to breathe.

Sure. Tell him 900 W Randolph.

A few minutes later, there's a cute, Sally Field look-alike knocking on the window of our storefront. What used to be a retractable garage door is now a single panel of glass, completely frosted except for the word *Here*, which is reverse-etched into the pane.

I unlock our front door, invite her in and shut it behind me. I can feel a burst of crisp, early October air come through the foyer. This is why Angela had heated coils installed under the tile.

"Wow, would you look at this?" Mom says, eyes wide like she's admiring the ceiling of the Sistine Chapel. "It's incredible!"

"Thanks," I say. "It's not quite done yet, but we're getting there. Take a seat." I pull out one of the stools at the bar and gesture for her to make herself comfortable. "Do you want me to take your coat?"

"No, that's alright. I'll keep it on the chair."

"Allie!" I hear Tabitha's thunderous voice coming toward me from the back office. "I need one of those tampons! Stat! I'm having a her-mergency!"

She emerges into the bar and I greet her with a silent smile.

"Oh. Hi. I'm Tabitha Johnson, chef de cuisine. Are you from the *Trib*?"

"No, Tab, this is my mom. Patty Simon."

"Oh, how lovely! How do you do, Mrs. Simon? Hey, are you hungry? I'm working on a new amuse-bouche concept and I want you guys to try it."

"She can't," I say. "She's going to an art show."

"Well, actually..." My mom shimmies the sleeve of her shirt back just enough for her to study her watch. "I have about forty-five minutes until I need to meet my friend at the Merchandise Mart."

"Perfect!" says Tabitha with the clap of her hands. "Hang right here and I'll bring something out in a few minutes. And, Allie?"

"Yeah?"

"Feminine products?"

"Spread out on the floor of the ladies' room. Don't tell Angela. I'm still working on it."

Tabitha scampers off to the bathroom, leaving just my mom and me in the chilly bar area. At least what's left of the sun for the day is still seeping through the front windows, which gives it a cozy feel.

"How's it been going?" my mom asks. She takes the liberty of flattening out some flyaways from my jagged part as she waits for me to speak.

"It's pretty nonstop," I say, figuring that's the most politically correct answer. "But I'm starting to get the hang of things."

"That's good. Any word from Benji?"

I shake my head and let out an audible sigh.

"I still think he's out there, Mom."

"I'm sure he is, sweetie." I want her to say more, offer more comfort, but I also realize she isn't entirely picking up what I'm throwing down. So I clarify.

"I miss him."

It's a tough thing to utter. Especially to my mom. There's probably not another person in the world she'd rather see me hung up on less than the guy who left her daughter broke, scared and alone. But she's loved an addict inexplicably before— her own brother. So I have to believe she'll greet my confession with a certain amount of compassion and understanding.

"I get it. But I don't think it's him you miss. He's not a good person, Allie. He's not well."

"Then why do I feel this way inside? Like I just cannot move on from him."

"Because you miss the good times you had with him. And the special way he made you feel. Those are tough losses because they're things you can't repeat with any other person. But you've got to leave room in there." She points at my heart. "For someone else to do their thing. Trust me on that, okay?"

"Alright, ladies." Tabitha comes back with two plates, each with three amuse-bouches. "Let me know what you think. Right here we have prawns grilled in sesame oil, avocado, mango, red chilis and lime juice. Then, there's a portobello oven-roasted, filled with ricotta, crushed garlic, chives, pine nuts, drizzled with premium extra virgin olive oil. And finally, this is a simple date filled with fresh gorgonzola and wrapped in prosciutto, drizzled with a balsamic vinegar reduction."

"You made these?" my mom asks, genuinely impressed. "These are so beautiful. So elegant. Are you sure I'm supposed to eat them?"

"Eat and critique!" Tabitha chimes. "I need help deciding which is going to be our go-to amuse on opening night. Take your time. Bon appetit!"

She scurries off as I come around the bar and proceed to fill two tumblers with ice and water. I peer over the bar and look at the plates. They are gorgeous. No matter which one she ends up selecting for opening night, our diners are in for a major treat. There are no wimpy flavor mousses, over-the-top essences or self-indulgent gastronomical touches here. Just extremely elevated dining. I can't help but note the glaring differences between Tabitha's style and Benji's.

By the time I place the cup of water in front of my mom, she has already taken her first few bites. Her eyes are closed and she's smiling as she chews. I know she's my mom, and she *has* to like Here, but I genuinely believe in this moment, she's enjoying herself independently of her connection to the restaurant. If this is the hospitality privilege that Angela says we get just by being in this business, well, then, I'll take it.

21

"You know what you need to do, right?" Angela asks, catching a glimpse of the complex spreadsheet open on my computer as she throws away her McDonald's detritus.

It's 10:00 p.m. and there are just two days left until our grand opening. Tabitha is in the kitchen organizing the shelves on her new walk-in cooler, Angela is chowing on a Happy Meal even though it's Wednesday, and I'm dunking her leftover fries into a cup of sweet 'n' sour sauce from yesterday's Chinese takeout in the back office. Suffice it to say, the three of us are extremely sleep-deprived and more down to the grind than ever.

"Yup, I think so. I have the vendor list in Column A, all the quantities in B and their payment terms here. Did you know our first liquor order has to be paid up front in all cash? Like, what is this, the fucking prohibition era? We have to smuggle it in with no paper trail?"

"Yes, Allie. That's standard."

"It is? Here I thought you'd get all hot and bothered about that."

"Don't worry, there'll be plenty of other opportunities to spike my blood pressure. Like if you wait one more second to press Send on this order."

"Don't you want to look it over?" I ask sheepishly.

"I don't have time to do the things I've asked you to do. Especially not after you've already done them. You're in charge of making sure that thing is right…not me. And, seriously, if

our produce guy doesn't get the memo in the next five minutes that we need twenty-five rutabagas delivered to that alley
in the next seven hours, we'll be serving chips and dip until
the angry mob shuts us down. So hop to it, Al-gal."

I spin my chair around to put the finishing touches on my
order forms and submit the first complete produce order for
Here. Next up, fish. Then meat, then dairy, then almost done.
Angela says once we get going, we'll eventually hire a bar director who'll take care of all things booze, but for now, I'll
order the alcohol—and get the cash ready—too.

Speaking of handling things, we hired an intern for social
media ("You're going to be way too busy to be live-tweeting
someone's foie gras, so don't even think about it," Angela had
said). It's a bit of a bummer that the one thing I know how to
do, and love doing, I won't be touching at all. But I see her
point. I've been too busy myself to scan social media anyway.

Also, I need to focus on floor managing. It's something we're
both set to tag-team once the restaurant is actually open but I've
had no practice in front of patrons since the last time I helped
at Benji's North Side pop-up. I'm sure that once bodies are in
the building, I'll pick up where I left off—big smile, question-
able wardrobe choices and all.

For as twisted as this all is, I actually feel for the first time
in forty-three days like I got it all—except for sleep, that is.

When I go to log in to our fish vendor's online ordering
portal I see a message come through the Here email account
from Benji's sous chef, Sebastian.

Hey Allie, this is super awkward I'm sure, the message starts
off. But I couldn't figure out how to reach you. I tried stopping
by your apartment last week to see if we could talk but your
doorman said you weren't picking up and probably weren't
home. Anyway, I looked up the Here website and found this
email address. I'm sure you and Benji are just super busy with

Here (congrats, BTW), but wondering if you know what's up with him? I helped him with his pop-ups last month and he was really mean to me. Worse than he normally is LOL. I walked off the middle of service on the second to last night and I haven't heard from him since. I fucked up. I shouldn't have left him like that, especially when he promised me I'd be his head sous at Here. I've tried to call him and apologize, but either his phone is off or he's just flat out ignoring me. If that's the case, could you tell him to call me? Tell him I'm sorry? Again, I hate to bother you. I'm just worried and kicking myself for throwing away the opportunity to work at Here.

I've been wondering when the rest of the world would catch on to the fact that their favorite hot mess was missing in action. Still, this message catches me off guard. Benji promised Sebastian a job at Here? Now that I've gone through my fair share of hiring, I can honestly say…that's not how this works. You don't just pinky promise you'll give someone a job at this level. Poor guy. And screw Benji and the effect he has on people wherein *he* can totally fuck up yet everyone else finds a way to blame themselves.

I ponder writing Sebastian back just for the sole purpose of telling him to grow a pair. To tell him to stop thinking it's his fault that Benji's not calling him back. But then I'd have to go into the real reason why he can't reach him, and also the fact he's not getting the sous job at Here.

There's another reason—a bigger, more important reason—I can't write anything like that back, though. Because whatever I say, even if I keep it vague, it could potentially blow the cover on what Angela has worked so hard to protect: the integrity of Here.

Plus, how concerned *is* he really? Enough to look up our website and send a single email? Please. I'm hardly impressed with the extent he's gone to try to piece this Benji puzzle together. But if I say nothing at all, and he adds my silence to Benji's, would that be enough for him to take his concern to another level? Would he call the police? Report a missing person? Put out a conflicting statement to *FoodFeed* and insist they demand proof of life pictures of Benji from myself and Angela? No. I don't think he cares that much, sadly.

I toggle over to our email settings, copy and paste Sebastian's email address and hit Block Sender.

"Are you sure?" a pop-up box reads.

I click yes and delete his email for good.

Two hours later, I'm finally done putting all the orders in. Everything is due to arrive tomorrow; truckloads of produce and proteins and pantry items all throughout the day. It seems like too much, but Angela and Tabitha assure me we'll move it all. Their confidence might stem from the fact that the press still hasn't been notified of Benji's "exit," an evasive maneuver Angela says she's employing on purpose.

"Trust me, we wait to announce this until tomorrow, a day before, and we use the pandemonium to our advantage. People are going to want to see how we recover from getting 'Benjied.' They're going to want to see who's filling his shoes."

"Don't take offense to this," I say, cognizant that Tabitha is three feet away from me. "But who's going to go give a shit when they find out it's *her*?"

Tabitha throws her hands up and rolls her eyes.

"Because, Allie, one bite of Tabitha's truffle ravioli and it's game over. It doesn't matter if she's not well-known now, she will be in about forty-eight hours. At the end of the day, if what people put in their mouths is good, then the name at the bottom of that menu will go viral. As far as I'm concerned, Bib Gourmand, James Beard, Michelin Man, here we come— with or without Benji Zane."

"I guess I'm just worried that we're going to get creamed by bitchy comments from a bunch of told-you-so haters." I can hear the hint of fear in my voice. "You know, like it's our own fault we hired a cokehead to run the line."

As the words come out of my mouth, I realize a paradigm shift has taken place. I don't know exactly when or why, but I catch myself saying "our" and "we," which means I'm officially lumping myself into this whole Here thing. Just a month and a half ago, I couldn't put a big enough wedge between me and *this place*. But now, whether it's success or failure I'm worrying about, the bottom line is it's ours.

"Two weeks ago I was about to order a fridge that wouldn't have fit in the kitchen and you're worrying about some internet trolls? Got news for you. We're for sure going to get those. So make sure you come into work with your big girl panties on tomorrow."

"Lovely," I say as I literally add the task to my iCal.

"Trust me, those are the same people who will be first in line to see how we clean up the mess. Hey, speaking of mess, how's your apartment post-Benji?"

Ahh...my apartment. My long-lost love. I haven't been back to my studio for longer than it takes me to shower, do a load of laundry and clean out my mailbox every few days. In all honesty, I should probably list the thing on Airbnb so someone else can pay my rent, but god forbid whoever stays in the place stumbles upon the mother lode of Benji's addiction I've yet to find. Or worse, they stumble upon him coming back to pick up his precious knife set.

So, yeah. Sleeping at the restaurant is terrible. But it beats being home alone in the official headquarters of what used to be.

Right after I surmised Benji wasn't coming back, about the same time I started sleeping regularly at Here, I was having these intense flashbacks to the *P.S. I Love You* night. It was the simplest moment of my entire life, despite how we arrived at it, and I was genuinely happy. And even though we're light-years away from that now, a temptation still exists to hold on for some hope that maybe one day, that moment could be replicated again.

Hope is the only thing that makes me feel good inside, that gives me just a little bit of a tingle. I think: if he hit rock bottom before and we were able to find smooth air, is it really that far-fetched that at some point in the distant future, we could have it all again? That he could come back and we could be even stronger than we were before? That the fantasy with the brownstone and the kids and the dog could still come true?

And if it did, would that mean I was the dumbest girl alive? Or the luckiest?

I could think about this all day, which takes away brainpower that needs to be dumped into Here if we're going to open with any trace of success. So the only way to prevent myself from going down the Benji rabbit hole is literally surrounding myself with Here—day in and day out. Which is why I've been sleeping in the restaurant for the last two weeks.

"It's fine, I guess. I haven't done a deep clean or anything, but I'll deal with that later."

"Why don't you deal with it now?"

"Because I'm in this prison cell. With you two. Come on, what's next in the book? I'm sure if you flip to page 93 there will be *something* I need to do—separate all the to-go lids from the containers in the storage closet…iron the tablecloths…run background checks on all the servers…"

"You haven't done that?" Angela's ears perk up.

"Please, of course I have. Everyone's kosher except one of the bartenders got a DUI in 2010 but I figured it gave him some credentials. I mean, the man knows his liquor apparently."

"Your perspective on things never ceases to amaze me," says Angela. "I think we're good for now. Tabitha, do you agree?"

"You put the delivery orders in, right?"

"Yeah, every last one. Triple-checked them, too."

"Well, then, knock on wood, but I think you can call it a day," Tabitha says as she pounds a fist on the top of her desk.

"Wait. Are you two fucking with me? Is this a joke? Am I going to go to leave and trip over some clear fishing line or something?"

"I was looking at the list of opening duties earlier and it appears we're caught up," Angela says.

"I guess that's what twenty-hour workdays will do," I say smugly.

"What's that I hear? Our first labor-law complaint?" she mimics back. "What time's our first delivery, Al?"

"Seven a.m."

"Great. Be here at six."

22

Quincy helps me out of the cab and holds open the door. "Miss Simon, I haven't seen you for a while. How have you been?"

I think he means to ask *where* have I been, but either way, it feels like I just came back from a ten-month stint in Iraq and boy, is it good to be home.

"I've been...busy. Really busy," I tell him as we walk into the lobby together. "I'm not sure if you knew, but I'm opening a restaurant called Here on Randolph Street in a couple days."

I notice that this is the first time I've been able to utter those words without having a nervous breakdown. There's an odd sprout of pride blooming deep in my chest, and talking about Here without any trace of panic feels like I'm pouring water into the soil beneath it.

"Randolph Street? Talk about the high-rent district! That's way too fancy for me, but congratulations to you."

Too fancy for you? I just overdrew my bank account by rolling up in that Uber just now, I want to say. But instead I smile and shrug, like I, too, am marveling at my new upscale status.

"I know, right? Well, wish me luck."

"Good luck, my dear. I'll tell everyone in the building to go to your spot for dinner. Great to see you, Allie," he says, buzzing me in from behind his post.

"Oh, hey, Q, one more thing." I double back to his desk and keep it vague. "No one has come looking for me, right?"

"No one that I know of," he says slowly with big eyes. I can tell he knows where I'm going with this.

"Alright," I begin, not fully believing it has come to this.

"Can you take Benji Zane off my list of approved guests? He doesn't have keys to the unit anymore, but he may try to come in through the parking garage, so could you keep an eye on those cameras for me?"

There, I said it. And of all the things I've been feeling lately—hope, false hope, despair, anxiety, etc.—a new one comes over me, just for a moment: relief.

"I will update your chart right now and let my team know. But between you and me," he whispers, leaning in close. "That fucker ain't coming by on my watch without a serious ass beating."

"I appreciate that," I say, and I do.

Once back up in my apartment, I inhale deeply, lock the door behind me and slide to the floor, where I collapse and sit. I know it's dirty, I know there's Sharpie marker still on the mirror (let's be honest, nail polish remover is not a legitimate cleaning hack), but the incubation period is over, I can tell. It's mine again and it feels good to be home.

Ding.

Why does Angela cut me to go home and relax when she just ends up sending me red flag emails twenty minutes later? That woman will be the death of me, I swear.

As I open my mail app, I'm surprised to find the message is not from her. It's from Hal Huckby, possibly the second most notorious druggie chef in the Midwest...behind my most recent roommate. He's been sober for just over two years, though, and celebrated the milestone by closing his restaurant for a week and taking his whole staff to Disneyland. *FoodFeed* covered it, which is how I learned about his checkered past and celebrated recovery. As soon as I read the articles on him, I figured Hal would be a great industry mentor for Benji, but surprisingly Benji wasn't as excited as I was about him and we never even made it into his restaurant. Which leads me to my next question: How did Hal get my email address?

Dear Allie,

Forgive the shitty grammar. I'm typing on an iPhone after 10 hours on the line. Big fingers, tired brain. You get the point. Also, forgive the random email. I know we don't know each other personally, but we know of each other and I'm in one of those "what the hell?" moods right now. Two years ago, that'd mean I'd go get a hooker and some blow. My, how times have changed!

So, you're the chick dating Benji Zane, eh? I wish I could say it takes a special girl to do that, but I know guys like Benji. And the girls they pick to be with, they aren't special. Stupid maybe. But not special.

I'm not trying to offend you. I'm just so fucking angry and confused as to how no one seems to get that he's a sad sack of shit. I've gotten high with him before on the north side (and south side, west side, etc.). You're not the first girl he's gotten to buy in on his crazy antics and you won't be the last.

Like I said, I'm not trying to offend you. I'm trying to help you. I've seen all the buzz about Here. I know you're part in it—or, I should say, your wallet's part in it. And if you give a flying fuck about that restaurant being even remotely suc- cessful or staying open longer than three weeks, break up with Benji and get his ass out of the kitchen. Keep him as far away from that place as you can. Okay? That kid's not sober, no matter what FoodFeed has to say. Unless he's got a clean mind and an honest heart, you're just a pawn and a flavor of the week at best.

If you've made it this far in my email, then what's it hurt to throw one more thing out there? The answer to "why do I care?" All I can say is I had an Allie Simon in my life once. She's the only one who won't accept my apology (that's some cathartic program shit in case you didn't know). It kills me every day that

I don't and won't have closure with her. So I selfishly decided the next best thing was to help save you.

Look out for yourself.
HH

I used to get kudos from everyone about my relationship status. From my coworkers to random strangers to glimpses even from my own mother and father—*everyone* was at least a little jealous of the guy I landed and what he could do with a sauté pan. Then I get this email from Hal-freaking-Huckby. A washed-up fortysomething chef with skin that looks like a broken-in saddle. This guy, short of calling me a chef-chasing ditz, calls it like it fucking is in an unprovoked, foulmouthed email. And somehow, I'm not offended. I'm enlightened.

There's a very good chance I'm too tired to care anymore. That I don't have the energy to find the words to fight back and defend myself and the relationship I very purposefully chose to have with Benji. But there's also a chance that I'm just really grateful to finally be understood by someone who has half a clue what it's like going through what I'm going through because years ago, he was the perp. He was the manipulative little bastard who worked his way through some girl's heart and her savings account because he could put the perfect med-rare sear on a steak, every time.

I reread Hal's email a few times. Dusting away some of the f-bombs, I see a correspondence laced with good intentions. I don't necessarily agree with his observation that I was one air valve away from being a blow-up doll that dispensed cash to Benji. There was merit in the way Benji held me. There was real care in the way he made my lunches. I believe when he said things about me were "nice," that he meant it.

But I do appreciate Hal's observation that when it comes to very expensive, very breakable things, Benji should be a lot further than an arm's length away. Rita called it first. I saw it second. And now Hal is a third, and an expert, opinion. Benji's not sober. And he's an asshole for trying to fool me by distracting me with a big, shiny investment and a tattoo that promised me a future.

So now what? I've been teetering this whole time, going back and forth between despising him for what he's done to fantasizing about the day somewhere in the future that this is all just a distant memory and my last name legally begins with a Z. It sucks because when I think of my past, it's him. When I think of my future, it's him. And when I think of the here and now (or, more appropriately, the Here and now), I see nothing. Because he's left me with nothing.

Until now. Until this note. It's the hard-hitting shake of the shoulders I needed to see something: clarity. And any other person trying to deliver this message to me would have failed. That, I know.

Up until now, I could never cut the cord. The distance and silence from Benji has been helpful, but in the back of my mind there's always remained the whisperings of "I miss him" echoing in my head.

But now I'm thinking that missing him wasn't quite it. If anything, that empty ache was just a symptom of withdrawal. It's been hard to come off the high of being the woman behind the man, no matter how mad he was. And it was more than that, too. It was the lust and sex and danger and difference and *other* about him that got me hooked.

But now, I see it. I'm not part of the cycle anymore. I'm not in his rotation, and more importantly, he's not in mine.

How do I repay someone I don't even know for helping me find closure in the oddest of ways in the latest of hours? By hitting Reply, and typing two words back:

Apology accepted.

23

Two hours of sleep isn't enough for me to function this morning, but that's what I get for deciding it would be a good idea to binge-watch one of my old favorites: *The Real Housewives of Orange County.*

My tiredness is enough to convince me to try drinking coffee. Plus, a $3,000 coffee maker was delivered to the restaurant yesterday and I figure I should take it for a test-drive. I have no idea what I'm doing but I press a few buttons, hold a mug under the spout and four seconds later a "vanilla latte" comes out. Okay, then.

"Miss Allie?" Hector taps me on the shoulder as I just take a seat at my desk. "The first delivery is here."

I check the time on my screen: 6:55 a.m. At least he's on time.

We walk back to the rear entrance and I step outside. The sun is just barely coming up and the air has a hint of fall crispness to it.

"Morning! Is this an okay spot to park and unload the truck for a few?"

The truck driver's guess is as good as mine, but I know better than to run in and check with Angela this late in the game. So I offer what's becoming my signature shrug and do a quick once-over for any pesky parking police. Before I know it, our delivery guy maneuvers his white box truck into the narrow entryway of our alley, hops out and unhitches the latch on the rear door.

He comes back into frame with a dolly full of boxes and I ask, all business, "How long do you think you'll be?"

"No 'hi, how are you, good morning, nice to see you again'? I see how it is." He winks at me and keeps on walking. "Fifteen minutes, Allie."

Nice to see you *again*? It's too early to rack my brain so I just cut to the chase.

"Have I met you before?"

The man skips no beats as he begins unloading boxes to our back kitchen. Hector is there to receive and put away in the walk-ins.

"Seriously? How quickly you forget our apple tasting. Have you found a better Honeycrisp? Never mind. Don't even answer that. It's impossible."

Oh. It's Jared. The really nice vendor with the good garlic that Tabitha loves. And yes, he came by with some apples, but no—no, I don't remember him having cheekbones I'm fairly certain can be seen from outer space.

It might be the caffeine kicking in, but I'm totally checking out our produce guy.

"Right. Hi. Sorry for spacing—these last few weeks have been a total blur and I'm not firing on all cylinders yet this morning," I say.

"No worries."

God, he's nice.

"Hey, Jared, the sign right there says we can only load for *ten* minutes with our flashers on."

"You think anyone is going to tell the pretty girl with the coffee she's got to move the truck that's in front of her restaurant? No way."

I look around expecting to find a polished Angela lurking somewhere nearby, but realize quickly I'm the only one here. I'm wearing ripped jeans and a sweatshirt with a bleach stain on it. My signature messy bun with a ballpoint pen is toppled on the crown of my head and my glasses have a smudge of butter on the right lens. No way could *I* be the "pretty girl." Clearly, he is blowing smoke up my ass so I'll tip him extra. Regardless, the sudden flattery makes my early wake-up call not seem as horrifying anymore.

"Do we need to hit a reset button this morning?" he asks, stretching out a hand to shake. "Jared Marcel, produce guy."

"Allie Simon, assistant general manager. And...owner, too, I guess."

"And *owner*? Well, you conveniently left that little tidbit out over apples. Congratulations."

He tips his beat-up baseball hat my direction, then hops back in the truck. He looks like he's stepped off the set of a Chevy commercial. Rugged and handsome. Where has Chicago been hiding all the men like him?

"Bring that dolly over here, would ya?" he shouts from inside the back of his truck.

I set my coffee down on the curb and wheel it over. Jared shuffles around some boxes and keeps on chatting.

"Manager, owner and cutest girl on my Randolph Street delivery route. You know what they call that? A triple threat!"

I can't believe how chipper he is as I try to match his energy without letting on that I'm taking all these compliments with a grain of salt. Imported pink Himalayan salt, but salt nonetheless.

"Here's the dolly. What would you like me to do?" I ask.

"These twenty-five boxes. Your walk-in cooler. I'll stack. You roll. Hector puts away. Think you can handle it?"

Wheeling ten-pound boxes a total of seven feet from the back of his truck to our doorway is so minor on the scale of "shit I've been asked to handle" in the past month, it's almost laughable. But it's nice to know that despite surviving a breakup with a drug addict, securing a restaurant deal in the most lucrative part of Chicago, quitting my day job and learning a new industry in practically no time at all, I still look like a damsel in distress. To Jared, I'm just a normal twenty-five-year-old with likely aversions to manual labor and getting up before ten.

"I can handle it," I assure him.

Fifteen minutes later, our first walk-in cooler is almost entirely stocked with produce. Next up is dairy, followed by meat, then fish. This is going to be a long morning of processing inventory, but at least I'm getting a workout.

"Alright. That's it, Miss Simon," Jared says, double-checking the back of his truck to make sure we aren't missing anything. He returns moments later with his clipboard.

"Signature here, here and here." He points.

I pull the pen out of my hair and begin signing.

"Have I mentioned that I like when the women in my life are prepared?" he remarks. "It's always the guy that's supposed to have the pen. I'm sick of it."

His roll-with-it sense of humor is distracting me from the ability to simply sign my name on a dotted line, but it's in this moment that I really look at Jared for the first time. With endearing smile lines and day-old scruff, there's something very rom-com about him. I don't mind it. I don't mind him.

I hand him back his clipboard. "Anything else?"

"Just your cell phone number here." He hands me his iPhone from his back pocket and I don't move.

"What? You have mine. I need yours. For business purposes," he says, urging me to input some digits. "You know, in case we get in some really nice mackerel that you absolutely have to have."

"Jerk."

"Kidding. Kidding," he says.

Early hour be damned; Jared is straight-up charming…and he's scheming. He knows full well my phone number is on the purchase order I submitted, but apparently he wants it a little more accessible. For "business purposes."

If this is the shtick he puts on for all the girls receiving deliveries on restaurant row, it's no wonder he is one wildly busy produce man that all the ladies, including butch lesbians, seem to love. Little does he know, he can smile through those boy-next-door brown eyes until the sun rises and sets, but Benji taught me well that any man trying this hard to make me feel good about myself wants something in return.

For now what Jared can have is my signature and, perhaps against my better judgment, my cell number. I give him back his paperwork and phone, and extend my hand for a farewell shake that I hope reads "strictly professional."

"Good luck with the opening," he says. His hand in mine is warm and rough. "I'll see you on Tuesday—same time, same alley, *Allie*."

"Can everybody please sit down?"

It's time for our first-ever staff meeting, led, of course, by Angela. I sit at one of the two-top tables with Tabitha. She slides the final version of our menu over the tablecloth toward me.

"What do you think?" she asks.

Here it is in the flesh, literally hot off the press. The single column of elegant text is printed on thick, manila card stock. Starters. Mains. Sides. I try to bend the card a bit to test the give; there isn't much. *Here* is embossed in gold at the top in a humble serif font. I run my finger over the word to feel the imprint.

I think we really threw down on these.

"Seriously, guys, today," Angela snaps, her voice commanding attention. "If sitting is too much to ask, then how about you find a place to put your body and not eye-fuck the person next to you for fifteen minutes? I know you're all attractive, young and just meeting each other for the first time, but this isn't speed dating. Exchange numbers *after* the dry run."

Angela is right. We are surrounded by gorgeous twenty-somethings. When they're all together, it looks as if I pulled our entire service staff from the ranks of a J.Crew catalog. I swear I did not do this on purpose.

Looking at them all in uniform—the girls in black pencil skirts, the men in black slacks, both with button-down, white, short-sleeve shirts—they look professional but sexy, like not-so-distant but much poorer relatives of Christian Grey. At first, I wasn't sure about the uniform selection, especially for the girls. But the final step in each server interview was to vote on the preferred outfit. By far, the ladies opted for the formfitting skirts (something about it helping generate tips) and the short-sleeve button-downs were the clear winner for both genders. Buttons down the front mean business, but it's a party down the sleeves considering that 90 percent of our staff has ink on their arms. As for shoes, all-black and at least a half-inch heel. When I made that regulation, I meant it as a way to encourage staffers to go with Danskos, the end-all, be-all shoes for professionals on their feet for longer than eight hours at a time. But that dress code was interpreted as clunky Nike Air Jordans for the guys and three-inch wedges for the girls. Kids these days, I swear.

Regardless, as they line up I realize they're mine—my village, my congregation. I *employ* these people. It's all too much.

Speaking of too much, I'm starting to wonder what specifically my $30,000 investment has gone toward. For instance, did I buy the fancy menus? The reclaimed 1885 barn wood in the foyer? The nine-inch bone china soup bowls at

$200 a pop that we only bring out to VIPs? Yes, of course, I know my money is mixed with Craig's and we're all in this together. But looking at this pristine restaurant piece by piece begs the question: how far does $30,000 really go in a place like Here where, at the end of the day, it's quite evident no expense was spared?

"A guest sits down and you find out what three things in the first thirty seconds? Anyone?" Angela asks, pacing the floor like she's giving a college lecture in her most sleek wrap dress yet.

"Booze. Time. Water," says our lead server, Jessica. All eyes zip to the tenacious blonde toward the back of the room. I can cut the jealousy with one of our hammered butter knives.

"Excellent, that's correct," Angela says. "First, you find out what they're drinking—whiskey, wine, one of the cocktails. Remember: you want to push them into something over twelve dollars if you can. If you think that's highway robbery now, you won't when you realize what ordering four of those expensive cocktails will do for your tip count at the end of the night. Then find out if they have anywhere to be after dinner. There are approximately five theatres just over that river—people are going to come here before a show and make a night of it. If they need to be out in an hour because that's when *Book of Mormon* starts, the kitchen needs to know so we can speed it up and turn the table. And finally, yes, we have tap water. But 'sparkling or still?' is the question to lead with. Our water bill is mammoth. Do your part to push bottled or we'll be losing money refilling pitchers all night. Moving on. What do you do when you see lipstick prints on a guest's glass building up throughout the night?"

"Swoop and swap," shouts Andrew, our other lead server. Not surprisingly, every girl in here just fell in love with his tall, dark, handsomeness.

"Folks, are we leaving it to the service captains to answer *all* the questions? Very good, Andrew. But let's try to hear from someone else with this next question..."

After a whirlwind review of several more points of service, Angela is satisfied. And so am I. Because even though I'm overwhelmed by the surfeit of information that seems so second nature to her and all the beautiful people, Craig's R&D budget is paying off. I'm answering her questions in my head and nailing most of them.

"Alright. Looks like you guys know your shit. As your general manager, I'm proud. I know training these last two weeks has been brutal. Memorizing every ingredient in every dish isn't fun, but it will be worth it. Any last questions?"

"I have one," says a redhead I barely remember hiring.

"Shoot," Angela tells her.

"On the bottom of the menu, it says the head chef is Tabitha Johnson. Soooo...what the hell happened to Benji Zane?"

A few muffled *yeah*s echo throughout the room. I have no clue how Angela plans to play this, but I pray to god it doesn't incite a mass exodus.

"Okay, relax, relax, relax, everyone. This restaurant is about good people. Good food. A good time. A good atmosphere. When people think about Here, they're going to have a picture in their head about what the experience of having dinner with us is like. And when they come back, or when they refer a friend, they're going to expect that experience is replicated. We are about consistency. If a vendor doesn't bring us quality beef week after week, we fire them. If we can only get the salmon to balance on the couscous nine out of ten times, we take it off the menu until we figure out how to plate it better. If a chef isn't going to show up to be a part of the best restaurant in Chicago, we find someone who will. And if a server is going to up and quit because they took a job only to get a front-row seat to a shit show, well, then 'bye, now. We don't need that either."

The room falls completely silent. This is the moment we find out who was here for Benji, and who was here for…Here.

"On that note, a press release was deployed approximately sixty seconds before this meeting kicked off introducing our chef de cuisine, Miss Tabitha Johnson." Angela gestures her way and Tabitha waves to the crowd. "By now, you've probably all seen her around here doing her thing, but let's give a formal warm welcome to the woman who will be making your staff meals, shall we?"

I clap louder than everyone and smile her way. We're really lucky to have her.

"Say a few words," I whisper to her. She shakes her head my way like she's refusing bad tuna. Oh, well.

"Now if anyone from the press comes to you and asks for a quote on what happened to Benji, I suggest you say 'no comment.' But if for some reason, you can't control your desire for less than fifteen minutes of pseudo-fame, I better not see anything outside of what I just mentioned hit the internet. Because the truth is, we don't know exactly what happened or what he's up to now. And we are not in the business of making shit up. That's how rumors get started. So if I see your name in the blogs, that's it. No verbal or written warning—it's straight termination. And I don't know about you, but I wouldn't want to be fired from a place where I'll likely be walking away with at least $300 in cash tips per night."

Holy shit, for real? Screw AGM, why didn't I just become a waitress?

"One final note before we move on to reviewing the guest list for tomorrow night. It's no surprise there was no soft opening for Here. I know that's not how several of you, including myself, prefer to roll. But unfortunately, for reasons you do not need to know, we weren't able to swing a Friends & Family Night. So that means tomorrow, starting at 5:00 p.m., you need to be ON. YOUR. GAME. Chug a Red Bull, get a blow job, give a blow job, whatever you need to do to clear your mind and be sharp as a tack…do it. We have one chance to be rock stars on night one. Heard?"

"Heard," everyone but me replies. I'll get it next time.

"Great. Now let's quickly go through what we have on the books for tomorrow night. Take out your Moleskines everybody, we're announcing VIPs and preferences."

In unison, the tribe pulls out small leather-bound notebooks from their aprons and clicks open the blue-ink pens we provided.

"Allie, you want to do this part?" Angela asks in side conversation. I pull a Tabitha and shake my head no. She rolls her eyes. I'll hear about this later.

"First VIP, 6:00 p.m., two-top: Aurora Jenkins, *Chicago Sun-Times*. Her husband has a dairy allergy. Tabitha, please note that."

"Heard," she replies without looking up from her own notes.

"Second VIP, 6:30, two-top: Mr. and Mrs. Bill Simon, parents of our AGM-slash-owner, Allie Simon. No allergies, no preferences. Whoever gets this table, start them off with two glasses of Moët, please."

"Noted," says Jessica.

"VIP number three, 7:00 p.m., four-top: Catherine McGee, *TimeOut* magazine. One pescatarian in the party. Tabitha?"

"Oh, for fuck's sake," she mumbles under her breath. "Yeah, Angela. Got it."

"Andrew, you'll take the McGee party."

"Heard," he confirms.

"Wonderful. All in all, 175 on the books. First seating is at

5:00 p.m. Final seating is at 10:30. We are fully committed. Each server should expect to turn their station at least three times. It's going to be a long night, I know. Now as far as the host stand, Allie and I will handle the majority of the seating for the night. We need to see firsthand how the flow of this restaurant is working. When we're in the weeds, we'll have a backup hostess. That's Becca sitting over there. I stole her from Florette. Say hi, everyone."

Becca is an eleventh-hour hire that Angela took the lead on. When she originally gave me the list of roles to hire for Here, I read the description of the host/hostess and thought: me. Greet guests, take their jackets, seat them, control the pacing and flow of our diners—I could do that. And to be honest, I wanted to save on the hourly cost of hiring someone else, so I told her that position was covered. When we went through some final notes a couple days ago, and she realized what I meant by "covered" she promptly texted Becca and asked if she'd be interested in moving on up to the big leagues. She said yes, which is why there's a ballerina-type-looking woman I've never seen before in my restaurant.

No hard feelings, though. Angela admitted I could take the lead on seating, and probably could have handled it all myself, it's just that there's no way to know how slammed we'll be now that we've released the news about Benji to the media.

"So, here's the scoop. There is no room for walk-ins in the main dining room, so nobody promise anything we cannot deliver. We'll be sending these folks to the bar until we run out of room. Then we kindly apologize and help facilitate a reservation for a future date. Allie, after this, please look over the reservation list in the system one more time and flag any VIPs I might have missed. Add detailed notes, too, okay?"

If I'd thought I was a computer expert in my time at Daxa, the software system we're using at Here has proved me wrong.

It almost makes me miss the job where all I needed to know was how and when to hit Retweet.

"Allie, did you hear me?"

"Heard," I assure her.

"Good. Make that known next time by giving me the courtesy of an audible reply, please and thank you."

Far from bristling at her rebuke, I like Angela even more in this moment. The woman has a zero-tolerance policy for bullshit. Sure, I might be (partly) responsible for giving her this job and changing her life, but that's not going to stop her from giving me hell if I don't do things the way I need to in order to make this restaurant work. There's no special treatment for me. For some reason, that's comforting.

"One final note," Angela says. "With or without a soft opening, it's crucial that no one has tunnel vision tomorrow night...or ever...in this restaurant. The biggest fuckup you can make is assuming your job is to keep your eyes on your table and your table alone. You need to see if the bar is backing up before you promise someone their Moscow Mule will be out in just a minute. You need to see if your hot food is coming off the line before you start to take an order for a table of six. You need to occasionally look toward the front to see if no one is at the host stand for some reason when a party walks in. Keep your eyes open, people. All night. All directions. Harder than it sounds, but absolutely mandatory if we're going to spot and correct small issues before they become full-blown crises. Okay?"

Even though I say "heard," it doesn't mean I got it. That task is going to be harder than the rest. I'm only one person. Two eyes. I can't be everywhere at all times, but I know that's what Angela is going to expect out of me—more than anyone else.

After the training meeting, I hobble over to the computer

screen to follow up on my task. It's crazy to see my parents' names on the reservation sheet. We've come a long way with this whole Here thing. I click on their names and make a note in the system to start them off with two glasses of Moët, just in case Jessica forgets. She won't, though.

Out of the corner of my eye, I spot two of the servers eating family meal at one of the tables in the bar. Family meal, aka staff meal, is cafeteria-style food that Tabitha prepares for us each night before service. Even though we don't open until tomorrow, we're going to do a mock-service in about an hour to help ease everyone's nerves about the lack of a soft opening.

Angela explained to me the importance of staff meal a couple days ago when I suggested we should make it a point to tell servers to eat before they show up for work or bring some granola bars to tuck into their apron. That way, they wouldn't get hungry running around holding plates of delicious-looking food all night. She shook her head at the cost-saving idea and I couldn't figure out why—labor laws don't mandate we feed these savages and I know money's tight with opening costs. Turns out staff meal gives everyone the opportunity to relax and enjoy each other's company before they're screaming at one another in the back for cutting them off while carrying a tray of hot soup. Time to eat, as short as it might be, sets the tone for service. Plus it'll start getting people on the Tabitha train once they eat more and more of her bombtastic food.

Of the two girls eating, one is the redhead who gave Angela sass about Benji's whereabouts in the preshift meeting. I can hear her whispering as she looks up at me intermittently. I casually walk closer to them for a better angle as I pretend to take stock of our liquor.

"He must have had a ten-inch cock because why the hell else would you buy your boyfriend a restaurant just so he stays with you?" says the redhead, who's skinny with a pointy nose.

"I heard she's never even worked in a restaurant before. I'm sorry, but I'm going to *make* my children be servers the day they're old enough to work. There's so much you learn about life here," says the other one, a chubby brunette with a pretty face.

"Like not dating a drug-addict loser who robs you?"

"Oh my god, did you see that photo *FoodFeed* posted a few weeks ago of her walking in here? She had a black eye, I swear. They're probably into kinky shit."

"You can totally tell she does tons of coke, too."

"Probably off his dick."

"I can't believe this bitch is our boss."

Annnnd that's about all I can take.

"Excuse me?" I say, walking over to the girls. "What did you two just say?"

"Nothing. We were talking about how many covers we have tomorrow," says Red.

"The hell you were. Look, I may not have spent the last five years of my life waiting tables every day and getting drunk every night, but didn't Angela just say something about having eyes and ears open at all times? Something about not having tunnel vision and spotting problems before they turn into crises?"

"Yeah, something like that," says the chubby one.

"Well, I'm spotting one right here. Two, actually."

"What's the issue? Talking behind your back? Got news for you, Allie, that's the way it is in the restaurant industry. First they love you, then they hate you," the brunette says. I really wish I knew their names, though that's becoming increasingly irrelevant.

"Yeah, just watch what happens after the press finds out about Benji being gone," the redhead adds. "People know you have something to do with the reason he left. And when they figure out what it is, they'll turn on this place. It won't be pretty."

I'm at a loss for words. These little bitches are intimidating me as they stuff their faces with homemade stir-fry. It's time to throw this thing into sport mode and remind them who they work for.

"This is *my* restaurant. Okay? I sign your paychecks."

"Which we'll mail you in a week. Now get up and get the hell out," says Angela from behind me. "You're both fired."

I lock eyes with Angela. She's firing two servers the day before we're expecting a full house. I don't want the girls to sense weakness, but is she crazy?

"You heard me. Leave your uniforms in the office. You have five minutes to be out of here. Get going, ladies."

The two scurry from the table. Whispers of "bullshit" and "fucking cunts" trickle back to us.

"I'm really sorry, Angela," I say. "I shouldn't have gotten so heated with them. I probably fucked us for tomorrow, right?"

"First of all, don't apologize. You're the boss and the owner. I'm not saying you should let it go to your head, but if someone doesn't respect you, they shouldn't be here. That said, if you feel like firing Tabitha, you need to run that by me first, okay?"

"Don't worry. Two staff members down with less than twenty-four hours until we open seems like enough excitement. Do you have any—"

"Backups? Always."

"I love you. You are seriously the Queen of Plan Bs. Where are the résumés? I'll comb through 'em."

"Easy, tiger," she says. "Don't get used to expecting we'll always be okay if something fails. There are only a handful of pillars that determine if you're successful in this industry. A quality chef and people to serve her food are two of them, so of course I had backups for both of those. But let me tell you, there are still a hundred-and-one-thousand things that can go wrong tomorrow night for which I have made absolutely no preparation. So from here on out, let's run a tight ship, shall we?"

"Aye, aye, captain," I say. Despite her grim pep talk, I found us a new head chef in a day, so I'm pretty sure we can find two half-decent servers before the doors open. Maybe even before the mock service if we're lucky.

"The résumés are in a green folder in the cabinet near Tabitha's desk. Can't miss it—it's labeled. Now if you'll excuse me, I'm going to smoke my last 'stress cigarette' as I go through the sixty voice mails on my phone from the press."

"Need any help?" I ask.

"I didn't realize you were so eager to converse with strangers about your ex-boyfriend."

"Oh. Right. Scratch that."

Angela lovingly flicks me off and heads out the back door. I pull up the YeltonXT and wipe the two defunct servers from the system. A few moments later, Craig walks in and greets me at the hostess stand. He's all but disappeared since signing the paperwork—though more than once I've thought that might be a good thing. Like our own personal Santa Claus, he comes down the chimney, drops off a nice present, then scoots out, never to be seen again. Having been in the trenches here these past few weeks, I have to admire a guy like that: one who can dump $300,000, plus a couple mil in cosmetic adjustments (on the restaurant, not his wife's face), into something, then walk away, leaving the entire operation to a former homeless chick and an emotionally frazzled twentysomething. That takes balls.

"Hi, Allie, how's it going, sweetie?" He kisses me on the cheek in a way that manages not to be totally creepy. I wonder if any of his spray tan is now on my face.

"It's going good, Craig. Less than twenty-four hours now, can you believe it?"

"Figured it was coming soon enough. You have to remember, not my first rodeo."

His lack of excitement is either concerning or calming, but I can't decide which.

"Yeah, I forget that you're a seasoned pro." A little stroke of the ego never hurt anyone. Damn, I forgot how shiny his veneers were.

"Well, Angela is. She's really the star of this show, no offense to you."

"None taken. I happen to agree."

"So are you nervous, Allie?"

"Incredibly. Angela thinks that since we dropped the news about Benji today, there's going to be up to five critics here tomorrow night."

"Blinds?" he asks, which is industry speak for a critic who is entirely undercover versus a known food writer.

"It's a mix," I say. "We've already got two from the media—both of whom have crazy allergies."

"Oh, fuck. No pressure, Tabitha," he says in jest.

"Yeah, exactly. But she's already prepping for them and fully expecting the blinds. In fact, I've got one of the barbacks in the office right now doing Google image searches of all the big ones. I mean, they obviously keep a low profile, but there are enough rumors out there about who's who, I figure it's worth taping some photos on the wall and telling the staff to keep an eye out for them." Admitting this aloud feels neurotic as fuck.

"And what about you? What are you doing to prepare?"

"Well, I'm going to study all the critic images really hard tonight, then go over all the starters again, and—"

"No, no, no. I mean what are you doing to *prepare*?" Craig

asks again, this time pointing toward my heart. I put my hand there to make sure there's nothing out of the ordinary—no nip-slips or mustard stains.

"I'm not sure what you mean, Craig. I've been studying the menus morning, noon and night," I say with a bit of defense.

"Can I give you a little advice, Allie?" he asks as he adjusts his Ferrari-branded cuff links.

"Sure, I'll take whatever I can get."

"Your job as the AGM is all about heart. Leave it to your staff to know how many ingredients are in the king crab appetizer. Leave it to your bartender to know how much bitters to add to an Old-Fashioned. Your job is to make people feel at home when they are here. That's why you guys named it what you did, right?"

Though being confronted with Benji's namesake day after day might have made me bitter, that's not how I feel about Here. When the clouds cleared from the shit storm he caused, Here is still the perfect name for what we've created.

"What's 'Here' mean to you?"

"I don't know. I guess it's the right place at the right time. Maybe, like, the one spot where you feel the most like yourself. Happy, lively, things like that."

"Alright, nice. But give me more. Dig deeper."

I look away from Craig and give myself a second to think.

The memory hits me all at once, from a time that seems impossibly far away.

"A couple years ago in college I studied abroad in France for a semester. God, I was so homesick. I thought it was going to be all glamorous like Carrie Bradshaw frolicking around Paris or something. Yeah, it was nothing like that. Anyway, my host house flooded and the school paid for me to get a hotel for a few days, so I picked the Ritz-Carlton. It was so over-the-top but at least they had super fast WiFi, so I Skyped my mom. It was daytime here in Chicago; my dad was at work. She left the laptop streaming in the living room all day. We watched a *Days of Our Lives* marathon together. Then my mom got up and said she'd be right back. She was going to go make herself some lunch—a grilled cheese and some tomato soup. I was so jealous. That was my favorite food and she knew it. Well, about ten minutes later, I get a knock on my hotel room door. It's room service. I tell him he's got the wrong room, I didn't order anything. But he says, 'Allie Simon?' I say yes and he says, 'Then this is for you. Can I set it here on the desk?'

"He walks by me to place the tray down, lifts up a heavy silver lid and guess what's there? A grilled cheese and a bowl of tomato soup. There was a note with it: 'Not quite how Mom makes it, but hope it'll do.' A few minutes later, my mom comes back into the Skype window with her meal and says, 'Eat up, honey!' I'll never forget it. An ocean away and I felt like I was right there in the house I grew up in, watching TV on the couch in my pajamas with my mom.

"I felt so loved. So cared for. So thought about. So comfortable. I remember talking with my mouth full of food and saying to her, 'It's so good! It's like you're here with me.' And she just smiled, pointed at her heart and said back, 'I'm always going be *here*, I'm your mom.'"

I finally pause and look back at Craig.

"Sorry. Was I talking this whole time?"

Craig laughs a bit. With me, at me—I can't be sure, but it doesn't feel mean-spirited.

"You know, if you weren't already the assistant manager of this restaurant, I would have hired you right here, right now based on that response. Because you get it, Allie. You may never have had to void a check or comp someone's appetizer, but I can already tell you understand precisely what your job is all about. Make everyone who walks through that door tomorrow—and every night after—feel exactly how you did when that grilled cheese showed up at your door in Paris, and you'll make your money back tenfold. Can you do that?"

Of all the job descriptions online I've read about AGMs, I've never had it put the way Craig did. And if that's what it takes to do this job, then I've never felt more confident that I got this.

"Yeah, I think I can."

"Great. Now, where's Angela? I've got some last-minute paperwork she needs to sign off on."

"Straight back." I gesture toward the office.

Craig raps the counter with his left hand on his way to the back. I hear his wedding band clank against the polished wood. I'm sure his wife is trophy in nature, but I bet Craig is a really good husband and father.

"Thanks again for sharing that story, Allie," he says, turning to face me again. "Angela was right about you being more than some junkie's enabling ex-girlfriend. I didn't believe her at first. I thought, what kind of an idiot hands over thirty grand to a guy who's just going to end up leaving her for another pussy and a bigger paycheck— and not necessarily in that order. But now look at you. Hospitality is in your bones. Who knew?"

I'm not entirely sure what to make of that. First of all, I generally don't do well with men over the age of forty using the word *pussy* in a conversation directed toward me, but okay. Secondly, Craig obviously doesn't realize that I didn't have a choice. Benji left me high and dry and it's his girl Angela who made it crystal clear that there was no way out. Craig seems to be operating under the very false impression that this has been my secret wish all along, which means Angela must *not* have told him the version of the story where Benji left me battered and broke.

And for that, I am really, really thankful.

24

I can now confirm that a mock service is essentially the same thing as "playing restaurant" as a kid. Only this time, we were pretending charred octopus was atop the plate, not hot dogs or birthday cake. And instead of being doting parents, Angela and I had to be tough critics, difficult customers and allergy-prone picky eaters.

It wasn't an Oscar-worthy performance by any means, but role-playing gave us a chance to quiz our servers on ingredients, have them practice the tableside setup for key items (oysters Rockefeller, the seafood tower and cheddar smoke biscuit), and identify any areas where servers would get clogged up on the floor. Having said that, tables eight and ten are now pushed six inches farther in opposite directions to create a wider pass.

Our two new backup servers weren't able to make it in for the trial run (something about having to go to school? God, how old are these people?), but they'll come in tomorrow and shadow the others. We need all the hands we can get with Angela predicting each section will turn *at least* three times throughout the night.

It's about 7:00 p.m. when I sneak out the back door for some fresh air and notice a box of iceberg lettuce sitting by the door. I lift the flap of the box and the lettuce is dead—totally browned and wilted—not to mention half-eaten by whatever lives under the Dumpster and between the cracks of the building.

Shit, shit, shit. I have no idea how this happened, but if I tell Angela, she'll happily point out it's my fault because I was in charge of the delivery. And even if I wasn't, it'd still be my fault because I am the AGM. Angela told me that in this industry, most things that go wrong will be our fault because of the nature of our job titles. Remind me again why I took this job? Or don't, actually.

Regardless, I need to make sure this is the emergency I think it is. So I run inside and open the walk-in fridge to make sure there are no other boxes of lettuce and that maybe this was a rogue extra that was meant to go back on Jared's truck. There aren't. Then I grab a copy of the menu to confirm what dish requires the iceberg lettuce. I should know this by heart, but I'm sleep-deprived and overwhelmed—more so when I see that a "Wedge of iceberg with house-made bleu cheese dressing" is up first on our list of greens. Yup, we're fucked.

I don't know what Step Two is, but I'm sure that Step One is destroying the evidence before Angela comes outside and notices that a basic item that's likely to be ordered over and over tomorrow night is already eighty-sixed. So I go back outside and toss the box into the nearest Dumpster. Then, I head to my desk, where I pull up the number to Marcel & Sons, more specifically, to Jared's cell phone. My tail is between my legs as I hear the first ring. I can't believe I'm requiring direct access to our produce guy this early on in the game.

"Hello, '*Allie Simon—Here Restaurant.*' Do you miss me already, or what?" he answers.

"I need lettuce," I say, cutting to the point.

"What kind?"

"Iceberg."

"STRAIGHT AHEAD!" he shouts in a British accent. "Sorry, that's a *Titanic* reference. Anyway, I brought you iceberg this morning. Thirty-five heads of it."

"Yeah, and I left it outside. It wilted and I think some rats got to it, too."

"Tsk, tsk. Allie. I bring you the freshest iceberg lettuce and you feed it to rodents? Too bad we're all sold out of lettuce. I guess you're just going to have to go grocery store hopping and see what you can come up with at this hour."

"Wait. Are you serious?"

"Nope. I'll be right over with a new box. Meet me outside in, say, thirty minutes?"

I take a giant breath.

"Yeah, that works. And hey, if you run into Angela when you're pulling up, don't say anything about this. Okay? Just text me and I'll be right out."

"Permission to text? Well, then, secret's safe with me," Jared assures me.

I head back into the office and Angela and Tabitha are looking over printouts of the reservation list with the updated notes I added earlier.

"Anything significant change since this morning?" Angela asks.

"Not really. I moved Tabitha's wife and mom over to the VIP list and requested Moët for them as well. That's about it."

"Oh, I didn't realize Johnson, Party of Two at 7:30 was for you," Angela says to Tabitha. "In fact, I didn't realize you were married."

"Happily. Going on five years next May," she says. "I don't wear my ring to work because if I get oil on that sucker, it's going to slip off and get chopped up in a Vitamix. Mary would kill me. How about you, Ang? Got anyone special?"

I realize then how odd it is that we've been spending virtually every waking (and sleeping) moment next to each other, but I know so little about their lives outside of Here—or that such a thing exists. My ears are tuned for her response.

"Me? Nah. No time."

"I call bullshit," I say.

"Seriously! I don't think I've dated a guy for..." She pauses and begins using her fingers as a calculator. "Man, it's got to be like ten years or something. Maybe even longer."

A decade-plus puts her at a time *before* she wound up on the streets. Unless I plan to dig in right here, right now about how that all came to happen, I better backpedal gracefully before an unknowing Tabitha probes further and accidentally unearths emotions that probably should stay put until *after* we clock our official first day.

"Well, you've got to at least have a crush on someone," I say. "Who's your David-Beckham-of-the-food-world?"

"Oh my god. Are we really doing this?" Angela asks. She looks irritated I'm inciting conversation about something other than employee scheduling or ramekin storage.

"Yes we are. And same question to you, Tab. But I guess, who's your..."

"Pam-Anderson-circa-1995-of-the-food-world?"

"Sure," I say. "I'll go first. Mine's Ross Luca of Republic."

"You sure it's not our produce guy?" Angela retorts.

"Or Andrew? I saw you eye-fuck the shit out of him in that preshift meeting," Tabitha jabs.

"What? No I didn't." I probably did. "Who's yours?"

"Easy. Don't tell Mary but...Giada De Laurentiis. I could watch her feed dough to a pasta maker all day."

"Nice. Ang, your turn."

"We're opening a fine-dining restaurant in less than twenty-four hours and the three of us nutjobs are sitting around the office talking about which celeb chef we'd like to bang? That's what's happening right now?"

"Quit being a prude and just spill it," I demand.

"I swear, you two either need to get to work or find Jesus," she says.

"We're waaaaaitingggg," sings Tabitha.

There's a long pause. Both Tabitha and I are wide-eyed staring at Angela waiting to see: Will she crack? Will she have a little fun? Will she show us she's human after all?

"Ugh. Fine. Curtis Stone."

The three of us hoot and holler and high-five each other like we're all hopped up on sugar at a sleepover party. I don't know what's so fun about sharing something so menial, but I do know one thing: I have craved silly fun like this for a long time now. Especially knowing that some of my most recent interactions with my normal besties (Jazzy and Maya) have been...tense. But this little charade in the back office at Here, as fleeting as it may have been, totally hit the spot.

My laughter is interrupted by a vibrating text in the back pocket of my jeans. I pull out my phone. Jared's here.

I slither out the back as Angela and Tabitha get back to reviewing their printouts.

"Almost didn't recognize you without your big truck," I call as I walk toward Jared, who's lifting a box of lettuce out of the trunk of his BMW.

"You know what they say about guys with big trucks..."

I roll my eyes. His sense of humor seems like it would scream cheese, but instead I find him endearing and cute. Dangerous territory.

"You ready for the big day?" he asks as he hands me the box.

"No. Not really. But I'll make sure to fake like I am when those doors open tomorrow."

"'Fake It 'Til You Make It' is actually the unofficial motto of this industry, you know. So I think you'll be fine." He gives me a wink and starts to walk back to his car.

"Thanks for doing this," I say. "How much do I owe you?"

"Consider it a housewarming present," he says. "Just don't use it as hamster food this time, okay?"

Angela spent the night at Here, insisting I "should go home and get a full eight hours of sleep" when I volunteered to do the same. Out of all the restaurant terms I've had to learn, "full eight hours of sleep" is the one that's been most lost on me of late.

When I left, she, Tabitha and our lead servers were blasting Queen's greatest hits and taking shots of Fireball as they gave the baseboards another once-over with a bright white semigloss. They waved away my halfhearted attempts to help. Apparently it was more important for me to go home, memorize the ingredients and try to clock the first real sleep I've had since before I knew what an amuse-bouche was. As I tossed my keys to the restaurant in my bag, Angela's parting words to me were: "Go forth and masturbate."

So I did.

Don't judge. It's been a while since I've watched *Lost* with anyone.

There's one other thing I did during my "time off"—and that's text Jazzy and Maya to smooth things over.

Opening a restaurant is a sobering experience, at least it's been that way for me. I look back on the me from weeks ago, standing in the foyer of my apartment, clutching that bottle of pills that wasn't mine, trying to bait and switch a brunch date with my friends into a field trip to the projects. I was out of my mind. It was like I was the addict in that situation. And I wanted them to know that I recognized that and I'm sorry.

It's now three thirty in the afternoon on Here's opening day. My Uber driver drops me at the front door even though I told him to pull around to the alley. "That's not safe, ma'am," he said.

"Trust me. If I get abducted, it wouldn't be the worst thing in the world," I said back. He didn't find that funny and I'm sure my passenger rating has since plummeted.

Before he drives off, I check my reflection in his tinted windows. The "five-minute French twist" I learned how to do on Pinterest is secured with a bottle of Paul Mitchell hair spray and enough bobby pins to set off a metal detector. The black, knee-length shift dress with a white Peter Pan collar feels just the right amount of professional and fun for a night like tonight and my high-waisted control-top tights are helping to keep the butterflies in my stomach at bay. As I head for the front door, my high heels click against the sidewalk exactly to the beat of my heart.

The restaurant is practically humming with barely contained energy. For the most part, I'd describe it as nervous—but not in a bad way. It's more like how you feel getting ready for a first date with a guy you met online. He looks hot in all his pictures, his profile checks out, but you can't be too sure he's not an ax murderer until you sit down and have dinner and feel each other out.

The smell of fresh paint still lingers on the walls as I weave my way toward the back office. My entire staff is in constant motion. Whether polishing silverware, steaming glassware or cutting up fruit for the bar, everyone is doing something with a highly focused look on their faces—all in the name of this little place we call Here.

Despite all the work I've put in, the reality is still as hard to digest as it was the day Angela wrote Benji to talk about a restaurant opportunity. But it *is* reality, I remind myself, and one with real consequences. The memory of my $30,000 lodges in my throat for the millionth time.

God, people better like the scallops.

"Who are these for?" I ask Angela, nodding to a bouquet of lilies smelling up the back office.

"You, buttercup," she says, not bothering to look up from the computer screen.

"Aw, thanks, Angela. You and Craig are seriously the sweetest."

"Bitch," she says not unkindly. She finally looks away from the monitor. "We already got your ass flowers once. The courting phase is over. Those aren't from us. Isn't there a card?"

I fish around for what I imagine will be a tiny white envelope. Knowing they aren't from Angela sends a mini wave of panic through my bones. Could they be from…I'm not even going to say his name.

Allie—
"Lettuce" wish you a happy opening day.
—Jared, Marcel & Sons

"So? Who are they from?"

"Our produce guy," I say, somewhat bewildered by the gesture.

She springs her chair away from her desk and looks at me for real.

"Okay, Allie. Eyes over here." She snaps twice. "I know I've thrown a lot of restaurant jargon at you these last couple weeks, but just so you know, Rule #77 is 'never sleep with a vendor.' Especially not a good one. Marcel & Sons has the absolute best produce in the city and we can't risk a bad delivery because you didn't put out, he came too soon or whatever else goes awry in those complicated millennial relationships you guys have."

Relationships.

The word jolts me just a bit. Short of fawning over our delivery guy's Gap model–looking face and incredibly palatable sense of humor, I haven't actually thought about what it'd be like to date anyone post-Benji.

It's a slow recovery. That's all I know.

"Please, Angela. The only relationship I'm in is the one with this restaurant," I say to quell her concerns.

"Good. That makes us Sister Wives, then."

She might have said it in jest, but I have to take a moment to acknowledge just how far Angela and I have come in the last forty-five days. When she first sent that email to Benji, all proper and hoity-toity, I was skeptical and predisposed to dislike her. A billfold straight to the boobs would put anyone off, right? I thought she was in it just to dethrone me from the privilege of working with the hottest man in the media.

But it's become undeniably clear that Angela couldn't care less whose name is on the marquee, so long as that person shares her passion, her vision and her drive. At so many points, she could have sided with Craig and convinced him to take his business elsewhere—leaving me an even bigger, broker mess than I was to begin with. But instead, she covered for me. She's kept a handful of my deepest, darkest secrets to date— that I unintentionally insisted on breaching an ironclad contract; that my ex-boyfriend took me down financially, then physically; that I haven't showered in days. She's guided me, carried me, taught me and seasoned me.

She hired me.

I know I never wanted to be a part of this restaurant—at least not in a front-and-center-on-the-floor kind of way. But here I am, assistant general manager at a fine-dining establishment in the most coveted part of the city. I don't necessarily deserve the opportunity I've been given—or rather, the opportunity I quasi-accidentally purchased for $30,000—but Angela has had perfect faith in me practically since the word

go. Clearly, she sees something in me that I don't yet. But I
owe it to her to discover that, cultivate it and keep at it.

It's 4:45 p.m., fifteen minutes from our first guests' antici-
pated arrival. I do a mental check of the dining room preshift
protocol: candles lit, chairs pushed in six inches from the table,
napkins folded the same, glasses crystal clear, music low, lights
dimmed, bar stools aligned at a forty-five-degree angle facing the door. Together, these things are greater than the sum
of their parts. Because standing back and looking at Here as a
whole, this place feels warm, welcoming. Like a total class act.

"I've got to admit it to someone," Tabitha says to me. "I
haven't been this nervous on a Friday since 2001 when the
first *Lord of the Rings* movie opened."

"Relax, Tab. I just did a forty-point check on the front-
and back-of-house and everything's locked and loaded," I assure her.

"So the only thing left to do is pray," she says.

Actually, that's not a bad first-night idea.

"Hey, can I get everyone together, please? Near the front?"
I say softly to a group of ultra good-looking servers standing
near us. They don't move.

"Everyone get your asses to the front of the restaurant,
please and thank you!" Angela shouts from behind me. They
scatter like the cops just showed up to the party.

"Rule #34: If you need something done a certain way, you
better be loud and you better be clear," she says more quietly, just to me.

I hear what she's saying, but it feels strange asserting myself
to these people so soon. They don't owe me any allegiance—
hell, they haven't even collected their first paychecks yet. Not
to mention the fact that it's not hard to deduce the only reason
I'm even here is because my ex-boyfriend was supposed to be

the head chef. Even though the details are fuzzy, people can (and do) safely assume it's because of an entirely fucked-up circumstance that I—the girl with no experience to speak of—am now second-in-command. For anyone who cares about the industry, like *really* cares, this is mind-boggling and borderline offensive. I get it. Which is why I'm desperate to prove I deserve to be here. Starting now.

"Alright, everyone," I say, weaving my hands together to keep them from gesturing awkwardly. "I just want to take a second to say how grateful I am for all of you. Forty-five days ago, this place was a shoebox. Now, from the looks of it, I'd say it's a full-blown fine-dining restaurant, wouldn't you?"

I don't know if I'm expecting them to answer out loud, but the blank stares and rogue pop of bubble gum aren't exactly giving me the confidence to continue. I swallow hard and start again.

"I know it wasn't easy moving a mile a minute to open by October fifteenth, but here we are and the place seriously looks awesome. I am so proud of each and every one of you. You've helped make Here a reality. I know this is kind of cheesy, but can you grab the hand of the person standing next to you?"

Again, no one moves. I remember Rule #34.

"If I have to ask twice for simple things, we're going to be in for a rough opening night," I say with some bravado. "So grab your neighbor's hand and let's bow our heads. Now."

Works like a charm. I see a smile play at the corner of Angela's lips as she offers her hands to the servers on her right and left.

"Heavenly Father," I begin. I don't pray much, but this feels like a solid start. "We ask you to bless us all with the confidence and strength to pull off a flawless performance tonight. Keep Tabitha safe and sane in the back-of-house, and keep our front-of-house lively and sharp. We thank you for this opportunity to inspire others through food and do what we love. Amen."

"Amen," I hear echoed back in a smattering of whispers.

As I look up, I see headlights pulling toward our valet.

A thousand questions flash through my mind: What if that's just the postman? Or just someone heading to their car? What happens if the power goes out later? Did I overpluck my eyebrows? I quiet the noise and make the official announcement: "First cover is arriving now. Places, everyone. Places!" I shout.

The crowd scatters and my heart flutters.

"Good evening, welcome to Here. Can we take your jackets?" Angela greets the first couple. They're model-esque hipster types. The woman is in a polka-dot dress and high heels. She's got a full face of makeup and brilliant smile. The man has salt-and-pepper slicked-back hair with a corduroy blazer and a bow tie.

My first thought? I would buy this porno.

My second thought? We are a place people get dressed up to go to. That's all sorts of awesome.

"Reservation for Miller," the man says as Angela hands off their coats to Becca.

"Absolutely. Allie, will you show Mr. and Mrs. Miller to their table, please?" Angela hands me two menus from under the host stand and taps table twelve on the YeltonXT. It turns red, meaning the table is now occupied so no one can seat another party there until the server has closed them out on their end.

"Right this way," I say with a smile as I lead the way.

And when we arrive at table twelve—without a moment's hesitation on my part, thankyouverymuch—I pull out Mrs. Miller's chair and comment on what a lovely table we have for them, right by one of the windows that looks out toward Willis Tower, one of the most iconic parts of our beautiful skyline.

"Enjoy your evening," I say before disappearing.

One down.

On my way back to the host stand, I keep my eyes peeled for someone to high-five. But I quickly realize there's no time for celebration. A six-top has just arrived, as well as our food critic from the *Sun-Times*, who is ten minutes early and giving our bartender a run for his money with a new take on a deconstructed Old-Fashioned.

"Allie, let Jessica know the deuce I'm about to seat at 28 is VIP and GF/DF."

"In English?"

"Two-top. Important. Gluten- and dairy-free."

"Okay. Got it. But I think she's busy right now pulling a bottle of wine from the cellar for 12."

"Then write it on a chit and stick it in her apron," Angela says moments before two walk-ins (*don't they know it's opening night and we're fully committed?!*) come through the door and her smile remerges like a hyacinth in bloom.

Chit. Chit. Chit. What's a chit? I sneak away to the coat closet, pull my iPhone out from my bra and Google it. Moments later, I have my answer. I go to the ticket machine and dispense a few inches of blank tape. On it, I write the note to Jessica.

Chit crisis averted.

"Allie, I just got double sat. What the fuck is going on at the host stand?" a server says in a hushed but frantic whisper. "Look at my section—it's packed. I'm about to be in the weeds here."

I glance over and, sure enough, six people have been sat within forty-five seconds, all in the wrong sections. I look up to the host stand and see Becca pressing all sorts of buttons on the YeltonXT while Angela is pouring wine at table twelve. I thought she was a pro, but apparently our computer system is way too technical compared to what she's used to at Florette. She must know there's a science to seating, so I'm blaming this one on technical difficulties. I've got to do something.

"Okay. Go greet the four-top at table fourteen. I'll take care of sixteen, those are actually my parents. Side note: they're huge winos."

"Yeah, I saw that in the reservation details. They're starting with comped Möet, right?"

"Exactly. So I'll go say hi, point you out to them and get them started with the glasses of bubbly. I'm sure they'll propose a toast while they have my attention, after which, I'll put in an order for an appetizer and send the somm over to discuss what wine they'll be starting off with this evening. That'll buy you at least fifteen minutes. In the meantime, I'll get with Becca and make sure you're not sat again until their dinner tickets are in and you're back on auto."

"Oh my god, thank you so much, Allie. Seriously, you're a lifesaver."

"It's fine, really. Remind me your name again?"

"Paul."

"Okay, Paul. You gotta breathe, buddy. You can't come off this nervous to your guests. Pull it together and command your table. You're in charge now."

The tension is coming off this guy practically in waves but somehow I'm able to deflect it, retarget it even. Angela's training is kicking in like a wine buzz from a Sutter Home four-pack and it's empowering beyond belief.

"Good evening, folks," I say to my parents as I drop off two glasses of Möet. This scene is not feeling all that unfamiliar compared to the last time I oversaw their evening at Benji's pop-up. In fact, my mom's wearing the same Tiffany's charm bracelet and my dad already has his iPhone out with the camera app open.

"Look at our baby girl, Bill! She's all grown up!" my mom says.

"I would, but I'm too busy looking at this restaurant. Have you ever seen such a beautiful place?"

"Listen, I've got to keep checking on things, but I wanted to start you off with some champagne and say how grateful I am for your support. I couldn't have done this unless I knew you guys were behind me at the end of the day. So thank you. I love you."

My mom and dad hold their flutes up, look at me, look at each other and cheers their glasses. I don't know how much more I'll get to interact with them tonight, but having these few minutes together gives me a sense of calm and confidence I'll take with me well beyond the time our last patron leaves. Now, with one fire out, it's time to check on another—the literal one in the kitchen.

"Fire one octopus, one date, one beet salad," Tabitha yells as tickets roar off the printer.

"Yes, Chef!" replies her team of cooks.

"Jessica, you've got to sell this polenta to twenty *now*. It's dying."

"Heard," Jessica says as she steps up to the line, cleans the plate with a white kitchen towel and scoots off to the dining room.

"How we doing back here, Tab?" I ask through the window.

"We're getting crushed with apps. Hector, how long on the squash?"

"Three minutes," a faceless voice replies.

"Three minutes?! My god, what's the holdup? Allie, I need you to expo for a few. I've got to get back there and step in. Food is not coming out quick enough."

I immediately regret checking on Tabitha. Expediting has been the hardest part of my restaurant boot camp, mainly because there's no real way to train for it. It's like a maestro practicing conducting with a phantom symphony. How can you test your intelligence until it's time for the big show? From what I learned watching this go down in the kitchen at Paragraph, essentially the job is this: as tickets come in, call out the orders—including any and all modifications—to the various cook stations in the back. When food comes up, make sure the plates look perfect, cleaning up any spilled sauces and finalizing the presentations with the correct garnishes.

If there was ever a time to know the precise difference between basil, parsley, cilantro and scallions—it's now.

I take a deep breath and assume my place behind the stainless-steel table where every plate will undergo a final check before being ushered to our guests. Right here, now, is when I put my mouth where my money already is. "Fire two duck and two scallop. I need one burrata flatbread, no sage, on the fly, let's go, let's go!" I call out.

"Heard, Allie," the kitchen chants back.

25

"Allie, I'm about to drop the check on table twenty and I found out it's their anniversary. Can you comp a dessert?" a server asks.

"Yes, I can do that. But go get a blank anniversary card from the back office and sign it before you present the bill. And remember to put a note in their profile in the system before you clock out tonight. That way this time next year, we message them and invite them back in to celebrate. Okay?"

"Got it. Thanks."

As I futz around on the computer adjusting table twenty's bill, Angela comes up beside me. I glance at the clock and realize it's been over an hour since I last communicated with her. Even though the dining room is packed, the lull in arrivals feels almost like a relief.

"You hanging in there, Al?"

"Yes, why? Is my BO saying otherwise?"

Before Angela has a chance to sniff me out, Jessica rushes up to us at the host stand.

"We're eighty-sixed on bison."

"What? Already? How can we be completely out of an ingredient halfway through our first dinner service?" Angela replies.

The news comes as a shock to me, too—part of which is due to the fact I actually remember what *eighty-sixed* means in restaurant speak and haven't had to pull up Google to stay involved in this conversation.

"Tabitha says it's no good. She just cut into it, and either it's old or it wasn't properly stored. Go back there. You'll smell it right away."

"Oh, for fuck's sake. Allie, who's the vendor on that?"

"Leo's Meats," I say with zero hesitation.

"Great. Can you please leave Leo a voice mail sometime in the next five minutes and let him know he's fired? Then find us a new provider before tomorrow. I'm going to go talk to Tabitha now and find out what the sub is going to be. You're in charge of the front. Smile. Looks like a walk-in is headed your way..."

"Good evening, welcome to Here," I say to the wannabe solo diner. She's middle-aged with frizzy gray hair, quirky red-framed glasses and a floral dress. It's a shame she got all dolled up for a dinner she won't be able to have here.

"Hi there. I have a reservation for two for Smith, but my dining companion unfortunately had to cancel at the last minute," she says with the hint of a twang in her voice as she writhes out of her wool peacoat. "I'm wondering if I can still be sat, even though it's just me this evening."

Technically, if she had a reservation and one person dropped, I really can't turn her away. Ideally, I'd like to put her at the bar and avoid an empty chair in the dining area, but every stool is full. I'm going to have to seat her.

I consult the computer and see two separate reservations for Smith, both at the same time.

"First name?" I ask to be sure I check in the correct party.

"Bonnie," she says.

Her reservation is flagged in the system as a potential critic. The name "Bonnie Smith" came off a little too fake for Angela's liking and so we went ahead and assumed she's a writer for one of the more influential food publications.

Upon seeing the note in the computer, I look up at her and ask for just another moment of her patience. And after locking eyes, even just for a split second, I, too, agree the name is a fake. But only the last name. I believe this is Bonnie *Zane*, Benji's mom.

I know Bonnie Zane is supposed to be a lunatic (hey, the apple doesn't fall far from the tree)—someone with marked depression, broken skin and a raging pill problem. But this lady is poised and elegant and soft-spoken. Still, something about her familiar chocolate-brown eyes won't let me drop my suspicion.

I know I've never seen a photo of her or heard her voice. I've just been told stories of what phone calls with her were like, which allowed me to form a picture in my head. But I'm willing to erase all of that and start fresh based purely on the feeling I have in my gut.

"Right this way," I say, marking table thirty as red. She'll be sat at the farthest table in the corner so as to hide the fact we have a one-off diner—a sight for sore eyes at a restaurant like this at a popular dining hour.

As I usher her back to the dining area, she walks next to me instead of behind me like most patrons would.

"Beautiful job," she says. "I've been following this restaurant in the news and counting down for this very moment."

I smile, unsure what to say.

"Traveled far, too. It's a shame my dining partner had to drop out at the last minute," she continues. There was never a *"dining partner,"* I can't help but think.

"Here you are," I say, gesturing to the banquette side of the table and motioning for Paul to remove the vacant chair that's across from her.

She settles in and I place the menu in front of her. She puts her warm hand on top of mine.

"I have a great appreciation for what you've done, Allie. I can only imagine what it was like to have to do this all on your own."

At that point, I know. And she knows that I know.

Not only is her identity clear to me, but so is the fact that the story Benji created about her being some absentee mom is most likely fabricated. Or at the very least, unfounded. All I see sitting here is another pawn that was part of a ploy to get me to amp up my empathy. And maybe that's why she's here. To show her unspoken support for a fellow woman who has been Benjied herself.

At that point, Paul is on his way back from removing the chair and is going to soon seek answers to the booze, time and water questions from this lonely patron.

"Enjoy your evening, Ms. Zane," I whisper just before Paul swoops in.

It's 1:15 in the morning. Our last guest left at 12:30 a.m. after being slightly overserved by our heavy-handed bartender, Brian. Since then, our servers have been working hard to finish their sidework—preassigned duties that must be completed before anyone gets cut to go home. When a server completes their designated task (coffee machine is cleaned, teas are restocked, silverware is polished, roll-ups for the bar are folded, etc.), they find me or Angela to check their station and then they can be dismissed if it looks like they didn't totally half-ass it. We're down to our last two, who happen to be the detail-oriented Jessica and Paul, who probably just feels like he owes me a solid after his near mental breakdown earlier tonight.

Meanwhile, the dishwashers are scrubbing everything down and Tabitha's team is wrapping and containing all the leftover food. I'm currently posted up on a stool at the bar, where we've flipped on the lights at full power. Damn, it's bright in here.

With a calculator in hand, I'm figuring out the server tip-out for the night. We held a team vote when everyone was hired regarding how they wanted to handle gratuities. Traditionally, a server keeps the total of what each patron leaves for them. But sometimes in fine dining, there's what's called a "tip pool." This is where everyone chips in the entirety of their gratuity and then we divide the grand total evenly by the number of servers who worked that night. They voted for the latter. Although it's risky, it forces everyone to be on the top of their game and work for the greater good.

Of that total number, I shave off a small cut for our busers and our bar staff, who deserve a portion of the server's pull since they greatly assist with the night going smoothly. When it's all said and done, my calculations are showing that each member of the waitstaff is walking with $305, which they'll be able to pick up from the office anytime after 10:00 a.m. tomorrow. Not bad.

As I walk back from officially cutting Jessica and Paul, I can't help but dwell on the fact my feet are killing me. I know I'm the one who made the half-inch heel rule, but as the AGM of this place, I felt like anything less than a three-inch stiletto didn't exactly scream "Head Bitch in Charge." Needless to say, these black leather Sam Edelmans were a bad choice. The thought of walking out to the street to catch a cab, let alone waking up and doing this again tomorrow, is frightening.

"So, how did we do tonight?" I ask Angela, who has all the printouts from the YeltonXT scattered across the bar along with a glass of Chambord and her own calculator.

"Two hundred covers. One-seventy-five on the books, twenty-five walk-ins."

"I thought you said we couldn't take walk-ins..."

"Yeah, well, I snuck a few in when you weren't looking. I saw a few pockets and knew we could handle it. If I explained to you how and why in the exact moment, your brain would have combusted. So that lesson will have to wait until next time."

"Fair enough. What'd we make?"

I'm fully bracing for Angela to tell me how I'm always about the money, but tonight I get to be.

"Just shy of 20K."

Twenty thousand dollars is only ten less than my original investment. Granted, I know that number has to now be split about 20,000 ways and probably only one of them is back to my pocket, I'm still proud. It sounds big. Is it?

"Would you say that's a good night?" I ask.

"No."

Fuck.

"I'd say it's a stellar night. Florette is much bigger than this, and our best night was 29K. To be less than ten thousand dollars under their *best* night is a big deal, Allie. Craig's going to be pleased."

Which I guess means I should be, too. If my feet weren't so damn tired, I'd be doing a little jig.

"Now what do you want for your shift drink?" she asks as she heads behind the bar.

"I'll take a glass of Malbec," I say.

"Malbec? You seated 200 people, handled an unexpected eighty-sixed dish and made sure none of our servers hanged themselves in the bathroom...and you want a *Malbec*?"

She forgot to mention surviving an unexpected encounter with Benji's mom, but who's keeping track?

"Fine," I say. "Give me a Johnny Walker Black. Neat."

"Attagirl."

She slides the glass my way; a few drips splash out onto the ledge of the bar and I wipe it with my sleeve. I take the first sip—it stings and burns as it hits the spot.

"So...how'd *I* do?" At least the flammable drink in my glass will make the harsh truth that I know is coming from Angela go down easier.

"B minus."

Thank god.

"I'll take it."

"We need to work on your serving skills," she says after gulping down a fair amount of the ruby-toned liquid in her glass. The smell of berries and vanilla wafts over the sharp tang of cognac.

"Why? We plate clockwise from twelve o'clock," I say with confidence.

"Yeah, but I'm not sure you know where twelve o'clock is."

"It's the wine cellar."

"It's...the bar."

"Oh. Then, yeah, that explains why everyone was shuffling plates to the right whenever I brought food out." It's a gaffe I'm sure the service staff won't soon forget, but what can I do other than get it right tomorrow?

"Don't worry about it," she says in an uncharacteristic lapse of stringency. "Oh, and one more thing. You've gotta get to know industry people better. Go spend some time Facebook stalking. Isn't that what you're good at anyway?"

"You mean...isn't that the job you made me quit last month? Yup, sure is!"

Angela lovingly flips me off.

"Really, though, what'd I miss?"

"It's not *what* you missed. It's *who* you missed. Hal Huckby was the solo walk-in you sent to the bar."

"Shit. I sent a sober guy to the bar?"

She nods as she sips on her drink.

"Now, don't worry too much about that. He's a cool guy now. He can handle being sat in front of a bottle of Jack. But had you recognized him, it definitely would have behooved you to have found me. We could have made space for him and given Tab a heads-up so she could have done her thing."

I can't believe I missed him, the guy who emailed me that

brazen wake-up call about Benji. He helped get my sorry ass out of the mourning period when no one else could. It would have been nice to say thanks. What's more is that I know what he looks like. So I guess I was just so taken aback by the whole Bonnie thing, I stopped looking people in the eye the rest of the night. But then again, seeing a tattooed chef out for dinner by himself in jeans and a V-neck is like spotting your teacher grabbing bananas at the grocery store. Without a white, sauce-stained apron tied across his waist, I just didn't realize Hal Huckby was in the house. Period.

"Sorry about that," I say back.

"Like I said, don't sweat it. Hey, speaking of solos, who was our other party of one tonight? The chick at table thirty."

I freeze up. I'm not about keeping secrets, especially not to Angela. But just like the details of her past, there are certain things that don't need to be bubbled up. This is one.

"No clue. Nice woman. Big fan of us. Dining partner bailed."

"Gotcha. Well, honestly, everything short of your com-pletely inappropriate shoe choice this evening was pretty damn spot-on."

This time it's my turn to throw a middle finger her way.

Just then, my phone buzzes on the bar with an incom-ing text. I've neglected all of my incoming messages—text, Twitter, you name it—all night and am now actively avoiding the task of combing through them. I know everyone means well, and I'm grateful for the support, but I am tired in a way I didn't know was possible. But then again, sitting here read-ing texts for a few minutes means I get to stay off my feet that much longer. I dive in.

Seven hours ago, a text from my mom: On our way! Where 2 park?

Six hours ago, also a text from my mom: Hi from table. Dad wants 2 kno where bathroom is?

Five hours ago, *another* text from my mom: Food = incredible! We R so proud of U. Call us 2mrw. Get home safely. No more sleeping @ the resto. UR gonna kill UR back!

Four hours ago, a text from Jazzy: Hey girl. Thanks 4 ur text. I'm sorry 2. Proud of U. U R killing it! M & I have resos next wk. C U then, K?

Three hours ago, an email from Maya with a link to the "Hot Opens" section of *FoodFeed* featuring Here: Congrats on the opening of your restaurant. I've heard nothing but good things. Thanks for your note. Love you, miss you and I'm so sorry about how things went down that day, too. See you soon! XO, M

Two hours ago, an email from Hal Huckby: Good job tonight, Simon. I was going to formally introduce myself, but you seemed focused, didn't want to distract you on such an important night. Hats off to Tabitha, too. Scallops were perfect. Take care. Hal.

One minute ago, a text from Jared Marcel: Dying 2 hear about opening night! We can wait til Tues when I'm up UR alley (NOT an innuendo), but thinking coffee Mon? UR off right?

A smirk settles onto my lips before I can think to stop it. Jared's charm game is on point.

No go on coffee, I write. Then, a calculated minute later, Make it a cupcake instead and U have a deal.

He wastes no time with the reply. An industry pro who prefers cupcakes to coffee??? WHO R U ALLIE SIMON?

This time my smile is augmented by the blush I can feel heating my cheeks. Angela raises an eyebrow when I look up to catch her watching me.

"Are you sexting with our produce guy?" she asks.

"No! No," I say, imbuing my voice with what I can only hope is professional sobriety. "I'm just…thanking him for the flowers."

26

When I turned twenty-one, my birthday was on a Friday and it was my first summer living alone downtown in the city. Finally, I would be able to have a drink with Jazzy and Maya and not worry if the place was carding or how I could wash the underage stamp off the top of my hand so I could score a Bud Light from anyone willing to buy me one.

I had my first drink that day around 9:00 a.m., when I arrived at the place I was interning for the summer. When my supervisors found out it was my twenty-first, they determined shots before the morning production meeting were necessary. After that, they took me to Happy Hour around 5:00 p.m. Then I stumbled home for a quick outfit change in preparation for my nighttime plans, which included barhopping with Jazzy and Maya through all the trendy neighborhoods in Chicago and telling every single person I passed, "It's my birthdaaaaaaay."

That night when I got home, I managed not to vomit but didn't quite escape unscathed—I drunk-dialed my high school sweetheart and passed out wondering if the world would ever stop spinning.

Then, I woke up the next day and did it all again.

And again that Sunday.

And when Monday came around, I felt like toxic waste—but totally okay with it.

That's how I'm feeling today, like I partied a little too hard, zero-regrets style. The only difference between clubbing and floor-managing is that my high school sweetheart was not part of the equation, which is a good thing considering I don't have to spend my first and only day off during the week (because the restaurant is closed) apologizing to someone I haven't seen in eight years.

I woke up sometime around 11:30 a.m., which sounds late, but by the time I finished the books and completed the few pieces of sidework that went undone, I didn't get home and to sleep until after three in the morning. So despite clocking a solid eight hours of rest, I am still very, very exhausted and am only just starting to pay off the immense sleep debt I've racked up.

My entire body aches, down to my pointer finger thanks to the serious workout the YeltonXT gave it. Angela said she's going to order stylus pens for us asap so we can still manage to have fingerprints this time next year.

I checked my Fitbit when I got home last night and saw that I clocked something like 100,000 steps this weekend alone. Lapping the restaurant, leading covers to their tables and just generally trying to stay one step ahead of the chaos constantly nipping at my heels beats anything I could have done on the treadmill. Apparently, this is how restaurant insiders stay so skinny despite being surrounded by rich food and a plethora of wine all the time.

Walking, and coffee…which I still don't like but everyone at the restaurant has conditioned me to believe is the only thing that snaps you out of feeling like a zombie extra on the set of *The Walking Dead*. So I dig out the coffee maker I bought from Goodwill for Benji and plug it in. I fish around for a filter and grab the canister of ground-up beans I bought him from a boutique coffee shop in Bucktown. I open it, inhale and let its one redeeming quality—the smell—remind me I'm alive and I survived the opening weekend of a big-shot restaurant.

I'm not sure yet how I take my coffee—hey, there's nothing to add to a Diet Coke but ice—but without sugar or cream in my fridge, I'll be preparing this morning's cup black.

I climb on a chair to reach the mugs I've stored on the highest shelf in my cupboard since I don't ever use them. In fact, Benji was the first and only person living in this apartment to tap into the collection of hand-me-downs, though the whole set of thick beige mugs has sentimental value: they're a relic from my parents' wedding registry circa 1982.

I rescue a mug from the top shelf, feeling oddly warm and fuzzy about this ugly blob of porcelain my mother picked out so long ago. But those feelings are dampened when I realize how filthy this thing is.

It's not just dusty or unwashed either. There's a thick black ash, almost like tar, caked to the bottom. Sure, Benji smoked in the apartment, but he always ashed out the window. That means this is residue from a far more sinister habit, a dirty, ugly thing I never allowed through the door—not knowingly anyway.

The thoughts that have been kept at bay by weeks of preparation and a weekend of hard work suddenly wash over me all at once. Though I haven't seen or heard from him in almost forty-five days, Hurricane Benji comes in for landing with crushing force. I've been too busy to keep my defenses up like they should have been, and now I'm completely overwhelmed by the realization of what went on within these walls. It's a violation only someone who has suffered a home invasion can relate to, but worse.

Worse because I know exactly who did this. I had sex with this person. I told this person I loved him. I actually *did* love him.

I make the choice to be angry, not sad, and spill the entire pot of coffee down the drain. The steam billows up and condenses on my face for a moment, stinging my eyes. I climb back on the chair and pull down every last mug from my parents' set as I fill the sink with half a bottle of Palmolive and scalding hot water. If they didn't have sentimental value, I'd throw them all down ten floors to the bottom of the trash chute and wash my hands of another piece of my past with Benji. But that's not an option right now, so I take a deep breath and focus on keeping it together. After all, I owe it to my parents and their thirty-odd years of marriage not to let these become collateral damage from the storm.

I scrub until the mugs are clean and my hands are red and cracked. With each rinse and repeat, I start to feel a little better.

Now that my coffee plans are foiled, I go back to basics and order a large Diet Coke and a Turkey Tom sandwich from Jimmy John's. While I wait for the delivery, I scan the social-sphere and see what I've missed while I've been running things at Here.

I may not work for Daxa anymore, but I certainly remember all the tricks of the trade. I set up a search to comb Twitter for any and all tweets related to the opening this weekend. My results push back a whopping 866 tweets, including retweets and replies, which automatically order themselves top-to-bottom based on how much clout the message's author has. Basically, I'm eavesdropping in the cafeteria, listening most closely to what the kids sitting at "the popular table" have to say about Here.

Zane out. New chef in. Thought it'd be a disaster but...top-notch. Insanely good foie gras at @HereRestaurant. Tweeted from the *Chicago Sun-Times.*

Job well done on an incredible opening @HereRestaurant! Place looks amazing, @AllieSimon & @ChefTab! #Foodie #Chicago. Tweeted from our friends at Paragraph.

Thought @BJZane was the chef of @HereRestaurant? Who's the chick in the back that made my dinner? Still yummy tho! Tweeted from a wannabe food blogger who apparently didn't read the press release we blasted out. Disregard/block.

My waiter is seriously the hottest thing ever. Totally getting his number. #HereRestaurant #Chicago. Tweeted by a cheerleader for the Chicago Bulls. I click into her profile and make a mental note that she and Andrew would actually make a beautiful couple.

While I appreciate the fanfare, I just know that at least *one* of these tweets has got to be less than flattering. I scroll on, just waiting for the bad one to rise to the surface like a game of whack-a-mole.

So Allie Simon is the AGM at @HereRestaurant? Pretty clear who she was blowing to get that gig. #dumbslut. Tweeted by an anonymous user with a cracked egg in a frying pan as his avatar.

Ouch—that one hurts. And not because I'm being cyberbullied by a nameless, faceless dickhead, but because I fear there are more cowards behind the computer screen who are just frothing at the mouth, waiting to call me out as the new laughingstock of the Chicago food scene. Let's just hope that was a one-off.

How come no one is talking about the fact that @BJZane has been MIA and failed to open yet ANOTHER restaurant? #LOSER. Tweeted by some random foodie chick who, as it happens, totally has a point.

And finally, before I force myself to look away, Did @BJZane and @AllieSimon break up? #sayitaintso. Tweeted (and retweeted 26 times) by the same dating blogger who said we were "relationship goals" not too long ago.

All in all, the feedback is good. Besides a few people who failed to get the memo that Benji was no longer running the back-of-house and his maybe-ex-girlfriend was now running the front-of-house, people generally stayed focused—and complimentary—on the things that matter most: the tasty food, the expensive decor and the overall aesthetic appeal of our service team.

Not bad. Not bad at all. I take a screenshot of the top tweets and email it to Angela.

By the time I sit down with my mercifully fast delivery and unwrap my first real meal in three days, Angela has already replied with links to actual journalistic responses to our effort. Apparently the *Chicago Tribune* completed their review of the opening and posted the article online.

I click the link embedded in Angela's email and have to consciously stop my hands from shaking as the article loads.

SERIOUS HEART IN 'HERE,' the headline reads.

My heart skips as I read the first few sentences.

Nestled on a stretch of Randolph Street previously occupied by a dilapidated concrete box, Here from the outside is all intrigue. Hints of motion could be seen through the street-side frosted windows as I vacated the taxi. I could tell already that my taste buds were gearing up to dance.

Inside, past a simple but well-stocked bar, is a dining space adorned with metal-bead curtains, vintage-bulb café lighting, and other visual tricks that make you feel like you are dining at a renowned architect's home. Hoity, no. Haute, yes.

I was seated amidst a packed dining room that looks as good as any of its neighborhood counterparts. Modern, yet comfortable. My nattily dressed server left me with a menu as she fetched my cocktail. Maybe there is something to this new kid on the block, I thought.

Too nervous to read the piece in full, I skim the article looking for anything alarming or unusual.

What was odd, however, was seeing Tabitha Johnson listed as Chef de Cuisine at the bottom of our gold-leaf menu card. Wasn't it just weeks ago that Chicago's culinary whiz kid, the erratic Benji Zane, was awarded the role? Regardless, the bait and switch was much appreciated, as Chef Johnson's roasted beet salad is the best in the city and not to be missed.

Benji may very well be doing coke by a rusty Dumpster somewhere on the far West Side, but at least the press is handling his absence well. I scroll down and read some more.

At the helm running the floor is seasoned fine-dining manager Angela Blackstone. Though this is her first stint in the city, she handled the razzle-dazzle of the big show quite well. The same cannot be said—yet—for her counterpart, Allie Simon. With zero restaurant history (that we know of), Simon flubbed a simple recommendation for a crisp white wine and instead wobbled away like a baby deer in a pair of high heels to pass the baton to the sommelier. Though charming and full of potential, she will have to realize that a bright, white smile won't be enough to cut it on Randolph Street.

Damn.

I remember this table. They started their night at the bar with Moscow Mules. I had a hunch they were critics, which is why I scheduled them to be put with a captain. Once they were sat in Jessica's section, I figured it would be smooth sailing from there. But when I stopped by to welcome them and see how their meal was going, they tested me on a wine reco. I thought I was doing the right thing by tracking down the sommelier and getting a professional opinion. I guess they wanted me to have all the answers, right then and there.

And alright already with the heels, okay? Working sixteen hours a day, seven days a week, doesn't lend itself to a quick trip to the mall for practical footwear. I'll get to it.

At least the article ended on a high note, awarding us three out of four stars and recommending the city make their way to the West Loop, if only for Tabitha's house-made bleu cheese dressing.

Bzz, bzz.

A text interrupts my research at my makeshift mission control center. It's Jared.

Cupcakes n conversation. 2pm. Molly's in Lincoln Park.

I wipe the mayo off my fingers, realizing how quickly I'd forgotten how good a simple sandwich from a chain restaurant can taste, and text him back.

Don't judge me if I order 2. Been a helluva wknd.

The last forty-eight days have been dedicated to Here. The four months before that I was with Benji, the ball and chain. I never strayed too far from home base, not even to grab wine with the girls or sneak an eyebrow wax unless he knew I'd be home soon and have access to my phone the whole time. So the fact that I've just left my apartment and am now on a leisurely stroll through Lincoln Park heading to a cupcake shop is just bliss. Pure bliss.

"There she is. How many Michelin stars have you won already?" Jared pulls me in for a hug and a kiss on the cheek, a gesture I'm not quite ready for. I'm sure he feels how stiff I am in his arms, because he pulls away fast but tries to cover by kicking at something invisible on the ground.

"Oh, please. It's more like how many prescriptions for Xanax have I filled. Man, no one ever tells you that opening a restaurant is going to be the single most anxiety-ridden, backbreaking thing you'll ever do."

"Yeah, those ice fishers on the coast of Alaska have nothing on opening a fancy-shmancy restaurant on Randolph Street, do they?"

Maybe it's just my close association with Angela this past month and a half, but I have a new appreciation for people who keep it real. And Jared does just that, letting me know he understands the struggle but also has perspective. His support is genuine but subtle. I like it.

The cool thing about Molly's Cupcakes—aside from the actual cupcakes, of course—is that they installed three seats near the counter that are swings. Usually, a free spot on one of them is unheard of. But at 2:00 p.m. on a Monday when most normal people are working normal jobs, the swings are vacant. So we post up there and order four delicious calorie bombs.

I watch Jared cut through them, creating a proper taste-test setup. Just like the first few times I've seen him, today he looks different again. Today, it seems like he looked himself in the mirror and gave himself the thumbs-up before he headed out to meet me. A black-and-red buffalo plaid button-down, slim-cut black jeans and what looks to me like a fresh haircut from Floyd's barbershop all contribute to him being the cutest guy in all of Lincoln Park, I'm sure of it.

I dig into the cupcake platter, and crumbs immediately plummet to my lap. Thank god my skinny jeans are dark enough to mask any chocolate that decides to melt itself into the fibers.

"This one is really good. It tastes like a Butterfinger bar.

Try it," I say as I point with one hand and wipe my mouth with the other.

"Nah, I'm not a chocolate guy," Jared replies.

I give him a death stare, though his smile tells me to go easy. "That's like saying you don't like *dogs*," I tell him. "Please tell me you're kidding."

He puts his half in his mouth, chews and replies, "I'm totally kidding."

Crisis averted. However, a new problem presents itself: I've been out of the game for a while and I think a cute guy might actually be trying to flirt with me.

"So can I ask you a question?" he says.

I know where this is going. It doesn't bother me. Hell, if anyone in my circle was dating a semifamous drug addict, I'm sure I'd want to know just how close it was to a real-life episode of *Intervention*, too.

But sitting across from Jared, contemplating why on earth I can't stop thinking about what this hazelnut buttercream frosting would taste like if I kissed it off his soft, full lips, I realize I don't want to talk about Benji. He might be just another character whose exploits are recorded in the morning edition to most, but he's a real person who brought real chaos and real heartache into my life. I'm hoping we don't have to go there right now.

But of course I don't say that. It's too early to demonstrate the baggage I carry. Instead I say, "Sure. What's on your mind?"

"I obviously know who you are. I mean, everyone in the industry knows who you are, even if it's just by association." Sad, but true. "So are you still...with him?"

Jared's gaze is fixed on marbled frosting as he asks. He sweeps his finger through the chocolate-and-vanilla swirl, scoops up a dollop and licks it off. I can tell he's embarrassed to have asked about my relationship status and won't lock eyes with me again until I somehow let him know it's okay.

"What, you couldn't figure it out from Twitter?"

"I'm not on Twitter..." he says.

"Never mind, I'm just joking. But the answer is no, I'm not." I pause for a second, wondering if he had some sort of a bet going that Benji and I weren't going to last longer than six months after the *FoodFeed* article came out. I hate how self-conscious this relationship has made me. Especially of industry people.

"God, I feel like such an idiot. I don't even know why I just asked that. It's really none of my business, is it? I'm sorry. I'm sure it was a rough breakup."

"No, it's okay. It actually wasn't really a breakup at all. He sort of just...left. I haven't seen or heard from him since."

"Wow, so you actually had the perfect breakup! No awkward 'it's not you, it's me' conversation," he says, clearly trying to backpedal us out of super-awkward, vibe-killing conversation territory.

"You could say that, I guess. The only downfall is I'm eating substantially less glamorously these days," I banter back.

He gestures to the myriad cupcake crumbs and colorful icing on the plates in front of us.

"I beg to differ," he says.

"Touché."

There's a beat of silence as we both take our next bite.

"So if he's out of the picture, why do you still want to run his restaurant?" Jared asks.

"It was never *his restaurant*," I say with what I sense is a hint of pride. "I spent my life savings to open Here."

"How old are you again?"

"Twenty-five."

"Barely able to rent a car." He smiles. "So I get that you're part owner, but explain the AGM thing to me. People work their whole lives trying to trade the apron for a suit and work the floor. Did you just kind of fall into it?"

More like plummeted off a high dive with ankle weights on.

"We had some unexpected staffing issues at the last minute that forced me to take a more active role. Otherwise, I'd risk this being a complete financial failure."

"Got it. So you're busting your ass to recoup your investment."

"And sleeping at the restaurant most nights of the week to make it happen."

"Wow. Allie-freakin'-Simon. You are an even bigger enigma than I thought."

"I'm going to take that as a compliment," I announce.

"Go for it," he says, leaning a little closer. "Or I can give you a better one. You're smart. And gorgeous. And holding your own at the helm of the most-talked-about new restaurant in the West Loop...all while under the scrutiny of an industry made up of gossips and assholes who want to see you fail just so they can feel better about themselves. I'm pretty sure you're Wonder Woman, and frankly I'd let you fly circles around me any day of the week."

I'm not exactly sure what I'd let Jared do around me any day of the week, but I'm certain it would involve a lack of pants and a bottle of pinot noir. At least, that's the gut feeling I'm getting as it dawns on me that he *is* flirting with me and that I'm attracted to him.

There, I said it. *I'm attracted to him.*

And what am I supposed to do with that? What *can* I do with that? There's no room in my life for a man right now unless he's a server asking me to comp a dessert at Here. And even if Angela let me break rule-number-whatever-it-is that says I can't date a vendor, I've got massive walls up from being burned by Benji. Walls that will require a few sticks of dynamite to even make a dent. I wouldn't go as far as saying I'm damaged goods, I'm just…temporarily eighty-sixed. I should pump the brakes here before one of us suggests watching a movie at the other's apartment next.

"Maybe not Wonder Woman," I say, returning us both to earth. "But yeah, I do what I can to make people want to come back and keep spending hundreds of dollars on tiny portions of really tasty food."

"So if Here wasn't your first career choice, what's your real dream?" Jared asks.

"You mean if I had another $30,000 to blow?" When I say it like that, it doesn't feel quite like this investment was one of the worst decisions of my life.

"Yeah, if you found $30,000 taped under your swing right now, what would you do with it?"

I check, just in case this is a massive setup from the Publishers Clearing House. Nothing. Jared grins at me.

"I'd probably buy every single cupcake this place has for a month straight."

"That's exactly what I was thinking, too," Jared says.

I know it's not the answer he's looking for, though he's politely playing along, so I hum a bit and look toward the ceiling for inspiration.

"I'd take my mom on an all-expense-paid trip to Paris," I say. "She's been a trouper throughout this whole restaurant thing."

"Oh, I bet. Clipping all the articles and sticking them to her fridge? Telling all the neighbors to make a reservation and ask for 'Allie'? Egging the house of the critic who said your shoe choice was subpar?" he asks.

"Yes. All that. And for not disowning me because of my horrible taste in men."

"Hey…" he says, gesturing to himself. "It can't be all that bad."

"Very funny," I say, not sure to play into or deflect the flirtatious fun. "I just think she deserves to be flown first-class overseas and then spoiled with room service, good wine, lots of cheese, dinner at the Eiffel Tower, things like that. I want to show her that I'm thankful to have her in my life and that she's still proud of me no matter what, you know?"

"Oh, I know." Jared stares at the crumbs on his plate, his voice taking on a more serious tone. "My dad passed away two years ago."

"Really? How?"

I immediately regret asking, but then remember he brought up Benji. Apparently tough topics aren't off-limits.

"Remember Snowmageddon two winters ago?"

"You mean when there was a sixty-degree temperature drop and two feet of snow in a matter of six hours? Yeah, that was brutal," I say.

"Well, my dad was doing a last-minute delivery for a place on the South Side and skidded off the I-94 ramp into a car coming the other way. He flipped the truck."

"Oh my god. I'm so sorry, Jared. That's really, really awful."

"He died at the scene. So did the other driver. Cops said they both died on impact, so I don't think they suffered much. It was just…man, it was just tragic."

I pause for a minute. I think of all the destruction that Benji caused and then realize something pretty simple: at least no one died. I know it sounds like a dramatic generalization of the rolling turmoil endured by being with him, but there's perspective here that I appreciate. There were dealer debts I almost volunteered to go pay. My home address was given out and made the epicenter for drop-offs of all sorts. I ventured into the city's most dangerous neighborhood for a casual look-around. The grip he had on me could get me to do *anything.* And somehow, through all that, I'm not just alive, I'm well. And at that, the care and concern goes back to the person who actually deserves it right now, Jared.

"God, I'm so sorry. How do you even *deal* with that?"

"Well, I suppose you could say he died doing what he loved, so I get some peace from that. The other driver I don't know much about. I suppose I could find out more if I dug through all the old news coverage, but it was hard enough moving on from my dad. I know it sounds heartless, but I really didn't feel like opening up a second wound, you know?" Jared sighs and pushes back in his swing. "I still can't even believe my dad's gone."

"So I assume that's when you took over? After the accident?"

"Yup. I mean, I never wanted to be a delivery guy or anything, but then again it's a family business and I was his only son so I knew it was coming eventually. I just thought I would have more time before I'd have to take things over officially."

"How old are you, if you don't mind me asking?" We've crossed enough boundaries already that I actually have zero qualms asking about his age.

"I'm twenty-nine."

"Ah, an older man," I say, trying to steer us back to light-hearted territory. "So then, Jared. What's *your* dream?"

"I want to be a dolphin trainer," he spouts off.

"Really?"

"No way, I can't even swim."

Our laughter seems to dissolve the buildup of gloom and sadness we've accrued in the last five minutes.

"I'd do what I was planning to before taking over Marcel & Sons—I'd become a high school history teacher."

"At least you didn't say math," I say.

"Fuck math," Jared says, clinking his plastic cup of water against mine.

Just then, I hear my phone ding with a new email.

"Sorry, that's probably Angela. I thought I turned it to silent," I say, reaching into my bag to switch the thing off.

"Don't worry about it. Hey, I'm going to run to the bathroom real quick. Don't let any bratty eight-year-olds take my swing." Jared stands and looks at me. There's a moment when it feels like he's going to lean in to kiss me on the cheek or something, but it passes in an instant and he's gone.

The feeling in my chest as I watch him walk away is... disappointment. Which switches to something else entirely when I see that the email I received is from someone claiming to be Benji's new girlfriend.

I thought you'd be curious about Benji's whereabouts. He is in rehab FYI. He'll be there a while. It's far away. Don't try to find him, we plan on picking up where we left off when he gets out and moving out of state. -Hannah

I spy Jared coming back, which means the phone needs to be put away and the look of sheer panic needs to be stripped from my face.

But not before I fire off a frantic text to Angela.

Benji's alive. In rehab. Has new GF, I write.

A second later comes her reply: Figures. PS. We need to up the order of paper towels.

27

"Beautiful, beautiful. Just like that," says the photographer. "Okay, just a few more—hold that million-dollar smile. Nice. Now, Allie, turn a little more toward me and drop your right shoulder. Perfect. Now pretend to bite the apple. GOOD! Hold still! Hold it!"

My name was first thrust into the public eye when *FoodFeed* broke the news of my last relationship. After seeing what that eventually led to, I swore to myself and Angela that I would never take part in another glorified piece of restaurant press again. But when Alexi Kolev, *Mag Mile Magazine*'s famed art director, contacted me and said he wanted to reenact the apple scene from *Snow White* with me wearing a beaded couture Marchesa gown and lying on top of our bar with Tabitha and Angela in the background, I immediately changed my mind. If anything, at least I'd score myself a new Facebook profile picture. Just like any twentysomething on social media, I still have my priorities.

"'One Bite and Your Dreams Will Come True,'" says Alexi. "Just got the email from the editor—that's going to be the title for your piece! Congratulations, dear. That's a wrap on the group shoot. Great work, everybody!"

It's been three months since we opened the doors to Here and not only has the place not burned to the ground, it's on everyone's short list of places to see and be seen in the city.

I'm not going to sit here and say I don't know how we did it, because I know exactly how it happened: we worked our asses off, gave up our lives and dedicated ourselves to inventing and defining a restaurant concept unlike any other in Chicago. A place where our guests can dress up and be treated like royalty but still feel like they're sitting at the dinner table with family and friends, eating a favorite meal they've never had before.

We've been in the black every week since we opened, and I've been trained to know that black—the color of Craig's AmEx—is good. With me in charge of the day-to-day books and Angela in charge of the overall budget, together our calculations show we are pacing to profit throughout the winter. Angela tells me that Chicago winters tend to destroy fine-dining restaurants because no one wants to put on twelve layers to stand outside in the cold for an Uber that's going to get stuck in the snow or slide on ice over the I-90 bridge into the West Loop, but so far, we are defying the wind, snow, ice—even the allure of ordering Grubhub in pajamas next to a fireplace.

What makes us so confident that this winter weather has nothing on the heated tile entryway of Here? Well, we sold out two separate rounds of seating on New Year's Eve, each with fifty covers. Tab cooked up a prix fixe meal with a price of $135 per person—$200 for the patrons that felt like celebrating with the boozy pairings. Then, with all the activity in the bar afterward, we pulled just over $40,000. Forty grand in a single night—twelve more than I'm due to make in an entire year according to the bone-dry salary presented in my offer letter from Angela.

Don't get me wrong. These last couple months haven't always been confetti and bubbly for us. I've had two waitresses up and quit because they felt the tip pool they voted to have was unfair. I replaced them fairly quickly, but it takes about two full weeks of training before anyone is able to take a table solo and upsell the shit out of our seafood add-ons. That said, we were a bit "compressed"—an industry term for totally stressed and feeling it—but have since managed to onboard the newbies and create a stellar team of servers that finally feels stable.

Our back-of-house wasn't immune to the HR drama either. One of the sous chefs was caught stealing meat off our delivery truck and carrying it around the corner to his wife who was waiting for him with a cooler. No wonder we were eighty-six filet mignon by 7:00 p.m. the first three weeks. Needless to say, the thief was fired and we held open interviews for a replacement cook.

Sebastian, Benji's former right hand, came in to apply for the job. I said hello and kept it short and sweet before fetching Tabitha to do the interview unbiased. She chose to pass on him for being a little too green for the fast-paced environment we have at Here, but she offered him the chance to stage on any Tuesday he'd like since Tuesdays are our least busy day. And by "least busy" I mean we feed 150 people a night instead of 170. I guess he took her up on it because I've seen him a few times since.

FoodFeed has been shockingly complimentary of everything Here is doing, but I think that's just because they want to keep me buttered up so I'll agree to provide a quote for a massive exposé they are doing on Benji, due out sometime next year. But unless they're calling me to see if I can squeeze them in for a seating on our sold-out Valentine's Day dinner service, I plan to reserve my right to remain silent.

So, yeah, that's what life has been like for the past three months: Here, Here and more Here.

With a hearty side of Jared.

Are we officially a "thing"? No. But knowing how I would feel if he found some other industry AGM to take to the movies or spatter off random historical facts to makes it feel like maybe we should be. Like maybe we should define this relationship.

Still, I refuse to put a title on what we are because if I fancy myself having a new boyfriend, that means I have to come to terms with what happened with my last one—and the truth is, I still don't know. Yes, he relapsed. Yes, it was bad. And yes, (apparently) he went to rehab. But for all intents and purposes, it's an open wound as far as I'm concerned. Every day, I do my part to patch it up, but there's a lot of healing left. That, I am not naive about.

The other reason I'm keeping this casual is that Angela will shit a brick if she finds out we've made whatever we are "official." I'm basing that purely on the fact she didn't take it well when I let it slip that I broke Rule #77 (or was it #34?) around our third-ish date. Yup, we slept together. And it. Was. Amaze-balls.

The sex is so different from what I had with Benji. I used to think nothing could ever top the carnality we shared—raw, hot, fast and furious. But I've come to realize that to Benji, my vagina was nothing more than a line of coke, a shot of dope. I was just another mood-altering substance in a life saturated by them. His passion for me wasn't a matter of love, loyalty or commitment—it was just a thing to get him high when he couldn't do cocaine. Kind of like a cup of coffee or bottle of cough syrup, but with a more intense climax.

Sex with Jared is exactly what sex should be: give-and-take and a good time for everyone involved.

Beyond just the physical, Jared and I have a connection. He's easy to talk to and we never go more than a few hours without a text. And not in that obsessive, manic, where-the-hell-are-you way. But more like the "TELL ME you watched this week's *Game of Thrones*..." variety. It's cute.

Another thing I appreciate about Jared is the fact that he

has helped me get my friendship back on track with Jazzy and Maya—and he doesn't even realize it. For our second date, we went to the Farmer's Market—first came cupcakes, then came cucumbers, if you will. While picking out fresh flowers, we ran into the girls. When I explained that these were my two best friends, he insisted that we all walk through the park together and he'd share who all the best vendors were. At first, I was uneasy going for a leisurely walk, crepe in hand, with two people who I was last seen with while begging for a ride to the projects. But the best part about Jared's "come on, it'll be fun!" attitude is that it leaves no room for details like that. I mean, who cares to discuss semantics of our past when the city's best tomato vendor is located just a few stalls ahead?

It wasn't long before the four of us were laughing, eating and telling stories like the cast of a TV series on the Lifetime Network. In a quiet moment, when Jared was catching up with one of his vendor pals, the girls told me how great they thought he was. How different from Benji—in a good way— he was. How perfect for me he was.

Jazzy and Maya are the only friends-and-family threshold Jared has crossed as of yet. My mom knows about him; he came up in one of our routine phone conversations. She'd probably still prefer I date a banker or an electrician, someone with less of a grip on this industry. But I think she's equally happy that I'm at least exploring my options and not hanging on to the could-have/would-have brought on by a certain someone.

While Alexi fusses with his camera equipment, I sneak a look at my phone after being largely detached from it during the morning.

How's the shoot? reads the text from Jared.

Got a pound of makeup on. Face hurts from smiling. Starving, I text back.

#BigShot. Lunch?

I wish. Still shooting. Can't believe we R nominated 4 a JBF award.

I guess that's another thing I failed to mention. Here is up for a JBF. In case you don't know, "JBF" stands for James Beard Foundation. And in case you're wondering, I'm in shock they consider us one of the best in the business.

The prestigious foundation is based in New York City and gives out annual awards in a multitude of categories ranging from Cookbook of the Year to Best Food Blog, Best Wine Program, Chef, Pastry Chef—you get the idea. It's a big night in the industry, like the Grammys for foodies. Winners give speeches onstage and losers give blow jobs in the bathroom. The event is broadcast on the web and the entire Twittersphere explodes when someone—either deserving or undeserving—picks up a win.

From what I hear, it's a cross between the best night ever and a total shit show. A prom throwback, if you will.

I'll see for myself, in person, in just a couple months—when the event takes place right here in Chicago. The award we are up for is a biggie: Best New Restaurant. In fact, it's the only award we even qualify for seeing that Here opened less than one calendar year before the date of the March ceremony. But because of all the buzz that's bubbled up about us having excellent food, drink and service, we qualified. And if you ask Tabitha or Angela, we're going to take the cake.

The girls tell me that Chicago restaurants have won this award for the Great Lakes region in the past, but largely because they were headed by celebrity, veteran chefs or because they had received actual Michelin stars (or at least a nod in their Bib Gourmand). We haven't received anything of the sort (yet), and, of course, the whole food world knows what happened to our "celebrity chef."

And, boy do they *love* to talk about it.

Jared was right when he said this industry was laced with gossip. I try not to look at the comments section of articles and blogs, but sometimes when I'm scrolling so fast, I stumble upon dangerous territory before I even realize I'm in the dead zone. I already knew that people can be cruel. It's not like I completely blocked out that one time I spent half a day at Daxa researching @BJZane and reading what perfect strangers had to say about him. But I guess I just expected that the hate and speculation wouldn't spill over onto me—a completely separate person with no ties, extraneous or otherwise, to illegal activity. Who knew that just things like the shoes I wear or the fact that I haven't spent my life in the industry would be enough gas to set the blogosphere ablaze.

I have to remember, though, that for every one hater, there are at least ten people raving about how good a time they had at Here. And how can you argue with that? It's evident we have an extremely talented and visionary general manager in Angela Blackstone, who understands the concept of Here on a deep and personal level. When I think about the fact we are up for a JBF, I'm not blind to the fact it's really *her* vision for this place that captured the imaginations of the JBF committee members. My name is just what got some people curious enough to come through the doors and shove an apple in my mouth.

Yes, I'm talking about you, *Mag Mile Magazine*.

Our JBF nomination is being covered by the luxury, who's-who, widely circulated Chicago glossy—and rightfully so. We're the only local restaurant in the running for such a high-profile category this year. And because I've got an investment to recoup, I don't really mind the camera flash in my face and request for an interview if it means we can trudge through this winter with a little more peace of mind. By the time this issue goes to print in the next week and a half, Angela predicts Here will go from booked solid for the next thirty-six straight nights, to somewhere around seventy-five. I can live with that. Correction: my bank account can live with that.

"Allie, can we get just a few solo shots of you in the dining room?" Alexi asks.

"My pleasure," I tell him. It's a phrase I've picked up from my time in this industry, and just one of the many little hospitable habits I'm starting to take on even while off the clock. Saying "behind!" when trying to pass someone in a narrow grocery store aisle and noting that my snack drawer is "eighty-six Hostess cupcakes" are two others.

I lead Alexi back to the empty dining area with my head held high like I do every night for the couple hundred diners who come into Here. In addition to the piece about Here's award, the *Mag Mile* article will also feature a small cutout about my debut into the restaurant world. "A League of Her Own" is the working title for the five-paragraph mini-story and, for once, it feels good be in the limelight. My contribution to this industry is just that—mine. It has nothing to do with a bad boy blurting out who he was sleeping with during a drug-induced Twitter rant. And that in and of itself is a priceless accomplishment, whether I take home the JBF award or not.

"This is incredible, Allie," Alexi says as he frames up the shot. "Can you snag the award for Best Interior Design while you're at it? The velvet accent wall behind you is to DIE for. Let's have you sit here and I'll shoot with it in the background."

"Thanks," I say, getting into position in front of the dark, luxe wall. "It's all Angela Blackstone's doing, really. She picked out these finishes."

"Well, kudos to her," he says.

Though she isn't within earshot, giving credit where credit is due is one of the ways I like to run my restaurant, even if I'm the freak show that everyone comes to check out. I know there's a bulk of patrons who just want to see what I look like post–Benji Zane. Did I go on a Ben & Jerry's binge and plump up? Do I look like I've been hitting my own crack pipe? I can't be sure what exactly they're coming to see, but they do come. And they do stare. And since they also pay a hefty tab at the end of the night, I let them. If sitting and wondering if I had anything to do with his disappearance makes me less broke at the end of the day, then so be it. Go on and get your fix, ladies and gents.

And then there's just the simple fact that Angela is my homegirl and deserves to be treated fairly by myself and the media. Besides Jared, Angela is a huge reason I haven't been crying on my bathroom floor each night alone for the last four and a half months. Her belief in me when it comes to being a strong, successful woman reminds me of the belief I had in Benji that he, too, could reach the stars. But her way of believing in someone is different than what mine was. Because hers is bulletproof. It's been tested before. She doesn't hand out acknowledgments for the fuck of it. If she believes in me, and tells me so, it's not to cheerlead me or to walk on eggshells. It's because that's what she sees for me and that's what she expects from me. And because I respect her, I make sure I do the best I can. That includes making it a point not to skimp when I give out nods to the press about my support team.

"Agh, crap. I think I'm going to need to bring in more light for this set," Alexi says, checking the shots on his camera.

"That's fine," I say. "No worries."

"Take five, will you? I'm gonna grab my umbrella and spotlight and be right back."

A five-minute break is actually on the long side of breaks I've been afforded since Here became my full-time gig. But for as fleeting as it will be, I sit and soak in just how beautiful this place really is. My role at Here might not be my dream job, but when I consider there was a time in the not-so-recent past when I really doubted the potential of this place to be magnificent… well, it's hard not to feel like I've come a long way.

Until, in a single second, I am right back where I started.

Because there, in a black wool jacket, is Benji Zane. He's blowing hot air on his cold, red hands as he stands right in front of me.

If it wasn't for the tiny snowflake that I just saw fall from his cowl neck collar and melt on the floor in front of me, I would have sworn there was something in that apple causing me to hallucinate. But, no. He's here. And so it's time for me to find my voice.

"What the hell are you doing here?" I say, shooting up from where I've been sitting to wait for Alexi's return.

"Wow," he says as he does a slow 360 turn right in the heart of the dining room. "This place looks great, Allie." When he makes his way back to me, he slips in, "And you do, too."

"Benji, I don't know why you're here or how you got in, but you have to leave. Angela!" I call at the top of my already-quivering voice.

I wonder if Benji can see the tremor in my hands, or if my face has gone that ghostly green you only see in cartoons. The churning in my stomach *feels* like that color.

"Relax, she's outside smoking in the alley," Benji says, placing his hands on top of my shoulders and directing me back to my seat at the table. How did he get close enough to touch me? It's like time is collapsing in on itself.

"So, she saw you?" I say, sharply arresting our progress and turning to face him. "And she just let you in? I find that *really* hard to believe, Benji. ANGELA, GET IN HERE!"

No answer. It feels like I'm a kid who has been abandoned at the park.

"Shhh, Al...*please*, can we talk?"

As Benji takes the liberty of casually sitting down at the two-top across from me, I can tell he isn't planning on taking no for an answer.

"In case you haven't noticed," I say, dropping my voice to what I hope is a dangerously low volume, "I'm sort of in the middle of something." Out of the corner of my eye, I see Alexi—or rather, his DSLR. Like the rest of the insiders in the Chicago restaurant scene, he knows exactly who Benji is, and who he is to me. I hear the whir of his camera shutter. *Click click click.*

"Allie, give me five minutes. Please. I've been in rehab. I'm sober now. Can't you tell? Look at me. Look into my eyes. I know you can tell, Allie."

Though I know it might be my undoing, I press my eyes closed tight for just an instant before opening them and looking straight into Benji's deep brown eyes. My kryptonite.

He looks good, I'll give him that. Though he's a bit on the skinnier side, his skin is clear and bright. His hair, still back in a bun, looks healthy—same with his nails, teeth and lips. I mean, without doing a strip search, I'd go so far as saying he looks better—healthier—than he ever did while I was dating him. What that *probably* means in relation to whether he was actually using drugs while we were together is slightly horrifying.

"Five minutes," I say, unable to quench my curiosity.

He lets out a sigh and leans back in the chair. I know he's thinking that clearing the first hurdle was cake. *Damn.*

"You. You are something else, Allie Simon. I know I've been absent..."

So that's the word we're using, *absent.*

"...but I've followed every piece of press about this place. And every good thing that was ever said, I knew was because of you. And when I saw your name, I'd lean over to whoever I was next to in the rehab center and say, 'This is my girl.' You know how many fist bumps I got?" He lets out a little laugh. I'm not coming with him on it.

"You're the strongest person I know. The best woman I know. And I see that in every inch of this place. My god, it's incredible. Better than I could have ever made it. You know, I never let myself visualize what Here would really look like when I was using. I sabotaged everything I ever had going for me—you know that. It was only a matter of time before I did that with this restaurant."

As if he's telling me something I don't already know.

"Yeah, this place is pretty fucking great, isn't it?" The snark rolls off my tongue, making me sound like the bitter ex I am.

"I know you're mad, Allie. You have every right to be. Every right. The things I did to you, the things I said to you—I look back on it all and I can't believe that was me. I'm not like that anymore—you have to believe me. I would never intentionally hurt you, Allie. Because when I hurt you, I hurt me. And I'm so tired of all the hurt."

My gaze is fixed in the distance and Alexi is no longer in the foyer. He's gotten all the paparazzi gold he could ever need and is probably off selling the shots to *Bon Appétit* this very instant.

"I had a slip," he continues. "It's no one's fault but my own. I take full responsibility for what I've done. And I'm sorry."

I let out a cold, uncomfortable laugh. "You're sorry? Oh, good. Let's hold hands and skip now, shall we?"

"Allie, bear with me. I'm working the program and I'm trying to make amends with those I've hurt and you're at the top of the list. That's why I'm here."

"Are you really using the program as an excuse for slithering in through the back door? I've thumbed through the NA literature, Benji. And I believe the stipulation in Step Nine is that you don't try to make amends in situations when doing so would cause more harm than good. Did it ever occur to you that waltzing unannounced into my restaurant—*my* restaurant, because that's what it became after you up and left—and taking a seat at a table so you could apologize like nothing ever happened might be a bad idea? That it might do more harm than good?"

It's unfortunate that I'm so angry I can't tell exactly how loud my voice is going. I can only hope these expensive velvet walls will absorb some of the sound.

"I know, I know. I just knew that you'd say no if I tried to organize this ahead of time. That's why I popped in."

Where the hell is Angela? The woman manages to be everywhere all at once whenever Here is in service but the second our lying, drug-addicted, sociopathic ex–chef de cuisine decides to stop by, she's nowhere to be found. My eyes settle back on Benji and I see him drawing a breath to speak again but I get there first.

"I THOUGHT YOU WERE DEAD."

I've never spoken these words before. In fact, I've never even allowed myself to think them. But in this moment that he's here—very much alive—the ugly truth of what has been locked away in my brain surfaces to the tip of my tongue.

"Shhhhh," he says again, like my volume will somehow further tarnish his reputation. If only *FoodFeed* had wiretapped me, they'd be doing the happy dance in their stakeout van right about now.

"No! Don't tell me to *shhhh*. You have no idea what I've gone through these last four months. No idea."

"Trust me. I know what goes into opening a restaurant."

"I'm not talking about picking out plates. Or…or…scheduling servers. I'm talking about *myself*. And my *emotions*. Remember those? Did you ever even know I had them? I've been broke, exhausted and depressed because of you. I even had to quit my job. Did you know that?"

He says nothing, just shakes his head.

"Yeah, I had to quit my job so that I could give this restaurant a fighting chance because who else was going to run it eighty hours a week for less than minimum wage and not report it to the government? Huh? Who? You? No. Because you left. And you washed your hands of it all as you got high. Fucking coward."

I catch myself pointing at him with a tightly clenched fist.

"What do you want me to say? I already admitted it. I lost my way," he says.

"And I lost EVERYTHING. I'm not just talking about my savings either. I gave up a promotion at Daxa—my dream! I could have been creative director at twenty-five years old, but that went down the drain. Oh, and my family had to go to counseling because of this and my friends just about gave up on me because I wouldn't give up on you. I wouldn't give up on someone who hit me in the face before turning his back on me for good. And now, after I finally came to terms with you being gone and this restaurant being my reality, I'm just starting to get it all back on track. We're climbing out of the debt—the debt of opening *your* dream restaurant—people like what we're doing, our chef is reliable, Angela is a goddamned saint in a Diane von Furstenberg dress and I finally don't have to sleep in the back office and shower in the slop sink anymore.

My life is starting to come back together after you ripped it apart and I think the key to that is you not being in it."

My monologue leaves me in tears and both of us speechless. All the words that have been brewing in me for months have finally been spoken.

"And no," I continue, drawing in a deep breath and willing my eyes to dry. "I don't believe you're just here to say you're sorry, Benji. I know you're sober now, and that's wonderful for you, but what do you *really* want? What did you come here for? What do you want from me *now*, Benji? Do you want your job back? Because that's not happening. That ship has sailed."

Benji puts his hands on mine. I would have thought I'd be able to pull them away as fast as I do when I touch a hot plate off the line. Instead, I just melt down.

The Benji Effect hasn't lost its power, it's just been dormant— and for the moment, I am paralyzed, at a loss for words despite wanting desperately to kick and scream.

Then it hits me. This is the moment. This is the moment that every girl waits for. It's the moment in the movies, the page in the book. The man of my dreams, my lost love, is back. And he's holding my hands like they are precious gems. This is the moment I give in, right? The moment I'm supposed to buckle at his touch?

"Look, I don't want my job back," he says, his voice quiet and sincere. "I'm living in a halfway house for the next six months, and I've got a cooking job there. It's not as glamorous as being up for a James Beard Award like this place is, but I'm committed to staying clean this time, so I'll do what I have to do. I'll sling peanut butter and jellies and grilled cheese sandwiches all day and night, no complaints. But you're right. There is something else I want. You, Allie."

I close my eyes and feel my makeup dissolve in dark tracks down my cheeks. The glue from my fake eyelashes pulls back ever so slightly on my lids, making it feel like my whole body is resisting the urge to shut down, shut him out, shut this off. But no matter what, I can't stop being here, with him.

"Oh, really? Then who's Hannah?" I say. "Do you realize your *new girlfriend* is the one who emailed me to tell me you were in rehab and to leave you alone, Benji? God, I don't even know which way is up right now."

"Oh my god, really? Hannah is *not* my girlfriend. She's just some food blogger chick who took me in when you kicked me out. It was a mistake, but I panicked when I realized I had nowhere else to go."

Rita was right. Or was it Hal? Regardless, whoever said I was just a flavor of the week and that he had backups was right. Damn it.

"It was a mistake. I should have just tried my hand at sleeping on the streets because I ended up spiraling out even more staying with someone who isn't even half the woman you are. I was so depressed at how I botched everything, I couldn't do anything to make myself feel better besides do all the drugs I could get my hands on and when I got to the point I knew I couldn't get a steady hit, I got really sick. She freaked out, brought me to a rehab center and damn near pushed me out of her car without so much as saying goodbye."

"So you aren't moving across the country with her?" I ask with a hint of skepticism.

"What? No. Look, I had no idea she emailed you. She probably figured because I talked about you so much, maybe you ought to know? I have no idea. The bitch is crazy. And the bottom line is, I've deleted all the contact info of anyone who was a toxic person in my life before getting help, so I couldn't even reach her if I wanted to. Hannah's been axed out of my life along with about fifty other scumbags. Trust me."

"Trust you, huh. Because that's gotten me far."

"Oh, come on, Allie. Drop the tough-guy act, will you? For one second?" There's a shift in his communication style. He's gone from complimentary to polite to apologetic to direct. Until now, I forgot that this man, who has struggled to keep his own body from slumping over in a dark alley on more than one occasion, is also the same guy who is known to have unparalleled confidence and command over a room when he really wants to turn things up. And I admit it, I am now listening.

"I'm serious. I will literally wait forever for you, Allie. I know you only had my best interests at heart and no one has ever put me first like that. The perfect girl. The perfect job. The perfect life. I wasn't in my right mind then to receive it all, and I know at least one of those opportunities is off the table. But I refuse to believe I've lost my chance with you and our happily-ever-after. Just tell me what I need to do and I'll do it, Allie."

I don't know if I believe him, or if these are just flowery words spoken softly by a guy with trusting eyes.

"Benji, don't take this the wrong way, but I wouldn't even know where to begin," I say with defeat.

"Look, I will never love anyone else but you. If you say no, I'll stay single forever, I swear."

Benji lets go with his right hand and digs into his pocket. Beneath his palm, he slides something toward me across the pristine white tablecloth—it's the Hail Mary. It's a ring. A thin gold band embedded with a small diamond.

"What is this?"

"You know what it is." A smile cracks across his face like a split in a windshield.

Okay, maybe *this* is the moment every girl waits for.

He's not brazen enough to put the ring directly on my finger so he plants it gently in my palm. He lets me hold it, examine it. It's like Novocain is running through my limbs, but I can feel the smooth, shiny band still warm from his pants pocket.

I look back up at him and our eyes lock in a silent stare.

"The Lincoln Park brownstone," he says. "The kids playing in the den. The pasta carbonara cooking on the stove."

"The dog," I whisper.

"Shit. Yes, the dog. I always forget about Pepper the chocolate Lab, but yes, he's there, too."

We both smile for just a second or two. It's the first time since he's sat down that the air has neutralized.

"It all starts right here, babe. Right now. I promise. I want you to be my wife. I want to spend my whole life proving to you that I got this. I got you. I got us."

He blinks hard and swallows loud, waiting for my words. But I don't have any. Instead, I grab his face from across the table and pull him toward me in a feverish thrust. I crush my lips to his and he intertwines his fingers into my hair with his signature "never letting go" grip. Nothing has changed. We still share the single-most undeniable chemical connection known to man. And that's what I wanted to prove.

Because here's the thing about chemistry. It's two unlikely substances coming together to make a reaction. And someone has to play maestro, blending the forces to make the magic. Without the deliberate mixing, there's nothing. No spark. No pop. Everything I think I know about being a woman tells me to stay in this moment until one or both of us needs to come up for air. Fuck what I think I know.

I push him away with the same amount of force. He wipes his mouth and lets out a huff like he just did a lap at the Indy 500.

"See? It's still there, babe," he says, gratified.

"It's always there. It's always going to be there, Benji. But how is it anything special when you know you can get up and leave it at any time and come back to it whenever you want and have it just be like nothing has changed? It's so convenient, isn't it? You can treat me like trash and six months, a year, five years, however many lifetimes later we can just come back to it and the sex will be wonderful and we'll both feel better about ourselves for a day or two before we end up inevitably hating ourselves more than we hate each other? I mean, what kind of circus is that?" I look to the ceiling, shaking my head. Benji's a trap that I'm prone to walking right into.

"Oh, hell no," comes Angela's alto, and it sounds to me like the voice of God. "No, no, no, no. You gotta get up, buddy. Up and out, you son of a bitch." Angela strong-arms Benji, prying him up from the chair. The ring is still in my hands.

"Yo, Andrew, can you give me a hand and get this asshole out of here? And, Jessica, call the cops—tell them there's a trespasser at Here Restaurant in the West Loop…they'll come right away." This chick never stops delegating, I swear.

"Jesus, Angela, would you fucking relax? I'm going. Okay? I'm going," Benji fires back.

"Not fast enough, motherfucker."

"Allie. This is the real deal," he says, pointing to the ring. "I can promise you that. Please think about it, okay? I know your love for me didn't just die overnight. I'm staying at that place on Monroe Street. You're on my visitor list. We can talk more about this there. I love you."

"LET'S MOVE, you schmuck." Angela turns Benji toward the door. "Get the fuck out before the police throw you out. I'm not fucking around, you piece of shit!"

Just like that, as quick as he came in, Benji leaves. Angela locks the door and tells Andrew to keep an eye on the front-of-house and Jessica to call the cops back; they can stand down now that our trespasser is gone. If it were anyone besides our two captains who witnessed this shit show, I'd be worried this whole thing would already be uploaded to Snapchat, but I can honestly say that everyone in the room right now has my back.

Angela rushes over to me and throws her arms around my neck. After my moment of strength, of honesty, my tears have started again unbidden, and it feels like my chest is imploding with silent sobs.

"I'm so sorry," Angela whispers in my ear. "I didn't see Benji come in. I just saw Jared."

"What do you mean you *just saw Jared*?" I ask, confused.

"He was in the doorway holding sandwiches from Graziano's." She draws back to look at me with sympathy. "I don't know how long he was standing there, but I'm sorry, Allie, I think he got an eyeful."

28

"If you want to go home, you can. Jessica can cover for you," Angela offers. "Just know I don't expect you to put the Here hat on tonight. Not after *that*."

I blow my nose and throw the tissue into a pile of them that's accumulated over the last hour in the wastebasket by my desk. Our preshift meeting starts in ten minutes. There's no way the puffiness under my eyes will go away by then, nor will I be able to concentrate on buttery wine suggestions if asked. But the thought of going home to sit on my couch and replay my afternoon just brings another round of nausea to cycle through.

"Look, Al. I wish I could sit back here and talk this through with you, but I've got to get out there. Family meal is already cleaned up, they're all waiting for me. We've got a four-top coming in at 5:00 p.m."

"I know, it's fine. You don't have to babysit me. I'll be okay," I say. We both know that's not true.

"Got any friends?" she asks as she sweeps a mauve-colored gloss over her lips.

"That I can call about this? No. Not really."

Even though we've patched things up, I'm not ignorant of the fact I have emotionally drained Jazzy and Maya when it comes to Benji drama. It isn't fair to bring him back into the picture, nor is it worth risking another setback to our friendship.

"Text me later. Please," Angela says. She throws an empathetic smile my way, then disappears through the double doors back into the dining room.

Alone in the back office, I pull out my phone and begin composing a text I'm ashamed to have to be writing.

Sorry, but I need 2 talk w/ U. Can I pls call U? I send.

The reply comes back within seconds and my heart sinks further.

I don't think that's a good idea.

Well, at least we're conversing, I console myself. I refuse to accept the text as a complete and total shutdown.

It's important, I nudge.

We should put some distance b/t us, Allie.

At that, I swallow all my pride and proceed to type one sickening word after the next.

Benji's back. He found me. I can't breathe.

Nar-Anon. 6pm. Lincoln Park Library. C U there, Rita responds.

Standing outside the library, I pace back and forth to keep warm as I keep watch for Rita. There's no way to tell if the people filing into the building are here to return a book, or attend a support group. But one thing does stand out: they all look kind of like me. Young, professional, *normal.* There's so much shame in loving a person like Benji. And up until now, I was embarrassed to be seen at a place like this. I wanted to find every reason that I didn't belong here. But today I finally see that I'm just the same. Just a girl who can't manage this on her own anymore.

A few moments go by and a black Range Rover slips into a narrow parking spot on the side of the street. Out hops Rita in a black blazer and Michael Kors crossbody bag. I never pictured her as a professional at anything other than organizing picnics by the beach, but she looks powerful and strong as she jaywalks across the street to greet me.

"Thank you so much for coming. I know I fucked up by not listening to you in the first place. And I know you don't owe me anything. And I shouldn't have texted out of the blue today. And I—"

"Shhh. Stop, honey. It's in the past. That's all in the past."

Rita pulls me in for a hug and I am careful not to get any salty-tear residue on her jacket. Even though I hadn't seen her again after our falling-out, her embrace feels as warm as the sun on the day we first met. It feels like relief.

She ushers me into the library and down a flight of stairs to a meeting room in their basement. We find seats near the front row underneath a heat duct. For some reason, I thought we'd all be sitting in a circle just staring at each other. Add that to the list of preconceived notions I was wrong about.

"So who's running the restaurant tonight?" she whispers.

"One of our head servers is covering for me."

"Gotcha," she says as she waves hello to someone she recognizes a few rows behind us. She really is an NA celeb of sorts.

"So how long has it been since you've gone to a meeting?" she asks.

"This is my first," I say. A wave of guilt washes over me. It's as if I just told my mom I can't remember the last time I went to church.

"That's okay. This is a good one—good people. You'll like it."

We shush our small talk and let the session begin. It opens with the serenity prayer. I've never said it out loud myself, but it was printed on an NA bookmark that Benji magnetized to the fridge after he moved in. Now the words are working their way through me, which is far different than just glancing at them as I help myself to a cold can of Diet Coke. As I let go of Rita's hand to my right and a stranger's warm, moist palm to my left, it hits me just how much I needed this.

Earlier today, Benji walked back into my life—man-bun and all—looking fine as hell and feeling great. And the sheer fact that his clear head could make me feel like everything he put me through was just a bad dream terrifies me. I want to forgive and forget, like he taped over my favorite show on the DVR instead of tearing through my life with the hurricane force that has come to signify his very existence. Something in me knows that isn't right, but that's the thing about getting caught up in a storm: it happens all around you regardless of whether or not you stand still and let it come. Now I have no clue how I'm supposed to feel, what to do with this ring or which man in my life I should text first when I get out of this meeting. I quiet the noise in my head and listen to the first person brave enough to take the podium.

"Uh, hi. I'm Sarah and my dad is my qualifier." Sarah is about my age with purple streaks in her hair and sparkly nail polish.

"Hi, Sarah," the room says back, not unlike the way my staff says "heard" at a preshift meeting.

"My dad got out of rehab two weeks ago," she shares. "And he just invited this girl from the market in his building to move in with him. I know her from when I stay over at his place. She's nice and all, but I didn't even know they were dating or that it was serious. It's hard because my dad seems so happy with her. I just feel like there's no way he's going to be able to manage recovery *and* a relationship at the same time and I really want it to work this time. You know? I want him to stay clean."

Sarah returns to her seat. *That's it?* I think. What did she do? How does it end?

But then I realize that's not what these meetings are about. This isn't Hollywood. Happy endings are anything but mandatory in this world. This is a room where you release the weight on your chest, if only for the moments that you're seated within these walls.

It's all the same story, too. Hers, mine, Rita's, everyone in this room. We're like a secret society that can't stop caring about the people who hurt us the most. Hell, Benji isn't even my boyfriend anymore. I should give zero fucks about him, yet the moment he's back, I have to march myself to a support group to triple-check that there's still nothing I can do to scare his demons away. Sarah's story reminds me that we are all in this together, doing the best we can not to get sucked under the wave. It reminds me that we don't have to have the answers planned or the ending plotted.

The moderator heads back up to the front and thanks Sarah for sharing. "Who's next?" she asks.

Rita stands up and takes her place at the stand.

"Good evening, I'm Rita. I'm celebrating twenty-five years in a couple of weeks."

The room erupts in congratulatory applause.

"As someone who qualified a lot of people throughout the years, I just want to take this opportunity to remind all of you that *your* wellness is just as important as ours. If you don't take care of yourself, what good are you to help us? Sarah, I can't imagine the hours you've already spent sitting and stewing over your dad and his girlfriend, teetering back and forth between 'Well, maybe it's good he's not alone' and 'He really needs to do this by himself.' You know deep down exactly what he should be doing if he's serious about his recovery."

I look over to Sarah. She's nodding intensely back at Rita, confirming that she is spot-on, per usual.

"That's maddening!" Rita professes. "That's no way for any of you to live—to be utterly consumed with how to keep *us* safe and healthy. He's gone to meetings. He's been to rehab. He knows what he needs to do for long-term sobriety. You can't help him work the program. You can help yourself, though. You can always help yourself. Remember that, and find strength in that. Thank you."

It hits me then that if Benji was really committed to his recovery, he wouldn't have proposed. The program says he shouldn't engage in any serious relationships until he's a year sober, and that's true for him as much as Sarah's dad—confirmed by Rita, who's been there, done that.

I haven't had a chance to tell her yet about his latest monumental ask—my hand in marriage. But I'm not sure it needs to be discussed. This meeting has confirmed what I already knew: I cannot accept his proposal. It'd just be another false start for us, and we all saw how well that turned out the first time. I just hope the conviction I feel now after hearing Rita speak sticks with me into the night after we leave the safety and comfort of this quiet, toasty room.

The meeting goes on another thirty minutes or so. A few more people speak, we close out with the serenity prayer once more, and I exchange numbers with Sarah before walking out with Rita.

"I don't know the rules here, Rita. But—"

"Fuck the rules. I'm here if you need me, okay?"

"Okay," I say.

"Do you need a ride home?" she asks. "I can drop you on my way to pick up Maverick from the sitter."

"I don't live far. I'm fine walking. I could use the fresh air."

"You sure? It's cold."

"Positive. I've got some stuff to think about anyway."

"Fair enough. It was good seeing you." Rita comes in for another hug before she crosses the street to her car. "Stay the course," she says before pulling away. "Stay the course."

I wave as she speeds through a yellow and I begin my walk home. A block and a half away, I pass a familiar storefront: Molly's Cupcakes. The swings are occupied by three little kids, all with frosting smeared around their lips. Their sugar-high smiles are enough to draw me in for a Red Velvet.

As the cashier boxes up my order, I know where I have to go next.

"Two forks, please."

It's around 8:00 p.m. when I build up the courage to take an Uber to the Marcel & Sons warehouse in the gritty Fulton Market neighborhood, next to the West Loop. While the rest of the world is winding down from yoga classes, heading to trivia nights at the bar or whatever else normal people do after work, Jared and his crew are diligently working to fulfill tomorrow morning's orders—Here's being one of them.

I hear backup beepers from their trucks, refrigerator hums and lots of shouting. Maybe this isn't the best time to stop by, but then again, what's the alternative?

I let myself in. Clearly their secretary has left for the day, which leaves me to meander through the chaos to find him.

"Yo, Roberto! Give me twenty pounds of spinach for Truck 13, please!" I spy him from afar. He's got a pencil tucked behind his ear and his signature beat-up baseball cap on. God, he's so cute. I fall into a daze watching him, the activity all around us and the very air itself seeming to slow and still the closer it gets to his calm, anchored presence.

I might have only just figured out today where I stand on things with Benji, but there's something else I realize. Except for this thing…I've known it for a while.

I could love Jared. In fact, I've felt the potential for the L-word ever since he doubled back to Here with a crate of iceberg lettuce and saved my ass the night before we opened. I just couldn't allow myself to go there yet. Not even now, really. But I'm heading down that path and it feels good.

I don't need a manual on how to date a guy like Jared. He doesn't require rules and regulations. No abstinence for alcohol, no support meetings, no ridiculous cable bill. And, not like it needs to be mentioned, but he'd never expect me to lie down for his dreams. Ever.

"You can't be back here," he says, drifting past me with a crate of carrots.

"I brought a cupcake," I say.

"That's cute."

He's battling me being here and I can feel my stomach sinking. I debate leaving the box on the front desk and hailing a cab home. A bottle of wine and too-big sweatpants are calling my name right now, but I think back on Rita's parting words. *Stay the course.*

"Can you take a break?" I try a more direct approach.

He pauses from counting out boxes and finally looks me in the eye. "Follow me."

Jared leads me back to his office and shuts the door. I want to absorb his headquarters, compare it to mine at Here, stare closely at the pictures he's tacked up on his bulletin board, but I'm aware time isn't slowing down for that.

"It's Red Velvet. I remember you liked their cream cheese frosting," I say, fidgeting with the tape on the pastry box.

"I'm not hungry. What can I do for you, Allie?"

Jared takes his hat off, runs his fingers through his dark,

messy hair, and puts it securely back on. He folds his arms and puts quite a bit of distance between us. I don't have a speech prepared. I'm not sure how to fix this.

"What you saw today…wasn't what it looked like."

"I'm going to stop you right there," Jared says. His voice is like poured cement. "First of all, as if showing up at my work in the middle of inventory isn't already totally inappropriate, you've come here to talk about your ex, who you're clearly very much still with."

"I'm not, though." My weak defense barely squeaks in before he fires up again.

"I've honestly had enough. I know you didn't want to put a 'title' on things, and I was cool with that because I really liked you and I respected what you had gone through with that monster. But if I had known the real reason you didn't want to be my girlfriend was that you were holding out for Benji to come around and put a ring on it, I would have walked a long time ago."

"I wasn't holding out for Benji—you have to believe that," I plead. "He just showed up out of nowhere." *At my place of business. Just like I'm doing to you right now. Oops.*

"Mmm-hmm, got it. Can I go back to work now, or…" He grabs his clipboard and turns his back to me.

I dart my eyes to the ceiling in complete frustration. "You know, I never wanted anything to do with this place and now look. Another thing that Here has royally fucked up."

"And that's another thing." He turns around. "I'm tired of hearing how Here isn't your dream. I mean, get over it, Allie. Do you think my dream job consists of schlepping around fifty-pound boxes of squash at nine o'clock on a Tuesday night? No. But I'm here. And guess what? That's my choice. It's not my first choice, but it's my choice. So I deal with it and I commit to it. You gotta grow up, Allie."

I can't believe how much his words sting, and from the way he's white-knuckling his clipboard, I have a feeling he's only getting started.

"You chose Here," he continues. "Own that! Boo-hoo, you got sucked into a wildly successful restaurant venture that you actually seem to enjoy being a part of most of the time. Every time I'm there, I see you and Angela bouncing around like sorority sisters as you count your cash. So my advice is you quit blaming the fact that you still can't choose him or me on your fucking restaurant. Okay? I'm done feeling sorry for you. There's nothing to be sorry about."

"It's not about choosing *him or you*," I fire back. He's struck a chord and now I'm a little pissed. "There was a time that I waited for him, yes, I'll admit that. Because I'm loyal. Because he was important to me—we were close, we lived together. Point is, that's the past. All of that is in the past," I say. When Rita uttered those same words outside the library earlier, they'd filled me with hope. I hope they have the same effect now.

"Thanks for those details, Allie. But I'm sure *FoodFeed* will run a refresher course on your entire relationship tomorrow and I can catch up on what I missed then."

"You know what? Fuck you, Jared. Seriously."

Now I have his attention. I let the closing argument begin.

"I didn't have to come here, you know? You ignored all my calls and texts today, I could have taken the hint. But I wanted to be here. To see you and tell you that what you saw today was just me going through the motions. It was one last pulse check to make sure that during the hurricane that was opening this restaurant, I didn't miss anything. I didn't forget that I'm much better off without him in my life. I know it looked shitty, and it was shitty. But I had to do it. I had to know for sure. I had to deliver the blow to my own gut and so, yeah, I kissed him. You don't have to believe me, but that would sure mean I'm a sick masochist if, after all that, I chose to be here with you only to get rejected and sent back home."

It feels like several hours pass when my little speech is done. How many would-be movie moments can a girl really have in a single day? Everything I've seen on the big screen tells me we can cut to the violins now, because Jared isn't just going to forgive me, he's going to pick me up, twirl me around and lean in close to my face as he whispers, "If you tell me you're mine, I want you to mean it forever. Forever, Allie. Because that's how long I will love you." Then he'll kiss me, all the complication in our lives will fade to black and the credits will roll.

Shock of shocks, that's not how it goes.

I can practically see the emotions battling for supremacy in his head. Rage, embarrassment, jealousy, maybe even something that looks like love—it's all there, trying to dominate. Eventually, he says, "So do you know now?"

"Yes. I'm not in love with him anymore."

Immediately, I get that there's another way of saying that: *I'm in love with you.* But clearing the Benji air takes precedence.

"Good to know."

Jared returns to his clipboard and his crates as if I just told him it's not going to rain tomorrow. The vertical blinds on the glass panel of his office door nearly fly off the hinge with the amount of force he uses to get the hell out and away from me. I'm alone in his office with the door open; I can tell he wants me to let myself out. And for the hundredth time today, I can feel tears welling up in my eyes. *Not here, not now,* I scream to myself. It's time for me to leave.

This is the first night that Angela has cut me and then not proceeded to call, text or email me with the slightest turn of events at the restaurant. Tonight, either her phone has died, she's completely in the weeds, or she's just respecting the fact my heart's been ripped out and pierced with an oyster fork. Depressing as it sounds, I'm hoping it's the latter.

How was resto tonight? I text her as I lie staring at my ceiling, unable to sleep.

Not the same w/o u. Need u back tmw.

I'll be in, I say.

Big girl panties?

Promise.

At that, I shut off my phone and let that little exchange sink in a bit.

It felt weird being away from the restaurant today even though I had an excellent excuse. It's just…working at Here is a testament to what can happen when you follow steps one, two and three. Things go down without a hitch and it's, well, it's just lovely. There's so much peace in watching events unfold sequentially, just the way you think they should. That kind of order seems like the antithesis of the chaos Benji brought into my life, which is maybe why I've been so resistant to embracing how much I love it.

Because I do love it. Even though I want to hate everything Benji Zane did and said and promised and destroyed, I can't help loving Here.

Maybe Jared was right to call me out. Sometimes the dream just changes, and maybe it's okay to end up not hating something you once thought was a miserable curse. The trick is to change with it. Adapt and respond.

Which I want to say is Rule #58 at Here, though it's late and my numbers might be off.

"Let me see your hands," Angela says as I throw my purse down on my desk in the back office. "Hold them out, spread your fingers."

I know what she's checking for, but she has nothing to worry about. Before the sun even came up, I took a cab to the halfway house on Monroe and put the ring and Benji's knives in a small shopping bag with his name on it and left it with the front desk attendant. I didn't leave a note or anything—not to be cold, but because there's nothing to say. All I want is to stay the course.

Will I wonder "what if?" Possibly. Will I picture our could-have-been wedding and how amazing the food would have been? Yeah. What our kids would have looked like? Sure, wouldn't be the first time. But that's okay. I'm going to give myself a hall pass to do all of that because I know that eventually, visualizing the life I would have had with that imaginary Benji Zane—the one who wouldn't have left me at the altar or been too drunk to hold down dinner or have left me barefoot and pregnant in whatever ramshackle apartment we could afford—will go from being a heartache to a foggy notion of something lost, to plain old silly daydreams of someone who never existed in the first place.

"No rings, okay, Angela? No rings," I say, flashing my hands front to back like I'm surrendering.

"Thank fucking god. Look, I don't want details. But I have to ask, is it over?"

"With who?" I need clarification.

"Good question. Let's start with your zombie ex."

"It's handled." I infuse my voice with that famous fake-it-'til-you-make-it confidence this industry is laced with. But between you and me, *we'll see* is probably more appropriate at this point.

"And what about the J-man? TBD?"

"Probably more like *PTSD* given what he had to see yesterday."

"Or what the whole city got to see today…" She tilts her computer screen my way. It appears Alexi has funneled a series of intimate paparazzi-style pics of Benji and me to *Food-Feed* and suddenly there's an article titled: "Are things heating back up between Zane and Simon?" up on Angela's monitor.

"God bless it," I say. "You know what, don't even forward it to me. I don't want to know what they're saying. Let's just hope Jared doesn't have access to the internet before I get a chance to tell him I love him."

"Um. Hey. What's up. Hello. YOU LOVE JARED???"

Shit. Did I say just that out loud? To Angela?

"I don't know." (Spoiler alert: I do.) "Maybe? But either way, it's a long shot that he'll ever want to go for *this whole situation*." I gesture toward myself from top to bottom.

"Well, if it turns out that it is *love*, just know that means Rule #77 is out the window. You have my blessing."

Angela's blessing is good—no matter what the subject is. But her advice is what I really need.

"So how do I do it, Ang? How do I get this simple, sweet produce guy to pick the bruised apple?"

She slides an arm around my shoulder and our silent accord takes us straight to the espresso machine.

"That, I don't know. But I *do* know we need our own reality show on Bravo. Stat."

29

I count off ten seconds in my favorite Mississippi intervals before I put my trusty tube of matte pink lipstick and my compact away.

"Babe, are you paying attention to me?"

I don't say anything, I just raise my eyebrows at him. Would I be paying attention to anyone else?

"As I was saying, I just think it's amazing that we're on our way to the James Beard Awards. I mean, not *me*, necessarily, I would be going regardless considering my contribution to this industry. But *you*. You totally don't belong here."

"Are you—" I start, practically choking on my rage. "Are you serious right now?"

"Deadly. I mean, the fact that you're attending this awards show with such a stud? Come on. Who deserves this? Look at this tux. Paid extra for the piping."

Mimicking Vanna White in the back of an Uber, he points out the silk black detailing around his lapels and pocket.

Raised eyebrows transition to rolled eyes and he can't hold back his laughter for another single second.

When Jared laughs, it's like the universe stops to listen to the joke. You can't help being drawn in—at least I can't.

"So you look like James Bond and I look like a sack of potatoes, right?" I adjust his bow tie for good measure.

"Well, actually, I have seen quite a few sacks of potatoes in my day, and you've got much nicer curves. Prettier hair, too."

"Gee, thanks," I say, about to give him shit about how *he's* the one with the real catch on his arm when our Uber slows to the curb of the Civic Opera House, the site of the James Beard Awards this year. My excitement nose-dives into a swirl of emotions that clog my throat. Jared immediately takes my hands.

"What is it, Al?"

"It's just…it—*we*—could have gone a different way, you know?" I let my voice get quiet so I'm less at risk for melting into a puddle of tears and ruining my makeup. "And if that happened, I wouldn't be here…in this dress…around these people…with a speech in my pocket just in case. I couldn't do this without you."

He plants a soft kiss on my mouth. I linger on his lips for a moment and soak him in. My nerves unplug for the time being as I breathe in my boyfriend's cologne.

How we managed to get to this place of peace is beyond me, and I try not to overthink it but I do like to relive it.

The day after I showed up at his warehouse, we were due for our next Marcel & Sons delivery. I figured he'd send Roberto to make the drop and avoid me that morning, but sure enough, Jared stuck with the route.

He didn't say anything to me as he and Hector unloaded the truck. I quietly supervised, carefully trying to sneak a smile in at any ounce of eye contact he'd give me. Just when I figured this was going to be our new normal, he came out with one final box. The one from Molly's Cupcakes.

"If I wait until a socially acceptable hour to eat this cupcake, it'll be dry. So, right here, right now…split it with me."

We took a seat next to each other in the bed of his truck and dangled our feet off the end. The cupcake was sickeningly sweet for 7:00 a.m. and crumbs found their familiar spot on my lap within seconds. But the sheer fact we were enjoying the moment in a dark, smelly alley superseded all the shortcomings.

"I'm not a jealous guy," he said. "And I don't like insecurity. And I felt both of those things back-to-back yesterday. Sucked the air right out of my lungs. And it scared me to think that some girl had that kind of hold on me. So I wanted to run. But I knew I couldn't so I just tried to push you away instead. Be short. Cold. Keep myself shut off from you. That didn't work either. Because I realized a girl with that kind of hold on me is the girl I want to be with. Allie, I believe you—what you said about Benji being in the past. But I need to know you want to be with me. All in. Officially."

"Am I being girlfriend-proposed to?" I asked.

"Two rings in two days is out of the question, Simon. But I'd still like an answer. Would you be my girlfriend?"

I kissed him and tasted just a hint of the famous frosting we both loved.

"So is that a yes?" he asked.

"It's a yes," I said. "Hi, boyfriend."

That was three months ago. And now we're here, about to exit the limo in front of the auditorium and enter what looks like a scene from the Oscars. Everyone is in evening wear, trying to smoke their last few cigs before having to find their seats on the other side of the baroque doors.

I don't recognize as many people as I thought I would, but that could just be because we all look equally incognito in our far-from-kitchen-appropriate attire. That said, all six feet four inches of Anthony Bourdain is unmissable out of the corner of my eye—as is the friendly wave from Hal Huckby, who's got a lady on his arm as he walks inside. I briefly wonder if she's the one who got away.

Jared squeezes my hand as we make our way in. "You okay?" he whispers in my ear.

I smile and nod, starstruck and terrified of snagging my beaded black dress on the heels of my three-inch pumps. It's the first time I've worn shoes like this since being shredded in the blogs for my footwear, and I'm a little rusty.

"You did great, Allie! Just broadcasted that whole thing live on Facebook from our page. 5,600 people tuned in!" Tabitha says as I take my seat back at our booth.

"And I just FaceTimed your entire acceptance speech to Craig," Angela adds. "Think he teared up a bit."

That makes two of us—three if I'm right about what Jared's wiped away from the corners of his eyes with his napkin.

It's unreal that we've just won the award for Best New Restaurant in our region. Technically, as chef de cuisine, Tabitha should have been the one to accept it, but she has a crippling fear of public speaking and, as Angela likes to remind me, I'm (still) "the draw."

It's crazy to think that there was a time I doubted we'd even be able to hire a chef, yet here we are basking in a round of applause that's already gone on longer than it should specifically dedicated to Here's greatness.

Jared pulls me in and kisses the top of my head. I fall into his embrace and slide the ribbon Angela and Tabitha's way for their chance to touch the elusive award.

"Is Craig proud?" I ask her.

"He is. Wants to know how we plan on displaying the ribbon."

Leave it to our too-busy-vacationing-in-the-British-Virgin-Islands-to-show-up-tonight investor to fixate on the logistical difficulties of winning a JBF Award.

"Jesus. Tell him we just won a freakin' James Beard and we'll get a task force going on Monday when our champagne hangovers have a chance to settle down," a 'tudey Tabitha says.

"Hey, I'll cheers to that," I say, clinking my glass against hers and chugging the rest of my bubbly.

I've had six drinks so far. The first two were to take the edge off. The second two were with dinner. And the last two were to celebrate the fresh win. I imagine that'll be reason for the next two as well. On that note, I need to use the bathroom.

Wandering through the lobby, I spy a familiar face that immediately sobers me up.

Though I haven't seen him in the three months since he slithered into Here, Benji's just outside the front doors, smoking a cigarette with a few local bartenders. He's in a suit, not a tux. I can't get a good enough look into his eyes to tell if he's been drinking. Why is he here? He wasn't nominated for shit, which means his general admission ticket was a cool $550. I can't imagine the cook job at the halfway house pays all that well, so I wonder what hopeless hanger-on dipped into her savings to take her adorably damaged new boyfriend on a field trip.

I duck into the bathroom before he has a chance to catch me staring.

But then it dawns on me that he's already seen me. I just fucking accepted the award for Here ten minutes ago onstage for crying out loud. *Everyone's* seen me.

I pull out my phone and, against all that is holy, I check Twitter for his reaction.

@BJZane: Coulda. Woulda. Shoulda. Tweeted five minutes ago.

It's vague and I have no proof it's in reference to having a drink at the open bar, sticking with Here or not blowing a future with me. For all I know, it's a compliment…or maybe it's a slight dig? Either way, the beauty is I don't dissect this kind of stuff anymore. Because I don't have to.

"Pardon me," a lady says, trying to dry her hands under the blower.

"Oh. Holy shit. You're Candice Allegro," I say with my typical eloquence. Standing before me, hands dripping, is the president of the James Beard Foundation.

"That I am. Allie Simon, right? Congratulations. Your restaurant is truly outstanding."

"Oh my gosh, seriously? Thank you so much. That means a lot. Like, a lot a lot," I say, sidestepping to give her access to the dryer. My brain keeps flitting between exclamations of *This is the Meryl Streep of food!!!!!* and *You sound like a teenager, Simon.* I feel myself break out in a cold sweat. What is my life?

In what seems like a nod to my fangirl status, Candice says, "Well, since you have your phone out, should we take a photo, no?"

I press the pause button on reality to let it sink in that Candice Allegro has in fact asked me to take a bathroom selfie. The lighting is surprisingly flattering as we get into position and smile for the camera.

"Tweet that to me, will you?" Candice asks as she pulls open the heavy swinging door and saunters back toward the auditorium. Now that's a chick who can walk in heels.

After I take a moment to make sure my eyeliner is still where it's supposed to be, I, too, depart the ladies' room. Outside the door, Jared is waiting for me.

"An elbow for the big winner?" he asks, offering to usher me back into the auditorium. I can't help but notice that Benji is back from his smoke break and in the middle of the grand foyer. The hungry media have tape recorders jammed in his face as he gives his two cents on what I can only imagine is the biggest win of the night so far.

"Well, that's kind of you," I say back. He's of course being a gentleman, but he's also protecting (read: distracting) me from the Benji Show everyone's suddenly tuned into.

"Please, this has nothing to do with you. Or him. This is about *my* ego. I absolutely must be seen with the most beautiful person in this place, who also happens to be a winner, *and* my girlfriend." He manages to make me forget about the circus in the lobby as we make our way back in.

It turns out the celebration doesn't end at the awards show. At an after-party at Acadia, a Michelin-starred restaurant in the South Loop, the chef there orders the somm to get the Veuve flowing and the next thing I know, I'm on the bar dancing to Journey with my ribbon around my neck. At least Angela and Tabitha are both there to sing backup, and Jared manages to make it look like we've choreographed the moment when he catches me as I stumble on my unfamiliar shoes.

When it's time to go home, Jared calls an Uber for all of us and we carpool it back to Here.

"Have I ever told you how great you are?" says a drunken Tabitha. "Like, you don't even get it. I'm living the fucking dream and it's all because of YOU. You're the best thing that's ever happened to me."

"Yeah, same," says a sloshed Angela. "You're the fucking best, Simon."

"Wait, can I get in on this?" Jared asks. "I think you're pretty great, too."

"KISS HER! KISS HER! KISS HER!" Angela and Tabitha chant. And when he does, the crowd goes wild. Our Uber driver can't kick us out fast enough, but to his disappointment, only the two of them get out at 900 W. Randolph. Jared and I stay in the car and head back to his apartment, our final stop for the evening.

When I wake up the next morning in the comfort of Jared's bed, he brings me a water and three extra-strength Advil. I don't remember much of what happened between the time I gave my acceptance speech to the time Jared and I had the most incredible sex to date, but thankfully Twitter and the hashtag #JBFChicago help me relive the magic.

As I scroll the posts, all I can think is, *Christ, Simon, you are one hot mess.*

But among the pics of debauchery, one tweet stands out. It's from @CandiceAllegro and it's been retweeted 2,500 times. A photo op with big winner @AllieSimon? #YesPlease #JBFChicago #BestNewResto.

"Why don't we have it matted and framed or something? We can put it up in the entryway and take it down when it feels gimmicky," Tabitha suggests.

"It's a ribbon. With a man's face on it. It's never *not* gimmicky," says Angela.

"It'd be one thing if Beard was hot," I add. "Then we could make it into a print and wallpaper the women's bathroom with it."

"That's not LGBT-friendly," Tab chides me.

"Yeah, and not sure Craig would go for us objectifying a founding father of food. Also, you know the two of us are meeting with him in, like, twenty, right?" Angela says.

"That's my cue to chop onions," Tabitha says before exiting the scene of the back office.

"I know, I know," I say. "And I'll put lipstick on when he valets. For now, I'm going to sit back, read the paper and enjoy feeling sober for the first time in three days."

"You do that. Because these press releases just happen to send themselves." She flings herself around in her chair and starts typing loudly on her computer to up the guilt factor.

"Oh my god, Angela. HO-LY SHIT. Look at this!"

She rolls over to me with a noted lack of hustle and looks down over my shoulder at the paper.

"'Congratulations to our friends & client, Here Restaurant, on their James Beard Award. Yours truly, Marcel & Sons,'" she reads slowly.

We lock our surprised eyes and let our smiles crack slowly across our faces.

"Okay. First question," she says. "You know that's a full-page ad, right? In the *Trib*."

I flash to the front of the paper to make sure I'm not seeing things.

"Second question: What is with guys marking their territory with you in the media?"

"Oh my god, I know, right?"

"Well, shit. Text him."

"Text him? It's a full-page ad. Shouldn't I call?"

"I have no idea. This is why I don't date and just stick with the one thing that never lets me down: seared foie gras. Either way, you need to thank his ass. Right now."

I pull out my phone and queue up a text. U R unreal is all I can muster. The butterflies in my stomach somehow paralyze my fingers and, apparently, my brain.

UR not freaked out, R U? Jared texts back.

No way. FLATTERED. And... I'm falling. I can't help it. I'm alluding strongly to the L-word. I have felt it for him for a while, I just haven't said it. Neither of us have. I blame it on the fact my life has been a roller coaster since he's known me, but for what it's worth, our relationship has been steady—and the best thing I've ever experienced. Now I only hope I didn't just freak *him* out.

A few seconds go by. It feels like an hour.

The single-word reply comes through and I feel my heart leave my body and float skyward. Fallen.

"Can you pause this particular episode of *Days of Allie's Life*?" Angela says, snapping her fingers in my face and pulling my phone out of my hands. "I just saw on the cameras, Craig is here. Get your lipstick on and your feet off the desk, please and thank you."

I give myself a five-second primp, fixing my hair with my fingers and rubbing my lips together to smooth out my lipstick. I'm already smiling a mile wide, which, of course, has nothing to do with Craig and everything to do with the man who is in love (!!!!) with me, but the warmth of Craig's greeting when he sees me lets me know he thinks it's all for him.

"Ladies, how are you?" he says as he sweeps into the back office, giving both of us a kiss on the cheek.

We shoot the shit for about ten minutes, not really addressing anything particularly regarding Here. The longer we chitchat, the more I realize I'm not entirely sure what the purpose of today's meeting is other than to talk about how nice the people are in the British Virgin Islands. I figure—hope—it will eventually have something to do with congratulating us on our big JBF win.

"So, Allie," Craig says, spinning his chair to face me directly.

"Yessir," I respond.

"How closely did you read your contract when you signed on to be a part of this restaurant deal?" The joviality in his voice is gone. If we weren't stuck in the back office of an urban restaurant, dark clouds would be rolling in on the horizon.

My stomach drops immediately and my palms begin to sweat. "I mean, it was all very quick. I think I just signed on a few lines and pulled funds from the bank, to be honest."

"Hmm. Interesting," Craig says. "You didn't have a lawyer or anyone look over the documents?" He makes a rolling gesture with his hand and organizes his face in faux concern, like he's talking to a child.

He's insulting my intelligence and I don't like it. Not one bit.

"You guys all rushed me so much, it's not like I had a choice," I say, not bothering to hide my defensiveness. "Besides, I never planned to be the manager or anything. I didn't realize there might have been some fine print I missed."

The room goes silent.

"Angela, should we fill Allie in on what she missed when she so nonchalantly put her name on a dotted line?"

Angela refuses to make eye contact with me and keeps her gaze fixed on the ground.

"Yeah, I suppose it's probably time," she mumbles.

"What the fuck is going on here, guys?" I say with zero regard for office-appropriate language.

"Well, there was a tiny little clause in there," Craig starts. "And it said that if you earn a Michelin star or a James Beard Award within the first year, and pull a profit of thirty percent or higher three earnings reports in a row..."

"Yeah?"

"You and Angela both take home a hundred-thousand-dollar bonus to be awarded on the one-year anniversary of our opening."

My jaw practically unhinges as my mouth drops open in shock. I feel myself turn in slow motion to look at Angela, who is red-faced and practically bug-eyed trying to hold back her laughter.

"Did you know about this?" I blurt out in her general direction.

She squints her eyes shut, determined to contain her hysteria, and nods vigorously.

"I should have figured you had that contract memorized like the Bible. Why the hell didn't you tell me?" I can't contain my shock and awe and start slapping her with the rolled-up newspaper. She and Craig high-five as happy tears well up in my eyes. "You motherfuckers," I mumble to the both of them.

In the past fifteen minutes, I've gone from high to higher to low to highest without so much as a hair out of place.

I'm in love with a man who loves me in return.

My nest egg is back, and it's on steroids. It feels like the shackles have been unlocked and I am free.

I am free.

"I knew it'd trip you up," Angela explains. "You'd focus on the money so hard, you'd forget to do your job and we'd slip. I'd never forgive myself for letting that happen simply because I couldn't keep a secret for a few more weeks. I mean, I know you have a copy of that contract somewhere in that unholy mess you call an apartment. You couldn't have read it on your own sometime before you depleted your life savings?"

"Right, because when I get home all I want to do is read more about the worst decision of my life," I say in jest. "And I'd like to see how clean your place is, please and thank you."

"Well, you ladies earned it," Craig says, bringing us back to center. "Fair and square."

"Wait," I say, remembering the way I like to run my restaurant. "What about Tabitha? We wouldn't be here without her."

"Christ, you *really* didn't read the contract, did you? Chef de cuisine gets a separate bonus. We were smart enough not to name anyone by name—if you know what I mean—in the fine print in that section, but don't worry, she'll be taken care of, too. All checks will be cut at the end of the summer. Keep doing what you're doing. Michelin's next, right?"

I'm speechless. I look from Angela to Craig and back again. Words just won't come.

"Yes, Michelin is next," Angela says, stepping in and speaking for both of us. I just twine my hand in hers and hold on tight as Craig takes his leave.

"Are you sure he didn't mean ten thousand?" I ask Angela, keeping my voice down. It's just the two of us again, but some of the servers have started to dribble in, dropping their purses and coats in the lockers beside us.

"I'm positive."

"I just don't understand how someone like that has so much cash to throw around."

"Because when we won our star at Florette back in the day, he tripled his initial investment in six months alone. The amount of people a nod like a Beard Award or a star brings in is insane. You'll see. We won't be closed on Mondays much longer. There's going to be way too much demand, way too much money to make."

I expect her to go on about all the extra hours we'll have to put in, what additions we'll have to make on staff to accommodate the extra volume, but instead the enthusiasm drains out of her body all at once. I watch her deflate like a tired balloon as she hunches forward, resting her elbows on her knees.

"Allie, we need to talk. Like manager-to-manager, serious talk."

"Look, if this is about the pictures that popped up on Instagram from the after-party, just know I've been detagging myself steadily all weekend. I shouldn't have gotten so wasted. I honestly have no recollection of doing that body shot off Jared and I definitely didn't know anyone was snapping pics." Poor conduct at an industry event is a fireable offense in the employee handbook I helped write.

"There's a photo of you doing a body shot off your boyfriend?"

"Off of his neck, actually. It's not something I'm proud of." I can feel my tail coiling between my legs.

"A, That's amazing, and B, I'd like it to be my new screen saver. But sadly, that's not what I want to chat about."

"Oh, thank god. What's up, then?"

I can practically feel Angela tamping down her nerves, girding herself to ask whatever it is she's got on her mind. "What do you think about...me buying you out?"

"Buying me out of…"

"The restaurant," she says, the sureness back in her voice.

"Come on. You serious? What are you talking about?"

"I know it seems out of nowhere, but I've been thinking about this since before we even opened," she says. "Knowing the bonuses were coming made me realize I could feasibly do it. I could offer to buy you out."

I pause and look away, not sure if I should be offended, flattered or something else.

"Why didn't you ever bring it up before?" I ask quietly.

"Well, for one, I didn't want you to freak out. It's a shitload of money and after the year you've had, I didn't want you to just take it and run if that's not what you really want."

"I mean, a Lexus and a Rolex sound good right about now, but I see your point. It'll be weird to have more than a crumpled five-dollar bill in my wallet at any given time."

"And then, also, I didn't want you to take it personally. Like that I want you out or something. Because I don't. I love you and I love working with you. I'm just open to the idea of being the sole captain of this ship if that helps you…I dunno, buy your own boat or whatever."

"Very poetic."

"I try."

"Well, it's not like you'd be firing me."

"No, of course not, Allie. But you know what I mean. I don't want you to think I used you for a means to an end. Like I needed you so badly and now I don't—that type of thing."

"I don't see it like that," I assure her. "You're not Benji."

"You're goddamn right I'm not. Look, consider it your way out. A chance to get back to the life you thought you'd be living," Angela says, placing her hand on my knee.

It hits me then that I've never shared my epiphany with

Angela—the one Jared inspired when he talked some sense into me months ago.

The truth is, I love Here. I love everything about it and everyone who's part of it. The notion that Angela has been coming to work every day to team up with a partner she thinks wants nothing to do with the place breaks my heart a little. How could I have not clued her in to the fact that I'm finally okay with things? That my whole heart is in it now? How did I manage to push her into thinking she needed to give up her hard-earned cash to stop my emotional hemorrhage?

"It's a lot to take in," I say, unsure of whether she's expecting an answer right at this exact moment.

"I get it. So just take your time and think about it. We've got to get out on the floor anyway for preshift. Can we shoot for an answer by Friday? I'd love to have our lawyers drum up the paperwork and give Accounting a heads-up so they can manage the financials one way or another."

The thought of Angela offering to buy me out of the restaurant with her $100,000 bonus is nothing short of blindsiding. But it's also enticing, no doubt about that. And not just for the dollar signs either. She's right: her offer is my exit ramp. Hell, with that kind of money, I could rent a bigger apartment. I could *buy* a bigger apartment. I could finally take my mom to Paris.

I can't tell if having an extra two hundred thousand dollars sitting in the bank is a problem or a solution, but I do know having the option to choose my own path for the foreseeable future is a luxury I'd be foolish to pass up.

Is quitting a successful operation worth having the chance to figure out the life I'm meant to live? I mean, in spite of winning awards and making bank, Here is still nothing but an accident at the end of the day, something I was never meant to touch.

On the other hand, Here has become just that for me. A

place that gives me purpose. The cliché makes me cringe, but it's the truth. I've learned the ropes in the last year and discovered what some might even consider a talent for restaurant operations and management. And this talent has given rise to passion. *My* passion.

The fact that I'm doing what I want to do and making a neat profit at the same time? It's a rare thing.

I try to imagine my life without Here. My mind buzzes through a half-dozen fanciful ideas that the business-minded part of me dismisses almost instantaneously. Sure, a bigger apartment would be nice, but I have all the space I need. Yes, Paris would be nice but how much does it really cost to visit for a week or two? And sure, a new business venture would keep me entertained for a few months and busy for a few years, but there's no family meal at a social media agency. There are no VIPs or ingredient trends or logistical fires to put out on a nightly basis. By 7:00 p.m. every day I'd be home with Jared— which is both a beautiful and terrifying notion.

I hear Angela's "please and thank you" float back to me from the dining room and can practically see our servers scurrying to do her bidding. Hospitality runs through that woman's veins. Here means something much different for her, something more than recouping a loss or sticking it to a crazy ex-boyfriend. She would never sit on the fence, not even for a second, if faced with the same choice she presented me with. She would say screw the money and she would stay. She would push Here forward, take it as far as she could, come rain, shine, stars or ribbons.

But I am not Angela, so maybe I just need to get out of her way.

Co-owning Here with Craig and Craig alone would mean Angela is one step away from eventually becoming the sole owner. And given her tenure with Craig, that would likely happen sooner rather than later. I admire what she's doing to make a dream come true, to make a particular situation come full circle for her. She's willing to part with a ton of cash and risk her relationship with me to achieve her long-term goals. She's focused, determined.

She's Angela.

I want to poll the audience, but I know they would all put this back on me.

"You have to do what feels right to you," they'll tell me. "It's no one's choice but your own."

Jared picks me up around midnight after all sidework is complete. We're spending the night at his place again. I'm still reeling from the fact that we did $38,538.14 in sales tonight. That's our second highest night ever behind New Year's Eve. And it's Tuesday. Just a random Tuesday! I'm starting to see what Angela and Craig meant about the "JBF effect."

"Sorry, you can just move those to the back," he says, waving away a stack of books sitting on the passenger's seat.

"Doing a little light reading?" I joke, heaving the thick tower of textbooks onto the floor behind him. I plant a kiss on his cheek and strap on my seat belt.

"Just a tad. I'm actually taking a history class at DePaul starting next week. Just one night a week."

"Really?"

"Yeah, I know. I'm going to be the old dude in the room, but it's something I've been wanting to do. You know I'm a history nerd and we've got some extra hands at the warehouse, so I can take a couple nights off now without the place burning down. I'm thinking I'll get bored if I don't plan something other than eating cupcakes with you."

"I love that idea," I say. "Best of both worlds."

As we take the highway up to Jared's place in Wicker Park, I gaze out the window at our twinkling city. I used to wonder if any other people zipping down the road were going through the same shitty times I was, but now that seems like a thought from someone else's life. Now I'm holding my boy-friend's hand, fresh off the second-best shift of my life.

I realize I'm in a position to have it all, in part because I only need a few things.

"Morning, pookie," Angela says as she files away a yellow request-off form from a server.

"Hi. I've made up my mind," I say, no hesitation in my voice.

She turns around to face me.

"Oh. Shit. Okay. And?"

For a second I think about drawing this out, making her wait for my answer. But I see the anxious questions in her eyes and I know this isn't a time for games. It's time for business.

"Buy me out for what I put in, thirty thousand dollars, and release me from anything binding in my contract as far as the fi-nancials and ownership are concerned. Just let me keep my job as AGM. I don't need to be the owner. I just want to stay the man-ager until either I quit or you fire me because more unladylike photos surface on the internet—whichever comes first."

Tears well up in Angela's eyes. I can tell that up until this moment, she suffered from her biggest fear: tunnel vision. She failed to see there was a chance for her to have the best of both worlds: Here can be hers someday, and we don't have to jeop-ardize what we both know is a once-in-a-lifetime friendship.

"Deal," she says, throwing her arms around me.

We both dab at our makeup, and the tension runs out of Angela like the yolks from a perfectly poached egg. The sound of shattering porcelain from the dishwashing station snaps our attention back to the present moment.

It's time to get to work.

★ ★ ★ ★ ★

Acknowledgments

Hot Mess isn't a textbook love story, but I'm in love with this story and have been since Allic's first words. I have a lot of people to thank for helping me share this book with the world. Some of them are below:

To my Harlequin editor, Margo Lipschultz, who made *Hot Mess* the first acquisition for the Graydon House imprint. From the get-go, you went to bat for this book and promised no one would be a bigger fan of it. To Melanie Fried, who hit the ground running and brought this book swiftly into production. And to the entire Graydon House team, thank you for seeing *Hot Mess* as the perfect fit for the imprint and working tirelessly on all angles of it.

To my agent, Danielle Egan-Miller, who is also my fearless leader. I trust you completely and am so humbled I get to work with you. I could have never imagined you reading about me while getting your hair done all those years ago would lead us here. Thank you, and Team Browne & Miller, for always having my back, lending an ear and kicking major ass.

To my critique partner, Becca, without whom I wouldn't have been able to write my first novel so bravely. Working on this manuscript with you was the most exhilarating experience of my life.

To Andrea, my inspiration for the character of Angela. I cherish our friendship dearly and look forward to our next dinner together. Even if it's at the McDonald's on Ogden.

To my family, especially my mother. Thank you for cheering me on louder and longer than anyone else. I can't do any of this without you. And to my dog, who kept me company while I wrote. Sorry for rushing our walks so I could get back to writing.

To those who have followed my writing journey, you make it all worth it. I look forward to seeing the selfies, responding to the comments and visiting your book clubs.

And finally to Matty B. My best friend, my biggest fan. Thank you for your unconditional support, your willingness to always get ice cream and, above all, your kind, beautiful heart. I love life with you.